EX LIBRIS

VINTAGE CLASSICS

HAPPY VALLEY

Patrick White was born in England in 1912. His Australian parents took him home when he was six months old but educated him in England at Cheltenham College and King's College, Cambridge. He settled in London, where *Happy Valley* was published to some acclaim in 1939. Graham Greene called it 'one of the most mature first novels of recent years'.

After serving in the RAF during the Second World War he returned to Australia with his partner, Manoly Lascaris. The novels, short stories and plays that followed *The Tree of Man* in 1956 – including *Voss*, *The Vivisector*, *The Eye of the Storm* and *A Fringe of* Leaves – made White a considerable figure in world literature. He was awarded the Nobel Prize for Literature in 1973.

In 2012 Jonathan Cape published *The Hanging Garden*, the first third of White's final novel, which he had put aside in 1981.

ALSO BY PATRICK WHITE

PATRICK WHITE

Happy Valley

WITH AN INTRODUCTION BY
Peter Craven

VINTAGE BOOKS
London

Published by Vintage 2013

2 4 6 8 10 9 7 5 3 1

First published in Great Britain by George G. Harrap & Co., London
Published by Jonathan Cape in 2012

Vintage
Random House, 20 Vauxhall Bridge Road,
London SW1V 2SA

www.vintage-classics.info

Addresses for companies within The Random House Group Limited
can be found at: www.randomhouse.co.uk/offices.htm

The Random House Group Limited Reg. No. 954009

A CIP catalogue record for this book
is available from the British Library

ISBN 9780099583677

The Random House Group Limited supports the Forest Stewardship
Council® (FSC®), the leading international forest-certification
organisation. Our books carrying the FSC label are printed on
FSC®-certified paper. FSC is the only forest-certification scheme
supported by the leading environmental organisations, including
Greenpeace. Our paper procurement policy can be found at:
www.randomhouse.co.uk/environment

Printed and bound in Great Britain by
Clays Ltd, St Ives PLC

CONTENTS

Jackeroo Epic
by Peter Craven

Happy Valley is the first of Patrick White's novels and it is a consistently compelling book, as well as the exhilarating performance of a great writer in the making. Everyone knows the legend, rooted in truth, that Patrick White finds his voice as a consequence of the war and after discovering the love of his life in Manoly Lascaris; and that the first in the long line of his masterpieces is *The Aunt's Story* which he brings back to Australia with him in 1946, the token of his love/hate for the country which provides the enduring matter of his great works, the intimately suffered homeland which he cannot separate from the compulsions of his own heart.

In fact *Happy Valley* is as self-consciously Australian a book as any cultural nationalist could hope for and it's not for nothing that the novel, published in London in 1939, was awarded the Gold Medal of the Australian

Literature Society in 1941, the year when A. A. Phillips, the future propounder of the Australian Cultural Cringe syndrome, was one of the judges.

Happy Valley is, in fact, a panoramic novel of Australian life which reflects White's own experience in the Monaro as a jackaroo, and the fact that it is situated in a country town and distributes the narrative interest fairly evenly among a group of characters gives the book a peculiar novelty and freshness—not least because White apparently forbade the book's republication, perhaps because of the way it reflects some unflattering details about a local Australian Chinese family, perhaps because *Happy Valley* is so manifestly the work of a young writer who is finding his feet.

But the latter point is easily misunderstood. The White of *The Aunt's Story* is fully formed, even though that drama of dreams and madness and spinsterly isolation is in some ways the dragon at the gates of White's work. Certainly from *The Aunt's Story* in the mid-1940s through to *The Twyborn Affair* in 1979 there is a consistent maturity and confidence in every page White writes and there is also—which is both a giveaway and a signature feature—an effortless sense of drama. You don't have to know precisely where you are in those dislocated and deranged sections of *The Aunt's Story* to know that you are in the hands of a great writer (which is not to say that White did not retain his unevenness throughout his career).

But the fact that *Happy Valley* is a rawer effort does not stop it from being a consistently engrossing novel. It confronts the reader with the pulsation and sheer narrative momentum which is one of the characteristics of Australia's always rather old-fashioned master of the novel form. This—together with the fact that the book has been out of circulation virtually from the outset—is likely to trick readers who think they know the early work (and that it is not worth revisiting), as indeed it tricked me. Hardly anyone has read *Happy Valley*, and if they have it is likely to be under the shadow of the later work.

Happy Valley is, in fact, the undiscovered country of Patrick White and it is a remarkable book. It shows the young White fiddling with the dominant influences of his time, and it may well be the case that he was even more embarrassed by the book's formalistic high jinks than he was fearful of its heavy-handed (actionable) bits of literalism.

He admitted that 'he was very much under the influence of Gertrude' (Stein) who is, among all the world's writers, the most improbable to have tinkling in the background of a novel of Australian pastoral and small-town life. He also saw himself as having been 'drunk with the technique of writing' and said he 'had gone up that cul de sac the stream of consciousness'.

In practice Gertrude Stein seems to have led him to a bit of decorative patterning, to rhythmic repetitions and paratactical touches of phrasing that sometimes make his sentences somewhat overloaded or too heavily coloured, but the other side of this, the so-called stream of consciousness, is in fact a pretty impressive and flexible adaptation of what can be learned from James Joyce and, rather surprisingly, doesn't get in the way of the narrative.

Happy Valley dispenses with quotation marks to indicate speech and it uses a very flexible roving point-of-view technique, with bits of inserted monologue, but the effect is the opposite of slow-moving or obscure.

It's fascinating to see an essentially dramatic novelist like White so enthralled by Joyce but the upshot is, for better or worse, much less brocaded and oracular than a lot of Faulkner, the obvious point of comparison.

Anyone coming fresh to *Happy Valley* would conclude that the twenty-seven-year-old Patrick White reflected the techniques of his literary elders that were in the air—Virginia Woolf's excruciated reveries, Dos Passos's roving camera eye with its hunger for communitarianism—but they will be more struck by the confidence with which he commands his canvas in the face of the most progressive and arty impulses in the world.

Happy Valley takes its epigraph from Gandhi ('the purer the suffering the greater the progress') and White proceeds to present the soul's dark night in a range of 'ordinary' human hearts.

David Marr says *Happy Valley* was White's best plot. Although this is not quite true, it certainly has the sketch of an elaborate one. The doctor, Halliday, is adrift in a dry marriage and finds himself falling in love with Alys, the piano teacher. She, in turn, is the ministering angel to Margaret Quong, the pensive child of an Australian Chinese family who has little time for her drunk father and querulous white mother, but communes with Amy, her very implicit and sympathetic aunt. She is a love object of a kind—though she's a few years older—to the doctor's son, Rodney. At a dramatic moment in the book she is struck by the asthmatic and frail schoolteacher, Moriarty, whose happy-go-lucky wife, Vic, is conducting an affair with the loud rouseabout, Clem Hagan. He, a saturnine figure with a remote resemblance to the laconic masculine figures of White's later fiction, doesn't mind tumbling in the hay with Vic but he would also like to get his hands on Sidney Furlow, the squatter's daughter who is captivated by him and treats him as her plaything.

Happy Valley builds up to a tremendous quasi-Joycean set piece in which all the voices wind in and out of each other at the races and then—just as we're starting to think it's all a bit orchestrated and lush—there is a murder, an act of mutilation and outrage, a further death and the hovering shadow of suspicion over one of the major characters. And then there is a solution to this which is breathtaking and weird, though very much in line with the heightened melodrama and chiaroscuro which the novel has been exhibiting throughout, where White (like Faulkner before him) comes across as a highbrow writer enacting a pas de deux with a much more red-blooded and populist conception.

After which the novel, in its last movement, ends much more elegiacally, in a return to the saddened but not hopeless faces of the young. There is a new-found monogamy, a departure and the intimation of a less illusioned future.

Happy Valley is a dazzling first novel in which Patrick White passionately attempts to ride the wild horse of his experimental impulses while also indulging, with extraordinary ambition, his inclination to write a saga of country life in the face of the most riddling existential and spiritual perplexities as well as every kind of violent dislocation.

In the end it is the narrative impulse that wins out but it is fascinating to see how much the decorativeness of a late modernist technique is made to contend with the sweep and fury of a writer who wants to create a landscape equal to the most savage and erotic drama he can envisage.

It's easy to pick holes in the upshot. The *bildungsroman* of the young boy could be more developed. We want more of his near-miss Chinese soul mate. All the women are a bit too much alike—as though sexuality was partly a matter of surmise to the novelist (and the siren of the squattocracy is a walking wet dream). The elements of melodrama have a slashing force but they could have been more fully and deliberately articulated.

And yet...what an impassioned, hopeful glory of a book *Happy Valley* is.

It shows Patrick White, as a seeker, at the crossroads from the outset. In *Happy Valley* White pays his dues to the towering shadows on the landscape—to Lawrence with his sexualised sense of the folk and his surging paragraphs as much as to Joyce's musicality and rhetoric. But then White goes his own way to create a book full of portent and drama and the compounding of the spiritual search with a stabbing sensuality.

This is not a major novel by Patrick White's standards but it is a hell of a calling card, and if it had not appeared so late in the 1930s maybe it would have riveted the world's attention. *Happy Valley* is a book we need to rediscover. It gives us White as a fledgling novelist, as fresh and wonderstruck and full of a desire to recreate the world as ever Australia was blessed with. It is a fitting thing and a fine one that in this centennial year of Patrick White's birth it should find itself back in print.

To Roy de Maistre

Happy Valley

PART I

It had stopped snowing. There was a mesh of cloud over the fragile blue that sometimes follows snow. The air was very cold. In it a hawk lay, listless against the moving cloud, magnetized no doubt by some intention still to be revealed. But that is beside the point. In fact, the hawk has none but a vaguely geographical significance. It happens to be in the sky in a necessary spot at a necessary moment, that is, at nine o'clock in the morning about twenty miles to the south of Moorang, where the railway line dribbled silverly out of the mist that lay in the direction of Sydney, and dribbled on again into another bank of mist that was the south. Moorang was a dull silver in the early morning. There was no snow there, only frost. The frost glittered like a dull knife, over it the drifting white of smoke from a morning train. But to the south, following the trajectory of the hawk up the valley and towards the mountains, everything was white. It was higher here. There was grey slush in the streets of the township of Happy Valley, but the roofs were a pure white, and farther up in the mountains Kambala was almost lost beneath the drift.

Happy Valley extends more or less from Moorang to Kambala, where originally there was gold, and it received its name from the men who came in search of gold, the prospectors who left the train at Moorang and rode out with small equipment and a fund of expectation. They called the place Happy Valley, sometimes with affection, more often in irony. But in time, when the gold at Kambala was exhausted, the name applied, precisely speaking, more to the township than to the valley itself. It is here that we have left the hawk coasting above the grey streets. There is not much activity in the streets. They are silent and not very prepossessing in their grey slush. And we have no business with them yet, rather with Kambala, which is almost hidden under the snow.

Ordinarily, if you could see for yourself, there would be about six or seven houses, inhabited by families of no particular distinction. The people at Kambala are a kind of half-bred Chinese, quiet and industrious, though perhaps a little sinister to the eyes of a stranger. But there is not much crime in Kambala, in spite of the large grey erection that is a gaol. There is no explanation for its size, except that perhaps the architect could not get out of his mind the days when there were nine pubs in the town, and colonies of tents down the mountainside, and English and French and Germans digging for gold. But now it is very peaceful. In the summer the police sergeant sits on the verandah of the gaol, tilts back his chair, and swots at flies. I repeat, there is not much crime. Only the publican before the man they had at the moment once set fire to his wife, and on another occasion a drover from the Murray side ran amuck and crucified a roadman on a dead tree. Old Harry Grogan found the body. It was like a scarecrow, he said, only it didn't scare. There was crows all over the place, sitting there and dipping their beaks into the buttonholes.

Now the gaol is covered with snow and the police sergeant is inside, writing an uneventful report that he will send later to Moorang. The gaol is an impressive white mound, the houses smaller ones. There is a general air of hibernation, of life suspended under the snow. Literally under, for in the winter the people of Kambala communicate with each other by channels or even tunnels carved through the snow. You seldom see any more than a streamer of smoke waving weakly from the arm of an iron chimney-pot or the eyelid of an eaves raised cautiously out of the snow.

In one of the hotel bedrooms the publican's wife was giving birth to her first child. She lay on her back, a big ox-like woman with a face that was naturally red, but which had now gone putty-coloured. Sometimes she tossed about and sometimes she just lay still. She was having a child, she told herself dumbly at first, until with the increase of pain she did not know what she was having, only that she was having, having, straining, it was tearing her apart, and the doctor's hand was on her. She closed her eyes. She had resented the doctor at first, did not want him to touch her, then by degrees she did not mind whether he touched her or not. Because the pain was there, whatever happened.

She had come from Tumut with her husband a year ago. Everyone told them they were mad. And now she began to wonder herself, somehow confounding her pain with Kambala and all that snow, snow everywhere, you could hardly see out of the window except at the top. She opened and closed her eyes and moaned. The doctor was still there looking at her.

There were two other women in the room, one a silent half-bred Chinese woman with a cast in her left eye, and the other an old woman with little greasy puffs of hair standing out over her forehead in a kind of arch. They had come in to help. Mrs Steele, the old woman with the puffs of hair, always came to assist at a birth or a death. She had helped bring a lot of children into the world. She could also lay out a body better than any woman in the neighbourhood. Now she stood by the bed and stared at the doctor with all her expert experience, and resented his presence a great deal, because apart from her own experience (she could have managed the lying in herself, only Mr Chalker, the publican, had to send to Happy Valley for the doctor), apart from this, the doctor was not old Dr Reardon who had left the district a year ago, and she could not help holding Dr Halliday responsible for this. She and Dr Reardon knew a thing or two. They were a source of mutual admiration. Dr Halliday told her to mind out. Very politely though. He was a gentleman. And this was an additional point for scorn. She refused to own that ability was a possible quality in a gentleman.

Dr Halliday stood by the bed, with his back to old Mrs Steele, looking at the patient.

You could put out the lamp, Mrs Steele, he said, without turning to look.

Mrs Steele stood like a post. The Chinese woman climbed up silently on a chair and turned down the wick of the lamp, till the light was out, and a white smoke meandered up through the glass.

The doctor looked at his watch. It was nine o'clock. He had been there since the evening before, and now it was light again, and there was a shadow of bristle about his chin. The rims of his eyes were dry and taut. They felt as if they might never close again, stuck there, glued. The calves of his legs ached. He had been there how many hours? He would not count, could not be bothered to count. But it was a weary business, and the way she moaned, weary, with that pale hair flattened back from her face. Somebody was cooking bacon and eggs. He could smell the fat, smell the wick of the now extinguished lamp, and the little oil stove against which the Chinese woman was warming her skirts. It was monstrously cold in this room, in this wooden house with the snow piled up outside. The little stove seemed to make no impression on the temperature. He shivered and put his fingers on the woman's pulse.

She opened her eyes and looked at him blankly.

It'll soon be over now, he said.

It was like delivering a cow, he felt. When she moaned it was almost like the lowing of a cow. And that same bewildered stare. Or perhaps he had become callous. Some people called it professional, when perhaps it was just callousness. Not like that first time, the woman in the tenement in Sydney, somewhere out in Surry Hills. She had screamed, or that was what it sounded like, something very personal and connected with himself, so that his own body had tightened up with the screams, and he sweated behind the knees, and the afterbirth had almost made him sick. When he left the house, when he got on the tram and found himself in William Street, he could still hear the screams. They were stamped on wax inside his head, the record going round and round. At the bottom of William Street he got out of the tram and had to go into a pub to get a drink.

The poor soul's havin' an awful time, said Mrs Steele behind his back.

She was having an awful time. But she was strong, strong as a cow. And in a little while it would be over.

In a little while it was. The child was born dead. It was a red, motionless phenomenon that he picked up and handed to Mrs Steele, waiting to receive it in a folded towel. Mrs Steele sucked her teeth. You felt that Dr Halliday was responsible for the stillborn child. She could have delivered it better herself, and that poor soul lying on the bed, it was terrible, Mary Mother of God it was awful what women had to go through. She carried the child out of the room still sucking her teeth.

But she was strong, he repeated, in the absence of any genuine compassion. He could not summon this. He began to gather up his instruments, while the Chinese woman floated round the bed, so silent that she almost wasn't there. He would wash his hands. There was a basin in the kitchen, the Chinese woman said. He would pack his bag, a small compact affair in darkish leather with his initials on the side in black. O.H. He had had it done in Sydney after taking his degree, correcting the man in the shop, saying it was not A but H, for HALLIDAY. It was good to have a bag with your initials on it. It made you feel important. You were less a medical student than a doctor. That was one stage, and the woman screaming in a tenement house in Surry Hills. Life in jerks, in stages. It ought to flow, theoretically, in an even rhythm, as he read (he was nineteen) in some book, and he must do something about his life, work it out into a neat formula, or make it flow beautifully. Everything would be beautiful. Then it began to move in jerks. And that was all wrong. He yawned. Perhaps Chalker would offer him bacon and eggs.

Mrs Steele was back in the room. While she was away she seemed to have caught on to the thread of the inevitable again, for she stood with her arms folded and began to compose a low, monotonous kind of recitative.

It's funny, she said, it happened that way. It happened that way with my first. All the rest boys but the first. The first was a little girl. They're good boys, my boys. There's young Tom, just got a job in the post-office at Tumut. He's good to 'is mother, Tom. Sends me money from Tumut. Tom says I oughtn't stay on 'ere. Kambala's no place for an elderly woman. When the summer comes I ought to go down to Tumut an' live.

She went on like that, and Dr Halliday did not listen to her. He would be getting on down to Happy Valley. He would be there in time for lunch, leaving the publican's wife to Mrs Steele. She would soon be about again. She was strong as a cow. Only the child was dead. So he went past the old woman, standing there as leisurely as a chorus from

Euripides, and out into the passage, where the publican sat on a deal chair smoking the frayed remains of a cigarette. He would have to say something to the publican.

Well, he said, I'm sorry, Chalker. We've done all we can. I'm sorry it's turned out like this.

The publican jumped to his feet and came forward, bending a little, nervously. He was relieved now that it was all over, even if not particularly moved, because he hadn't really stopped to think about the child. Only his wife. The possibility of reproduction only moved dimly at the back of his mind. Sometimes it moved farther into the foreground, and he thought, well, a kid would show you there was nothing wrong, and afterwards it could lend a hand in the bar, give Rita a chance of laying up. So when he sidled nervously to the doctor there was a propitiatory smile on his flabby face.

Better luck next time, eh, doctor? he said.

Then he laughed. It was a wheezy, semi-coagulated noise. Halliday found it rather unpleasant. He refused to encourage Chalker's relief and asked if he could wash his hands. There was yellow soap in the kitchen sink. Chalker hovered, talked, coughed. He was a big man, perpetually in his slippers, with yellowish whites to his eyes. A stream of soft platitude fell about Halliday as he washed his hands, as he accepted a whisky in the bar, as he refused an offer of bacon and eggs. No, he'd be getting down. His wife.

All right, doctor, said Chalker, unlatching the front door. If there's ever anything I can do. You never can tell, eh? You never can tell.

Tell what? How these people talked, just another

minute, as if they were afraid that this was the last human contact they would make. Halliday bent down in the tunnel of snow to fasten on his skis. And it might be up here, so quiet in the snow, a long, slow, seeping quiet. Chalker clung to the door. Literally clung. He was afraid of something slipping away, smiling feebly, and trying to make a joke. Halliday straightened up.

Good-bye, Chalker, he said.

So long, doctor. God, it's cold, ain't it? Freeze the snot on your nose.

He was shivering. Halliday was conscious of his own brutality as he felt his way along the tunnel and out towards the light. But he could not stop. He did not know what to say, and the man was not so much worse off than anyone else, if it came to that. Up here at Kambala or down at Happy Valley was a choice of evils. Only here the isolation was physical. That was why Chalker shivered like an unwanted dog.

At the end of the tunnel the valley widened out into a long sweep of snow. He slid off on his skis, his bag, fastened with a cord, bumping against his back. How the air cut. It shaved the flesh off your face. It made you feel lean, leaner, almost non-existent, as you arrived with a rush at the bottom of the slope. He was a little out of breath, for physically he was thirty-four. But it did not feel like that, feel like anything. He was sixteen, that night on the ferry in Sydney when he knew he could do anything, and Professor Birkett had said there was something in his poems that was not just adolescence, and he would be a writer, he would write poems and plays, particularly a play with some kind

11

of metaphysical theme, only the trouble was to find the theme. A crow flew out of a tree with a half-hearted caw. He had not found the theme. He was now thirty-four. Hilda said she thought it was a lovely poem, she hoped he would write one for her, one she could feel was her very own, he must call it To H.G., though she knew he must wait to be inspired. She had grey eyes that were full of sympathy as they sat on that seat in the Botanical Gardens and there was a smell of old banana skins and squashed Moreton Bay figs. It was so easy to get sympathetic on a warm morning in the Botanical Gardens. You began to talk about ideals. It was Hilda's sympathetic eyes. Later on you began to realize that sympathy in women was largely compound of stupidity and anxiety for the future. However, that was later on.

It was warm now, tramping along the level on skis. He would be in a sweat by the time he reached the place where he had left the car. You left the car at Halloran's Corner when you came up to Kambala in winter time. Snow never fell very heavily as far down the mountains as that. But it was cold. It was colder at Happy Valley than anywhere else in the world. Take your scarf, dear, Hilda said, poke it into your waistcoat over your chest. She coughed as she served apple dumplings to the boys, and Rodney said he hated apple dumplings, they stuck in his throat, he began to cry. Hilda said, dear, dear, Oliver, you'll have to do something about that child, he'll finish by driving me off my head, I can't stand any more.

Oliver Halliday, father of a family. That's what he was. And it didn't feel any different, in essentials, from what it was at sixteen. Wrongly, no doubt. Just this coating of the essential sameness with superficial experience. There hadn't been any adjustment, he hadn't had time. The way you were going to do everything, make your life flow in an even rhythm, like that damn pretentious book. He had copied out bits of it, too. It made you feel rather intellectual to write down things about the Life Stream and Cosmic Force in coloured inks. That was sixteen, Cosmic Force, and cultivating an expression of intensity in the glass before going in to tea. He works very hard, said Aunt Jane to Mrs Meadows, so that he would not hear, but he did. He wrote interesting letters too, bits of thoughts and things going over on the troopship, and sang bawdy songs in the evening. There was a man called Wright, a shearer with cross eyes, singing, and the streamers that morning as the boat slipped away, and Aunt Jane saying, this'll kill me, Oliver, why you had to do it I'll never know. He felt very proud when he told them he was nineteen. Nobody would have known. He was big. But he was frightened lying in his bunk at night, and the way the men snored, and the sea seemed eternity, and perhaps Hilda would forget what she said, that she would marry him when he came back, because she was proud he was going to the War. On the newspaper placards in Sydney the War was cold print. You went to the War. Then suddenly in the Indian Ocean you were going to God knows what, and it wasn't so good, but it couldn't go on for ever, it was already '18. Perhaps he would get a medal, and newspaper placards in Sydney, because he was sixteen, would say...Once he was sixteen.

Oliver Halliday wiped his face with a handkerchief. There was something vicious about letting your mind run

13

on like that. You felt a bit ashamed as soon as you pulled yourself up. It was like reading in the lavatory or lying too long in a hot bath. If he had a gun he'd take a pot at that hawk, put a shot in its belly for lunch, and it would fall down and lie on the snow, its blood red on the snow, dead. But there would be no pain before annihilation. All its life it would probably know no pain, not like Mrs Chalker writhing about on the bed at Kambala. The hawk was absolved from this, absorbed as an agent into the whole of this frozen landscape, into the mountains that emanated in their silence a dull, frozen pain while remaining exempt from it. There was a kind of universal cleavage between these, the agents, and their objects: the woman at the hotel, forcing the dead child out of her womb, or the township of Happy Valley with its slow festering sore of painfully little intrigue. It was a medieval attitude perhaps. But they were still living in the Middle Ages with their dark fears and antidotal faiths. His skis made a long slurring noise on the snow. A handful of snow rattled from off a tree, falling down out of the interstices of twigs. The arches of the trees were white with snow, almost Gothic in structure. Like a cathedral, he felt. Miserere of the crows. A plump black crow peering out of the window of a briar like a priest from his confessional.

There was still some use for the Holy Roman Church. It taught you to turn pain and the fear of it to some spiritual use. But you weren't a Catholic, and pain only made you bitter, or made you ashamed because you were bitter and afraid. He said his prayers every evening on the troopship, quietly to himself in his bunk. He lay there feeling afraid,

14

getting closer, and closer, and then the War stopped. Of course it had to stop. He was sorry in a way, because a gesture like enlisting when you were sixteen, and afraid, wasn't as big when you couldn't carry it through to the logical conclusion and give everyone the impression you were brave, even though bravery was something forced on you whether you liked it or not. But he went to London. He had two weeks in Paris, where everyone was very tired, and old, spiritually, and nobody took any notice of him at all. He felt far younger than he had ever felt copying Great Thoughts into a notebook at home, but it was a fresh sensation, he appreciated it, walking about the streets in Paris and everyone else preoccupied. But he was worried because everyone was old and when he went out of the city into the country, to Saint Germain or the forest at Fontainebleau, the country was young. That was the strange part. It was stranger because at home everything was reversed. The people were young, adolescent, almost embryonic. When he got back from Europe he looked at them and there was nothing there. Life was a toy, you rattled it. But the country was old, older than the forest at Fontainebleau, there was an underlying bitterness that had been scored deep and deep by time, with a furrow here and there and pockmarks in the face of black stone. Over everything there was a hot air of dormant passion, of inner war, that nobody seemed to be conscious of. In Sydney you went to parties. In Happy Valley you fornicated or drank. You swung the rattle for all you were worth. You did not know you were sitting on a volcano that might not be extinct. It puzzled him at first.

And he wanted to get away again. Even when he was married he wanted to get away. And Hilda said, you're restless, dear, you're tired, if only you could take a week or two we might drive down to Wollongong. He married Hilda when he was twenty-four. That was eight years. But waiting was Hilda's strong suit, for more than eight years. Rodney was nine and George four. And he was still only sixteen, which was something that Hilda did not know though she knew pretty well everything else. It was far better to be like Hilda, complete in superficialities, complete in your own conception of completeness. He had only once felt complete. It was an accident, he felt, and being in Paris, it was somewhere round about the Luxembourg, and he had gone into a church, he did not know why, it was an ordinary church, but perhaps there was a cold wind, anyway he went inside. The organ was playing. He could remember that his feet were cold and there was a smell of varnish. The organ was playing a Bach fugue. He knew it was Bach because he had picked out bits of Bach on the piano at home. And then he was at home again, but not at home, it was in the church in the neighbourhood of the Luxembourg, it was in France, with old German Bach streaming out of the organ loft, and the War had stopped, and he was losing his breath, he was losing...Then he sat very still. He supposed he was breathing. He did not know. But he knew he was crying. He did not care if he cried; there was nothing wrong with this sort of crying and nobody would see. The music came rushing out of the loft, unfurling banners of sound. You could touch it. You could feel it. You could feel a stillness and a music all at once. You were at once floating and

16

stationary, in time, all time, and space, without barrier, passing with a fresher knowledge of the tangible to a point where this dissolved, became the spiritual.

A great boulder of black rock rose nakedly at the edge of the whitened road. He stopped and kicked at it with his ski. The tangible. There is a stubborn, bitter ring if you kick at a piece of black rock. And how would serene, Christian, German, eighteenth-century Johann Sebastian have dealt with a lump of antipodal rock? Serenity perhaps was the effect of environment, not so much the result of spiritual conflict. At least you would like to think that. It would make things easier. You could give up the ghost at the start. But you did not give up the ghost, you went on swerving, wheeling, in the direction of Happy Valley, ducking beneath the arm of a tree when it nearly hit you in the face, half closing your eyes to keep out the spray of snow and the wind, and it was exciting, and you held your breath, hoping this wasn't your last moment, almost, but not the last.

Oliver Halliday caught the point of his ski in a trough of snow and fell over in a heap, though it might have been a knot, it felt like a knot. He had that blue, constricted sensation of being winded. He felt that his face was a distinct, bright blue, then that his toes were hurting. He put his hand on the snow to raise himself up, sank in an inch or two, touched the ground. He was almost out of the snow. He would take off his skis and walk, if he could walk, if he wasn't dead, but he felt he was dead, physically more than thirty-four. So he lay back on the cold snow, to consider the situation, and it was good and cold lying there, the way the ribs moved with his panting, in and out. His ribs moved in and out the day he won the quarter-mile, and the cup he received from the Governor dropped on the gravel drive as coming down, and somebody sniggered, he was very foolish bending to pick up the cup. He laughed. He was lying on his back in the present. His bag made a pillow under his neck. He was laughing up at a patch of sky that looked rather chaste and bewildered in the scud of cloud. Once he had written nature poems, on clouds and things. But he did not do that any more. He would get to his feet, and take off his skis, and after reaching the car he would drive on home to lunch, probably find cold mutton and pickles out of a bottle, it was a Monday, and Hilda said, you can't expect anything hot on Monday, there's always the wash. So the present was cold mutton and pickles, not nature poems about a cloud or mountains, he used to be keen on the idea of mountains, they recurred over and over again, generally blue, or else there was a mist, but that was before he had heard of Kambala. The way that man clung to the door, shivering on the mountaintop, perhaps standing there still, waiting for someone to come, and the whole winter nobody would come except a half-baked Chinese, creeping along the snow tunnel from one of the other houses.

But you needn't think, of course. The Miracle of Thought, he had read somewhere, in a Sunday newspaper. God making a clockwork toy and feeling pleased with it, then scratching his head and seeing that it might work too well, so he put in an extra mechanism in a moment of compassion, you just pushed down a lever and the action was held up.

He walked along slowly. He would not think. There was

the car now, with a thin powdering of snow on the roof. He began to whistle a tune, a Ständchen. Elisabeth Schumann sang it on the gramophone. It was thin and very cold and very sexless, but there were moments when it persisted it coming into your head, jamming down the lever, on cold, thin, sexless mornings walking over the snow.

2

The hawk continued to circle in wide, empty sweeps. It might have been anywhere, heading towards Kambala, over the roofs of Happy Valley, or aimless in the sky above the Moorang road.

I'd shoot that bird if I had a gun, Clem Hagan said.

He hadn't a gun, so he knew he was perfectly safe. It was probably a damn side too far off. You couldn't tell. But he hadn't a gun and it was all right.

It's a hawk, said Chuffy Chambers, hunched up stolidly at the wheel.

Go on! You're telling me something new.

The mail truck churned its way from Moorang. The road was a sticky yellow-brown, for the little snow that had fallen on the lower slopes had thawed, and the country was visible now in its customary nakedness. The mail truck groaned and laboured on its way. On either side of the road there were stretches of grey winter grass, and trees that were grey in winter and summer too. A flock of ragged ewes scampered with a scattering of black dung into a hollow and out of sight. In the back of the truck the mail bags jostled. There were also some bags of corn, Hagan's luggage, an incubator, and a separating machine. When the truck skidded the separating machine struck the incubator with a loud metallic ring.

That was a near one, said Hagan, holding the door.

Yes, agreed Chuffy Chambers, that was a near one right enough.

He settled over the wheel again. He was not conversationally ingenious. He liked to sit and spit, or smile at other people's remarks, and when no remarks were made he merely sat. As Hagan was a stranger, to-day he sat. Every day he drove the lorry from Moorang to Happy Valley twice. His chief significance was as a link between two geographical and economic points, though he could also play the accordion and was consequently in demand when there were dances at Happy Valley at the School of Arts. Twice a year there was a dance at the School of Arts, in race week and during the agricultural show. Then Chuffy Chambers sat on the platform with the rest of the band, his yellow hair smoothed down, and the girls smiled at him as they danced past, and he felt extremely satisfied. There was no one could play the accordion so good as Chuffy Chambers, they said.

Hagan began to shiver. He turned up the collar of his overcoat, which was a greenish grey and fell to his ankles when he stood up. He had never felt so cold. Not even up in the north, he came from New England, had he ever felt so cold. It was a godforsaken part of the world. There was probably worm in the sheep. And perhaps he'd been a fool to come, only the money that Furlow offered was a rise on anything he'd had before. And what you couldn't do with money! In Sydney, in at the Australia or the Metropole, you weren't an overseer any more. This was what made you stop to consider money, all those faces in a ring round the bar. So he wrote to Furlow that he'd come. He was going to have a cottage to himself, and a cook, and there were also a couple of jackeroos. He would feel no end important as overseer to jackeroos. But the country, it made you sick, just to look at, not a blade of grass, though they said it was the country for sheep. Still, you always said that once you'd landed yourself in a mess just to make the best of things. He took out a tin of tobacco and started to roll a cigarette.

It's cold, he said.

Yes, said Chuffy, it's cold.

Anything doing out here? In Happy Valley, I mean.

Oh, I dunno. Now an' again. There's the races. There's the pictures once a month in a 'all that belongs to Quongs'.

Chows, eh?

Yes. There's Chows. Quongs is Chows that run the store. They got a good shop. You can get anything at Quongs'.

Hagan rolled his cigarette. You could never say much for a place that was run by Chows. Chows or dagoes. They always took away the profits from anyone else. He spat out over the side of the truck, to emphasize his dislike of Chows. His fingers were very red as he smoothed out the

22

white cylinder that soon would become a cigarette. On the backs of his hands there was reddish hair that had crept out as an advance guard from the wrists.

What about girls? asked Hagan, licking the flap of the cigarette.

Yes, there's girls, said Chuffy.

What sort of girls?

Same as most places I suppose. All sorts of girls.

Oh.

Chuffy Chambers did not like to talk about girls, because they were a sort of unrealized ambition with him, and even if they said, Chuffy, you play the accordion so good, they never said more than that. They laughed. They said he was loopy. Though he treated his mother well, he was a good boy, Chuffy, but—well, he wasn't quite all there, and you couldn't treat him altogether serious because of that, or go with him or anything like that. So Chuffy Chambers always squinted and felt embarrassed when anyone spoke about girls. He felt a hot sensation inside his shirt next to the holy medals and the sacred hearts. For Chuffy was religious, he was a Catholic. When Father Purcell came from Moorang to Happy Valley he went to Mrs Chambers' for tea, and it made you feel good to have a priest in the house. It was a great consolation to be religious. The Protestants called him a Micky, but he didn't mind. It gave him a kind of secret superiority over the other boys who went with girls, and when things got too bad he told himself he didn't want to go with girls, it was bad, he touched the holy medals and told himself it was wrong.

Like most places, eh? Yes, I suppose you're right.

Men who work a lot in the open, especially men who work with sheep, have a habit of repeating things, even trivial things, several times, perhaps because conversation is scarce and it gives them a sense of company to have a phrase coming out of their mouths, even if the phrase is already stated. Clem Hagan was like this. He repeated a remark ponderously, sometimes with a different intonation just for variety's sake. He stared out in front of him with an expression that might have been interesting if you didn't know it was due to his having spent most of his life looking into the distance for sheep. Anyone who stares long enough into the distance is bound to be mistaken for a philosopher or mystic in the end. But Hagan was no philosopher, that is, he searched no farther than the immediate, sensual reality, and this translated into simpler terms meant a good steak with juice running out at the sides and blonde girls with comfortable busts.

He had the immense self-confidence of men who are successful in their sensuality. If you saw him walking, he walked slowly with his legs a little apart and his arms a little bent and the trousers tight across his behind. Or when he smiled there was a bit of gold in one of his front teeth that flashed, and they liked that. He only had to lean up against a bar and smile and they were ducking about behind the bottles, yes, Mr Hagan and no, Mr Hagan, and pouring out whisky when it should have been gin. Everything happened so easily. He tilted his hat over his eyes. He wore his hat perpetually on a tilt which made him look rather lazy, as if he had had too much, and you were just a moment too late, a pity, but there it was, and opening your mouth and breathing hard wouldn't help matters at all.

Hagan sighed. He was getting cramp in his legs. His trousers were catching him in the crutch. And he wanted to make water too. There was no end to the yellow pasty road. In the back of the truck, if you could judge by the jangle, the incubator had come into permanent conjunction with the separating machine. There was the hell of row, and the country going on and on, it was how many miles, mean and sour, there was probably fluke in the sheep, and he did not know why he had come. She said her name was Bella, that red-haired one. She had a behind like a cart-horse, wicker-patterned, after sitting in that wicker chair drinking a gin and ginger beer. She said she got the wind awful bad, but she just loved ginger beer, and wasn't it funny the way it got sticky on your fingers, she said. She liked ginger ale too, but didn't it prickle up your nose. On the whole it was pretty dull. He had torn up her card and thrown it down the lavatory in the train. That was the worst of women, they were dull, talking about ginger beer, or when you began to tell them about yourself they shut up at once and began to hum and then came out with something about a paper pattern they'd got out of a magazine or who was taking them to the races Saturday week. You cut up rough with them sometimes, and you wouldn't go with them any more, and then you went. Or sometimes you gave them a date, like that night about eleven girls waiting outside the King's Cross picture show, and you went past in a tram and laughed to see them all there, looking at each other and waiting and people wondering what was the gala show.

25

But it served women right, coming up to you in the street, served them bloody well right.

Hagan laughed.

Eh? said Chuffy Chambers.

All sorts of girls, said Hagan, spitting over the side again.

Lurching away, he'd have to get down or...

Here, you, he said. What's your name?

Chambers.

What Chambers?

Chuffy Chambers.

What sort of a name do you call that? Anyway, stop this bus. I've got to get down and have a leak.

The truck gave a complicated emotional groan and stopped to let Hagan get down. Chuffy Chambers sat at the wheel. He had gone a little red because he had said his name was Chuffy Chambers, but he couldn't help it, they called him that. He could not remember how it began, but it had always been like that, they said come here Chuffy, and he came. His real name was William.

3

If you could go up with the hawk you would see Happy Valley there in the hollow, the township I mean, still some way from the truck. The truck won't get there till later on. But we have to go on a bit, only spatially, that is. For it is still pretty early, and not much activity trickling through the streets, not that there ever is in Happy Valley, except for the show or the races or polling day. So now there is very little doing, and we are looking down from above, and we are not particularly impressed by any beauty of design. Because somebody once built a house, I think it was probably old Quong, and someone else come along and built another, some little way off, just far enough to show that there was no love lost in the act. And it went on like that, just building here and there, without co-operation. There never was co-operation in Happy Valley, not even in the matter of living, or you might even say less in the matter of living. In Happy Valley the people existed in spite of each other.

To go one step farther, the country existed also in spite of the town. It was not aware of it. There was no connecting link. Just as Oliver Halliday noticed when he got back from Europe, the country slept, inwardly intent on some secret war of passion or trying to separate the threads of old passions spent. This made the town seem very ephemeral. In summer when the slopes were a scurfy yellow and the body of the earth was very hot, lying there stretched out, the town, with its cottages of red and brown weatherboard, reminded you of an ugly scab somewhere on the body of the earth. It was so ephemeral. Some day it would drop off, leaving a pink, clean place underneath.

But that day has not arrived yet. And as it is not even summer, the town does not look so much like a scab, though most of the snow has melted to slush and you can see the country round about, and the road to Kambala, and the road to Moorang, and the less official road out to Glen Marsh, which is the Furlows' place. Up at the top of the hill, where the Belpers live, there is a bright red water-tank. It is a nice bit of unconscious colour. I say unconscious because nobody thought about that sort of thing, not even Mrs Belper, who in spite of breeding dogs had her Artistic Side. She even did pokerwork in her spare time. But mostly at Happy Valley you just lived. That was unconscious too, but more unavoidable. You ate and slept and dusted and cooked and hung out the washing on Monday morning.

It was Monday morning now, so there were several lots of washing hanging out in the backyards and beginning to look white against the dirty snow. Then the drizzle began to come, so you had to go out and gather your washing in. You shouted remarks on the weather over the fence, then billowed away. There wasn't much else going on. A pounding noise came out of the blacksmith's shop, and a smell of burning hoof. A pale little yellow sheep-dog bitch, with a collar several sizes too big, pointed a pink nose to the wind and trod delicately down the street.

I'm going up to Moriartys', said Amy Quong.

At first Arthur said nothing at all. He never said much, but he knew that over the present case there was less to say than he usually said. He took up a bunch of liquorice straps and hung them on another nail.

I've said all this week I'm going to Moriartys'.

Arthur grunted and turned away.

Somebody's got to go, she said.

Arthur dusted a flitch of bacon. The texture was a kind of smooth-rough. It was also pleasant to smell. The whole store was pleasant to smell if you had a taste for incongruities. That is the particular advantage of a general store. Arthur nervously dusted the bacon and said:

Somebody's got to go.

He was small and brown and gentle. He had a soft, gentle voice. He didn't like people, except Amy, who was his sister, and that is why he did not want to go to Moriartys', because he did not like people, though he knew he ought to go. Amy would go to Moriartys'. She usually went. He looked at her slowly out of a pair of eyes that most people in town thought queer. There was a white rim near the edge of each iris. The iris was brown. So the general effect

29

reminded you of marbles, the superior glass taws that you kept in a bag by themselves. The children were a bit afraid of Arthur Quong on account of his eyes. If they came into the shop they hoped they would encounter Amy, who was also small and gentle, but with a black bun at the back of her head and without the white rings in her eyes.

Amy was also more European. They were only half Chinese. Their father, old Quong, had taken a poor Irish girl, who was the mother of Amy and Arthur, and of Walter Quong, but Amy and Arthur did not speak about Walter much. And now old Quong was dead, and the Irish woman he married, she died first, because she hadn't much vitality. But old Quong lived a long time. He had come into the country with a bundle on his back, and sold things to the miners at Kambala, bootlaces and things, laughing a lot and being cheerful, and they liked him up at Kambala and showed him how to wash for gold. So old Quong sometimes washed for gold, but he continued to sell things to the miners, and then he put up a hut at Happy Valley. The miners used to get off the coach and talk to Quong on the way down. Now the hut was a weatherboard building with an upper story and General Store painted on the front. This happened about seven years before old Quong died.

You shouldn't've let her have that ribbon last week, said Amy.

All right, said Arthur, you would have thought sulkily. All right, he said, we'll leave it at that.

But he wasn't sulky. He just didn't want to think of ribbons and things like that, or of what Mrs Moriarty owed. It was Amy who ran the store. Arthur thought of bigger things. The hall where they had the picture show, that was one of Arthur's ideas, and he speculated in land, and he had a racehorse in a stable out at the back. The horse was a neat bay colt that stood deep in straw all day and neighed if you went across the yard. Arthur Quong spent most of the day going across the yard. He squatted in the corner of the stable, or rubbed down the horse's back with a slow and gentle purr to match the delicate progress of his hand. But he hissed when he finished off on the flank, he gave a sharp electrical flick, making a pattern on the horse's flank, he quivered with a wiry intensity standing up on the balls of his feet. He loved the colt. He put his hand on the horse's neck, something almost emotional in his touching the muscular neck, a tautness in his body, a tautness also in the horse that arose from the conjunction of skin and hide. He wanted to rest his head against the horse, and close his eyes that were no longer brown and gentle, but brown and sharp.

The Quongs also had a big new Buick which stayed in the garage most of the time because they seldom went out. I can't see the use of that car, said Mr Belper grudgingly. People used to make guesses at how much the Quongs had got. You never knew. You never knew with Chows. And this was a source of bitterness. Because when a man has money and you think it's probably a lot, not that you've ever found out, it's a constant source of bitterness. At least, in Happy Valley it was that way.

Amy Quong put on her mackintosh. She wore a brown skirt with a blouse, and black shoes that laced up, with the laces dangling in a bow. She also wore gold-rimmed spectacles. Taking an umbrella from the back room, she prepared to go into the street.

These Moriartys, murmured Amy Quong, that voice blurred and indeterminate like the corners of the shop.

Walking up the street, she held the umbrella to shield her face from the rain pitching on a slant. It was muddy in the street, but not very far to where the Moriartys lived. Amy walked with short steps, plumping into the mud. She smiled a little because of the way Arthur looked when she told him off. Arthur was one of the passions in her life, of which there were three, very deep and difficult to extricate. But there is no point in taking out Amy's passions in the street, and, besides, she had come to Moriartys' door. To the back door, that is. You went round to the back.

Good morning, Miss Quong, said Gertie Ansell, the girl that helped Mrs Moriarty in the house. She wore a pale blue woollen dress and her hands hung down, red and blunt.

I want to see Mrs Moriarty, said Amy Quong.

Yes, Miss Quong, said Gertie.

She went back into the house.

A brown, feeble hen was pecking at the ground just inside the wash-house that was across the yard. It was a poor layer, Amy felt, you could tell that by its comb. The mangle looked as if it was broken, gaping there with that chemise hanging half-way out.

Oh, Miss Quong, said Gertie, coming back, Mr Moriarty's down at the school. I'm afraid he won't be back till lunch. I'm ever so sorry, she said, simpering a little and rubbing her dress.

I want to see Mrs Moriarty, said Amy.

32

Oh.

The girl stood in the doorway rubbing her dress.

You'd better come in, she said, but she seemed uncertain as if—well, it wasn't her fault after all.

Amy waited in the front room. It was rather pink. She put her umbrella in a corner, standing it against the wall. Then she sat down to wait. On the centre table there was a cyclamen in a big silver lustre bowl that caught the light and gave out reflections of the objects in the room, all of them a bit distorted, the lampshades drawn down into nightcaps, long and pink. It was a lovely bowl. She had to get up and touch it because it was so lovely, and the reflections there, she had never seen anything so lovely before. Her breath made a cloud of mist on the lustre surface. I wouldn't mind having that, she said.

Because, after Arthur, you might say that Amy's passion was things; she would have called them things herself, and she had a number of things, the lids of scallop-shells and a Chinese dressing-gown that she bought at a shop near the Central Station in Sydney. She lived in a kind of mystical attachment to her things; she lived with them in the cocoon of custom that led her to dust them, to take them up and put them down. And she wanted more; she was always anxious to add a thread to the soft and necessary structure of the cocoon.

She gave a little sigh and sat down again to look at the bowl. She would have put it in her room under the picture of the Virgin Mary, and she would have stood a tin inside and burnt incense there. She liked the smell. She lay on her bed on a Sunday afternoon and smelt the smell of incense and looked at the picture of the Virgin Mary that hung near a crucifix in varnished oak. Incense made her close her eyes. She lay on her bed on the cotton quilt and there was a strange, beautiful atmosphere that she could not explain, only that it was bound up with the Virgin Mary and her things, and Arthur was pottering about in the yard, perhaps carrying feed to the horse. So on Sunday afternoon the three threads of Amy Quong's passion became tangled in a complex knot that she did not know how to untie. She did not want to, only to close her eyes.

The cyclamen in the lustre bowl sprawled in wide, voluptuous curves.

Yes? asked Mrs Moriarty, opening the door.

She did not waste a good-morning on a Chow, you didn't beat about the bush, especially if you knew that the Chow had come with the inevitable and tiresome demand.

I'm sorry, she said to Amy. You see, I haven't had time to dress. Working about the house in the morning, it spoils your clothes. Gertie, she called back through the door, don't you dare forget that steak. These girls, she said to Amy, you can't call them servants at all.

Mrs Moriarty was, in fact, not dressed, or only half. She only explained to Amy because she didn't know what to say. She had a kind of pout that was turning from charm to fat, and you had to admit that Mrs Moriarty was fat, even if her admirers called her plump. She was little and pink, with the pink pout underneath a lace cap, and there was the ribbon she had bought from Quongs' about a week ago. Sometimes she said she was thirty-two and sometimes

34

thirty-three, but that is only by the way.

I've come about the five pounds, said Amy, looking down at the floor.

Oh, yes. Yes. Is it five pounds?

Yes, said Amy, looking at the floor.

Dear, said Mrs Moriarty, the way these things mount up!

She stood by the mantelpiece. She was wearing a skirt, and a pink jacket, a bed-jacket perhaps, for there was a swan's-down round the neck. It was fastened across her bust with a paste brooch.

I wouldn't've come, Amy said, only—only the time before...

Mrs Moriarty frowned, because having her up on the mat like this, and a Chow at that, but it was all you could expect from a place like Happy Valley, why Ernest had ever brought her there, when they could have lived in Sydney in a flat. So she pouted and frowned, and picked at a spot or two of egg that had dried in the region of the paste brooch. It was very silent in the front room, only the silly tick of a brown mahogany clock that someone had given Ernest for a wedding present, they had made it clear that the clock was for Ernest, and she hated it, she wanted a French gilt clock like her sister had, only that one wasn't French.

Let me see now what I can do, said Mrs Moriarty, delving down apparently into the depths of her mind, and the sigh gave you to understand it was a considerable depth.

The Chow woman was saying something about small profits and quick returns, or small returns, or something, or something. It was a lie. Mrs Moriarty smouldered. The

35

way they let Mrs Furlow and Mrs Belper and that doctor's wife run up bills, it was humiliating, she said, just because she wasn't one of the Upper Three, but the schoolmaster's wife, and the way that old Belper woman ran about smelling of dogs, poking in her nose, that was what made her sick. She tapped with a finger on the mantelpiece. You couldn't help it if your face got lines. She must remember to write to Sydney for that lotion, perhaps they would give her a bottle on trial. And the Quong woman was sitting there, and she would have to give her a pound, so perhaps the postal note was more than she could afford, or go into Moorang on Saturday, or...

Mrs Moriarty fished out her bag; it was poked down behind a pink satin cushion, not on account of burglars, but because it usually got there on its own. It hurt her to part with a whole pound.

There, she said. There is a pound.

She held it by a corner, munificently. Her little finger was crooked.

Thank you, said Amy. I shall come on Saturday for the rest.

She got up. Her yellow face was slightly pink. She took up her umbrella that was standing against the wall.

The cheek of these people.

You should have left your umbrella outside, said Mrs Moriarty sharply, looking down at the pool.

I'm sorry, said Amy.

I shall have to wipe it up.

It's not on the carpet.

No. It's not on the carpet. Gertie! she called. Of course

she's gone for the steak. I shall have to wipe it myself.

. It was humiliating. She ought to have servants. Showing people like Amy Quong to the door, that was what Ernest had brought her to, if only he could get that job up on the North Shore. She watched Amy go down the street, treading calmly in her mackintosh, with a black bun that glistened behind her head. God, what a place it was, that street that you looked down every day and nobody ever came.

Poor Vic, you're not very happy, said Ernest sometimes, and patted her hand, and she felt a bit warmer towards him then, because he could see, though it wasn't a helpful remark, and it would not make her happier patting her hand. She went back into the sitting-room. There was something she ought to do. Lucy Adelon's Almond Lotion whitens the hands, an application morning and night, perhaps if she wore gloves, if she slept in gloves, with Ernest patting her hand and wheezing, she could not sleep for hearing him wheeze. She had liked his moustache. It looked distinguished, a schoolmaster with a moustache, and Daisy marrying a grocer, and she could not live with Daisy and Fred, in Marrickville at a grocer's shop. She had learnt to paint flowers on crêpe de chine. Ernest said she had beautiful taste, which was beautiful coming from behind his moustache that made him distinguished, that made her cultured, crêpe de chine flowers, and marrying a school-master was one up on Daisy and Fred. He collected stamps. He brought his album to show, bending over and telling her the names, it was an educational hobby, he said, he believed in educational hobbies, and if she liked he would show her how he stuck them in, you licked the end of the funny tag,

37

would she like to lick, and she had a lick, that funny taste on your tongue, and she licked a lot, she licked one that Ernest licked, oh dear, she said, going quite red and Ernest going red, he asked if she went to the pictures ever, he had seen the Shackleton film and wasn't it an education to see what Man could do, so perhaps she would come with him one night, there was a film about Queensland aboriginals on at the Rialto all next week.

She sat down in the sitting-room. There was something she had to do. She yawned, her whole face yawned, the little golden curls quivered at the side. When she went to bed at night she took a comb and frizzed them out. Ernest said she had pretty hair. Oh dear, she said, this place isn't good for your asthma, Ernest, she said. They don't give you a proper screw. You're killing yourself, she said, which was as good as saying you're killing me. Only I'm fond of Ernest, you can't live with anything long without feeling it's the furniture, that suite Mrs Belper has, running up bills indeed, and if only you had money you could show them what. You could live in a flat in Sydney, you could have a cook, and a maid with a cap. If Ernest got that job up on the North Shore she would have breakfast in bed, she would join a library and read in bed. She would be in the Sydney Morning Herald on the Ladies' Page, because of course she would play bridge, you had to play bridge, even if you hated cards, because it was a social obligation, and the paper would say: On Tuesday afternoon Mesdames Smith, Brown, Moriarty etc. etc. had bridge tables at David Jones's, and perhaps a description of her dress, she would wear powder-blue.

She sat with a chilblain on her foot, the window letting in the rain. That was Happy Valley. God, that street. And the window was stuck. Across the way a geranium had died in Mrs Everett's pot. And this damn window stuck, breaking your nails, and the rain.

Walter Quong drove past in a brand-new Ford. He had a round, fat yellow face that closed itself in smiles. He was waving his hand, and that was just like his cheek, as if she was one to spend her time waving from her window at Chinamen. She never waved to Walter Quong. He had tried to help her across the street, in Moorang, because it was dark, he said, and couldn't he drive her back, as he took her by the elbow, his hand, but she said she thought she would wait. After all the stories you heard about Walter Quong, it was like his cheek, what with that Everett girl at the cemetery, and old Mrs Everett jumping out, from behind a stone, they said, and hitting him over the head with a jar that someone had taken to fill with flowers. All the same it made you laugh, Walter Quong finding old Mrs Everett instead. Then he wanted to help her across the street. Those yellow, puffy hands.

Mrs Moriarty closed the window with a bang. Her bosom rose in an access of breath. There were little dots of sweat on her upper lip, on her pout. She rubbed her hands, Walter's hands that were small and plump. The very idea of a Chinaman. Then she went out to the back to see if Gertie had fetched the steak.

The pool from Amy's umbrella lay on the sitting-room floor.

4

Alys Browne lived by herself on the outskirts of the town just near a kink in the Kambala road. There were no other houses very close to her, though from her bedroom window she could see the bright red water-tank near the Belpers' house that provided such a nice piece of unconscious colour in the midst of the town's otherwise neutral tones. As a matter of fact Alys disliked the water-tank, because it slapped you in the face, she said, and she was rather given herself to a compromise in colour, something in the nature of a pale grey, or mauves. Mauve is a dangerous colour. If you see a woman who is wearing mauve you can bet right away she is a silly woman, and if you get close enough up to her she will have a particular scent that always goes with mauve, and if you are introduced to her—well, you will wish you hadn't been. But Alys Browne was not in every respect a mauve woman, though she liked to wear mauve, for she had at least a spine, you did not feel she was a dangling bundle of chiffon rags. And she had some definite opinions of her own, which nobody had the opportunity to hear because she always lived alone.

Mrs Moriarty said that Alys Browne was a snob. Mrs Belper said she was neurotic, whether it hit the mark or not, for this was a word Mrs Belper had learnt from an article on popular psychology in a woman's magazine, and having learnt it she had to use it somehow, she just had to, and of everyone in Happy Valley Alys Browne was the most likely mark. Anyway, she lived alone and seemed to like it, and that in itself was something queer.

Like most people who live alone, Alys was lonely, and like most lonely people living alone, she said she liked living alone. She was the daughter of Butcher Browne, who had owned land up at Kambala in the gold-rush days and had made money and lost it before Alys had time to think what money was. He speculated a bit. He drank a lot. He once rode a heifer down the main street. In fact Butcher Browne was a character. Finally he died of delirium tremens in a ditch while Alys was away in Sydney being companion to a Mrs Stopford-Champernowne.

Alys had not known her father very well. She was an independent sort of person, she liked to get away by herself. So she said, Father, I am going to Sydney, I am going to a convent. So she went to Sydney—this was when she was fifteen—and she stayed at a convent for four years, and learnt the piano and needlework. This did not worry her father, because he was too busy speculating in land and being a character in pubs. He said, all right, if Alys wants

to be a lady and learn needlework in a convent, all right.
So it suited everyone, especially Alys, who got on well with
the nuns without being particularly tractable, for she did
not want to become a nun herself. She did not know exactly
what she wanted to become. She read books. She thought
it would be nice to fall in love, if only she knew how to go
about it, and there was not much opportunity in a convent.

She read a lot of books, and she read poetry, particularly
Tennyson. When she was seventeen she had the reputation
of being pretty well read and rather a mysterious person,
which pleased her a lot. She began to cultivate a mysterious
look. She wrote a concentrated backhand with the greatest
ease. And then she thought she would change her name.
Because she had been christened "Alice," and that of course
did not go at all with mysterious looks, so she began to sign
herself "Alys" Browne, which was more to the point, she
felt. But that was a good many years ago. It was a long time
since she had stopped to write in a concentrated backhand,
and in Happy Valley there was nobody to appreciate mysterious looks. Only the name "Alys" remained, had become a
habit, she really did not know why. It was on a little brass
tablet at her front gate, ALYS BROWNE, PIANO-FORTE.

Teaching the piano at Happy Valley put her in a
pretty good position. She could have gone about with Mrs
Belper if she liked. And it was partly because she didn't
that Mrs Belper said she was neurotic. But Alys liked to
be independent. When she left the convent—she was then
nineteen—she went to be a companion to Mrs Stopford-
Champernowne, an old lady who did tatting and snored.
Mrs Stopford-Champernowne should by rights have been

a bitch, but she was nothing of the sort, and Alys was very happy there, living in Sydney, and picking up the old lady's tatting, and practically running the house. She even got rather fat. But she did not feel particularly independent. She thought she would go to California. So she went to a shipping office and got some pamphlets. But she did not go to California; she sat with the pamphlets in her lap in the evening at Mrs Stopford-Champernowne's, and she began to ask herself if she knew what independence was. She could not altogether decide. Sometimes she thought it was something to do with money, and sometimes something more abstract, more spiritual. She had read a poem by Henley, something about My head is bloody but unbowed. It was all very difficult, what was she going to do.

It was about this time that she got the wire to say her father had died in the ditch. This was disconcerting. She began to feel she was alone, and not independent, or was independence being alone, or what. Butcher Browne left her very little money, so she was not independent in that respect. Some acres of land near Kambala and a weatherboard house at Happy Valley, that was what she got. She began to grow thin again, consoling herself by saying it was better that way, she was thin by nature. She made herself a new dress to celebrate the change, and said to herself when she put it on, I was falling asleep in all that fat, I look a hundred times better thin, though I am really rather plain.

Here I am, she said to herself, Alys Browne, thin and plain. I cannot call my hair anything but nondescript. My eyes are not so bad, though of course that is only an excuse. I have nothing to stop me from going to California, except that I cannot make the effort, and after all it is such a long way, and they say the Tasman Sea is rough.

In the end she went to Mrs Stopford-Champernowne and said:

Mrs Stopford-Champernowne, my father has left me a little money and a house at Happy Valley. That is where I come from, you know. I have decided to go back to Happy Valley to live. I shall give piano lessons. And then I can also sew.

Very well, my dear, said Mrs Stopford-Champernowne, if you've made up your mind. I suppose you know best.

So it was all settled. Alys was rather surprised. It had settled itself, this going back to Happy Valley, she did not know exactly why. She could not explain. But anyway, she told herself, I shall be more independent giving music lessons, more independent than picking up tatting and walking with Mrs Stopford-Champernowne in Rushcutters Bay Park.

She had been back now what seemed a long time, it might have been six years, or was it seven? Nothing had happened to her. She felt she was just the same, though of course she wasn't. There had in fact been a young man in Sydney, a young man in a bank, who brought her chocolates, but she had never cared for chocolates, and there was nothing in the young man to make her start to like them better. There was nothing in that, she said. And, after all, falling in love was a secondary process. She might still go to California. She had sold her paddocks up near Kambala and had given the money to Mr Belper to invest. There were no dividends yet, but when there were she might

44

go to California. But why California? It suddenly struck her like that. And she did not know. Perhaps that was a secondary process too. Perhaps she did not want to go away, or wanting to go away had got itself into her head as a substitute for something else. Sometimes she stopped to think about that, but she could not discover a satisfactory answer. Satisfactory answers are generally scarce.

In the meantime there was plenty to do. Before the dances she made dresses for the girls. They came up to see her, bringing their patterns, and she generally helped them to decide whether it was to be taffeta or something else. She also did most of the sewing for Mrs Furlow at Glen Marsh. Mrs Furlow drove herself in, perhaps with Sidney, bringing anything she wanted done. And it was a kind of royal progress, Mrs Furlow's visit, because she was the wife of the richest man in the neighbourhood. But Sidney Furlow, who was her daughter, usually sat in the car. She had a very red mouth and had been to a finishing school.

If I were Sidney Furlow, Alys sometimes said. Then she stopped. Sometimes you want to go on being yourself, if only for very inadequate reasons, as if you know you will suddenly turn into a direction that is inevitable and you only have to wait. So she continued to sew and give music lessons. She could not play very well, but well enough. And sometimes she played for her own pleasure, she played Schumann, and after that Chopin, and then Beethoven with anxiety. But she liked Schumann best, because he made her feel slightly melancholy, and she just went on and on into a mental twilight and a finale of original chords.

She read too. She had started some of the Russians, Anna Karenina, and Turgeniev, but Tennyson sounded funny now, she could not read him any more. She liked to sit down at tea, and take off her shoes, and read a chapter of Anna Karenina, though sometimes she found it a bit of an effort and lapsed to the Windsor Magazine. Tolstoi was interesting though. She had spilt some tea on the seventy-second page. It gave the book a comfortable, intimate appearance, and she liked it better after that, as if she had always had it with her and had read it several times.

This was Alys Browne. She had got up early on the morning that Dr Halliday delivered the publican's wife, that Hagan came to Happy Valley in the truck, and that Mrs Moriarty had been visited by Amy Quong. She did not know why she got up early, but she pushed back the bedclothes and got up. There was snow on the ground. And later in the morning it began to rain. It will rain and rain, and I shall not go out, and to-morrow perhaps it will rain, she said, and I am perfectly happy, why, she said.

It was then that she cut her hand. She was slicing some onions in the kitchen for lunch, and the knife went down on her finger into the flesh. And she looked at the blood as it ran from her finger and soaked into the cracks in the wood. That just goes to show, she said, and knew at once that it sounded stupid, that she must do something, because her finger, and the blood. She wrapped her hand in a hand-kerchief. The rain was coming down on the roof, it made a noise on the corrugated iron. She was holding her hand in the handkerchief, staring stupidly out at the rain. This was the spirit of independence, cutting your finger on a wet

46

day, and everything went out of you as you felt the blood through the handkerchief. They said if you tied a tourniquet, if you had some string, if you held it under the tap, the cold water would congeal. The rain kept coming down as she held her finger under the tap, in spouts, the rain, the waterspouts. And the string was loose. She couldn't tie it with one hand. Perhaps I am affected, she said, playing Schumann and pretending to like Anna Karenina more than the Windsor Magazine, though I like it quite a lot. But if I were not affected I could tie a piece of string, or stand blood, and I can't stand blood, the way Mrs Everett when she tore her leg.

It was nearly lunch-time, she saw. But she did not want any lunch. She thought she would like to cry. But it's never much good crying on your own. That hill up there was grey, with a feathering of grey grass. In the spring it was green. She went up and lay on the hill in spring, that was a long way off, it was not spring, everything was a long way off.

Then she saw that the bleeding had stopped. I have been a fool, she said, as she wrapped up her hand again, but there was nobody here to see, that is one of the consolations of living alone. There was a pool of darkish blood on the table-top. But I don't like blood, or iodine, I ought to have iodine, to keep it in the house.

So altogether she felt very much alone. The fire in the sitting-room was almost out. It was exhausted, she was exhausted, she felt. She would go down to the doctor's and get him to bind up her hand, even if Mrs Halliday was cross to see her arrive in the middle of lunch. She would go down in spite of that. She would walk perhaps through the dining-room, disturbing them at their lunch, and she would be glad to see them sitting there, because it was good to look at faces after you had cut your hand, after you had discovered you were not as self-supporting as you thought. So she put on her coat and she went down the hill, holding her hand inside the flap of her coat. She walked in the rain without minding. It did not seem very relevant, or the mud, if only she could get to the doctor's house and see them sitting at their lunch. Passing people in the street you did not think, walking without a hat, and that man in a hat looking at your face.

When she got to the Hallidays' Mrs Halliday came to the door. She was having a busy morning, she let you know. Her hair told you as much.

The doctor isn't here, Mrs Halliday said. He's up at Kambala. To see a case. He's been there all night.

That was not helpful, to say the least.

But he ought to be back soon. He can't be away much longer. If you would like to wait.

I'll wait a little, Alys said.

Mrs Halliday took her into the doctor's room.

There, she said.

Then she left her. It was Monday morning. There was such a lot to do.

48

5

The truck drew up in front of the store. A face peered out, stared, retreated with the information that this was a stranger, a man in an overcoat.

It must be the man for Furlows', said Amy Quong. She put down a bottle of olive oil and went outside to see for herself.

Hagan was fishing in a trouser pocket for his fare. It was hard to get inside, under the overcoat. The wind cut into his face making it red. A drop on the end of his nose hung distinct and luminous.

You the man for Furlows'? asked Amy Quong.

Yes, he said.

This was one of the Chows, a squat little thing with a yellow-brown face, standing there like a schoolmistress, not all Chinese perhaps, but very like that schoolmistress in Muswellbrook.

They're sending a truck, she said, but it isn't here. The road's bad from Glen Marsh in weather like this.

That's a fine look-out for me, he said.

Oh, it'll be here all right if you wait.

Then it looks as though I'll have to wait.

In all this rain, or go into the store, and sit about with a lot of Chows. She stood there watching him with folded hands. It took some time for a strange face to sink in.

Got such a thing as a pub? he asked.

Round the left and up the street. You'll see it up at the top.

Well, I'll go on up and look for it, he said.

About time he had a drink, sitting in the truck with a loony all that way, there was nothing like a drink for company. That girl poured the gin into the ginger beer, sitting there cool as if it was water, then drinking it off. Said her name was Bella, sitting in Sydney drinking gin. He went on up the street. His walk was stiff from sitting cramped in the truck, and his coat hung down nearly to his heels. He turned the corner and there was a girl walking quickly down the hill, her hand held inside her coat. Flat and sour she looked, the kind that stared the other way when you gave them a smile, not that you'd waste your time, it was only friendly to smile. That was the sort of place you'd struck, you could see that, you were not a fool. It was a dirty joint. The houses looked as if they might fall down. It was poor and dirty, with skinny old women rooting about in their backyards, like so many rickety fowls. But he might have known, there was nothing but cockie farmers from Moorang to Happy Valley, and that was always a poor sign.

It made him feel superior to come from New England, where the big squatters drove into Muswellbrook for the picnic races. You had money to burn. You hadn't, but somebody had, and that was the point. Somebody always stood you a drink. As you leant up against the bar somebody always said, come on, Hagan, what'll you have? And it was intimate and friendly. You told stories, about the time the drought, about the time the floods, and they were always pretty tall, and everyone knew and tried to spin a taller one themselves.

He couldn't see any pub. She had said at the top. But all he could see was the pale road meandering out of the town and two old shorthorn cows standing nose to nose at the bend. A little miserable sheep-dog bitch quivered at the side of the road and gulped down a piece of bone. He felt like a dog in the rain. He felt like a fool.

Of course there were houses. You could always ask. Over there for instance, that woman in a cap peeping out of her front door, seeing what she could see, and she looked a bit of all right with that jacket hiding only half the goods.

I say, he called. Then he took off his hat. Excuse me, he said, can you tell me the way to the pub?

Yes, she said.

She came out on the steps.

Yes, it's just at the top. On the right. You can't miss it, she said.

She got back on to the porch out of the rain. This was a bit of class, he felt, with all those ribbons and the brooch. You could see she took her time, probably ate breakfast in bed. So he stood with his hat in his hand.

There's another one on the left, she smiled, but that's closed. They couldn't make two of them pay.

Well, that's a pity now, isn't it?

He had made her laugh. It came panting out very easily, perhaps a little too easily, but it showed she was ready to please. And when she laughed the little curls at the side jogged up and down.

Oh, she said suddenly, closing her mouth.

She ran back into the hall, as if she'd been bitten, as if...

No, she said, coming back. You're all right, she said, smiling again, they were old friends. I suddenly thought of the time. But you're all right. How the morning flies! And anyway you're a traveller. They'll always sell a traveller a drink.

That's one advantage, I suppose.

Makes you want to keep on the road.

He laughed himself. His hair was getting wet in the rain. He ought to put on his hat.

Well, she said, up on the right.

As if she was telling him he'd better move, and he couldn't stand there, right in front of her porch, but she'd like to keep him there all the same, or ask him in, or...She had a mole on her left cheek. And here he was standing in a puddle, and he ought to go.

So long, he said.

She nodded her head, smiled, her lips sank back again into a pout.

As she said, it was just a little way up on the right. It was a big brown building, wood, with baskets of ferns that hung down dead from the verandah ceiling. They drooped down very black and spidery out of the baskets of net. The verandah had a dirt floor. A child's celluloid doll was lying on its face, one leg cocked up in the air. Well, this was the place and a drink was a drink anywhere. He looked back down the road. She was still standing on the porch of her house. As soon as he turned she went inside as if she did not want him to know she had watched him up the road. He waved, but already it was too late, she had gone inside, she had not seen. He smiled and opened the door of the bar.

Morning, said Hagan, going into the black atmosphere of the bar.

He slapped the black wood with his hand, just in a spirit of friendliness, to show he knew what was expected in a place like this. The publican nodded. He had a sharp, drawn face, his lips going in on the gums. It was not what you expected of a publican, any of this, or the bar, but it was Happy Valley after all, so he said to the publican sharply:

A double Johnnie Walker, Steve.

In a dark square that was all you could see of an inner room (it was probably the kitchen or a scullery) the publican's wife and two girls paused in wiping dishes and stared at the strange face. He did not feel moved to return their stare. It made you feel lumped down in nowhere, this black room. Only the woman standing at her front porch waving the direction with plump hands gave you a sense of being anywhere at all. You could see she was different, and that she saw you were different, a kind of mutual sympathy.

There were two men in the bar. One was perhaps a drover, wearing a plaid overcoat and spurs. The spurs tinkled when he moved his feet. And he had a black leather stock-whip over his arm. But the other was an old man, one of those static old men you see in country bars, who seem to have no significance at all, except as recipients of drinks that they pour in through the meshes of a yellowish moustache, just standing and nodding, willing to listen to a story, but never giving much in return. They are generally called Abe or Joe. Though this one was called Barney, as a matter of fact.

Just a dried-up old post, like a post rotten with ants. Hagan swallowed his drink. And the snakey drover, with a stock-whip coiled like a black snake.

Yes, said the drover to the old man, that was a nice little mare. Carry you a 'undred miles an' not a sore on 'er back. She was game. An' not too big. She was a pretty little mare. So I said to Walter, 'ow much do you want for your mare, Walter, I said. An' Walter said, look, 'Erbert, if I was to sell that mare I'd be sellin' me bloody self, 'e said. An' I said, you're right, Walter, you wouldn't see a finer little mare in the country, Walter, I said.

The man nodded his head.

You wouldn't see a finer mare, he agreed.

Hagan had another whisky. It made him sick, talking about some runt of a horse, as if you could breed a horse on sour country like this, that wasn't a bag of worms with a couple of gammy legs. It just made him sick.

What you know about horses? he said.

Eh? said the drover, opening his eyes.

Hagan plunged his mouth in his glass. He would take his time. He would make them open their eyes. And he wished she could have seen, with her pink ribbons, how

54

he dealt with people in bars, or how he got on a horse, that time in Singleton, and that was a horse. So he filled his mouth with whisky and swallowed it down, and it was no doubt whisky made you feel good, made you open your coat. He stood there with his legs apart staring impressively at the two men.

You haven't got horses down here, he said, and waited for it to sink in. You won't breed horses in hill country, nothing but runts, he said. Give us another whisky, Steve. You won't have seen horses if you haven't been up north. Nothing but runts down here.

An' who said I haven't been up north? said the drover, shifting his whip.

His spurs tinkled as he spat straight on the floor. The lip of the old man hung pinkly, stupidly, down.

Nobody said, said Hagan, taking his glass. I was making a statement, nothing more.

Two can't play at that, I suppose?

Hagan bent his knees. He was talking to people in bars, and they listened because there was something to hear, because he could tell a story well, and he was feeling good for the first time, just as if the pub was full, in race week up north, and people coming in, and girls in the bedrooms upstairs changing their dresses for a dance.

There was a horse in Singleton, he said, swallowing down. That was a horse. A big brown colt. They couldn't do a thing with that bloody colt. And there you could see, he was a beauty, plenty of bone and size, nothing runty about a horse like that. But there they were standing round, bringing twitches and God knows what, and the colt shaking them

55

off, and the saddle-cloth they threw over his head. It made you laugh. There was a cove called Rube Isaacs, and Rube got a kick straight in the pants. Well, you couldn't help laugh to hear Rube letting on. And the horse just stood there snorting, flattening his ears. So I up and said, what do you say if you leave off arsing about and let me have a go at the horse. The brute wasn't having a chance. And I grabbed hold of the brute by the ear. I twisted his bloody ear all right. And I got on his back. And Christ, he didn't half let fly round and round that yard, and everyone climbing on to the fence. I thought I was losing me guts, the way we kept on hitting the ground, with that big bastard heaving about. And then...well, what do you think?

Nobody thought. The three women in the inner room paused with their napkins and stared out. The drover wiped his nose on the back of his hand.

He cleared the fence, said Hagan, taking a drink, and started on a five-mile lick. But he hadn't got me beat. Not me. I haven't had a horse that could beat me yet. I just gave that colt his head and let him do what he liked.

Wonder 'e ain't doin' it yet, said the drover, slamming down his glass.

Doing what?

You ought to know, said the drover, shifting his whip. You're tellin' the story. It isn't me.

Now look here, if you think...

There ain't no cause to get nasty, gentlemen, said the publican, leaning over the bar. His lips flapped in on his gums. For he only wore his teeth on Sunday afternoons.

Who's getting nasty? said Hagan.

56

You ought to be able to tell us that. Don't let that one beat you, the drover said.

The old man simpered into his beer.

If you think I'm a liar...

You're a touchy one, sighed the drover. You'll be telling a bloke 'e's got 'is 'and on your watch-chain next.

This was what you got for telling a story to a snake-face, and you couldn't argue with a snake, you broke its back without waiting to ask what it thought. You told a story and you knew it was a story, or a lie, or a story, but you didn't tell a man it was a lie because it was a story. But those mean snake eyes, he'd like to push its face, and she'd see he was pretty strong, like the time he bashed that shearer up at Werris Creek, she'd like to see, standing there with a bit too much on view, and white, with that sort of fur around the neck. He wanted to hit somebody, something. He wanted to land out, show that it wasn't being drunk, because anyway it wasn't drunk, and eating at seven o'clock, she said was time to beckon him past the clock, to look, to eat, looking at the clock to see if a traveller or what.

Keep it friendly, gentlemen, said the publican.

That's right, Bill, said the drover. We're all pals, ain't we? Bloody pals. 'Ere you, Mr Horsebreaker, what are you goin' to have on me?

I'll have the same, said Hagan.

You couldn't refuse the offer of a drink.

It was a lovely horse.

You bet it was, said the drover.

Yes. A lovely horse.

Even if he hadn't ridden, not that horse, he had ridden

a horse, and here they were leaning with their arms on the bar, their elbows touching, and it was better now, a familiar glow in the bottles, the publican's face filled out into a plumper curve. There was a clatter of plates from the kitchen inside as the publican's wife piled them up, and the two girls hung their cloths to dry by the stove. The drover was telling about the time he was caught in the snow above Kambala with a mob of sheep, it was early snow, he was bringing them down from summer pasturage, but the snow caught them and the sheep died, and once two men had died in a drift at the same place, and someone saw one of the men about five years after, only it wasn't the man, it was something like him, moving about among the trees, or perhaps it was only a grey tree. Then Hagan told the one about how he swam the Barwon in flood. And the one about the girl and the motor-bike. They all laughed, the old man very high up, so that you wondered a bit. But they were all friends.

I'll have to be getting along, said Hagan. They're sending a truck from Glen Marsh.

He patted the drover on the back. He wanted to lie down on the floor and let the drover walk over him, they could all walk over him, he loved them all. But instead he had to go to Glen Marsh. He always had to move on just as the geography of a place began to get familiar, and altogether it was very sad.

I'll be seein' you, the drover said, returning the pat on the back. He was going down to Tharwa in the afternoon, he came from there, he would not come back for a year or two, but you said things like that.

So long, Barney, said Hagan. So long, Bill.

Then he went out into the slush. The rain dribbled down, dribbled down, and the ruts coming up to meet, because you were drunk, because Furlow said, and damn Furlow, money or not, to sober up on the way. He felt just that, splash splash the mud. She waved her hands, they always did, though only as a formality, and you went straight ahead, if you saw a blonde hand waving out of a window-pane. But he did not see her. The windows were blank. A feeble hen had come round to the front and was picking at a garden bed. Dead. The house was dead. There was no sign.

A brand-new Ford came bumping along the street, swerved, cast up a spray of watery mud on Hagan's over-coat. The yellowish, cheerful face of a Chinaman looked out from the steering wheel, tried to frown, but smiled. The car bumped over the ruts and down the hill.

Hagan swore. To be run over by a bloody Chow right in the middle of the street. It made him angry again. He scraped off some of the mud with his fingers and flicked it back on to the road. He looked at his fingers stupidly. They were thick and hard, with a mist of reddish hairs on the back. He would like to feel that Chinaman's jaw. He would like to finger a paste brooch or to probe beyond swan's-down into a region that was mysteriously pink. But instead he continued uncertainly down the hill, and when he reached the store there was the truck waiting to take him out to Glen Marsh.

6

They stood about in a little aimless group behind the urinal. There was Andy Everett, and Willy Schmidt, and Arthur Ball, besides Rodney Halliday. Willy Schmidt was chewing a liquorice strap from Quongs', so that his ordinarily well-formed pink, if insipid, mouth had become a blue-black smear.

'Ere, said Willy suddenly, you can 'ave a piece of this 'ere strap, Andy. I'll give you 'alf if you like.

Andy Everett was throwing stones at the corrugated iron of the urinal wall. The stones went bang, bang, and plumped down into the mud.

I don't want your strap, Andy Everett said. I'd've taken a bit if I wanted to, but I don't like lickerish strap.

He continued to throw stones.

Of course 'e'd've taken a bit, laughed Arthur Ball. An' so 'ud I.

Willy Schmidt went very red.

Rodney Halliday stood apart, he was with them, but just a little way off, kicking a hole in the ground. It gave him a queer, horrible thrill to hear Andy Everett speak like that, to hear the omnipotent smack of the stones, and to wonder what would happen next. They always went behind the urinal in the break. Rodney watched the face of the clock, knew it would happen in so many minutes now, the hands turning, the heart. Then they would go down to the bottom of the yard. His heart fell. He hated Andy Everett and Arthur Ball. Willy Schmidt he just despised, sucking liquorice there, with the strap dangling from his mouth. Willy Schmidt, like Rodney himself, merely hovered on the edge.

Andy had stopped throwing stones.

Rodney still looked at the ground. He wished that he had not followed them down the yard. It would be so easy to go and play with the girls. He lay in bed at night and said, I shan't go with Andy Everett any more. But he went. Once he woke from a dream of Andy pulling out his teeth, that were as big as logs, and he lit the candle, and his face was yellow in the candlelight looking over at the mirror at the other side of the room, his face dancing in reflection and wet with tears. The silence was a ticking clock, substance a great shadow that bent down over the bed, the form of Andy Everett past and present and inevitably future.

Look at Green-face there, said Andy Everett.

It was dull behind the urinal. There was nothing to do. He felt a sudden contempt for Rodney Halliday. You could see it coming on his square red face. Rodney saw it. His stomach quailed.

Green-as-grass Halliday, chanted Arthur Ball.

Willy Schmidt sniggered through a liquorice pulp.

Rodney kicked at the ground. You could not say anything, because your throat, that hot swelling, and a sick tingle in your stomach, or turn, because to-morrow came, and you followed them down the yard. He hated Andy Everett's face under the cropped hair, he hated the red mottled skin, his hands were very strong and muscular because in the evening he helped his father milk the cows.

What shall we do to Mumma's boy? asked Andy, taking him by the arm.

The face was very close, those red spots, and the body hard as it pressed against your side. There was a lingering smell of cows on the old serge coat that Andy Everett always wore.

Give 'im a windmill, chanted Arthur Ball.

Once upon a time you resisted windmills, fought against the sharp twisting of the hair above your ears, and they all laughed, but you fought, and then it was no good. You did not resist. You let it happen. The ring of faces, with Willy Schmidt putting out an adventurous hand, and the toothy mouth of Arthur Ball, and Andy Everett's bullet head. If you tried hard enough you became a thing, a dull whimper that did not come out, or only half, because they must not know.

I'll give 'im the windmill, said Willy Schmidt.

But they all gave the windmill in turn, Andy Everett holding his arms, Andy Everett's body pressed up against his back. They said you got lice from cows. Perhaps Andy Everett would give him lice. He did not care. Perhaps they would tear out his hair by the roots. Willy Schmidt had now gathered courage enough to give him several windmills in succession. He darted about from foot to foot, chewing wildly at the liquorice strap.

There are times when you've got to run your head against the inanimate agents of pain. Even though you know you're mad, that they cannot feel, it is some relief to your feelings to increase that pain by venting them on the feelingless. It is desperate but necessary. So you kick the chair, so you bang your head against the wall. And it was in much this spirit that Rodney Halliday burst from Andy Everett's arms and gave Arthur Ball a crack on the mouth and Willy Schmidt a kick on the shins. But then he was afraid. At once. It is only a momentary and stupid respite to attack the agents of pain.

I'll break your bloody neck, roared Arthur Ball.

And Rodney Halliday knew that, metaphorically speaking, his bloody neck was as good as broken, knew he was lying on the ground with Andy Everett sitting on his chest and his ears singing from repeated clouts. There was a bell that rang erratically in his head. What have you done to your coat, all that mud, his mother said. He did not cry. There was no breath in his body. Or breath had curdled. There was a hard kernel of petrified breath that would not come out, and the bell ringing.

Better leave 'im. There's the bell, said Arthur Ball, a thread of blood trickling from his lip.

Andy continued to deal monotonous clouts.

That'll teach you, he said.

Then he got up grinning slowly, slowly wiping his

hands. The small knot unravelled itself, the threads trailing across the yard, Andy and Arthur and Willy, their heads turned back, their faces still intent on reluctantly relinquished pleasure in the form of Rodney stretched still on his back.

P'raps something's up, said Willy nervously at the door, but after all it was Andy's fault, it wasn't him, he hadn't wanted to.

Then Rodney got up. Andy grinned. The three of them went inside.

It was over, Rodney Halliday said. He would go inside and do arithmetic. But it was over for the day. He tried to brush the mud from his coat. He was aching. He was bleeding. He was also free. And he would go home for lunch and read that book on Columbus till it was time for afternoon school. There was no break in the afternoon. He used to run home as fast as he could. Sometimes they chased him and threw stones. But he could really run very fast. And now there was a feeling of exhaustion and of triumph, almost like leaving the dentist's in at Moorang, only Mother was not there to buy him an ice-cream. Instead he would go inside and wrestle with sums.

They did not look when he went in. They bent their heads over exercise books. Only some of the girls had a look. Emily Schmidt tittered behind her hand, because it was Rodney Halliday. She whispered to Margaret Quong. But Margaret Quong leant over her book, doing a leaf design in the margin, not looking up. And Rodney sat down. It was arithmetic. One of his knuckles had lost some skin.

If A and B are given a bag of one hundred and eighty

apples, said Mr Moriarty, writing it up on the board. And A eats two a day, and B eats three, and after a fortnight they are joined by C, who eats seven, how long will it be before they've emptied the bag?

He spoke in a dry, precise voice, like chalk dust falling. Or he paused and you heard a wheeze that Willy Schmidt could imitate, though of course not loud enough for the old cow to hear. The chalk squealed on the board. Margaret Quong writhed and drew down her head, like a tortoise, into her jumper neck. One hundred and eighty apples, breathed Willy Schmidt. Somebody had upset the ink. Somebody made a smell. The stove crackled. The clock said a quarter past.

The school at Happy Valley was built like the rest of the town, with a purpose, and not for beauty. It was also built without regard for time, that had already made considerable incursions on its body, softening its joists, weakening its joints, blanching its colour, and scoring its face with cracks. The school was squat and completely drab. It lay on its square of bare yard with the two lavatories at the end, one for Girls and one for Boys, and almost seemed to totter a bit when the wind came down from the mountains and struck its side. A corner of the corrugated-iron roof flapped in the wind. It ought to be seen to, Mr Moriarty said, but as nobody saw to it, a basin continued to stand in the corner of the larger schoolroom to catch the water that fell inside.

In the smaller room sat the younger children with a pupil-teacher, a young Miss Purves, who suffered from chronic catarrh and chilblains on the feet. Altogether her time was pretty well taken up in straying from her nose

65

to her feet, with dabbing and scratching, and rolling her handkerchief into a smaller ball or hanging it out to air on the desk. She had another handkerchief stuck through an armlet, as a kind of reserve, but this she seldom used. She just used to dab and scratch, or rest her receding chin on a cold hand.

The big children were dealt with by Ernest Moriarty in the larger and more imposing room, that smelt of a coke stove and clotting ink and settled chalk. When it rained you could hear the water dripping down into the enamel basin from the roof that nobody came to see about. But the room was not so lugubrious, in spite of Mr Moriarty sitting in his overcoat and scarf, for the sake of his asthma, he would have said, sitting there correcting exercises with his bluish hands. It was not so lugubrious. There were maps of Asia and Africa, and a larger one of Australia over the desk. And you could lean on your elbow when you were bored and wander up the Ganges or wonder about Irkutsk. There was also a stuffed fox in a case, and some jars of spirit containing various snakes. And somebody sometimes brought some flowers.

Rodney Halliday sighed. A and B and C. Sharing apples with Andy Everett and Arthur Ball. He experienced a mild shiver of recollected discomfiture, from contact with Andy's body that smelt of cows. And he could not do sums. If you leant on your elbow and waited till it died, you were lost in the Indian Ocean's turquoise glaze, you jogged across a saffron steppe east of the Caspian Sea, and the plain of India was a field of blood. But his knuckle no longer hurt. It was numbed from paying tribute to A, B, and C. He sucked his knuckle. His breath was a silver cloud, in spite of the restless coke stove his breath sailed out silverly into the Yellow Sea, beyond this the god's face in the encyclopaedia, and a bearded cinnamon-tree, and a god squatting on a kind of plant, like Margaret Quong. He looked across at Margaret Quong, who sat, not on a lotus, but on a bench doing sums, and she was good at sums, she was the best, she was thirteen, and she helped her aunt make up the books at the store. He would like to play with Margaret Quong. She had a soft voice. But she was thirteen, and he was only nine. She was also a girl. So he had to go down with Andy and Arthur and Willy behind the lavatory, and you knew, and you knew. But you did not think of that. You turned over a page in the mind till A, B, and C were facing you. It was better like that.

It was better like that, said Ernest Moriarty, correcting an essay by R. Dormer on the Cow and Her Relationship with Man. She kept on saying, it'll kill you, Ernest, and look at the screw, it's shameful the way, and a man with all those years of service, and if you got that job up on the North Shore we could easily keep a maid. The Cow is a useful animal. She gives us meat, milk, and menewer. In the evening the Cow went slowly home and they milked her dry. She was content. He was content, of course he was content. He had his stamps. He was secretary to the Moorang Philatelists' Society. Only Vic, sitting in the front room, said that the sofa was wearing out. She was still very pretty, like those evenings in Marrickville when they licked stamps together and he touched her hand. And then he could not restrain himself, and he had to go home, and perhaps the people in the tram knew why he was wheezing, and it was uncomfortable to walk. The Cow has an udder with four tits. I don't want to complain, she said, only I'm fond of you, only it's for your own good. He wrote and nothing happened. He showed her the letters before he sealed them up. And nobody came to mend the roof. It made him feel bad, in spite of those new powders, and at night he could hardly breathe. So he could not very well do more than write. Poor, pretty, pink Vic. It made him proud to possess her, not physically, that is, because that always made him wheeze, but to know that she was there, like the three-cornered Cape of Good Hope blue and the surcharged German New Guinea. He arranged R. Dormer's exercise book on the pile. It was very neat, a perfect square of exercise books with a rubber on the top. There were four pencils and a pen in a little wooden tray in front of the ink.

I've finished that one, Archie Braithwaite said.

Then he cringed back on the desk. Andy Everett had given him a kick.

Turn to page ninety-four. Example number thirty-six.

The Cow resumed her laborious Relationship with Man.

The Yellow Sea and the Red Sea, and the Blue Pool near Moorang, where you went for picnics in the summer, if it was a good summer, if there was no drought, but if there was a drought. Arthur Ball had blood on his face. The way your knuckle stung as it landed on Arthur's teeth.

Emily Schmidt smelt her handkerchief, passed it to Gladys Rudd to smell. Her lips spelt Parma Violets behind her hand. Emily Schmidt smiled in a vastly superior way and played about with her ring.

It was dull, because this was school, because the feverish chant of the younger children burst in a thin unison through the wooden wall, intensifying the monotony with a twiceoneatwo, twicetwoafour, twicethreeasix, seeming to paralyse the progress of the clock. And there is no monotony so desperate as the activities of A, B, and C, nothing so definitely guaranteed to work havoc with the nails or to make you groan inwardly at the endlessness of time. Until, with the ultimate gesture of a formal hand, the clock points beyond these deserts to a luxuriance of sound and motion and sensation suddenly revived.

Conversation became intricate at twelve o'clock. Somebody banged the door. Somebody dropped a book. Somebody bounced a ball. Then they were going out. Their voices distributed themselves in the open air as they started to walk home, or ran. Rodney Halliday ran very lightly up the road as hard as he could go. He drew his legs up under him and jumped a ditch. He ran on past the wire fence, under the telephone wires, under the truculent murmur that telephone wires have, and a knotting of small birds.

Emily Schmidt walked with Gladys Rudd, letting her smell the handkerchief.

Are you coming up this evening, Emily? asked Margaret Quong.

No, said Emily.

Why ever not?

Because.

Emily Schmidt compressed her lips. She had a face that

69

was small and pale and concentratedly vicious under her pale slender curls.

My Mumma said I'm not to go to Quongs'.

So did mine, agreed Gladys Rudd.

All right, said Margaret.

Her voice was very resigned. She began to walk on ahead, looking down at her feet. Behind her Gladys and Emily began to giggle. They began to sing high up in voices nasally intense, and remarkably alike:

My Mumma said I never should
Play with the gypsies in the wood.
If I did she said she would...

Margaret walked on quickly bending her head. She did not listen. She tried to avoid unpleasantness. She did not ask for reasons, because reasons were unpleasant, and she knew already, vaguely underneath, that it was Father that made Emily giggle and compress her lips. It was that time about the Everett girl, and Mrs Everett going to court, and Mother had gone to court, and there was that time in at Moorang when they ran Father in for doing something you did not think about.

She hung her head and walked along. She was thin and straight, with her hair cut straight in a fringe over the eyes that were more oblique than Amy's even, or Arthur's, or Walter's eyes. Chinese eyes, said Ethel Quong with very definite bitterness. Ethel Quong was Walter's wife, and before she had married Walter, before Margaret was born, she had been a housemaid at Government House. How

Ethel married Walter Quong will keep till later on. It is sufficient to know that she is bitter about it, and that when she looked at Margaret she often said, your sins will always find you out. Only she did not think it was fair that she should pay for her sins on her own, she always insisted that Margaret should share the debt.

And that is why Margaret had acquired the habit of looking down and closing her ears to unpleasantness. She did not hear what Emily and Gladys sang. She would go back to dinner at home, and she did not care, and Father would come in from the garage wearing overalls and make a lot of pleasant jokes. She found it difficult to connect Father in overalls with the things you did not think about and which made Mother bitter, because she had married a Chinaman, Walter Quong. It was too much to unravel, all this. And on the whole she was happy, helping Aunt Amy at the store, or going for a music lesson at Miss Browne's. Only sometimes, walking home, she felt unhappy. There was a lot inside her that got churned up.

There was a dull, mysterious moan in the telephone wires.

Rodney Halliday no longer ran. He had passed the road that led to Andy Everett's and Willy Schmidt's. He felt larger now. He began to whistle. Stooping down, he pulled up his socks and glanced back down the road to see the others straggle along in little groups, preceded by Margaret Quong. He liked being alone. Only sometimes he didn't, and then he thought about it a bit, and then he preferred to be alone.

He looked from side to side of the road. The air was

very sharp. In one of the paddocks a bull was serving a cow. He looked, and he looked away. He remembered the time— he was a good bit younger—when the dogs came into the yard, and his mother went red and shooed them away, and he had cried because she would not let them play. Mother said, later you'll understand. And later he did. And it made you look sideways at the bull out of the corner of your eye. But of course you understood. A bull and a cow. He stopped at the side of the road and had a proper look. He would have liked to stay there by the fence and see it happen again. He jingled some pennies in his trouser pocket, and a shell he always carried about. But somebody was coming and perhaps they had seen him look. It was Margaret Quong, walking along the side of the road. If Margaret Quong had seen, as she must, then he felt ashamed. But she looked down at the ground.

They both continued to walk along.

He took a look at Margaret, at that funny black hair like a doll's, and the eyes. He saw that she was almost crying, and that made him embarrassed too, because he didn't know what to do, or say, or if he should do nothing, or what. But Margaret did not speak. It made him uncomfortable to see her cry.

Margaret, he said.

Yes?

She did not look over from her side of the road.

Look, he said.

What?

She turned her head, biting her cheek inside. She was like that picture in the encyclopaedia.

72

I'll give you that, he said.

What is it?

It's a shell.

They began to walk in the centre of the road. He held the shell in the palm of his hand. It was pink, of curious shape, folding like the bud of a flower with brown spots on the underneath. Margaret put out her finger and touched the shell.

It's pretty, she said.

When we lived in Sydney, he said, there was a French woman used to come to teach me French. She gave me the shell. She said it came from the bottom of the sea.

Really? said Margaret. How did she know?

I don't know. That's what she said.

It's pretty all the same.

Rodney put it into her hand. Then they walked along a bit. The mud splashed up on Margaret's stockings. She began to wipe her nose.

Her name was Madame Jacquet, Rodney said.

Margaret looked down at Madame Jacquet's shell.

When I'm twelve I'm going to go to a proper school, said Rodney. Father says I shall be a boarder. I'll only come home for the holidays. But now I'm only nine. I'll have to learn Latin as well as French. Because I'm going to be a doctor. You have to know Latin for the prescriptions, I suppose.

It was good to talk to Margaret Quong, and there was a lot he wanted to tell her, about what he liked and what he didn't. He wanted her to know. But now they had come to the turn, and she stood waiting to say good-bye.

73

Thank you for the shell, said Margaret Quong.

That's all right, he said. It wasn't much use to me.

She began to walk on, uncertainly, up in the direction of her father's garage, where a truck had stopped for a fill at the pump. Her black woollen stockings were dotted with yellow mud. He would have to go in to lunch.

Rodney! called Margaret Quong. You can come one evening and see our litter of pups. Only if you want to, she said.

Then she went on up the hill clutching Madame Jacquet's shell.

Somebody leaves you alone in a strange room, in a house you have scarcely been in before, and this is the surest way of feeling detached from all possible sequence of events. You are no longer part of the whole, to which in your saner moments you like to think you belong. You wait in the strange room and this is another life. You try to reconstruct this other life from the objects you see in the room, and it is all on another plane, a little monstrous, and you even think in an undertone in case it should be heard.

Well, Alys Browne was feeling something like this as she waited alone in the doctor's room. There was no fire, and this intensified the feeling of detachment, making the objects sharper in outline, distinctly part of a life that was not her own. She sat for a bit in a leather chair holding her cut hand in her lap, feeling cold and forgotten, especially the hand, and the chair, there is nothing so calculated to make you feel forgotten as somebody else's leather chair in a fireless room. Then she got tired of sitting. She walked about. The woman who helped was sorting out linen in the wash-house across the yard. Alys could see her from the window, and a toy cart filled with stones lying in the middle of the yard. But there was not much to see from the window other than this.

So she went and sat in the chair again. It was still a little warm from her body the time before. The air perhaps was a little bit warmer too. And on the mantelpiece there were photographs of two little boys, one of them sitting on the floor with some bricks, looking very absorbed, and the other a few years older, standing with his ears sticking out. The elder boy was Rodney; she knew him by sight, they said good morning or good afternoon whenever they passed in the street, and she liked the way his ears stuck out. Only he was rather pale out of a photograph. And there was Mrs Halliday too, sitting on the doctor's desk with an air of having only a moment to spare, she must jump up, the photographer mustn't mind.

She remembered when the Hallidays came, about a year ago. She supposed that she ought to call, but she didn't call, and she said she would call later on, and then the intention lapsed. Mrs Belper called. She said that the scones were stale, and Mrs Halliday—well, there was no atmosphere in the Hallidays' home, and Mrs Halliday such a stick, though you could see the poor woman was ill, but you must have atmosphere in a home. By atmosphere Mrs Belper meant dogs, and pokerwork candlesticks, and people dropping in and out.

Mrs Halliday sat nervously in her frame. Alys felt sorry for the doctor's wife. She began to be more at home crossing her legs in the leather chair, for even a railway waiting-room will slowly fit itself into your scheme if you are forced to stay in it long enough. She looked at the black rug with the hole that something had burnt, falling out of the fire, or a cigarette. There were pipes on the mantelpiece. There were books, medical books, Urn Burial, a volume of poems by Donne, and a book on Kant. She had read about Kant. She was rather impressed. And perhaps the doctor would have read Turgeniev, or Anna Karenina. But you did not talk about things like that, you came for something out of the dispensary, and then you went away again, because Dr Halliday did not encourage you to talk. He said good morning in the street. Otherwise you did not exist. His eyes were very cold. They were blue, she thought, or grey, she could not be sure. He was going grey. And now they were starting to have lunch, she could hear the plates, but the doctor had not come, or had come, and Mrs Halliday...

Then somebody opened the door.

Hello, said Rodney, looking in.

He looked a little surprised. He stood awkwardly by the door. Then he went outside again, finding nothing further to say.

He wanted to get the book and read about Columbus after lunch, but with that Miss Browne sitting there, he would go away, he could wait, he did not want to talk to Miss Browne, talk to anyone, Margaret Quong, he was glad he had given the shell, and now he could go up to Quong's garage and have a look at the pups. He went along the passage to the dining-room.

Rodney, called Mrs Halliday, where is George? Look at your coat! What have you done to yourself? Look at that mud!

Which was just what he knew she would say.

I fell down in the yard, he said.

Oh dear, she said, the way you ruin your clothes! Go and find George.

He's coming, he said, sitting down.

Whether he was or not, he was hungry, even if cold mutton, he hated that. He took an onion out of the jar. Mother was standing there carving the joint.

I wish your father would come, said Mother, slicing a piece of fat. George! she called. Where is George? Rodney, you *never* help. Put those onions down at once.

All right, said Rodney. George'll come.

He sat back and scratched his head. He wished he had someone older, like Margaret Quong, and the pups, but George was young, playing about in the backyard with a cart, or falling down and hurting himself.

There is great indignity attached to having a brother younger than yourself.

Mother! called George. I can't, I can't open the door.

Rodney, said Mother, can't you see my hands are full? Can't you open the door for George?

Oh, all right, he said. If only you would give me time.

But they drove him about. He would not take long over his lunch. He would get that book and read it alone in his room. Perhaps he would be an explorer, not a doctor after all. But perhaps there was nothing left to explore.

George was fat, and uncertain on his feet. He nearly fell over when Rodney opened the door.

Don't fall over, said Rodney.

I didn't!

Don't tease him, said Mother. Georgie, darling, look at your nose! Be a man and give it a wipe.

I don't want to wipe my nose.

It'll fall in your food, Rodney said.

Don't be disgusting! Mother said. Come here to Mother and let her wipe.

George was crying. He always cried.

Oh dear, coughed Mrs Halliday, what a pair of children I have!

She sat down to mutton and pickled onions, coughing still, even after a mouthful of water she coughed. She rested her elbows on the table, looking as if she wondered whether she had time to eat. Because that sheet that Mrs Woodhouse tore, and darning wool, there was no feed for the fowls, Oliver come, or Rodney call in at the store, his coat all mud like that, and the sick hen with the scaly eyes, Oliver take a gun, but a long way off, holding ears.

Hilda Halliday pushed back her plate of mutton and pickles and sat with one elbow on the table holding a hand to her chest. The thought of sickness, even in a hen, always made her put her hand to her chest.

Eat it up now, George. There's a good boy, she said. Mother isn't hungry. But you eat yours.

Hilda Halliday was almost forty. Oliver was thirty-four. But they were happy, she said. Sitting on the seat in the Botanical Gardens, in the warm smell of Moreton Bay figs, he said he would write a poem. She was wearing a yellow hat that made her look slightly pale. And of course Rodney was pale, he took after her, not Oliver, and it was not anaemia as everyone said. Fancy falling down on his back.

You didn't hurt yourself, dear? she asked.

Why?

Falling down on your back.

No, said Rodney.

He would make a paper aeroplane and climb up into the girders at the garage at Quong's and let it come floating down. Margaret would stand underneath. Walter Quong gave him petrol for his lighter, which he only kept to see the flame, for of course he did not smoke.

You must be careful, Hilda said.

Oliver said it too, and that Dr Bridgeman they called in about her cough, but she had not wanted to tell Oliver, and Bridgeman advised the country, somewhere bracing, it would be all right, nothing to worry, only she must have plenty of air. Air. Hilda Halliday sat at the table and took in a good breath of air. It would be all right. And Oliver was pleased, the way she had soon picked up. Only sometimes at night she began to cough, stifled a cough so that Oliver would not wake. Sometimes at night she thought what she would not think, that Happy Valley, if only they could go to Queensland perhaps or somewhere warm, she was afraid, only it was for the boys, not for herself. She could not afford to become a drag. Oliver really must shoot that hen limping about in the yard.

Rodney, she said, you've hurt your hand.

He was sailing in the Yellow Sea. He had forgotten his hand. Now it came back.

Yes, he said, sullenly. I hit Arthur Ball on the face.

Then you were fighting. I thought as much. You didn't fall down on your back. I don't like to think that you tell untruths.

He thought it sounded silly to call it an untruth when it was a straight-out lie. He bit his lip and frowned.

Oh well, he said.

No. I like to think I can believe what you say.

It was all coming back, Andy Everett, that big cow smelling of cows, and perhaps lice, with a bullet-head, bending over your bed in a dream and twisting your arm behind the lavatory at school, and going to a boarding school Father said, away from Andy Everett, if you could go, or go to your room, and it wasn't any good trying not to think because it only came again, was no use, was again and again.

Rodney, darling, you mustn't cry. You're much too big to cry, she said.

But that made him cry. He hated it all. She looked at him and made it worse. He would go to her. He would go back to school. He went and put his face against her neck and cried.

There, there, she said, patting his back with her hand.

George opened his mouth. He sat, fat and surprised, with his spoon raised and a piece of potato tumbling out of his mouth.

There, said Mother. You'll soon be going to another school. There'll be lots of nicer little boys.

81

Her neck was soft, and feeling her hair against his face he whimpered softly into her hair, wanting to stay or have her come in at night when he woke, like bronchitis, with a candle, and he felt better, there were no shadows on the wall, smoothing his hair and sitting on the bed.

What's Rodney done? said George.

Nothing. Rodney's done nothing. Eat up your lunch.

Rodney's crying, said George, beginning to cry.

Oh dear, she said. Which of them did it, Rodney?

No one.

He blew his nose. He felt silly. He'd go away to his room.

Don't you want any pudding? she said.

No. I don't want any more. I'm going to go play in my room.

Seeing him go, she turned to George.

Now there's nothing wrong. Rodney's upset. Who wants some apple pudding? she said.

Apple pudding, sighed George.

She put her hand to her chest. She must speak to Oliver about the boys. Rodney had bronchitis that last winter in Sydney. He said the shutter banged and woke him up. He looked like Oliver sitting up in bed, as the troopship, and she stood on the wharf with Aunt Jane, and they said the War would be over soon and it was. The country doctor's wife showing patients to the waiting-room, only they hadn't a waiting-room. She must tell Oliver about Miss Browne. About her cough. She must not think about it, because it made her cough, she could not eat apple pudding, but cough, and a handkerchief.

Mother's coughing, said George.

Hilda Halliday recovered her breath. It left her uncertain. You did not know what to do next. There was nothing you could put your hand on with any certainty, except marrying Oliver, she had waited and he came back and he brought her a scarf from Paris and a paste pin. When they were married she wore the scarf. She felt safer being married to Oliver. They were very happy, she said. Six years did not make any difference, because their interests were the same, and she appreciated him, she had ideals, and she wanted to help him, if he would let her, and anyway there was a lot she could do, and he sat in his chair and told her about the patients at night. That is why it would be so terrible if anything happened. She must be careful of her health.

Oliver Halliday came into the dining-room. He was tired. His face was shadowed with the first stages of a beard.

Well, here you are at last, said Hilda.

He bent and kissed her. His face was very cold.

Yes, he sighed, here I am at last.

Father's back, said George, dropping an apple ring on the floor.

Hilda began to carve the mutton.

You look tired, she said. How is the poor woman?

She's all right.

And the child?

No.

She wrinkled her face in sympathy over the mutton. She would not penetrate any farther, not before George, asking about the child that...If it had been Rodney or George. She thought she would have died when George, and that poor woman up at the hotel. She was intimately connected with the publican's wife by a link of pain.

Here's your lunch. You must be hungry, she said.

He was hungry, and his muscles ached from the skis and his fall, wrenching his toes like that, as he sat down on the chair. But he was back, he was home. The dining-room table was a round mahogany pond with the sauce-boat pushing whitely into port. You sat and ate. Just to eat mutton was good, Hilda sitting there with folded arms, but pale as if she had not slept. She smiled, or at least she moved her face in the way that she always did when she caught him looking at her. It was a sign of intimacy and encouragement, or a symbol of what either of these ought to be. He was fond of her, that was what made it difficult, desperately difficult, when you were fond of a person and tried to grope behind the fondness and bring out something else. There is something so passive and taken-for-granted about the state of being fond. And he did not think he had ever been anything else.

Where's Rodney? he asked, with an onion on his fork.

Poor Rodney, sighed Hilda. He's...

Then she thought better.

He's finished. He's in his room.

Then why poor Rodney?

I don't know. He seems to be out of sorts.

She would not tell him now. He was tired. But later she would speak to him about Rodney and the boarding-school, and the fowl feed, and the sick hen. She would not tell him about the sheet Mrs Woodhouse tore because he might be annoyed. Detail irritated Oliver.

Rodney's been crying, said George.

Run along out and play, said Hilda. Look, it isn't raining any more.

The fire burnt with the intimate crackle of a wood fire when the heat has almost dried the wood. Oliver did not look at Hilda. He ate. You knew she was keeping something for later on. You ought to be grateful for all these little subterfuges. You were in a way, only, only there was something both irritating and pathetic in a perpetual cosseting that was only so much time squandered in the face of the final issue. Hilda tried not to see this, or would not, was afraid to see. She built herself a raft of superficialities and floated down the stream. She tried to drag him on to her raft, and when he almost upset it she did not complain. I must be nice to Hilda, he said. I am growing morose and introspective. It's the climate, or age. Those evenings going to Professor Birkett's and talking over beer, the inner life provided a series of formulas for pleasant solution, and you came away with a mind neatly docketed for future reference. Nothing could jostle a theory, it was cut and dried. Then you lost the labels in time, and you started again, or tried to start, and it was a case of order out of chaos, and you wanted to tip the whole lot overboard, only that was impossible, because Hilda and Rodney and George clung to the fragments, were founded on something that you thought had existed before. And why had Rodney cried? He went on cutting up the mutton, listening to the fire. It was peaceful, and he was glad it was peaceful. His legs ached. He was very tired.

Oh dear, said Hilda suddenly. I'd quite forgotten, Oliver. Miss Browne is waiting in your room.

She can wait a little longer, he said flatly.

Perhaps you ought...She must have been there three-quarters of an hour. She said she had cut her hand.

Oliver put down his knife and fork. He went down the passage towards the room that he used as a combined dispensary and consulting-room. When he went in he was still finishing a mouthful of food.

Good morning, she said, getting up out of the chair. I didn't want to disturb you at your lunch. I could go away, she said, or, or just as you like.

Because he frowned it put her off, taking away the words. She saw that his eyes were blue, not grey. She saw that he had not shaved. But of course he had been away all night. He looked rather gaunt, like a saint with a beard in that book of saints, or not a saint at all, just tired and unshaven. But she wished she had not come at all, the way he frowned, she blamed the sudden spirit of panic that had made her long for company.

Let's see, he said. You've cut your hand.

She took off the handkerchief.

There's not much wrong with that, he said. I thought it sounded like six stitches at least.

Oh no. I hope not. I should hate stitches. Don't they hurt?

He had taken a bottle of iodine and a swab of cotton-wool.

Of course they hurt.

He said it almost between his teeth, she thought, as if...

86

Then the iodine plunged down into the cut, and suddenly she was hot behind the knees, and she laughed rather stupidly, holding her wrist as hard as she could. She wanted to walk about, and bite her lip, she could feel the breath mount in her throat, pushing to form itself into a moan. Then she looked at him. He was looking at her. He was very detached. She had shrunk to the significance of something pinned to a sheet of paper or writhing underneath a lens. Then he was not looking at her, she saw, it was her imagination, or he had been looking and suddenly withdrew into some world of which she may or may not have been, and probably not, some possible indication. He turned away and brought a bandage and some lint.

That hurt quite enough, she said.

He did not answer. He bound her hand. His fingers were cold. He manipulated her hand as if it were a parcel of bones and tissues, detached from the body, no connection with this. She did not feel there was any necessity to be quite so professional, it reached a point where it became rude, and she found herself thinking of Mrs Stopford-Champernowne, the old lady whose tatting she used to pick up, and whose mind and body had the soft, comfortable texture of an eiderdown. She did not like Dr Halliday, because he did not like her, and she grew ashamed of a whole lot of things, half-formed thoughts connected with Dr Halliday, how she had imagined as she sat alone in the room that she would ask him if he had read this or that, and perhaps he would have thought she was distinguished. Because in her more private moments Alys Browne wanted very badly to be thought distinguished, and that is why she read Anna Karenina and played Schumann in the late afternoon.

There you are, he said, in a voice that suggested now I can get back to my lunch.

There was nothing more to say. She let him show her out to the door, she ran down the steps, she went on up the street. She felt more sober too, as if she had rid herself of the waste ends of a lot of surplus and superficial emotions. There was that dress for Mrs Belper that she must do. And she tried not to think of Dr Halliday, who thought she was a fool, and it is always uncomfortable to put yourself in a light in which you shine only as a fool.

You'll have to shoot that poor hen, said Hilda.

She was standing by the dining-room window when he got back. Hilda finding the substance of pity in a hen trailing across the yard, or Hilda herself was pity, he felt, like an allegorical figure he had seen in a French church, the sad Gothic emptiness of the hands, standing in Happy Valley, only it was Hilda, and she was inclined to wear jumpers, blue or grey, that she knitted herself, and she wore her hair in a kind of coil with strands falling, straggling at the side. He put up his hand to his head. That Browne girl pitying herself because she had cut her hand was unreal, or he, or Happy Valley, was unreal, removing itself into a world of allegory, of which the dominating motif was pain. Sitting on the ferry he had wanted to write a play, but he could not find a theme, not like a sculptor who carved Hilda on an altar-piece. You looked through the Browne girl and there was nothing, except a little veil of self-pity. It is half-past two. You stand in the dining-room and pity yourself, and that is different, but the same, appalling in someone else, inevitable in yourself, but the same.

You haven't had your pudding, Hilda said.

I don't want any pudding.

Oliver...

She was looking at him, wanting to say something that wasn't easy to say, and she rubbed her hands together as if they were cold. Both of them wanting to say something and then it only came in words.

It's about Rodney, she said. He'll have to go to another school. He's beginning to see that he's different. Different from the others, I mean. They persecute him. We'll have to send him to Sydney to a proper school.

Yes, I know.

His head ached.

We'll have to make the effort, she said.

All right. I've got to think. It'll mean expense. You must give me time, Hilda. I can't manage it all at once.

Here he was defending himself. She looked anxious, anxious for Rodney, or anxious for herself. Hilda coughed in bed at night. She turned about in bed at night and said, I can't sleep, Oliver. What time is it? I can't sleep, she said. My mouth's dry. Perhaps you'd get me a glass of water. Because I can't sleep. And now he looked at her as she stood there speaking for Rodney, and again there was so much he wanted to say, remembering Dr Bridgeman and how she hid her handkerchief. But there seemed no words in which to express compassion for a human being with whom you were in close relationship. It became even more difficult then.

He went and touched her face with his hand, pushing back a strand of hair.

All right, he said. We'll see. We'll all have to get out of this.

He thought she recoiled.

I didn't mean...I only meant Rodney ought to have a chance.

It hasn't started again?

I'm all right, she said, lowering her eyes. Only sometimes I don't feel very well. Only a little cough. It'll be better when the summer comes.

He held her hand. There ought to be so much that two people could say. He was fond of her. There ought to be so much. But they were like strangers standing on the railway station waiting for the train to go. You were always waiting for something that you did not say, that perhaps after all you could not say. But you felt you ought.

Now look here, he said, sitting on the table edge and starting to be matter-of-fact. There's a man up in Queensland Birkett knows. He wants to exchange his practice for something in the south. You'll be better there. And we can leave Rodney in Sydney on the way.

She was very still. But he could feel her relief, the gratitude inside her, because they would go away, Hilda receiving one more chance to put out her hand towards certainty.

I didn't mean, she mumbled. I only thought that Rodney...

I'll write to Birkett to-night, he said. Ask him to get in touch with this friend of his.

90

It would be better in Queensland. It would be warm, said Hilda slowly, slowly beginning to clear away the things.

She was tranquil now. He seemed to have stopped the quivering of some little nerve that whipped her into a ceaseless running to and fro. But she looked tired clearing away the things.

You ought to lie down, said Hilda, because she was like that, she had to transfer her own sensations and emotions to those she came in contact with.

He kissed her on the back of the neck, very lightly conscious of the scent of her neck which he knew so well, the scent and shape, sitting on a seat in the Botanical Gardens, when he thought he knew everything. And now he knew nothing, or at least he did not know Hilda, nothing more than the scent and shape.

He opened his mouth to say—what? Something that he would not say. So he went away along the passage to the dispensary, where he would lie down. He was tired. And later on she would bring him tea. Out in the yard George played with a cartload of stones, and Happy Valley stretched away back in grey sweeps, the child playing in the foreground unconscious of what had been arranged. He would write to Birkett to-night. And Happy Valley stretched away, greyly sweeping, the curve of telephone poles. He was standing in the window at the head of that great unconscious plain, how very grey, putting a hand to his beard, he must shave, he must sleep, he must leave Happy Valley to-night, to-morrow, sleeping for an hour or two on the hair sofa in the dispensary, it would take a month or two at least to drag up the roots and deliver safely on a towel that red child and she said hurt. He had been rather short. The way she held her wrist. She said Miss Browne. He would go up there in the evening and see, because he had not meant to be rude.

8

Mrs Furlow tried the door. It was locked.

Sidney, dear! she called. Sid-ney!

Yes?

What are you doing, dear?

Nothing, Mother.

Mrs Furlow stood by the door, one hand raised in perplexity to her mouth.

Hadn't you better go out and get some air?

I can't go out in the wet.

It isn't raining now. You ought to take some exercise.

Silence made Mrs Furlow frown. She bent her head to the door and frowned.

You ought to go for a ride, she said. I'll tell Charlie to saddle your horse.

Then she went away. She was passably content. She had arranged that Sidney should go for a ride.

Mrs Furlow's habitual expression was one of puzzlement, because frankly her daughter puzzled her, and her chief preoccupation was her daughter. She used to say, when I was a girl I didn't do this or that, but it was a statement that did not help matters at all. I do my best, she said, which meant that she made arrangements. She made many arrangements. She had arranged that Sidney should marry a young man called Kemble, an Englishman, who was A.D.C. at Government House. The young man did not know. But Mrs Furlow did, and that was half the battle. Mr Furlow only grunted and left her alone to do her best. Mr Furlow was very equable, and his daughter loved him. Sidney is *passionately* fond of her father, Mrs Furlow said, this without any bitterness, or as if she had resolved to make the best of a galling situation by suggesting that Sidney's passion was a flower fostered by her own hands. For Mrs Furlow's consolation was her own capability, whether as a president of charities or as the disposer of other people's affections.

Sidney puzzled her, but did not otherwise upset her comfortable confidence. Mentally, Mrs Furlow always wore a tiara. She had an actual tiara too, which she kept put away in a velvet case, and wore on state occasions for dinner at Government House or the Lord Mayor's Ball. And she looked very fine in her tiara, was a fine figure of a woman, in fact, with her head held up and her chin only just beginning to go. When she swept into a room in an excessive number of pearls everyone said, MY DEAR, which, if overheard, Mrs Furlow always interpreted to her own advantage. This because she held an innate belief in her own importance as a public figure. She liked to pick up the Herald and read a description of her dress. She had also a private passion for the Prince of Wales.

But Sidney was difficult, she said, moping away in her room and reading a book. Now when I was a girl. Not that Mrs Furlow didn't read books herself, she paid a country member's subscription to Dymock's library, and received a parcel now and again, Hugh Walpole and travel books, though what she liked best was a travel book with a plot. But Sidney moping in a room. She had not paid for her to go to a finishing school in town just to mope in her room. So that is one reason why she had just been to knock at the door. It would do her good to ride across the flat. It would do her complexion good. One had to think of the dances, and Race Week, and Roger Kemble, the A.D.C.

I've told them to saddle Sidney's horse, said Mrs Furlow, going into the office where her husband sat.

Mr Furlow grunted. He always sat in the office to allow his lunch to digest. And he was reading Saturday's Herald because Monday's had not arrived, and because he always had to have a newspaper in his hand. He peered at the fat stock prices, which he had read several times before, but which, to Mr Furlow, appeared inexhaustible.

I don't know what to do with Sidney, Mrs Furlow said.

Her husband grunted.

She'll be all right, he said. Leave her alone.

But something ought to be done. She has no interests. Perhaps if I let her arrange the flowers. Yes, that will be something. Sidney shall always arrange the flowers.

Then she went out to write to a Mrs Blandford, not

that she had anything to write, but it was soothing to cover a clean sheet of paper with words. Like Mrs Furlow herself, Mrs Blandford was a Pioneer. That is to say, their people had immigrated at an impressively distant date, not in suspicious circumstances of course, though an obscure relative of Mrs Furlow's had indeed married a man of convict descent. Mrs Furlow tried to forget this. She did not think that Mrs Blandford knew. Anyway, they were both Pioneers, and that, like a tiara and a close connection with Government House, was a considerable asset.

If only Sidney would be reasonable, said Mrs Furlow. She was pretty, but she was a stick, the way she sat at dances and did not give young men a chance. Now if it had been Mrs Furlow herself. Roger Kemble had a handsome face. It was pink and faintly embarrassed. So very English, Mrs Furlow said, which was almost the highest compliment she could pay. The highest, in point of fact, was: so like the Prince of Wales. But Roger Kemble was not quite like that, though in every respect fitted to marry her daughter. Marriage was the sole, the desirable end. To be able to say: Mrs Roger Kemble, Sidney Furlow that was. Mrs Furlow's letters to Mrs Blandford were full of such remarks, once she got past the weather and was able to settle down.

It was difficult to settle down. She was very volatile, she told herself. She wondered if Mrs Blandford had heard that the Vinters were getting a divorce. Actually Mrs Blandford had told her, but she had forgotten that.

Mrs Furlow sat at her writing-desk at the window of the drawing-room. Down on the flat the wind was rife, the brood mares huddled with their rumps to the wind, the cattle clustered in groups for warmth. Such very *trying* weather, wrote Mrs Furlow to Mrs Blandford. The weather had ceased to be a conflict of natural phenomena, it was a state conjured for the spiritual trial of Mrs Furlow. Just as the cattle and the brood mares, the rams that moved gravely, overweighted by their sex, in a paddock across the river, the ewes on the hillside, the maids in the scullery, and the little fox-terrier that was now almost too constipated to walk, were symbols of her material prosperity.

That is the sort of thing which tends to happen when you have lived on a property most of your life, and your family have lived on it most of theirs, it tends to become an institution. This is what had happened to Glen Marsh. The landscape had lost its significance as such, to Mrs Furlow at her writing-table, to Mr Furlow in his office. You lived in an intimate relationship with it, but the land existed because of this, turning itself to good account by the unostentatious changes of its appointed seasons.

Mr Furlow turned to the racing news. There was a gentle rumbling down in the region of his paunch. He would take his time. Besides, the new overseer would arrive during the afternoon. He sighed gently, and tried to study form. Checkmate and Salamander at Warwick Farm, Gaiety Girl at Rose Hill. And Sidney sitting in her bedroom, perhaps he should go and see, or not go and see, it was so much easier to study form in the Herald. Because Mr Furlow's life was based on a line of least resistance, unconsciously, for he never paused to ask himself if his life was based on anything at all.

Mr Furlow hadn't a mind, only a mutual understanding

between a number of almost dormant instincts. He was vaguely attached to his property, still more vaguely to his wife, because these were habit, they were there, he accepted them. He also loved his daughter in a fumbling, kindly way. He took her riding on her pony when she was a little girl, or to eat ices at a soda fountain when they were in Sydney, perching her up on a stool, and looking at her proudly as she chose the most expensive ice. He said, there, pet, wipe your mouth. He was happy, he wanted her to be happy, eating an ice or doing whatever she wanted to do. It surprised him to see her grow. It came as a shock. Already she was painting her mouth. But of course she knew best. He liked to feel her hang over his chair, to hear her say, darling, I haven't a bean, her face on his shoulder. He gave her a five-pound note instead of an ice. He did not worry as Jessie worried, everything would solve itself in time, everything always had, and Sidney grow and paint her mouth, and marry or not, just as she liked. A fly had settled on Mr Furlow's nose.

He got laboriously out of his chair. He had not measured the rain. He went down the passage towards the verandah, stretching his legs, and trying to control his wind. Outside Sidney's door he paused a moment. Then he went on with the easy smile of someone who always believes in letting the situation handle itself.

Sidney Furlow was lying on her bed. She had taken off her shoes. She pointed one foot at the ceiling, raising her leg as high as it would go, and watching her instep arch. She drew her suspender taut and let it snap back against her leg. She sighed and her leg dropped back on the bed, Oh dear, she sighed, biting her lip. The pillow was warm underhead, the kind of warmth that is slightly perverse and misplaced, the warmth of a bed after lunch, as you rub your cheek against the linen and wonder what you can do. It made you cry, having nothing to do, or read a book, or read a book. She looked very pretty when she cried. She did it sometimes in the glass. Or she picked up a book and glanced, between phrases, into the more interesting, if desperate, territory of the mind. Oh dear, she sighed. Je me crois seule. As if she wanted to go riding across the flat in all that wind. And Mother said Charlie must go too, just in case anything happens. But I won't be followed about by a groom. En ma monotone patrie—et tout, autour de moi, vit dans l'idolâtre d'un miroir. With that stupid face that said, Miss Sidney, I'd better tighten your girth. The hell of a girth and she did not care if she fell, or broke her arm, they would carry her in, and Mother running down the passage to see. Qui reflète en son calme dormant Hérodiade au clair regard de diamant, what did it all mean, o charme dernier, oui! je le sens, je suis seule. Reading French and that old fool of a Madame Jacquet in cotton gloves coming to teach French at Miss Cortine's, ma petite Sid-ney, and Helen and Angela waiting to be taken to a dance by a couple of naval men, they were pretty lousy anyway. The book dropped to the floor.

Sidney Furlow was nineteen. She had been two years at finishing school in Sydney, at Miss Cortine's. She had not learnt very much, but it was not part of Miss Cortine's curriculum to teach. Only to mould my girls, Mrs Furlow, to prepare them for life. Miss Cortine prepared her girls for life with a course of tea-pouring and polite adultery. Consequently most of them were considered a very good match.

They did not sulk, like Sidney, they said pretty things to young men who came to take them to dances, and cuddled up very prettily when they were expected to. Perhaps if you leave her another year, Miss Cortine said.

She was damned if she would stay another year. She wanted to go home. So she went home and it was all a bloody bore, and Sydney was a bloody bore, and reading Mallarmé after lunch. Je me crois seule en ma monotone patrie, Hérodiade au clair regard. Her arms were very brown and thin. She stretched them over her head, catching the bed-rail over her head, and feeling a strange lassitude that crept along under her skin. Her breasts stood up, thin and abrupt under her dress. Her hair spread out over the pillow in little snaky tongues.

Oh hell, she said, jerking herself up. She wanted to cry. O charme dernier. She jumped off the bed and went and sat at the dressing-table, looking at herself fiercely in the glass. He had wanted to touch her at that dance, putting his hand. She stroked her breast sulkily, between her breasts that were warm and firm, it made her smile. And she told him to go to hell, it made her laugh because he looked so surprised, sitting there on that battleship where orders were always obeyed. Only she hadn't, she had put back her head and laughed. Helen said she had a laugh like a piece of wire, and that thin mouth—well, it was thin, she supposed.

She took up a lipstick from the dressing-table and began to work on her mouth, pressing it down hard on her lips, as hard as she could. Her mouth looked like a wound. She took up the eye-shade and blurred the lids, sitting with her eyes almost closed to watch the effect of that blue blur, and her mouth, and her dress falling down on to the point of a breast. She laughed, or at least a little contemptuous snort came out of her nose. Oui! je le sens. She was like a whore.

Sidney, called Mrs Furlow from the other side of the door, haven't you gone for your ride?

Yes, I've gone.

There's no need to be rude, complained Mrs Furlow from her side of the door.

She was going away. You could hear her feet protesting down the passage. She had gone.

And now what, said Sidney, or her breath said now what, as she took up a paper tissue and rubbed the lids of her eyes. She put her head down on the dressing-table and began to cry. She had no control over it. It was like the flicking of a piece of wire.

Stan, dear! Stan! Where are you? called Mrs Furlow.

Then she reached the verandah and saw him with a beaker in his hand measuring the rain that had fallen into the gauge during the night. Oh, there you are, she said. The new man's come. You'd better go into the office and see him. I told him to wait in there.

Mr Furlow held up the beaker, half closing his eyes to read the number of points.

He's a very large man, said Mrs Furlow rather pensively, but without any accent of approval, for she thought he was rather uncouth, in fact definitely common, though she did not know why she had expected the overseer to be anything else. He would probably be a good worker, she felt, which meant he knew about sheep, which meant in the long run that Mrs Furlow would take many delightful trips to Sydney, on the strength of the overseer's knowledge of sheep. This had always been Mrs Furlow's attitude to overseers. They were a race of golden geese that you encouraged enough to ensure a profitable return, but avoided killing by an overdose of attention.

You'd better go in and see him, she said. You must have measured that drop of rain.

Mr Furlow had measured the rain, although he was staring still at the scale of points. It was a gesture of postponement. He stood holding the beaker between himself and the necessity of going to interview the new man. Actually, he would say he had to think things out, he was now expected to say impressive things as the owner of Glen Marsh, but Mr Furlow never thought, he relied on a process of slow filtration and trusted to providence to give the mechanism a jog. The process of filtration was still in a state of doubtful progress when, mastering an incipient belch, he went into the office and found Hagan sitting there.

Good day, said Mr Furlow, cautiously closing the door.

He tried to look solemn and businesslike as he sat down in his chair. He tried to find something to say.

You've been having a drop of rain, said Hagan.

Yes. A nice drop of rain.

Hagan sat there holding his hat. He had sobered up.

Nice mob of ewes up on the hill, he said.

Yes. A nice mob of ewes.

Merinoes?

Eh? said Mr Furlow. Oh, yes. Merinoes.

He sighed and folded his hands on his paunch.

I'm trying a Lincoln cross, he said.

102

He felt he had made a contribution to the conversation. He was satisfied.

Mutton? asked Hagan.

Yes.

A dopey old fool, you could see that, and the money rolling into his pocket, it beat you the way it happened, just for sitting there, it made you feel sore, working for a soft old bladder and trying your luck at a ballot and never doing any good, you hadn't any luck, it seemed to be fixed in a ballot who was to draw the land, but you were as good as any of them if it came down to brass tacks, only you hadn't a chance. Hagan shifted in his chair. The silence was getting him down. He beat a tune with his fingers on a typewriter lid. Then he realized what he was doing and stopped.

Mr Furlow cleared his throat.

Well, he said, that's about all I've got to say. If you go on round to the back the groom'll show you where to go. We can talk things over to-morrow. We can take a ride round the place. I hope you'll be comfortable, he said.

Then he opened the door.

I'll be all right, Hagan said.

Out in the passage there was a woman, it was Mrs Furlow, beating against a door.

Sidney, I insist! she called. I insist that you go out!

She stood there in the passage, her voice pretty high with anger, knocking away on the door. Hagan went along the passage towards the back. She did not seem to notice him. She was too busy banging on the door, hitting it with her rings. You could see well enough who ran the place, not that old coot talking about his Lincoln cross. She was making the devil of a row on that door.

Oh, for God's sake, cried another voice, and it was harsh, it sounded as if it would tear. You treat me like a blasted child!

A great scurrying then, and he was at the back door, and someone was coming, he wanted to look back, but he had to open the door, and he couldn't very well look back even if...He opened the door on to the back verandah. And somebody was coming, coming slap up against him, almost jamming him in the door. A girl ran out on to the verandah. She was a white blur, her dress, as it pushed past him, and the feel of her arm on the back of his hand. She looked back a moment angrily, taking her anger from the woman and fixing it on him, he felt. She looked a bit of a bitch, with that sharp, red, painted mouth. Her breath had come past him with a rush. But she did not stand there looking at him, or say anything, say she was sorry, she ran on.

What's been happening now? asked Mr Furlow fretfully.

She, she..., wailed Mrs Furlow.

Hagan did not hear what She had done. She was running down the hill in the mud, in a pair of high-heeled shoes that went over as she ran, and the mud splashed up on her dress. She was thin, there wasn't much of her, not his type at all. Anyway, he couldn't stand on the verandah all the afternoon. He would have to find that groom. He went down the step and across the yard. The girl had reached the bottom of the hill, had pulled open the door of a shed and gone inside, slamming the door after her. She had some guts the way she ran, even if that little behind, he'd never had

104

anyone thin, not like that woman in the jacket, you couldn't see her running down the hill. He went on across the yard. His hat was tilted over his eyes, he walked with his elbows slightly bent, stiffly in his suit of best clothes. He whistled a tune that he had heard somewhere on the gramophone. In front of the stable door a red cock was treading a hen.

9

When Margaret Quong had finished dinner she helped her mother wash up the plates. She stood with a towel waiting to receive the rinsed plates. And she was at once both deft and absent, wiping, staring out of the window, and digging with her tongue into a hole in one of her back teeth. She began to hum. She had eaten a bit too much. It was still too early to go back to school. In fact, she had just that feeling of detachment and suspended time which makes your eyes expand, or at least it seems like that, and it is difficult to think of much, or thought has no connecting thread, and reaching back with your tongue to a hole in a back tooth is a gesture of well-being, comfortable, almost voluptuous.

Anyone'd think, said her mother, that this was a hotel.

Margaret did not answer. She seldom answered her mother. Words beat on the border of her mind, but did not penetrate. If she selected a remark from out of the habitual wash of words it was one that needed a reply, one of those remarks that form the structure of an inevitable relationship. So now she hummed, and let her mother look at the clock, and frown, and say:

Coming in at any hour for meals. Just like a hotel.

Mrs Quong flicked the water from her fingers. It fell back into the sink. It spattered with a little hiss, like the voice of Mrs Quong. Then she drew down her sleeves.

Ethel Quong was sour and thin, her whole aspect was a little virulent, so that people avoided her, and she said she had no friends at all because she was married to a Chinaman. And why had she married Walter Quong, they said. Well, it had happened like this. Ethel had a friend called Mabel Still who lived at Clovelly and was married to a man who travelled in Ford parts. Still took in a number of the towns in the south of the state, like Tumut, and Batlow, and Moorang, and he went to Happy Valley too, not that there was much business there, only a Chinaman called Walter Quong, Mabel said. He kept a garage. He was ever such a good chap, they said, and you had to be broad-minded, and what was a Chinaman, they said. At this time Ethel was a housemaid at Government House. She used to visit Mabel Still, go out to tea on her afternoon off, or in the evening to a movie. Yes, she said, you ought to have a broad mind. She agreed with Mabel over that. Mabel lent her books on sex. She felt very proud of her broad mind. You had to move with the times. She went a lot to the Stills, and there she met Mr Quong, he was up in Sydney, on business, he said, and Harry Still had asked him along. Mabel said, couldn't you see Walter Quong was a good chap? Ethel had to agree. She didn't really like the idea of hobnobbing with a Chinaman, but if you had a broad mind, and anyway you called him a Chinese, and he was only half. They had a game of cards after supper. Walter asked if he could take her home. She let him drive her some of the way.

She had to admit to Mabel that she liked Walter Quong. He took her over to Manly one day. It was rather hot. Walter took off his coat, and made some jokes, and nobody stared too much, so she enjoyed herself. A Chinaman was like anyone else, she told herself. They went on the roundabout. He gave her an ice-cream in a cone. Then they sat on the beach and it began to get dark, with the sea coming in very cool and continuous and a hot scent off the pines. It was very pleasant running the sand through your fingers and listening to the sea and Walter's talk. But she said that she ought to go. Now, he said, why did she have to go, when he knew that she had the evening off, was she meeting a friend, and she laughed and said, no, she hadn't a friend, but they ought to be getting back. Walter said it was all nonsense. Well, perhaps it was. You could see the surf whiten on the shore through the darkness. It was cooler in the dark. She lay back on the sand. That was the way it happened when she hadn't meant it to, she told Mabel afterwards. She didn't know why she had let it happen, only something came over her on the beach, and she was letting Walter, but of course she needn't see him again. Only supposing. Yes, said Mabel, supposing, only it wouldn't. But it did. And that is why Ethel married Walter Quong. She called the child Margaret. She had narrow eyes. There's no mistake, said Ethel, your sins will always find you out.

Margaret was spreading the towel to dry.

You're growing out of that dress, said her mother. You're all wrist.

She looked at Margaret and frowned, because she was long and gawky, those long straggling legs under the dark woollen skirt, and the drawn-out wrists, and the eyes. Margaret continued to pat the towel. The woollen pocket of her dress hung down with the weight of Rodney's shell. She was feeling happy. She would go for a music lesson after tea.

Look at the time, said her mother. Anyone'd think it was out of spite.

What is? said Walter, coming in.

I don't know what you expect, she said, coming in at such an hour. And look at all that mud on your boots.

Yes, he said. It's muddy outside.

He looked at her and smiled. Walter was always ready to smile. It was the most natural activity of his yellow face.

Well, she said, we don't want to have it muddy in here.

Where d'you expect me to put my feet?

I don't mind where, she said, only I don't want mud on the floor.

I can't walk on the ceiling, Ethel. I'm sorry, it can't be done.

And I don't want cheek. Dinner's over, anyway.

Good, said Walter. I had a bite down with Arthur. I just dropped in to see how you were.

Then he smiled yellowly out of his fat and went outside to tinker with the Ford.

She looked out of the back door. She was thin and sour. She watched him, fat and yellow, crawling under the car.

She was exasperated, she was drying up, and Walter only smiled. Or put her to shame with that girl he asked to the cemetery, or the time he got drunk at Moorang and tried to make water through the keyholes all along the main street. And then he only smiled. Mrs Quong's face was taut with bitterness as she turned away from the door.

You'd better look sharp, she said to Margaret.

Because it irritated her to see that child looking at herself in the glass. Margaret in a red tam-o'-shanter pulling it down over her eyes. You would hardly believe she had a dash of anything but Chinese.

There's no need for *you* to go wasting time on the glass, said Mrs Quong.

But Margaret let the stream of her mother's bitterness flow over her, because their relationship was like that and the voices of some people, like the beat of a clock, like the creaking of the furniture, part of the exterior envelope of sound, beating and creaking, but failing to penetrate to the substance. At least, as far as we are aware. For there is a general cumulative effect and sometimes an ultimate explosion. But Margaret said placidly:

Good-bye, Mother. I shall be late. I'm going to tea at the store. And there's my music lesson after that.

Then she was clicking the front gate, and it was part of custom, like her mother's voice, it was part of what you took for granted, that slid away consciously, when perhaps all the time it was making a more indelible impression. Then she was going down the street, skipping a step or two every few yards. The sky was blue again, but cold. The houses huddled wetly between their sodden strips of garden

110

and their backyards. There were wet nettles in the ditches beside the road.

In summer there was a hot, pungent smell about the nettles in the roadside ditches. It was one of the predominating smells of Happy Valley. It made you feel warm and indolent, just as the cold sky isolated you from the landscape on certain winter afternoons and you were walking on top of the earth, against the sky, and it made you feel cold and strangely unattached to even the most tangible and conspicuous objects. But all of this may seem very irrelevant to the figure of Margaret Quong, skipping puddles on the road, and walking schoolwards. Only the landscape sometimes felt like that, it became the scent of nettles or a fragment of cold sky and she was very conscious of these, she was more conscious of them than the beat of her mother's voice, or perhaps because of it, she was thrown back into a world of sensory experience.

When she went into school they began to do geography, they were considering the rainfall of Central Asia, and it did not seem very necessary, this. The stove cracked. The chalk squealed on the board. Geography did not move her at all, not like it did Rodney Halliday, who leant forward on his elbow with his ears sticking out. She took out the shell from her pocket and had a look. It was smooth and pink. It was very satisfying to touch the shell under the desk, and he said it came from the bottom of the sea.

What's that? whispered Emily Schmidt.

Nothing, said Margaret.

She put the shell in her pocket again. Emily Schmidt stuck out her tongue.

111

Margaret looked at the desk. Her hair hung down black and straight, or rested on her shoulders at the back. She would put the shell in a box which already contained the harebells she had picked with Miss Browne, an ivory rose, and some silkworms' eggs. Uncle Arthur had given her the ivory rose. It was real ivory, Aunt Amy said. Rodney Halliday was very pale, leaning forward on his elbow like that. Aunt Amy was an old maid. Rodney was nine years old. Miss Browne was twenty-seven, she had worked it out. I am thirteen, she said, and when I am a little older I shall go and work at the store, I shall help Aunt Amy, two old maids, because that is what I shall become. I shan't care, she said. Miss Browne's hands were smooth and white, smooth as a shell, as she taught a scale or tacked down the hem of a dress. And Rodney had a cut on his hand. Miss Browne was almost an old maid. Rodney looked at a cow in a paddock. Miss Browne washed her hair and knelt in front of the fire to let it dry. Miss Browne smiled. She liked a lot of butter on a pikelet, she said.

Margaret sighed. They were still doing geography.

When afternoon school was over she went along to the store where Aunt Amy was serving Mrs Schmidt with some candied peel. It was getting dark in the store. They had lit the lamps. The jars shone, and the scales, and the bacon-cutting machine. Aunt Amy laughed as she weighed the peel. It was a little, glistening, humorous laugh.

Hello, Auntie, Margaret said.

She was fond of Aunt Amy. She had finished school. She threw her tam-o'-shanter on the chair and went on out to the back. It was all over for the day, or the day had just begun, you noticed things, you wanted to skip, you hung over the stable door and watched Uncle Arthur giving the colt a bran mash. The colt whinnied and tossed his head, the light on his flank from the lantern that hung by a nail on the wall. And Uncle Arthur purred, or swore a little at the horse as he laid back his ears or pawed the bedding with his hoof. The hoofs were black and clean, painted over with oil and tar.

Come on round now, Uncle Arthur said as he smacked the horse on the neck.

Uncle Arthur did not speak to her. He knew she was there, but he did not speak, and she did not expect him to, only she liked to be there, hanging over the stable door. They never spoke very much, the Quongs. They sat there at tea, eating a tin of herrings, sitting in the room behind the store, Amy and Arthur and Margaret, and they were very complete, they ate stolidly, they passed each other the things, their hands touched and sundered, and it was enough to be there, the three of them, that was quite enough. Margaret would have liked to live at the store, Amy and Arthur would have liked it too. But this was a state they did not consider, they did not mention, though each of them knew what the others thought. There was a silent mutual agreement in almost everything the Quongs did.

Amy rumbled and poured out the tea.

Another cup, Margaret? she said.

Yes, I'll have another. Then I must go.

She felt grown-up having tea at the store, not like at home, because Aunt Amy always made her feel like that, she talked about grown-up things. Margaret sat up straight and sipped at a cup of tea, her eyes round with abstraction, it always happened when she drank hot tea. She encouraged this. She relaxed and opened her eyes. It was warm and steamy in the back room.

May I take a quarter of bull's-eyes? she said, when it was time to go.

All right, Amy said. It's cold. You ought to be wearing a coat.

I'll run, said Margaret. I'm only going up to Miss Browne's. Thanks for the bull's-eyes, Auntie, she said.

Amy and Arthur sat at their tea in the back room. Arthur was quietly picking his teeth. You did not say good-bye when you left, you just went out, and Amy and Arthur stared at the tablecloth, Amy rumbling, Arthur picking his teeth. You would soon come again. There was really no need to say good-bye.

Margaret Quong ran up the hill. She would be out of breath. She was always out of breath when she went to see Miss Browne. The bull's-eyes stuck to the paper in the warm pocket of her hand. But the air was glass, the ruts sounded metallic under her feet. There was a sort of culmination in going to see Miss Browne, as if the day had slowly mounted towards this peak, this running breathless up the hill towards a rite. Tea at the store was a rite too, but calm and emotionless. There was no effort attached to having tea at the store. But I am a different person at Miss Browne's, she said. I must sit and speak in a special way, which is the way Miss Browne sits and speaks. I would like to be like Miss Browne. I would like to wear a mauve dress. I would like to have been in Sydney, to be able to talk about the nuns.

114

Talking to Miss Browne was delicious with regrets and also possibilities.

Margaret knocked at the fly-proof door and went into the sitting-room. Miss Browne was kneeling on the floor. She was cutting out a dress, the patterns spread on the carpet, holding the scissors in her hand. But there was a white bandage on her hand.

Margaret dropped on her knees. She wanted to touch the hand.

Yes, said Miss Browne, I cut it. Wasn't it stupid? I almost cried.

I once cut my knee, Margaret said.

There was a mingled pleasure and pain in pain shared with Miss Browne. And again she wanted to touch the hand, and because she was rather afraid to, she reached out with her voice instead, in a way that the voice does when it acts as proxy for a more emphatic, an unequivocal gesture.

I was in the yard, she said, playing with the chopper by the meat block. And there was a turkey came into the yard and I got frightened. I wanted to frighten it away. It was blowing out its chest. It looked so fierce. And then I dropped the chopper and cut my knee.

She was out of breath. It sounded silly to tell Miss Browne something that wasn't to the point, only it was, and Miss Browne did not know.

Don't let's talk about it. We mustn't be morbid, Miss Browne said.

Margaret was not sure what morbid meant, only that Miss Browne objected, and it sounded like a hot day, the

115

sounds in the yard after dinner, or a thunderstorm before it broke.

Look, I've brought you some bull's-eyes, she said.

Bull's-eyes? Margaret! said Miss Browne. When I was with Mrs Stopford-Champernowne...

There is a kind of past experience that always serves as a point for anecdotal departure, and for Alys Browne, Mrs Stopford-Champernowne was just such a past experience, a signpost pointing to a region in which Alys Browne was the heroine. And she liked to talk about herself. She liked to talk about the past, because it was something achieved and distinct, if only in small ways, like walking in Rushcutters Bay Park, or buying bull's-eyes at a shop in Darlinghurst, and these events had crystallized, they were not like the future, formless and volatile. Margaret also liked Miss Browne to talk about herself, because in listening she became an inhabitant of that same corner in time, the recollected past, she knew the park, she knew the cupboard where they put away brown paper and string, she sat with Miss Browne in a window-seat and the Salvation Army played on Sunday evenings in the street below. Kneeling on the floor they became drunk with anecdote. The clock hung up its purpose in the sitting-room, did not exist.

We must get to work, sighed Alys Browne, because it needed an effort to extricate yourself from the past.

Then they sat at the piano, and Margaret did her scales, and Miss Browne was beating with her hand, and Margaret frowned as a note escaped control, and she wanted to play well. She was not naturally musical. Only the piano was Miss Browne. They were trying a Beethoven sonata. And

Margaret frowned. Miss Browne bent over her shoulder and made a note on the sheet. The pencil quavered in the bandaged hand. And you played with feeling, you wanted the whole of what you felt to come rushing out in a sudden chord, because the hand was a note in music or a link with Beethoven, was Miss Browne.

Alys Browne sat with a bull's-eye in her mouth, wondered why she had become a music teacher, because it was like leading somebody in the dark. It was a false pretence. She had said very glibly: I shall teach music. She did not know what it meant. Sometimes her audacity frightened her. But nobody knew what frightened her, there was that consolation at least, just as nobody knew she had wanted to cry when she cut her hand. The bull's-eye was warm and soothing in her mouth. And the way the doctor had spoken, he was rude, she had almost cried as the iodine plunged down into the cut, he was watching her. She was watching Margaret Quong make a mess of a Beethoven sonata. She could not help her much. And Margaret sat receiving assistance that almost did not exist, only for Margaret she would be an endless well of experience, the child would not know how shallow this was. The doctor knew. He looked at her and knew there was nothing there, she had felt it, he made her feel inadequate and naïve. There was a hard efficiency in the doctor's face, like the face of someone who does things well facing somebody who. She turned over a page.

It is beautiful, felt Margaret Quong, she is beautiful, if only my hair was not quite so straight. I am nothing at all, sighed Alys Browne, he made me feel I am nothing at

117

all, and why did I think his eyes were grey, or look, but you had to look at somebody in the street, even if he meant nothing at all.

May I come in? he said.

He was standing there at the door. He had shaved. They turned round on the music stool, the two heads in the circle of light.

I don't want to interrupt, he said. I was passing. I thought I'd see how your hand.

Oh, said Alys Browne. My hand. You'd better sit down. We shan't be long, she said.

He was sitting down by the table, taking a book, or no, it was the Windsor Magazine. She knew it was this. She knew she wished it was not. And then she was ashamed. She could feel that her face was red. But she would have liked him to know that she read Tolstoi too, even if he thought it was affectation, he would surely think it that.

A little slower, Margaret, she said.

Margaret was taut, her back. She could not play. She would never play, with the doctor sitting behind.

Have a bull's-eye, said Alys Browne, and she made her voice as nonchalant as she could.

I think I'll go, said Margaret. I promised I wouldn't be late.

She got down off the stool. Miss Browne was looking at the wall.

Oh, she said, and her voice was vague. There's still a quarter of an hour. But of course we can always make it up.

Miss Browne was looking at the wall. Her hands lay in her lap. And there was a shadow on the wall, grotesque, where Margaret's head hung down, her hair hanging straight and her body drawn out into the shape of a post.

I promised Mother, Margaret said.

Don't let me interrupt.

You're not interrupting, said Alys, and her shadow turned.

Miss Browne wore her hair drawn back, looking over at the doctor who sat in a chair, because he had spoken, looking at a magazine. And there was nothing to say, but go to the door, Margaret trailing her shadow like a post, heavy as a post.

Good night, she said.

Oh, good night, Margaret, said Miss Browne.

Margaret opened the door and went outside. He was sitting in the chair. She looked back and his jaw was swollen with a bull's-eye, his shadow bunched on the wall. I shall come again, she said, and we shall make up the quarter, many quarters of an hour. Then she went slowly down the steps and her feet were stubborn on the frozen path. Withdrawing into distance the shape of door dimmed, out of focus as you looked back. Her throat was tight, cold.

That silly magazine! said Alys Browne.

He did not hear. She picked up the music sheet. She wished that he had not come. She did not think she would have very much to say. She felt about seventeen, or younger than that, because reading Tennyson at seventeen, they had said she was old for her age, and looking at herself in the glass she was very wise.

Why? he said.

She laughed.

119

Why not?

Somebody said she was enigmatic, which meant, she knew, that you made something of nothing, a word or a glance, helping out your own inadequacies, but the doctor saw through.

Because man must cater for his imperfections. After all, he said, there's a reality about his imperfections it'd be a pity to deny.

She could interpret that how she liked. He threw down the magazine, conscious of his own pomposity. He looked at her, saw her floundering, and said:

Well now, what about your hand?

Oh, that's all right, she said. That was nothing at all.

She was moving about the room. She was patting things. He had put her to flight, and now she was defending herself, moving about with uneasy grace, a hardness in her voice that perhaps he ought to soften somehow, allow her to play her part. Because after all if what he said about man and his imperfections, and it had been damnably pompous, he knew, she ought to be allowed to play her part, and he would sit with his hands on his paunch, acquired to match his pomposity, and listen and applaud. Then suddenly he realized it was difficult, and perhaps he could no longer make a contact, sitting at home and talking to Hilda. Other people don't play much of a part in our lives, said Hilda, with the conviction of a knitting needle, we don't need them, she said. So it was rather difficult. It made you sit on the edge of your chair.

How long, how long have you been at Happy Valley? he said.

She shrugged her shoulders.

A long time. Quite a long time.

He had spent a long time diagnosing the disturbances in people's bodies, that now had become bodies or a source of behaviour. I have got pretty smug, he said. He sat with the bull's-eye in his cheek trying to think of something to say, but in the end he would most likely go away, admitting he was a failure, say, it is so much easier to be professional.

I used to play a bit once, he said. I used to play Bach.

Oh, she said. Bach.

She looked at him sitting there. He was rather absurd with that bull's-eye in his mouth. He was not so formidable and going grey.

I think Beethoven means more to me. More, more feeling, she said. And depth.

But perhaps he would see through that too. She blushed. Seeing or not, he had gone across to the piano and was looking through the music lying there.

But you also play Schumann, he said.

Why not?

She had said it before, as she said it knowing, also that it meant nothing, or acted as a defence.

I mean, why shouldn't I play Schumann? Because I like him. We can't keep to the heights, she said.

God forbid!

He sat down and began to play something from the Kinderszenen. There was a kind of sweet enervation about the music of Schumann, just going on and on, and it was easy to succumb, as she probably succumbed, sitting up here alone and playing Schumann to herself. Hilda sat in the Botanical Gardens on an iron seat. He bent over and touched her cheek. He said he would write a poem. There was a gentle titillation of the senses in the morning sun, in Schumann's music. How soft you went if you gave yourself a chance. His hands became still on the keys, his shoulders bowed. She was watching him.

Why don't you go on? she said.

Not now.

Man must cater for his imperfections.

He looked at her and smiled. She was smiling. She was standing by the fireplace, and her body had lost its rigidity, and he was looking into her, at a core that he had not noticed as she winced in the dispensary and pitied herself.

We all say lots of silly things, he said. I ought to be getting home.

He had come to look at her hand. He was the doctor manipulating a bandage. Hilda would send out the bill.

There's one thing I've sometimes wondered, he said. Why are you "Alys" Browne?

I think I wanted to be different, she said, and she was surprised, because her voice did not falter, because she did not want to look down. She looked at him and said:

That's the only reason, I suppose.

It's a pretty honest reply.

You don't leave many loopholes, she said.

When he had gone she sat down, she was upright, she was firmer, something had happened to her, she felt. As if her body, and perhaps her mind, had suddenly grown taut as he touched her hand, tightened the bandage, touching some nerve that had always hung slack. What is it, she

122

said, and why am I sitting like this, waiting, like sitting with pamphlets in my lap about California, and then not going, I never went, there was no significance in it at all, and what am I waiting for? It was one of those questions you could not answer. And why California now? she said. I don't want to think. She went into the bedroom and lay on the bed in the dark, against cold sheets, and promptly thought harder than before, or the mind wandered in its fashion, like Schumann, and she asked herself if Vronsky or Karenin, if either of these was parallel. But that was no good. She lay on her back looking upwards into the dark. Then she began to realize how cold she was.

Where have you been, Oliver? said Hilda.

I went up to see Miss Browne. To look at her hand.

Hilda yawned.

It's late, she said. Rodney's been having a dream. It's that school. He's unhappy there.

Oliver went into the dispensary. He did not light the lamp. He stood there in the dark. Then he wondered why he had gone into the dispensary, there was something, but of course it was Birkett, and Hilda was sitting outside waiting for him to write. Rodney lay in bed afraid. Rodney was his son. He would write and they would go away, his wife and two children, the situation enforced by their going away. That was a reality, not playing Schumann in a mauve dress. Hilda and the children were all that he had ever wanted, he said, he wanted no more than affection, they were fond, they were happy, and he would write to Birkett. There was still a flavour of peppermint in his mouth. She was after all a human being, very silly perhaps, but looking at her he was glad she was silly and that underneath the silliness there was a core, an "Alice" Browne. But it was quite irrelevant, this. Only it made you a little surprised to discover a human being. You got out of touch. And Rodney was his son, was a human being, was more than a biological fact. He must try to remember that. He must not go off at a tangent into a world of his own, until a face pointed to the possibility of human beings.

He lit the lamp and sat down to write to Birkett. He would not think about a face that was in no way remarkable. Only that she had leant against the fireplace and looking into her face had been to look into an avenue that made him feel suddenly unfulfilled and cold.

Mr Belper had just said that Australia was the country of the future, he said it as if it were a fact that had not struck anyone before, the discovery was his. He sat there in his chair, a kind of Captain Cook of platitude, only the natives made no stir, Moriarty was almost asleep, his wife was a plaintive yawn. Mr Belper loved to talk about things in a general way, things like natural resources, the national physique, and the canalization of surplus energy. Moriarty half woke up and drew his attention to the irrigation area round Mildura, but Belper coughed, and pretended he had not heard, anyway Moriarty was half asleep. Mrs Moriarty dug her finger-nails into the sofa and yawned. She was past the stage of putting up a hand. And take industry, Mr Belper said, now that new industries were opening up, which by the way reminded him of the Salvage Bay Pearl Fisheries and that was something he could recommend if Moriarty should think of a flutter, with 640,000 5s. shares issue at par, on application 1s. on allotment 4, a very attractive speculative enterprise that he could recommend to anyone, he was in touch with the company, was interested himself, and he'd bring along a prospectus and let Moriarty have a look, because he did not believe in pushing a man in a direction he didn't want to go.

But what can a man do on a miserable screw like mine? Moriarty said, sitting up with a fretful wheeze.

His lips were thin and blue. There was a suggestion of dry mucous in the corners of his mouth.

Now if I could get that post up on the North Shore, he said. I write. I've written how many times.

Yes, said his wife, it's a crying shame. And Ernest's health. Look, Mr Belper, he writes and writes, and what does the Board do?

For Mrs Moriarty the attitude of the Board of Education was a case of personal animosity, and she was the martyr, living here in Happy Valley listening to Mr Belper talk, if only he would go away.

You might be a lot worse off, Mr Belper said, his voice very comfortable and rich with phlegm.

Mrs Moriarty pouted and looked away. It was all very well. A great swollen gas-bag like that living in a brick house, it was all very well for the bank manager to talk, because he had a position, not a penance, and the school-master was nothing at all, did not count, and she was as good as anyone, whatever that Mrs Belper might say with her red face and her coming-it-over-you ways, that told you about her cousin who was secretary at Government House,

126

if you liked to believe that, she didn't for one.

Why should I be ignored? Moriarty said.

He shuffled with his slippers on the floor, his hands restive and complaining in his lap.

Don't you worry, Ernest. Mark me, she said, there'll come a change.

Though what the change would be, meaningful as it might sound, she really did not know. She wouldn't let Belper get away with it though.

Mr Belper knocked out his pipe, leaning forward red and apoplectic, deciding it was time to leave. He had said what he wanted to say on the future of the country, the national physique, and the canalization of energy. It bored him when the conversation grew particular and people began to grouse. He did not like people who groused. He and Cissie never did that, removed as they were from all source of complaint. They were large and red and comfortable. They lived at the bank. And everyone called them Good Sorts. This, like most reputations, required some keeping up, though none perhaps to the same extent as the spirit of the paper cap. It became a lifelong enterprise, being a Good Sort.

You're not going, Mr Belper? said Mrs Moriarty, surprised.

Yes, he said. The old woman. She'll be wondering what I'm at.

Dear Mrs Belper! Mrs Moriarty sighed. She spoils you, really she does.

Bursting out of his clothes, and that woman, dirt-common, in silk jumpers swaying about, a wonder she had the nerve, if it wasn't to put a stamp on a letter, and Ernest was clever, he had a mind if you drew it out, not like Joe Belper, coming and talking for hours on end till you didn't know if your head, without a cachet in the house, she fancied herself of course because that cousin at Government House, well, if you liked to, and Joe if you like, but she didn't, not in a public-house, and then come to the back door with her, oh, Mrs Moriarty, I'm collecting things for the church bazaar, as if you was a working woman where front doors don't exist.

Night, Moriarty, Belper said. Keep the flag flying, eh? You'll have to try the Board again. But what'll we do without him? That's what I say to the wife. Who'll keep them up to it at the school?

Moriarty did not answer that. The Inspector told him that the standard of intelligence at Happy Valley was the lowest in the state. He wondered if Belper knew.

He sat slumped down in his chair when Belper had gone, alone in the room with the ticking of the brown mahogany clock that the Smiths had given him when he married Vic. He was going to have an attack. At night he usually had an attack, and that powder he burned made him sick, the fumes, as he leant over the tin and the smoke went into his lungs and he dropped back exhausted on the bed. He would burn a powder now if he had the strength to drag as far as the cupboard where it was kept. But Vic would come. He closed his eyes, intent on a series of previous attacks, that time in the bus, or at geography, or the party at the Chubbs' when everybody gathered round and it was almost a distinction to be asthmatic, with Vic holding his

hand and saying, it's always like this, Mrs Chubb, it'll pass
if only you give it time.

Well, said Mrs Moriarty, that man has a blooming
cheek. Dropping ash all over the carpet too. He might as
well spend his evenings in a public-house.

She had come back into the room and was moving
about in a formal attempt to restore an order that she liked
to think Mr Belper had dispelled.

Oh dear, she said, you're not going to have an attack?

He nodded his head, his eyes closed, waiting for
sympathy.

She looked at him and frowned, as if it was too bad,
and it always came at night, and she couldn't put up with
it, she was human after all. She looked at Ernest and her
whole life was a series of attacks. She looked at him in his
chair, the man she had married; who was so distinguished
behind his moustache, licking stamps at Daisy and Fred's.
But she hadn't bargained for this. It's a wonder I'm not a
virgin, she felt, and distinction is all very well. But he's thin,
with that moustache getting into the tea, and those long
pants he wears, says he feels cold, and fancy a man with
pants showing above his socks. She punched at a cushion
and frowned.

It's too bad, she frowned.

But I can't help it, Vic.

No, of course you can't.

The cyclamen in its lustre bowl sprawled in wide,
voluptuous curves and brushed the nap of the tablecloth.
She saw her face in the bowl, looking out of shape, and pink
like the flower of a cyclamen. It was funny that yesterday

the cyclamen had stuck up straight, always changing, sometimes as straight as a poker and tight in the mouth, almost
spinsterly, and now it lolled, couldn't hold up its head, it
looked sort of abandoned with its droopy leaves.

Ernest said:

I'll be getting to bed.

He began to pull himself out of the chair. He sat on the
edge, his mouth open, the breath harsh on his moving lips.

Vic Moriarty looked at her husband in an access of
compassion. You could see he was sick, and it made you
ashamed sometimes the way your thoughts, but you could
not help your thoughts lolling, those droopy leaves, wanting
something else and wasn't you human but nobody had ever
called you bad, except perhaps that Mrs Enderby next to
Daisy's because the postman, he had a drooping lip, and the
door closed and you stood behind it with the letters, you
were all right, then Ernest came and you were all right, till
the day I die, only sometimes something happened and that
bloody plant drooping all over the table, you must get Ernest
to bed, his poor face, and that powder, you would not sleep
for hours, the smell, and he must sleep with window shut.

Come along, Ern, she said, putting a plump and
momentarily tender hand into his armpit and helping him
up. You poor thing, she said. It's cruel.

He leant on her. He had always leant on her, and
somehow she had buoyed him up, pneumatically, helped
him along the passage, or composed a sentence for a letter
that he was writing to the Board. He walked slowly with his
head bowed. His chest was tight, removed, but there was
a kind of exultant pain in breath torn with an effort from

130

the lungs, and she was supporting him.

We'll get you into bed. And then you can burn your powder, she said.

He sat down on the counterpane. There were still six or seven essays on the Cow and Her Relationship with Man that he could not, not correct. He said:

Vic, there's still...

Don't you talk, she said.

He lumped down and let her take the slippers off his feet. The Cow gives us What. The Board of Education in how many ha'penny stamps he'd spent. But there was always Vic.

Vic Moriarty bustled about the room. God, she tried her best, she did, nobody could tell her that she didn't make a good wife, fetching and carrying and handing pity on a plate, and of course she was sorry for him, she sat and watched him wheeze till it hurt, was what any normal person would call a sacrificing wife, those slippers she had made for Ernest who was like a stray dog, that little shivering whippet she found, poor Tiny that died of a chill and she nursed him in blankets, and cried, it was when she was trying that stuff on her lashes which ran when she cried, till Ernest said, and she said I must make the best of meself Ernest and you can't complain of that, because she was good in deed, only a thought sometimes slipped, and she defied anyone to have a mind free from recreation, she did.

God, I'm tired! she said when they had got into bed and the fumes of the powder, mingled with the quenched candlewick, had invaded all the corners of the dark.

He patted her hand. He lay in bed and tried not to

131

wheeze so that she would be able to sleep. That water dripping in the schoolroom maundered through his head. His head was confused with fume of smoke, with the crumpled train of cows, their horns tilting at the basin on the schoolroom floor.

I had to give that Chow a pound. Oh dear, she said, we'll have to get the mattress teased.

It was funny the way that plant sometimes stuck up straight, like an old maid that had listened to a dirty joke by mistake. She sat by Ernest in the evening and tried to take an interest in his stamps. He was holding her hand in bed, perhaps asleep, and she wished she knew if he was asleep, so as she could take away her hand. That Walter Quong driving down the street in his car and waving a yellow hand that touched her in Moorang as she wanted to cross the street. They said a Chinaman, who was it said that, it must have been Fred, the dirty brute. She took away her hand from Ernest. She thought he must be asleep. Lying there, my hubby's blue, can't help that, because he's asthmatic, the poor soul. And that young chap went up to the pub, turning to look back and wave, as if, well, somebody noticed anyway, and Gertie Ansell said he was the new man for Furlows' because her brother was down at Quongs' when the truck, he was a man anyway, water the plant to-morrow, not much, perhaps that was why it sprawled, like that time that chap at a party Daisy had on the couch, touched his muscles, he had red hair waving back down the street, and Daisy turned on the light, said, Fred, oh go on, you couldn't help it, go mad if you didn't, and what was he doing going out to Furlows', that girl there dolled up to

132

kill, and you never knew if Vic oh what Ernest I am almost asleep asleepernest.

Stabbed in sleep then legs apart licked a stamp or went up the hill on the curve the moon played Schumann it was chalk chalk in his bones or heartburn as he tossed the ticket took a train Rodney Rodney there on the map is Queensland yellow for Sun A for Andy when it blew blood like the spermwhale she stretched out her arm that clove white a slice of the darkness she put up her face with pins drawn back into a roll and then crackled the arpeggio you could always tack down the hem and write and write to blot out another purpose if you write.

So on, so on, with the diversity of detail and the pathetically compulsory unity of purpose that informs a town asleep. Smoke mounts faintly skywards from the chimney-pots. Dream is broken, turns, sighs. She said, she said, the wind. The cat walking on the water-butt touches with her cold pad a star, claiming it as her own, like Happy Valley extinguished by the darkness, achieving a momentary significance.

PART II

It was no longer winter at Happy Valley. You began to wonder if it could ever be anything else, and there was really no reason why it should, why Happy Valley should take part in the inevitable time process rather than stay concealed in some channel up which either time or circumstance had forgotten to press. Then it happened when you forgot to wonder. On the hillside you began to see the whorls of barley grass, wavelike and consolidated when there was a wind. Lambs tilted at the ewes. The frost thawed early under the sun. But all this was incidental, you felt, there was no reciprocation on the part of man, almost no connection with the earth, or else it took longer for the corresponding tendency to penetrate and touch the instincts with which he is endowed. It was like this, very slow, until with an undertone of protest that time ignored, flowing blandly, even through Happy Valley it flowed, he was caught up, whatever his private argument might be, and pitched beyond reach of his own intentions. At Happy Valley man was by inclination static. That was the rub. Watch a man complaining at sundown over a glass of beer, watch him wipe the dust off his mouth, listen to his pale, yellow voice, if you want to understand what I mean. Because there you will find that static quality I'm trying to suggest, I mean, the trousers hanging on, but only just. Well, time got over this and any more positive protest, though things continued much the same, the washing on the line Mondays, the geranium dead on old Mrs Everett's window-sill, with Mrs Everett's geranium face wilting and inquisitive above the pot. Mrs Everett, like her geranium, no longer underlined the seasonal change. She twittered in a dead wind. She clung on through habit adhering lichen-wise to the rock.

Mrs Everett's brown face was more than this, was the face of Happy Valley seen through dust, those dust waves churned by a car passing down the main street. Because it was no longer spring. Spring was a transitory humour or exhalation that dried and evaporated, disappeared with the barley grass and the weaned lamb. Happy Valley became that peculiarly tenacious scab on the body of the brown earth. You waited for it to come away leaving a patch of pinkness underneath. You waited and it did not happen, and because of this you felt there was something in its nature peculiarly perverse. What was the purpose of Happy Valley if, in spite of its lack of relevance, it clung tenaciously to a foreign tissue, waiting and waiting for what? It seemed to have no design. You could not feel it. You anticipated a moral doomsday, but it did not come. So you went about your business, tried to find reason in this. After all, your existence in Happy Valley must be sufficient in itself.

Oliver Halliday had written to his friend Professor Birkett one night in winter as we have seen. He wanted to go and live in Queensland, ostensibly because of Hilda, his wife, actually for many other reasons, some of them conscious, more of them not. Birkett will arrange it, he said, with this man Garthwaite, who wants to exchange practices with somebody in the south. Hilda will be better in a warmer climate, her health. And Rodney will go to school in Sydney. We shall all be better, happier. We have said that before, in Sydney, in coming to Happy Valley, but this time it will be different. It is always different the next time. So he waited for Birkett's reply, and Birkett said he would see, and now it was no longer spring, it was summer again, and a hot wind blew down from the mountains, and Hilda said, hasn't your Birkett done anything yet? She began to look anxious again. You've got to have patience, Oliver said. He had written to Birkett. He felt absolved. Even Hilda's anxious cough did nothing to his conscience now it was as if he were responsible for nothing, least of all for himself.

There has been no change that I am aware of, he said, or at least I don't think so, even if I am honest with myself. But I don't want to ask myself too much. I am happy as I am, even stuck here in this hole, it is not so important now, perhaps after all it was only a matter of time, kick against the pricks and you hurt yourself, stop and you forget. It was like that. Or perhaps the possibility of Birkett's arranging something was designed as an envelope against discomfiture, mental discomfiture, that is. For it is miserable here in summer, that hot wind beating against the gauze with the hum of flies, and the dead bodies of flies bloated and obscene upon the window-sill. But I take off my coat and it is better. The shirt clings to the skin. There is no draught of air in the dispensary, only the passive blanket of heat threaded with vague chemical smells. This is nothing but an external discomfiture. Just as bumping along a dusty road, hanging to the wheel, when I go to see a case, the act itself recedes, together with purpose, and the trees blur, and the murmur of advice, the yes, doctor, and no, doctor, in the kitchen afterwards.

So he began to feel lighter. Hilda could hear him whistle in the dispensary, laugh as he told a patient what to do. She watched him with George in the yard, twisting a piece of tin into the shape of a boat, and sailing it in a tub. On the whole she was glad. But she waited for the mail, to see if anything had been effected to change Queensland from a possible future into an immanent certainty.

Don't you worry, Hilda, he said. We can't fix everything in a day.

This was when he found her looking out of the window with that air of hopelessness that seems to attract people to windows, as if they only have to look outside and find a solution stalking up the road. He patted her on the back. He thought, poor Hilda, and all my present tranquillity is nothing to her, it cannot reach inside and touch that kernel which, incidentally, I have never touched and don't know how. It either comes in a flash, or it doesn't, and here it didn't, but all the same we have made something of our lives, there are Rodney and George, and I am something to Hilda, apparently some kind of necessary stay.

To the people of Happy Valley Oliver Halliday became what old Dr Reardon, lamented of Mrs Steele, had been before. It was once What Dr Reardon Said, it was now What Dr Halliday Says. He drove up to Kambala, in summer you could drive all the way, and treated Mrs Steele for ulcer of the leg. She had it very bad. Of course she had not gone to Tumut to live with her son Tom, she would try another winter, she said, even though she had an ulcer awful bad. She said, did Dr Halliday remember that night when poor Mrs Chalker? Well, Mrs Chalker was expecting again, and she hoped, the ulcer willing, to help Dr Halliday at the lying in, because it would take the two of them, Dr Halliday and Mrs Steele, to deliver Mrs Chalker, it would. So it was quite an occasion when Oliver went up to look at Mrs Steele's ulcer at Kambala. She gave him a basin of potted meat and some cuttings of plants. Because, she said, he got the money out of the insurance and she did not want him to feel he was getting nothing out of her. Her potted meat was famous, she said. When he got it down to Happy Valley the heat had sent it bad.

Driving down from Kambala along the hot metal road, you passed the bright red water tank and the house where Alys Browne lived, standing a little back. Sometimes he went to see Alys Browne. He went up the path and, listening for the level silence or a groping peace, he would either continue up the path or else retreat. She was never surprised to see him now. She had reached the stage when she no longer felt bound to say to her friends; oh, Dr Halliday was

141

here to-day, only as she had few visitors she had skipped that stage, and nobody really knew. She felt she would not have minded if they did. But, as they didn't, there was no necessity to tell.

So Oliver Halliday called in on her sometimes on his way down from Kambala. He began to think it was the natural thing to do. After all, it was only sociable. You couldn't shut yourself away, or you had too long, and now it was time you made the effort, and Alys Browne gave you pikelets for tea. You dropped your hat on the floor and fell down without any ceremony into a chair. Like going across the bay to see Birkett, at sixteen, and forgetting ceremony as you talked, as you put up your feet, before Hilda said the cretonne would have to be cleaned. Now again you remembered how to unbend. It was hot drinking tea in the afternoon. Your shirt stuck to your skin. But Alys Browne's sitting-room seemed to encourage a breeze, perhaps the way it was placed up on the hill, perhaps because of that. Anyway a breeze, actual or otherwise, meandered occasionally through the room, without apparent purpose, like the conversation of two people drinking tea in the heat, a kind of accompaniment to the act of drinking, with nothing deliberate about it.

When he came to think about it Alys was on the whole far from being a deliberate person herself. There are people who imply things deliberately by their conversation, or whose whole personality is a deliberate implication of their particular tastes and antipathies, so that their whole existence suggests they are hitting the nail on the head. But this was not Alys Browne. Her life was if anything an under-statement of the fact, a system of delicate, and undoubtedly unconscious, indirect implication. That was why you did not notice her at first, why he had looked through her in the dispensary and seen nothing worth noticing. You thought she was vague and rather silly. Well, perhaps she was silly, but not fundamentally so. She suggested things in a glance or a phrase that were an emphatic denial of this. And then, because of that, you got to like her for her silliness too, or for your own stupidity in not seeing through it before.

Sometimes she played for him when he went up there in the afternoons. He said:

Play me something. Play me some Chopin, or Schumann, or something like that.

Is that how I stand? she said.

Not altogether.

But almost.

She protested, but she played it, and he knew that in spite of her protesting she liked to play it, and he knew that she knew. They both knew it was what they wanted. What he did not know was that he had wanted this so much, for a very long time, suppressing the fact till Alys Browne released it.

That sort of thing happens and you can't think why you have put it off so long, almost as if there was a certain amount of immorality attached, or a sense approach to music like a sense approach to a person. But there was nothing erotic in his attitude to Alys Browne. He wasn't in need of anything like that. He was not in love with her. She was a necessary accompaniment to Hilda, who was his wife, who was the mother of two children, which were

143

also his. If I have never loved Hilda, he said, it is because she has never wanted love, at least, love in the sense that Chopin or Schumann implies. You could never connect Hilda with that, it was just incongruous. For that matter, nor did you connect Alys Browne with more than the outer form of the music that she played. She did not, he did not expect anything else, otherwise he would not be sitting here listening to her as she played, would have stayed away, would have...To think of falling in love with Alys was to take up your hat and go.

All this was happening in the summer. He went about and he began to see he had wasted a lot of time in just going about. It was hot, but he did not mind it. It would be hotter, he said, when they went to Queensland, for of course they would go in time, but it was a pity it should have to happen just when he was getting to know people, and it was almost like getting to know people for the first time.

When Moriarty, the schoolmaster, took to his bed with asthma he went along to see him. Moriarty had been worse ever since the winter. Now when he took to his bed his wife sent for the doctor to give him an injection, and incidentally herself a little spiritual support.

Dr Halliday, she said, you don't know what I put up with, living in a place like this. It isn't the sort of thing I'm used to. Now if Ernest could get away. Yes, I'll take you in to see him in a minute. As I was saying, if Ernest could get away it would be so much better for us both. Perhaps you could do something, doctor. A doctor's report might help with the Board. Of course I don't want to complain myself. But I'm getting a nervous wreck.

She dropped her eyes and sighed, in a way she had when she wanted to impress, but there was something of the basking seal in Mrs Moriarty that made Halliday want to laugh. A pink seal basking on its rock of complacency. Then it made him angry.

I'd better give him that injection, he said.

Mrs Moriarty began to pout, as much as to say, she didn't expect this, and changing her dress, because she liked the doctor if only he gave her a chance, only she wasn't going to waste her time blasting a piece of stone. So she got up.

I'll take you in to see him, she said, pattering, her voice shrugged, her hand already dimpled on a china knob, though with a certain reluctance, as if...Halliday forgot her, Mrs Moriarty withdrawing angry or not, forgot her and went in.

Moriarty was lying in bed, eyes closed. His face was a dirty grey, except for the stubble pushing blackly through, and his lips, which were violet and very thin. His body made a thin ridge under the cotton counterpane that quivered when he tried to breathe. Watching him, Halliday suddenly became conscious of his environment again, that it was summer, a hot arid brown, that the flies were stinging the gauze with a repeated buzz and burring of their wings, that somehow he had been existing for a time apart from this, apart from the reality of Happy Valley, carried bodily out of it by some form of mental levitation. This was Happy Valley now, with Moriarty on a brass bedstead and the wash-basin unemptied from the day before. He went up to the bed and took Moriarty's pulse.

145

It was like this and Hilda was right, knowing through some protective instinct that they must make an effort to escape, while he went up and listened to Alys Browne, and here was Moriarty, or Happy Valley, or the embodiment of pain, or Happy Valley instilling pain into the passive object that was Moriarty lying in his bed. When he plunged the needle into Moriarty's arm there was no sign of acceptance or of rejection, it was as if a surfeit of pain had effected, to its own loss, a kind of anaesthesia. But the flies buzzed. But the roof cracked with the heat. He looked down at Moriarty's face with an expression of disgust that turned to pity as the body stirred, relaxed, as the tension of the face withdrew.

Looking at Moriarty it was possible to conceive of the intense kind of mystical satisfaction that might arise from the healing of pain, if you were that way inclined, like on the ferry going home when you decided you would be a doctor, it was that attitude which attracted you. It was funny the way you made decisions on ferry-boats, something in the flow of water that made you think you would write a play, you would go to the War, you would become a doctor, or more accurately an instrument of mercy, because you were young at the time and the prospect had the appropriate sheen or became almost abstract in the soothing, escapeful susurration of the water, as the ferry refining thought. Moriarty moved and coughed. Then you became a doctor, a sort of hack, and getting up in the middle of the night or taking a test of water in a beaker divorced the decision from its mystical element, and you became a kind of machine for doing, it was altogether material, and of course it was only because you were young that you imagined you saw an aura round the figure of empirical reality.

How's it going? he asked.

Moriarty opened his lips, wordless, but with a lessening of tension in his eyes, a freedom of breath in his throat. Looking into Moriarty's eyes you saw, sitting on the ferry-boat, yourself, and I shall be an instrument, you said, not a hypodermic and adrenalin. The adrenalin working in Moriarty's body was responsible. Of course it was this, you knew, that unknit nerves. Only it gave you a sudden irrational satisfaction to feel your power, almost in your own hands a power to heal, like a quack, only not. You hadn't felt like this before. It was different. As if you suddenly saw yourself at one extreme and Happy Valley at the other on a kind of balance, and now you had begun to tip it down, standing in the scales, touching with your hands Moriarty's arm, as the scale swung with the weight, and you began to feel you had made some considerable onslaught on the battalions of energy cased up in rock and earth with which Happy Valley bludgeoned a hitherto feeble human opposition.

Halliday sat down on the bed. He leant forward slightly and listened to the loosened breathing, watched the gentler rising of the chest.

How long do you think this'll take? Moriarty suddenly asked.

How long'll what?

Moriarty tried to sit up. He said:

I can't spare more than a day or two. I've got to get back. Or perhaps they'll send someone, he said. Perhaps they'll see I ought to get away. But I oughtn't to leave the school for more than a day or two.

We'll have you right pretty soon, Halliday said.

To say something to Moriarty, this poor misery, even if it is just something for something to say, to ease him back on the pillow, and now he has fallen back, taking my word, depending on me, when I can't offer more than illusory comfort, and it is mostly like this, dealing in illusions in the face of the material, and becoming reconciled to it, until now I want to give Moriarty something else.

It's good of you, doctor, Moriarty said. My wife wants you to send a report of my health to the Board. I expect she told you. It's very hard on poor Vic. And of course she deserves more than this. And it's mostly been like this. I wouldn't complain for myself, doctor. But it gets me down, her, and the school. Sometimes I can't stop thinking about the school. The inspector tells me the standard of intelligence is very low. Of course that isn't all my fault, but... You see, there's nothing I can do. I can only do my best.

There was a dead hum of heat in the room. An intruding fly spun in a brown circle over Moriarty's head. Halliday reached and swept it away.

But the fact is I'm a failure, Moriarty said. I can't cope with them. All those children. Sitting there. You don't know, doctor, how children can hate. Half their life is pure hate. They hate you when they know you're weak. They hate you when they know you're strong, because they're afraid, they think you're going to make use of your strength. And d'you know, doctor, I—I'm afraid of them, I think.

It upset Halliday to see someone caving in like this.

It upset him because there was nothing to do. It was like looking at some private emotional mystery that you had no right to be looking at.

I dare say most of us are afraid, he said. Not of the same things perhaps. We start off being afraid of the dark. Then your fear probably moves its centre to something more tangible. And most of it rises out of a feeling of being alone. Being alone is being afraid. Perhaps one day we'll all wake up to the fact that we're all alone, that we're all afraid, and then it'll just be too damn silly to go on being afraid.

Moriarty lay there, detached. He was not listening. You could see that.

I'm a failure, he said. You see, I'm a failure, he said.

It all depends what constitutes success, Halliday said. Being a politician and running round in a limousine on other people's money, that's success of a sort. Or writing books for a few million middle-aged ladies to read themselves silly enough at night so that they can sleep. A very laudable success. But there's a worm in the kernel of most of it. Look, Moriarty, if you could persuade...

He looked down and the face had fallen asleep, or appeared to be. It was a good thing, because here he was talking about god knows what, but probably tinctured with the sourest grape. It was a dangerous theme, success.

The patient's asleep? whispered Mrs Moriarty.

She had come all a-tiptoe to the door. She put her head round the door, taking an excessive amount of trouble to balance herself, as she thought, elegantly on her toes. She was rather wide-eyed and very pink. She had put some rouge on her cheeks, he saw. Altogether she was like that woman standing in a doorway in Paris and trying to beckon him in.

He got up and went out of the room.

I'll make up some medicine and send it down, he said shortly. And I'll come and give him another injection to-night.

Oh, doctor, she said, I'm so grateful.

I'm only a doctor, he said.

Her lip that had begun to tremble, heavy with self-conscious gratitude, swelled itself into a pout. She frowned.

Yes, she frowned. All the same, you must be busy. We don't want to take up too much of your time.

Your husband's having a bad attack.

You don't have to tell me that. Don't I know it? she said. Hasn't he had me up all night?

She put up her hand to her head.

It makes me feel quite bad, she said. I would have come in, but my head. I'm awfully sensitive, doctor. I just can't stand it any more.

He'll be up in a day or two. Then there won't be anything to stand.

He took up his hat and went out into the garden, into the sun and the smell of earth that is very hot, and nettles in the sun. It licked up the smell of Mrs Moriarty, the powder caked in sweat, and he was glad, while feeling a twinge at the same time, because Moriarty there in bed, and I'm awfully sensitive, doctor, perhaps not emptying the wash-basin because of this, because an erotic blonde. There is something distinctly nauseating about love in its obese blonde aspect. Though Moriarty was not conscious of this, that wedding group over the bed, the gloves and the flowers

150

and all the paraphernalia of a stiff photographic convention that was almost cynical in its confidence, placing a head here, turning a shoulder just an inch towards the bride. It's very hard on poor Vic, he said. But she pitied herself enough for two.

He trod carefully in the dust to avoid a cloud, walked at the side of the road along a margin of dead grass, kicked a bottle shard, green and swimming in the sun. Mrs Moriarty molten with self-pity and sweat. But Alys Browne had come into the dispensary that day and he had despised her for the same reason before probing, but Mrs Moriarty was not Alys, even if to her husband, she was perhaps Alys, and Alys to him. He brushed a shoal of flies away from his face. Thinking about it again, he said, and her room so cool, why do I think of music, glistening in the chords a breeze. He must send medicine to Moriarty, though more, he could not give him more, he wanted to give him more, he wanted to give so many people the impossible through the existing wall that somehow the human personality seems to erect. Only she played Chopin and it crumbled to non-existent brick and they looked at each other, each time for the first, or looked at Moriarty for the first time, as if she had made it possible. I am not in love with Alys Browne, he said, and his foot, slurring the dust, sent it up in a fine cloud. I am not in love with Alys Browne. It is only a matter of gratitude for this fresh chord struck, with something universal in its tone, that penetrates isolation, even the farthest planet, lending significance to the hitherto insignificant. It is only this.

Alys Browne and Mrs Belper, the patterns scattered and the cutting scissors, were drinking tea in the sitting-room at the bank. Alys had gone down to help Mrs Belper run something up. That was the difference between Mrs Belper and the other people, Alys Browne went to Mrs Belper, whereas the others went to Alys Browne. Another difference was that Mrs Belper thereby got something off, an issue at first illogical, but consider the distinction of Running Up, I mean as apart from Making a Dress, and she always gave a slap-up tea and really it was only right. Not that Mrs Belper was mean, she practised what she called economies. So here they were having tea, in the sitting-room at the bank, with its encrustations of pokerwork and pervading smell of dog. Mrs Belper had a passion for dogs. There was always one in her lap, or one protruding from under her skirts, the little fox-terriers that she bred, or if she answered the front door there was always a screaming, and snarling, and gnashing of teeth from little flighty, spring-toed dogs and laborious bitches about to whelp, the pandemonium threaded through with Mrs Belper's soothing voice, her there, there, Trixie, you know who it is, or, how nice to see you, Mrs-er, no, no, Box won't bite, will you, Box, my lovely boy? So on the whole it is not surprising that the sitting-room, or even Mrs Belper herself, should be redolent of dogs. For she did smell of dogs, and nicotine, and she had a rich rasping cough, of which you were never certain how much was laughter and how much cough.

God bless my soul, said Mrs Belper, I'm sweating at every pore. Like a pig.

Mrs Belper is very unconventional, said Mrs Furlow once upon a time, unwilling to launch a suspicion that Mrs Belper was common, I ask you, using expressions like that. This was before she learnt about Mrs Belper's cousin who was secretary at Government House, which made her decide that after all Mrs Belper was just a Good Sort. It did not worry Mrs Belper. Nothing annoyed her, except when other people refused to trumpet like herself, or somebody cast a disparaging eye at the pool that one of the puppies had made, as if they could help it, the lambs, she said. The Belpers' house was like that, you had to tread warily on account of pools, and sometimes even worse.

Drink up, Alys, cried Mrs Belper. And you're not eating a thing.

Alys Browne, sitting with her cup in her hand, removed from Mrs Belper, let her mind wander vaguely, wondered if he would come this afternoon, though of course it was not to be expected, coming the afternoon before, when she had played that polonaise that he said. And why was a polonaise in stripes, the pink and black and yellow stripes, unfolding like a roll of stuff. All that on the floor, and the pins. And he would come perhaps and find that she was out, could not be in always, and why should she be in? Elbow on knee, she leant forward suddenly and said:

I was wondering about flounces, Mrs Belper. How they'd look. Starting perhaps from the knee. And there could be little flounces at the shoulders too.

Walking up the path would hear no sound, open the door perhaps, sit down and wait in room, waiting, while...

Me in flounces? My dear girl!

Then Mrs Belper began to laugh. It was too good. The idea. So she had to laugh, rich and rasping from cigarettes, and her breasts stirred happily beneath the large-mesh silk jumper that she wore.

Cissie Belper in flounces! she laughed. Alys, you must be off your head. And what would Joe have to say to flounces? Oh dear, no, she said.

I once had a dress with flounces, said Alys, looking down into her cup, the leaves spread like a fortune for Mrs Stopford-Champernowne to tell. It was when I was at the convent, she said.

That's all very well, said Mrs Belper. You in flounces and a convent. But that has nothing to do with me.

She continued to shake all over, spherical and convulsed, her hands working on her skirt or over the body of a little dog crouched in the hollow of her quaking lap.

You shouldn't've left that convent, she said. You should

154

have become a nun, Alys. But I don't understand you, of course. Living up there all by yourself. You'd have done much better in a convent, even if it's only hens. Because, I mean to say, well, company, and somebody else's face. And they can't have such a bad time there or they'd all come pouring out. Take my word, it's the priests. They get all the entertainment, and there's no talk of the tax.

From the convent in those blue afternoons you watched the bay, white with yachts, spread out like a book when reading, an illumination, or the Lily Maid upon a barge when Tennyson was always in your lap, and the wax face of Sister Mary cut in above the rustle of her skirt, made you think that perhaps after all you should have become a nun, even without vocation, as Mrs Belper said, and not look into teacups and wonder if in the leaves, but walk in the garden by the laurels, and the variegated laurel clump, with Sister Mary holding a hand, and it was evening, and the trams hung an unimportant apostrophe between the laurel clump and the lights. Perhaps I should have done all this, she said. I don't know. Perhaps I shall never know.

That's what you ought to have done, Mrs Belper said. We'll never find you a husband here.

And if I don't want a husband? said Alys.

Well, there's not much chance of your going off the rails. No one even for that.

What's all this? asked Mr Belper, coming in suddenly and clapping his wife on the back.

Look out, you clumsy brute! she said. You've startled Trixie out of her skin.

Poor little Trixie! Trixie! Trixie, come to Father, dear.

155

Trixie doesn't love Father any more. Do you pet? Joe, duckie, pour yourself some tea. If I touched the pot I'd stick to it. When d'you think it's going to rain? We were finding a husband for Alys, Joe.

Tell it not in Bath! said Mr Belper, rolling a slightly bloodshot eye.

Always a tease, murmured his wife, feeling perhaps through her latent conscience that some excuse was necessary.

She looked at her husband all the same and waited for him to follow up, because the Belpers were like that, a kind of perpetual vaudeville act, or concert party, The Good Sorts, who bandied about a clumsy ball both for their own entertainment and their audience's discomfiture.

I think I shall have to go home, said Alys.

Go home for what? Mrs Belper complained. What a girl you are, to be sure. Of course I don't understand you, Alys. You could have stayed on to supper. We might have had a game of cards.

Always on the make is Cissie Belper, said her husband, faithful to the act.

Oh, shut up, Joe, for God's sake! But doesn't Alys make you sick?

Jostled redly the Belper faces counting through lines of intricate sound the veins and a dog's bark one two shattering the lampshade beads. Yes, thought Alys Browne, it is time I left, though why, he will not have come.

What about the shares, Mr Belper? she said as she took her hat.

Shares? Oh yes! The shares! Don't you be impatient,

my girl. Just you trust to your Uncle Joe. He'll hand you a nice little nest-egg, though we can't produce any dividends yet.

Joe, you're a marvel, said his wife, not altogether sarcastically. Mrs Belper always held her breath before the faintly miraculous conduct of stocks and shares.

But Alys thought she would go home, went out into the sunlight that was heavy on her hair, and it made her altogether heavy to walk in the hot sun, even as far as home. She walked along the road and smiled to herself until she thought it must look silly that anyone passing her on the road would wonder what she was smiling at. So she stopped. It seemed a long way home. Nowadays she always seemed to be on her way between two points, or waiting, she waited much more than in the past, though now with a sense of fulfilment in waiting as if it were some end in itself. She could not think what would happen, but she did not much care. Most things were irrelevant now, having tea at the Belpers', or buying shares in a company on Mr Belper's advice. But she had sold the paddocks at Kambala that once her father had owned, and buying the shares she had said, I shall go to California soon, this is almost on the way. But this was when she was buying the shares. I shall go to California soon. Now she did not want to any more, it did not seem worth while. And the Salvage Bay Pearl Company, a prospectus in a bottom drawer, had lost the romantic possibilities which were such an inducement to buy. Those men who went down in helmets, the dark faces behind glass, walked on the bottom of the sea to gather pearls, walked through forests of sponge, like dark flowers encased in glass, it was all there behind the printed word, the ropes of weed that swayed without a wind. Reading the prospectus was to get rich, she would go to California, and all this would be on pearls, though nobody in the boat would know that Miss Alys Browne was made of pearls, a kind of pearl queen in her way. This was how many months ago? She wondered, but she did not know, and anyway she was not rich yet, and—well, she did not altogether care. Though this would be nice, she said, a change to have people like you just for your surface value, quite a change.

Her feet caught in the heavy surface of the road. If he would approve, just for a while, a certain amount of frailty, like the books she had scarcely read. But she could not always be thinking of someone else. She brushed away a face with her hand. Because she must go on being herself, or what was herself, that was what made it difficult, being herself, or thinking of someone else, which was herself? She thought of him and became at once a different person, yet in a way more herself, firmer, and more distinct. Perhaps this was it. And she wanted it like this, the start of something positive. All those superficialities, she said, all these must fall away, all that I was building up, because I was afraid, it is because I was afraid that I wanted to be different, that I wanted California, because I was afraid.

The shadows were longer on the road as she turned up towards her house. It was still sunny and hot, but with that quietness which anticipates the decline of the sun, and there was a brassy sheen on everything. In summer when your sense of perception has been numbed all day by the light and the heat, and you have sunk down into a blurred

158

world, of which the reality is less actual than your own, because you have constructed something in desperation in which to take refuge with yourself, you first become aware again in this softer but still florid light, you discover in the external its proportionate significance. So to Alys Browne opening her gate objects became distinctly defined, as if she had been looking through a gauze all day and now it had dropped, and the fence-posts stood up with a kind of sober, detached beauty, very distinct from their environment, and the house with its long, slender shadow, and the potsherds bordering the flower-beds, and the corrugated water-tank, all these had an existence of their own, only united in this moment of depreciating sun.

Alys Browne clicked the gate. In the stillness it made a loud click. It was so still that she felt he could not be there. There was no reason why he should. She was as nothing to him, as his wife was something, and she must not think. My husband is up at Kambala, she said. She was Mrs Halliday and at the same time almost an impersonal entity, to her, personal to him. He said, you must come down and see my wife. She felt she must ask about his wife, but they talked about music instead. The way her hair that morning, slightly grey, as if she were older than he, falling down at the sides, and she said he was up at Kambala. Alys Browne walked on up the path. Suddenly she hoped he would not be there.

On the edge of the verandah sat Margaret Quong, leaning against a post, and her legs hung down into the flower-bed underneath. She sat there playing with a shell, holding it in her hands, looking at it, not at Alys Browne, as her feet stirred poppy and marigold. Oh dear, thought Alys, that child, then he is not here, and isn't she thin, those long legs.

Hello, Margaret, she said. I could drop.

She went and sat down on the edge of the verandah beside the child. She rested her head on Margaret's shoulder and closed her eyes. Margaret stopped playing with the shell. Down the slope Schmidts' cows were arriving to be milked, walking heavy with shadow into the curve of the hill.

It isn't your lesson, is it? said Alys.

No, said Margaret. I just came.

She spoke very softly. She sat stiffly and still, holding with her shoulder the burden of Alys's head. There was something pained and almost Gothic in the angle of her body, like a figure in a niche embodying pleasure and pain.

Have you been here long? asked Alys.

About half an hour.

So he had not come, for she would have said. Alys got up and went inside. Margaret followed her in. This silent child, and if he were to come.

I've been down at Belpers', she said.

Oh.

Yes. Mrs Belper is having a dress.

She must look round the room, she felt, but not without an attempt to disguise, because Margaret might see a note, where of course there was none, or had blown away perhaps if a wind, was no wind. And why was she looking at her, this child, knowing, if only she would say, the way that children usually know and say, but Margaret different in this, her face closed up.

160

Why, what's the matter, Margaret? she said.

Nothing.

You look so strange.

Margaret Quong turned away. She began to kick the floor with her heel.

The doctor was here, Margaret said.

Alys put down her hat. Yes? She wanted to say, yes, what else, tell me what else at once, and she looked at her hand that was trembling on the brim of her hat.

He was, was he? she said, and it was not her voice at all.

Margaret was very still.

And what did he want? said Alys.

Nothing. He didn't say.

She began to arrange things, things there was no need to arrange, because Margaret looking, and yet would know. She looked at Margaret, that sullen stare that was almost tears.

I'm going now, said Margaret. I'll come to-morrow for my lesson, she said.

Then she went very quickly, and Alys could see her marching quickly down the path through the tarnish of the late afternoon. She had wanted to say to Margaret before she left, to say what? She even called out through the door, Margaret! Margaret! to a figure that was almost distance. But anyway if Margaret turned she really had nothing to say, or so much, so much that she could not say, to Margaret whose face was heavy with tears. She felt a bit ashamed too. I am to blame for this, she said, or is one to blame, is it just that one is part of a movement for which one is not responsible, a note joined to other notes to complete a bar, and these repeated in a pattern forming part of the general scheme. She hoped it was like this. She did not like to think she was responsible, the way Margaret looked, and she was fond of Margaret who could not see that this was different, when he came to the house and she played him Schumann, as she and Margaret played, only the whole tempo was different then, and there were moments experienced with Margaret that always must remain separate, if she could tell her that.

She shook back her hair. She went and lay on the sofa, on her back. Her throat was white in the shadow. I must think it out, she said, how I can tell her this, the silly child. She lay there with the very best intentions, knowing she would not think of Margaret, but let the mind follow its own curve, and she smiled because she knew this, like coming up the road, only now she did not check herself, she smiled.

Mrs Furlow hovered in the passage. She had hovered, both
mentally and physically, for the best part of a week. Her life
was on tenterhooks. Nobody can say, she remarked to her
husband more than once in that memorable week, nobody
can say I haven't done everything I can, it only remains for
Sidney to do the rest. Whether Sidney would was a different
matter, but it afforded Mrs Furlow some satisfaction to
cherish a mental image of herself as the pelican offering its
blood, and at the same time there was the possibility of an
improvement on the fable if the precious nourishment were
refused. Because you never knew what Sidney would do.
It is *supremely* trying, she wrote to Mrs Blandford, Sidney
is quite incomprehensible. Once she used to put original,
but the credit of giving birth to originality is exhausted
by degrees as this quality develops its resourcefulness. So
originality was now a trial.

Mrs Furlow sighed when she thought of herself as a girl. She had been what is known as a Lovely Girl, and not altogether devoid of originality herself, though she knew just how far this might hinder an economic and social success. Whereas Sidney was quite devoid of a sense of obligations. Life, for Mrs Furlow, was a series of obligations, to her class, to her daughter, to her friends, and more especially to herself. There was something revolutionary for Mrs Furlow in her daughter's attitude, as if at any moment she might pitch a bomb into the elaborate edifice that it had taken a lifetime to build. So you cannot be surprised if she waited on tenterhooks, sometimes catching her breath, sometimes punctured with relief as the structure still remained. And now Sidney's engagement to Roger Kemble, which would provide through marriage the topmost pinnacle, swayed in mid-air on the crane of Sidney's wilfulness, dangled, threatened to drop.

Mrs Furlow decided not to recognize this possibility at all. She had fixed a smile on her face that was a badge of future success. My son-in-law, Roger Kemble, she would write to Mrs Blandford. The bride left for England in a mink coat and a tiny hat well off the face, the honeymoon will be spent, the Sydney Morning Herald would announce. But now she hovered in the passage, waiting, while Roger put on his riding-boots, he looked so handsome, so English in boots, and Sidney did something in her room, one hoped not sulk, before what must be the crowning spasm of a week of agony. To-morrow he would go away, back to vice-regal duties at Government House, thought Mrs Furlow not without a twinge. She looked at her watch. She had ordered the horses for three o'clock, time for lunch to digest, and all that, and the day was mercifully not so hot, as she looked out of the verandah door, almost willing a decrease in the temperature.

Roger Kemble came out of his room, in the boots, and a shirt that was open at the neck. It was a blue shirt. It made him look very pink. Mrs Furlow hoped that his skin would not peel, sending him out in the hot sun, but as it was all in a good cause she decided she might be excused.

Ah, there you are, Roger! she said, a little too precipitately, as if he had just come out of a conjurer's basket and not from his bedroom door.

I see you're staging a heat-wave for the Last Ride, he said.

Whatever he meant by that. She could see a suggestion of perspiration on his skin. A slight suggestion of perspiration was very attractive, she thought.

Isn't it hot! she said. Shall we go and look at the thermometer?

A thermometer's never much help, do you think?

No. No! I thought...Sidney! Hurry up, dear. Roger's waiting, you know.

They stood there awkwardly. If he knew how much she felt for him, if she could put out her hand and say to him, there, Roger, we both know how it feels, we're inexorably linked, it might help quite a lot. But instead they stood awkwardly waiting for Sidney, and she found herself wondering about his moustache, if it went that way of its own accord or if he stood in front of the mirror every morning and twisted it up. She could not imagine Roger

Kemble twisting his moustache. He was so gentle. A fair moustache. Or a blond moustache was perhaps the term. On the whole she preferred a blond moustache.

A penny for them, said Mrs Furlow skittishly.

I was wondering about the ultimate effect of a Mediterranean climate on an Anglo-Saxon race.

Oh, she said. Yes. Yes.

Then Sidney came out of her room. Mrs Furlow recoiled with relief out of range of the Anglo-Saxon race.

Come on, said Sidney briskly. We've got to get this ride over. There's no use hanging about.

Sidney! protested Mrs Furlow.

Well, we know it's a bore, don't we, Roger? Going out in all this heat.

Mrs Furlow persuaded herself that he blushed.

It's hot enough, he said. But, after all, it's the last time.

No, she said, it's the prelude to lots and lots. Mother will ask you again.

She looked at him with a smile. It was almost a straight line, her lips very thin and red, cleft by the sudden imposing of a smile, and then suddenly still again. He felt a long way off from her, that in spite of the smile there was no contact at all. He felt at once both excited and uncomfortable.

She's going to be difficult, her mother sighed, clenching her rings, and said:

Shouldn't you have worn a hat with a larger brim?

Sidney opened the fly-proof door with a bang.

Or a pith-helmet? she asked.

You know that time you got sunstroke.

Yes, she said. It was bloody.

Sidney, *dear*!

A red, lean kelpie met them on the verandah and began to jump up to Sidney's thighs. She held it by the paws a moment, her thin brown hands on its thin red paws. There is something here completely foreign to anything I know, felt Roger Kemble, those hands that touch a different substance, and despising what I touch. Then the bottom fell out of the afternoon. He did not want to go for the ride. He knew he would have to, but it was like going up to your homemaster's study during prep, you knew what it meant.

Mrs Furlow took root on the verandah step.

Good luck, she said.

Then she was immediately horrified, in case they might interpret, though it was a thing people said, young people, she had heard them say it, and perhaps Sidney and Roger would only think. She had only said it because she liked to imagine she was one of them. For Mrs Furlow was one of those parents who, in an effort to keep in touch with contemporary slang, are determinedly B.O.P.

They left Mrs Furlow on the verandah step. They went across the yard to where the horses hung their heads, or flicked with a warning of steel in the thin shade. There was an odour of sleep from the stables and the sound of sleep in the throat of a red cock, prowling on no apparent errand, but with the conviction of his kind. His colour burnt across the yard, was harsh to the eyes. Then they got on their horses, Roger and Sidney, and rode down towards the flat. It was yellow and burnt up. The hills were burnt brown, and scabrous, quite bare in the heat, in the shimmering of heat that was liquid and apparent, the whole landscape melting

167

and fused into an indeterminate shape beyond the margin of the eyes. You wanted to close your eyes as you rode along, to shield them from the light and the crusting of black flies.

But perhaps he is getting something out of it, Sidney felt, the way men do in their peculiar way, just from a presence, though by this a prelude to touch is generally implied. His boot touching. Sitting at dinner, the dessert came and he began to tell us, what was it, about Toc H and lighting torches, and peeling an apple his voice meant no more than this, an unwinding of surface skin. There was something decidedly pathetic about earnest, worthy men. So little defence and you wanted to see just how far you could penetrate without hurting, or perhaps hurting a little, to see. Like kicking a dog. As if he were a dog, something with wire hair. She jabbed the spurs into her horse. It gave a little whinge and sidled along.

This time to-morrow, he was saying.

This time to-morrow, she said quickly, and with no attempt at succour, you'll be going in to Moorang to the train. It'll probably be just as hot as this. You'll be awfully sorry and we'll be awfully sorry. And then you'll write a bread-and-butter letter and say how awfully good. N'est-ce pas?

He bit his lip. It was just what he had expected. Going up to the study step by step, and knowing as you got to the top step that you were in for something unavoidable and unpleasant. She rocked along on that chestnut horse, part of the volatile, heat-tinctured landscape that was like something unfolding in dream dimensions, because unreal, you could not say that the present moment was real.

Roger Kemble sat and held hot leather in his hands. His hands were hot. He used to stutter when a boy, and they laughed at him at school, and it was pretty beastly till he got over it, but there was always something of the stutter remained, in his manner if not in his diction. Women liked him for it. So that it might have been an asset, if he had been conscious of assets of that particular kind. But he was the sort of Englishman whose women are not material for barter and exchange, creatures rather seen through the distance of a speech-day cricket match or a May Week haze upon the Cam. You employed a different vocabulary for their benefit, almost a different tone of voice. They were, in fact, Women, an abstract concept, which did not altogether gainsay the possibility of a concrete example to be welcomed with all due deference as a wife. He had hoped that Sidney would become that concrete example, would have written home to say that of course she is unconventional when judged by ordinary standards, but that is only the effect of environment, and their standard of values is different from ours. Roger Kemble clung doggedly to the idea of environment. It was the nucleus of all his favourite clichés, it made him feel intellectually safe, just as a politician erecting a safety barrage of party catchwords, and Roger Kemble would probably succumb to politics later on, standing for somewhere in Wiltshire and thought a lot of by farmer Conservatives. It was the inevitable conclusion, not Sidney Furlow, and vaguely he knew this, that Sidney Furlow would not fit in. His mother sat on the lawn and poured out tea. Girls came and sat beside her, resting from tennis in white frocks, nice girls who behaved towards

Sidney Furlow with a not altogether effortless attention, because of the Dominions, those pink daubs on a map and subject of the King's broadcast speech. Sidney Furlow a Wiltshire lawn, was not this, in a white frock, was a brown sterile spur that you saw in a heat-haze, a long way off. That was the difference.

You can't think what a vast difference there is, he said, between what you're used to out here, and what we've got at home.

Are we so inferior?

I didn't mean that.

He blushed red in the sun.

I mean, he said, it's *so* different. The landscape, for instance. Environment must eventually be responsible for a lot.

Saying this when he meant to ask her if she would like to see England, if she would like him to show it to her. His skin prickled with futility.

Yes, she yawned, I suppose it must. Thank God I shan't be here to see it.

He tightened his hand on the bunch of reins.

Why all this discontent? he said.

Am I?

Well, yes. I should have thought. Something must be responsible. Perhaps if you got away.

She pursed up her lips.

You know, Roger, you make me laugh.

Why?

Oh, I dunno.

They rode on a bit. The silence was jerky with the

170

flicker of grasshoppers, the air yellow with their wings. On the horses' necks the veins stood sculptured through the sweat.

I often think, said Sidney, it'd be rather fun to blow out one's brains. Only one mightn't be able to watch the reactions of one's friends. And that of course would be the whole point. There's something so cool and soothing about the barrel of a gun. To feel it up against one's forehead.

Sidney, he said.

Oh, you needn't make me promise you things. In the end one doesn't do it.

But I wanted to ask.

Look, she said, I'll race you down to the bend.

Because only by this you could feel the wind, in the heat soothing as the barrel of a gun, the horse stretched and breathing under your legs. He was going to ask, well, what Mother for the last week had been wanting him to ask, as if this were the price of a week at Glen Marsh. The Furlows of Glen Marsh. The Glen Marsh stud. I am a Furlow and object of deference, because God knows why, why the Furlows, if only you could strip off and become some, something, something, anything, or even naked. And he was going to ask me about England, Sidney Furlow, change the initials on my dressing case, because married to Roger Kemble is only an exchange of labels, would not be essentially different, going up to bed and sleeping together would not change all that. She pressed her legs into the sides of the horse, feeling the weal of the stirrup leathers pressed in to her legs. Hurting Roger Kemble if she said no, hurting him more if she accepted, he did not realize what

171

it implied, that she wanted more than deference, even if she did not altogether know what it was she wanted yet, if definitely not an English accent and a fair moustache. Though it would have been so easy. It would have been such an easy way out. Of course I shall marry, Helen said at Miss Cortine's. Helen was not a virgin. There was that little naval man, very smooth, looked as if he must have been shaved all over. Oh well, that, said Helen, that won't make any difference, and you can't be a prude if they want. Lying in bed and wondering if Helen and that man, it made you stuff the sheet in your mouth, though Helen said. The horse cantered towards the bend. She drew him in, her hands whitened by the straining of the reins. But if I married Roger it would be different, would not touch unless. She jerked at the horse's mouth.

Come up! she shouted. Come up, damn you!

This old post of a chestnut gelding that they gave her to ride, as if she were a child and couldn't manage, or didn't want to manage, even if your hands hurt or breath beat out of your body, or hoofs trampled blood upon your mouth. Her lips were white as she reined in the horse.

Roger came up behind her. She looked at the tension of his face, working up, working up to say...

Look, she said, there's Hagan over there with the men.

Then watched his face slacken as the moment slipped and they rode closer to the group of men.

They were working on the fence, pulling out the rotten posts and twitching up the wire. The two men turned to look. They wiped sweat from their faces and watched the horses approach. Hagan, his back turned, tamped the earth

172

round the butt of a new post, and the tamp rose and fell through his hands like a piston-rod. He stood with his legs apart, slowly tamping. His arms were a burnt red.

Afternoon, Miss Sidney, one of the men said.

Both of them touched their hats. Hagan turned.

Good afternoon, Hagan, she said.

She looked down at him, at his face shiny with sweat, and screwed up as he looked through the glare. He nodded at her and smiled. The way that gold flashed in the sun. Did not take off his hat. She frowned at him as she passed close, looking down. He could have put out his hand. She saw the reddish hair on his arms. Hated him ever since that day when, running down the hill and glancing back from the shed door, she had seen him standing insolently up in the yard, owning the place, and watching her make a fool of herself. He always felt she was a fool, looked at her like this. Our *Mr* Hagan, she said. And now he watched them as they rode by, standing propped upon the iron tamp, looking through her body and making her conscious of its movement, its curve and sway, even though her back was turned she felt that he stood there looking with his eyes screwed up. His hands were hard. She had touched them that night at supper, handing the salad, and the skin was cracked, the broken nails. She had looked up into his eyes and they were hard too above the salad-bowl.

Let's go back, she said to Roger. We can go up that gully and round. I don't know why we're trailing about like lunatics in this heat.

After all, it's the last time.

She looked at him.

173

If you say that again I'll scream. No, I don't mean that. I'm sorry, Roger. Only I wish we had gone another way.

She had let fall upon him a cool word that another time would have been exquisite, now only a reminder of things still undone. He took out his handkerchief and slowly wiped his face.

She looked back over her shoulder. Hagan was tamping the earth. She turned again and frowned. As if there was something in the denial of a supposition that galled. She hated him because he had stared, she hated him more because he had not.

Sidney, said Roger, and it all came rather quickly, as if there was not much time, and turning the shoulder of a hill she might canter out of his vicinity. Sidney, I want to ask you something. Something I've wanted to ask you for a long time. I wonder if you'd marry me, he said.

Oh Lord, she groaned mentally, now it was all coming, and why was a proposal so just like what you had expected, coming from Roger anyway it was. If only it could stay like that, but you had to say something in reply.

Well, she said, do you feel any better now that you've got that off your chest?

No, not a bit.

I'm sorry.

You've rather left me in the air.

You don't think I could marry you?

I don't see why you couldn't.

His voice was stripped rather painfully of its reserve. There was always something rather painful, she thought, about a voice that had lost its insulation.

174

Think a bit, she said, and you'll see.

Which was what he had done already, denying the rational conclusion, because Sidney was like that, because he wanted her, because he could not understand her, which made no difference, for somehow the unattainable puts a stronger accent on desire.

I don't see why you couldn't, he said again.

Like a schoolboy, he felt, his voice, a schoolboy who produced a lamentable defence, clung to a shielding phrase, in the face of the inevitable.

She began to hum.

What do you want? he said. What do you really want?

I don't know, she said.

Her cheeks looked hollow as she turned.

But I don't want to talk about this. See? It's all over.

Her voice flipped out. Then they rode on silently.

He had done it. It was over. He felt he had been whipped all over. He would write to his mother and say, dear Mother, say...Nothing at all. Because there was no need, sitting on the lawn, to explain that Sidney was a kind of paradox, still in fact, though non-existent as far as Wiltshire was concerned. But he did not want her any the less, his words flung back, and that look, when he fell down a cliff-face in Dorset his hands on shale, he looked up the sky white and sheer as silence.

I suppose you'll come up for the races, he said, in the kind of voice with which he made conversation at garden parties, and which made old ladies murmur, Roger Kemble, so attentive, so kind.

I don't expect so, she said.

Damn these grasshoppers!

Yes. There's a plague.

Australia, the land of plagues.

She looked at him, twisting up her mouth. The lids of her eyes hung low against the glare.

A second Egypt, she said. Only not so full of allegory.

The voice was heavy in her mouth. What you said in this heat was somehow immaterial. About allegory. I am dying, Egypt. Those silkworms, shrivelled up and made a smell and you ran away out of the room because the smell of putrefying silkworms was too much. Sidney, dear, said Mother, we must throw the poor little silkworms out, you won't mind, darling, Daddy will get some more. More and more and more. We must feed them on mulberry leaves to keep them fresh and fat and smooth. Then they lifted him up into the tower and it must have been hard work, though of course there would have been someone underneath to push, and that woman slobbering, it was a monument, with his mouth on Egypt. Roger Kemble with his mouth tight pressed. Helen said you opened your mouth. Tamping that post hole and he got a sunstroke, it would take him down a peg, or would go away and then. It was too hot, too fly, and the house like a red wound on a burnt face with a tank that flashed, not gold, that was too hot, hot.

They rode back again into the yard. It was hot and foetid as they left it, a smell of dung, of ammonia from the stables, and no shadow anywhere. The red cock was a flame licking up the dust near the pantry window, quite solitary beside the dead house. They led their horses into the stable. They walked across the yard. Each step was of consequence, only so many necessary steps, the rest dispensable.

Mrs Furlow had taken off her shoes and her dress. She had lain down to rest. I shan't sleep, she said to her husband, who was dozing in the office beneath an ark of newspapers constructed to protect him from a possible fly. Mr Furlow did not even grunt. He was asleep. So Mrs Furlow lay down on her bed, in need of sympathy, thought she would like to pray, if that were not blasphemy, was it, she wondered, and one always prayed for rain, not that it did any good. Mrs Furlow lay on her bed and sighed, tried not to accuse the Almighty of perversity. That was till she heard Sidney come. She heard the bang of the fly-proof door, their feet in the passage going to their rooms. Mrs Furlow's heart banged. She sat on the edge of the bed. Then she got up slowly, put on her dressing-gown, and went down the passage to Sidney's room.

Sidney, she said.

She looked over her daughter's shoulder, at her daughter's face in the mirror, sitting there at the dressing-table, quite still. It was the stillness that perturbed Mrs Furlow.

You've got back very soon, she said.

Yes. It was a bore riding about in the heat.

Sidney took up the powder-puff. She dabbed at her face with the soft puff. She looked at her mother in the mirror, standing there in her stockings, on soft, puffed feet, soft, very soft, looking ludicrous with her head stuck forward, waiting. It made you want to hurt something, take it in your hand, not a flabby insipid puff. She threw down the powder-puff. It made a faint protesting cloud as it hit the dressing-table's glass top.

177

And Roger? said Mrs Furlow. Roger wanted to go for a ride.

He's in his room. You'd better ask him if he enjoyed it.

Sidney, you didn't quarrel?

Why should I quarrel with Roger?

No. I wondered. I wondered if he...

Sidney got up. She was trembling. She couldn't control her mouth, no longer pressed into a line, but forced open by the breath, that was hot, that was rasping on her lips. She quivered like a wire.

No, she screamed. No. He didn't. Or he did, if you like. Only I didn't. Now get out. For God's sake. Go! Go!

Mrs Furlow retreated on her stockinged feet. Her face was a quaking mass of afternoon despair. She began to cry.

For God's sake, go! For God's sake, get out!

Like a wire struck and still vibrating, Sidney Furlow had that zinging in the ears. Her hands fumbled at the lock, and with less directed purpose on her own face. Back to the door, she trembled in the glass. There were two lines of red down her left cheek, fresh from the passage of her nails.

Mrs Furlow stood outside in her stockings, whimpered desolate against the door.

178

14

Clem Hagan had finished work. He stood in the wash-house at the back of the cottage where he lived. The light was frail outside, the landscape gentler, the cows in acquiescent groups. Hagan looked out of the window, though not at the landscape, not conscious of this or the activities of natural phenomena, except as a source of economic advancement, and now that work was over he did not even think of this. There was a smell of yellow soap in the wash-house and of boiling water in a kerosene tin. He stood at the basin, bare to the waist, and the water ran down his shoulders, down the channel of his spine and the valley between his breasts. There was a foam of soap at his neck. The water glistened in the hollows of his neck. When he had washed he took the razor, and with the same inevitable rhythm, he began to shave his face. You heard the tottering scrape of the razor, the seeping sound of the lathered brush. You saw him, half-shaved, eye himself in the glass with the satisfaction of one who has confidence in his body, both as a physical structure of muscle and bone, and as a source of endless possibility. He smiled at the glass, not exactly at himself, but at an array of achievements for which he had been responsible. Then he continued to shave himself.

Clem Hagan riding into town for the evening and risking a new pair of pants on the saddle. Clem Hagan whistling and testing his spurs on the horse's side. Clem Hagan mounting the hill and letting the horse go in the almost darkness, opening her out along the road, so that the trees flew and the letter-box at Ferndale, and then just the hissing of the darkness, as it got dark, and there was nothing but darkness to fly past. This was an apotheosis. A shave and a wash made you feel like new, and the sound of metal as the horse galloped along. You were a new man. You bent forward along the horse's neck and the wind was in your teeth. Your teeth bared to the wind. Clem Hagan going into town.

Would go and try his luck, there was every sign, and that Saturday in the store brushing up against him as if there was no room, and apologizing, and a tin of dog biscuits falling on to the floor. Oh, Miss Quong, she said, aren't I clumsy, she said, but it's dark, my eyes aren't used to the light, though she could see like a cat rubbing up against him, you must come round, she said, my husband and I will only be too glad to see you, because one never sees a soul in Happy Valley, does you, not like in Sydney where Daisy, Daisy's my sister, you know, they have a business at Marrickville, she said, I used to live there before I

180

met Ernest, that's my husband, that she slipped in for luck when she asked anyone to come round, that little runt of a schoolmaster. He said he'd come round perhaps Saturday night. She said she'd be ever so pleased. It was a pity they didn't see more of each other, wasn't it? He must be lonely out there at Glen Marsh. They might have a game of cards, if he liked cards, she didn't much. Then she went out of the store, pneumatically down the steps, and he could see the ridge of the corset on her behind.

Hagan whistled between his teeth. It was a tune he had heard somewhere on a gramophone, long enough ago to forget the circumstances, though he could have made a pretty good guess. He yawned. It was all pretty much the same, a different gramophone to the same tune, and sometimes you wondered if it was worth turning the handle, wondered that is, until you thought you'd give it another try, see if you still had the knack, and then the bloody tune was the same. He stopped whistling. He could have done with a drink. Perhaps she would give him a drink, or perhaps that little blue-faced slate-pencil of a Moriarty was T.T., looked as if he might be anything, or a Baptist, or anything. Take her to the pictures perhaps. Only there was Moriarty. Might take her to the pictures and get her in the middle with Moriarty the other side, kid Moriarty there was nothing up while working on his wife, which would make an easy job a little bit difficult. It was all so easy, all so much the same, turning the handle for the same tune. He could do with a Scotch. Working on those fence-posts it made you dry, and drinking out of a canvas bag the water soft and warm, that you spat out of your mouth, wiped sweat from your eyes as she came past, and good afternoon Hagan she said, with that pink-faced pommy chap that they said was going to marry her—well, he had a tough job there, the poor bastard, like getting your crowbar into the rock, and she thought she was doing you a favour as she rode past to say, or up at supper that Sunday evening with doyleys on the table and passing you the salad-bowl. He began to whistle in thoughtful scraps. The wind flirted past his face as they went down Tozer's Hollow where the water-hole was now bone-dry. Passing the salad-bowl and jumping as if she was shot, made you think a bit as you looked at her, saw she was hard as a nail, and not for you if you wanted, even if you wanted what you didn't want, not a virgin anyway, it was too much like hard work, and holding you responsible, as if you wasn't doing them a good turn. Sidney Furlow could keep herself.

He rode on towards Happy Valley. There were lights soon and someone in a buggy going into town. Somebody said good night. Good night, he said. They were almost into town. Funny the way you even got a kick out of going into a one-horse joint like Happy Valley that made you cry just to think about, and then started you up when it turned into lights and the barking of dogs.

He left his horse in a yard out by Schmidts', that Schmidt let him use to save putting up in a stall at the hotel. He took off his spurs and put them in his pocket. He went along the road past Schmidts' and up into the main street, where there was a hurricane lantern hanging from the verandah at Quongs'. A dog barked at him from Everetts'. People coming down the street. Somebody singing at the pub.

That day going up the street, was winter, to the pub, and standing in the rain at the gate, he was going in, farther along, she said, Mrs Moriarty said…Mrs Moriarty.

Mrs Moriarty sat at the piano in the sitting-room. She had sat there for some time, because she did not want him to miss her, as he came along, her voice singing, because Daisy said she had a fine contralto, if only she had had it trained. So Mrs Moriarty sat at the piano and sang in her fine contralto with great feeling those scraps of Charmaine that she could remember. It was old but somehow appropriate. I wonder when bluebirds are mating, sang Mrs Moriarty. Then she came to a bit she did not know and she la-la-ed with even more feeling than she put into the words. La-la la-la-la la-la LA LAR, sang Mrs Moriarty. She had once thought about going into vaudeville, a tasteful act with a grand piano and a pink bead dress and a big black curtain with parrots appliquéd on it. DOROTHY CHALMERS—THE SILVER VOICE on the bills. Because you couldn't call yourself Victoria, or even Vic. It was always a sore point with Mrs Moriarty that she hadn't been called Dorothy.

The brown mahogany clock ticked with the annoying obtrusiveness of Ernest's mahogany clock.

Damn that clock, she said, which included somebody else.

It made her restless, waiting like this, her nose. God what a sight, and that cream didn't close up the pores, didn't give you your money back. Perhaps you ought to be discovered on the sofa, glancing through a magazine, rather casually, because that was the point, and the piano was not so casual after all. Then Mrs Moriarty had to frown. She realized she could not be discovered anywhere, because Gertie Ansell had gone home, because she would have to let him in herself, and that was what happened when you couldn't keep a maid. She struck a chord on the piano. It quite hurt her hands.

Then Hagan knocked on the door.

Ah, she said. How nice to see you, Mr Hagan. It is so nice of you to come.

I expect I'm late, he said.

Oh no, she said. That is, I was just trying over some old favourites. I love a good tune, don't you?

It all depends on the voice, he said.

Well, now. What am I to say to that?

She laughed and put up her hand to her shoulder, the way she had seen that mannequin, when Daisy and she at David Jones's, and the sleeve fell down to the elbow showing off the arm. She laughed very prettily.

You'll pass muster, he said. I heard it coming up the street.

Mrs Moriarty laughed again, even more prettily than before. Because she had charm, if only people gave her a chance, were appreciative, but she wasn't going to waste it on people who did not understand. Hagan looked at her, smiled, that gold in his teeth. He understood.

I expect you're quite parched, she said. This heat. Won't you let me pour you a drink?

I don't mind if you do.

Thought he didn't expect that Moriarty, and two glasses, and a siphon and all.

I'm going to keep you company, she said. Ernest's gone

184

up to talk to Mr Belper. They're such cronies. I hope you don't mind. Anyway, drink's always the same.

I guess it is.

Waving her glass at him, and she knew a thing or two anyone could see, a fast worker, sending him out and...

Yes, he said, drink's always the same.

Cheers, said Mrs Moriarty, waving her glass.

I'm glad I came, he said, getting his breath out of the glass.

It's a change to see people now and again.

She rested her face on her hand, making her eyes big, because sympathy, she knew, was always her long suit.

I was up at Muswellbrook, he said.

Happy Valley makes me cry.

I'm sorry about that.

She giggled at a bubble in her glass, that she was emptying too quick, and he'd think, but she wasn't like that.

Have another drink? she said, after they had talked a bit, decently, about the rainfall in New England and the wool clip at Glen Marsh.

Thanks, he said. What about you?

I don't mind.

That's the way.

Oh, I'm not frightened, she said.

What've you got to be frightened of?

That made her pick the braiding on the sofa.

Well, she said, slowly.

He came and sat down beside her on the sofa. It was only the second drink, but panting like that, you could see it was time to take her hand. But she got up and stood by

185

the table and began fingering a plant.

What have you got to be frightened of? he said.

Oh dear, Mr Hagan, she said. It's hot. It makes me perspire.

Mr Hagan? You can call me Clem.

Do you think I might?

I never say yes when I mean no. What do you go by, now we're on it?

Vic, she said.

It made her blush. She wished she had been christened Dorothy.

Go on! he said. Vic.

Yes, she said. It isn't my fault, you know.

Like the Queen.

Perhaps.

Vic, eh? Come and sit down again, Vic.

She stood fingering that bloody plant, as if she didn't know, as if he was a zany, and you could see she was excited the way she heaved under her dress.

It's so close, she sighed. Wouldn't you like to go to the pictures, Clem?

It'll be closer there, he said. But just as you say, Vic.

So they started off to go to the pictures in the hall that belonged to Quongs. She said it was so nice to have his company, somebody who understood, as she walked along with her hand under his arm, and he could feel her hand under his arm getting a bit inquisitive. He began to feel good. Yes, he said, yes, giving her hand a squeeze, and it was a pity they hadn't got together before. That first day he had wanted to know. Most people were in the hall, but there were still some walking up the hill, some girls, and behind them Chuffy Chambers, who drove the lorry from Happy Valley to Moorang, walking on his own. He walked up the hill, his mouth slightly open, and out of breath.

Look, said Hagan to Vic. Look at Chuffy Chambers chuff-chuffing after those girls.

Ssh, she said. The boy isn't right in his head.

But she laughed a bit all the same, because it looked like that, the girls and that loopy boy, oh dear, he had a sense of humour, you could see that, and she'd mixed the whisky pretty stiff, and she felt as if there were sparks in her head.

That's good! she laughed. Chuffing Chambers.

Chuffy Chambers shambled slower, suddenly ashamed, saw them as they passed on. It made him cold down his back. He had been named William, only they called him Chuffy, even his mother. Chuffing after those girls. Somebody said, come here, Chuffy, and he came, but could not remember how it started, why. His skin felt cold against the holy medals that he wore beneath his shirt. Father Purcell said. He hated Hagan. He lagged back, would not go to the pictures now. The others went up the hill. You could see the lights through the girls' skirts as they turned in at the hall door. That day on the lorry Hagan had said what sort of a name was that, and he did not know, could not tell, except that down on his knees Mrs Everett's skirts went by, and she said, come here, Chuffy, stand up, you're a big boy now, don't you worry, Mrs Chambers, he's only slow in developing. He was all right, Chuffy Chambers. They got him the job driving the lorry when he was old enough.

Hagan said. Chuffy Chambers turned back down the hill in the opposite direction from Quongs' hall.

There was a western on in the hall. It was pretty full, except for the more expensive seats at the back, which of course he would buy her, because that would show he meant to do her well, and you always got back your money's worth, that time in Sydney at a revue, in a box, but there weren't any boxes here. He bought the tickets from Amy Quong, like a brown owl in a box. They went on into the hall, full of darkness and the titanic exertions of figures on the screen. He took up his whip and it curled right round the ranger's head, making a weal on his face. Vic Moriarty squealed. That was the trouble, she always entered into everything, Daisy said. They began to bundle into the expensive seats. The air was hot with cigarettes. She was sorry that no one could see, because of course the darkness, that the overseer from Glen Marsh was taking her in the most expensive seats. If Mrs Belper was there. She clung to her moment of superiority, getting down into her chair, and pushing her shoulder up against him when she had sat down, just as much as to say, we'll watch it together, shan't we, and he wasn't at all averse.

Happy Valley bathed itself in a stream of excess-reality, as the great hoofs came out of the screen almost beating upon its face that, upturned, open-mouthed, demanded no answers to questions, only a statement of energy. He's going to kill her, they said, or no, he can't, that man behind the tree, that boy with the gun will shoot, oh, oh, yes. That boy with the gun who would populate the life of Mrs Schmidt for another week as she washed the separating

188

machine, kneaded dough, or lay beneath her husband on a feather-bed. These figures would assume almost a normal, an everyday proportion of washing-board or butter-pat while maintaining their dream texture, that kept them apart in substance, and so ideal. Tie her on the horse and send her out across the desert till your mouth was dry as a cigarette, and those big prickly pears that tore her dress. Arthur Ball, biting his nails, wondered if Emily Schmidt, who was a good smell, that ball of a handkerchief that smelled so good, would faint tied to a horse, the day Gladys fainted in geography and they put her out on the porch, and under the prickly pear an old man sitting, a swaggy in rags, would take Emily down from the horse and dip her handkerchief in a water-can. Arthur Ball put out his knee and encountered the thigh of Emily Schmidt. The old man sponged her face with a handkerchief.

It's interesting, said Vic, to think of all that desert. It must be Texas, she said.

For a moment she forgot it was not Ernest, and not an educational film that demanded the sort of remark you made to Ernest, who was so good, and that asthma. She sat up a bit straighter. She had not meant to do this. That night she could not get him to bed and he had to stay all night in his chair with three or four pillows behind. You can't say I'm not a good wife to Ernest, she said, love Ernest, and this, God, you got to do something all the same, sit down there and listen to Belper talk about industry.

What's up? said Hagan in the dark.

Nothing.

Thought there was something up.

189

No, she said.

She relaxed again. He put his arm round her. You had
to do something, she said, whatever he did, not care, sitting
in the dark and that music and your head, it must have been
the drink, but you meant it like that, hell you cared what.
She sighed, or his arm squeezed out the breath, as she leant
against him, and his shoulder was rather hard.

Like it? he said.

Yes, she sighed. I love the pictures, don't you?

He began kissing her neck. She put up her shoulder as
a kind of protest that only held on to his face and she could
feel his lips distended in the hollow she had made. There
was plenty of her that, without the corset she had left off,
flowed into his hand, like standing under a tree and having
apples fall right into his hand, or melons, only melons didn't
grow on a tree except in a story, and what was that. She
began to wriggle as the Indians rode down the gulch. Of
course it was a gulch.

I can't bear it, she squealed. I can't bear Indians.

Would you like to step outside? he said.

Look at their knives!

You haven't got to look, he said.

He twisted round her face. That was a bit of cheek, she
felt, and perhaps not so dark that someone would not see.
She felt his tongue on her mouth. You could not help it, she
sighed. The darkness was heavy with arms. You could not
help it, she sighed.

He's going to get killed, she said weakly.

He said something between his teeth. The way some
women carried it off, born with a sort of ventriloquist's gift,

would shout from behind the door to the grocer while, and most of them like that, and it was damned uncomfortable in this bloody seat that got you no closer, like an eiderdown, like two, bundled up into a ball, or cleft, and you thought you knew all about the eiderdown when suddenly you didn't, and she wasn't born yesterday, hanging on like that to your mouth, which she didn't learn in school from a pair of spectacles, would soon be over, shooting them down right and left with his arm round a girl, shoot 'em down and they went over like ninepins, if you were lucky, in spite of leaning against your shoulder, it was a different matter near the equator, sailing into those Indians, help help, they cry, and the sheriff's men, come here Mr Sheriff, have you in court and come over all innocent at the judge, in a circle ending with lights.

That was a lovely film, she sighed. I shall always remember that, she said.

All films are the same to me.

No doubt, she said.

She shrugged her shoulders, getting up, walking out. All the same. Going down the street she began to hum. I wonder when bluebirds are mating, she hummed. Her hips brushed up against him as they walked.

It's going to rain, she said.

Let it, he said. I don't care. Do you?

I don't want to get wet.

They were all the same. Call the tune and leave you to whistle it. Oh no, mister, don't touch me, brushing up against you like a cat.

You're not going in yet? he said.

His voice sounded a bit hoarse.

Yes, she said.

She walked along and she felt that she had Poise.

You oughtn't to go in yet, he said.

Down in the lane by Everetts' he got her up against a paling fence, so that she could not get away, did not want to get away, as struggling, her arms went out, and her hands were going up and down his back as if they did not know where, did not want to settle. You would have thought he was strangling her, the way her breath came into his mouth. He pinned her up against the paling fence with his knee between her legs.

Now d'you want to go in? he said.

She hung on to him, her breath coming fast. Saying something incoherent, or perhaps nothing at all.

God, she said. We're crazy, she said. In this lane.

Who in blazes cares about that?

I'm the schoolmaster's wife, she said.

Then she began to extricate herself. He might have known. Saying this and that, she was.

You mustn't think I'm like this, she said. Because I'm not.

Oh hell. What's the use of talking?

You're very impatient, she said.

What've I got to expect from that?

I said you're very impatient.

He knew she was smiling at him, the way you do know when someone is smiling in the dark. Then she began to move away. He could hear her heels going over on the stones. He waited there for a bit, he was irritated, he was smiling, feeling sort of let down, before he went into the main street.

Vic Moriarty had got home, out of breath, to a siphon and glasses on the table that were a memorial to more than the pleasures tasted in the glass. Her bosom went up and down with ease, because she had left her corset off. But she didn't feel giddy any more, had taken herself in hand, what could she have been thinking of, she said.

The cyclamen stuck up straight in the lustre bowl. Queer the antics of that flower. Anyone would think it had its ears back. Bitchiness in a flower.

Or a bitch up against a fence, pressing into you, it gave you goose-flesh now, and Ernest in bed, was not like that, you said, was not and nobody believed it true, Ernest perhaps, with veins on his hand that nearly burst, and suppose your gown tore on the fence, or splinters sticking in, it might go septic, his breath said why not, ugh, and the leaves funny with that flower, because Vic loves flowers, pottering about the garden, he said, Ernest pottering in slippers she embroidered with a pricked finger, and then his arms you couldn't help it, being the schoolmaster's wife, you said.

She jostled the glasses viciously on the table and went into the bedroom.

Is that you, Vic? Ernest sighed.

Yes, she said.

Where you been?

Mr Hagan took me to the pictures.

Poor Ernest. But I can't help being being, whatever I am, and what am I, creaking the bed, and that smell of asthma powder as he turns.

The pictures was lovely, she said. It was about a ranger. And he was in love with the daughter of the sheriff. It was in Texas, you see. And there was another chap called, called...I forget. Anyway it doesn't matter. Well, this chap insulted the ranger with a whip. About the girl. It was a double insult, you see. And he was also in league with the Indians. And...

The bed groaned, snored. Vic Moriarty sat down on the chair and began to draw her stockings off.

194

15

It had begun to rain. The sound of rain on the iron roof gave you a feeling of isolation, something in the hollow sound, as if you were contained in this hollow and hung in space. Oliver Halliday and Alys Browne. He leant against the mantelpiece, silent now. He ought to be going, he felt. I have been here an hour or two, talking, she has laughed, sitting there on the couch, we have both laughed, and it has been very pleasant but unsatisfactory. And now we have exhausted all those pleasant, unsatisfactory things, and are silent, waiting for something essential that does not, perhaps will not come. It is like this with Hilda. I have never spoken to Hilda using anything but the outer convention of words. We look at each other, hoping for something that does not come, it is now too late. And Alys, it is going to be like this, there is no reason for anything else, I come here to talk or to drink afternoon tea.

She sat up straight on the sofa. Her hands were in her lap. Now that he had stopped talking she waited, not conscious of time, though it was late, with a tautness in her ears, any renewal of sound would shatter the membrane, she thought. She sat bolt upright. She had no connection with anything else. The silence made her feel like that, or the hour, as if twelve o'clock robbed your body of its awareness and tightened up your mind, making it function more acutely inside the insulation of the flesh. The rain kept coming down on the roof, regularly, then broken by a wind. He was standing there by the mantelpiece. It will happen soon, she said. She felt that she had lived only in preparation for this, that she had not dared to formulate, resisting because of many things, but conscious all the time of the trend her life was taking.

Alys, he said.

She did not answer him. She sat there on the sofa, very straight, with her hands in her lap. Her face was a bit drawn, as if she were trying to restrain emotion, like him restraining for years something he did not need. Then it began to come awake. For weeks it had been happening, he felt. And now he wanted to give expression to this, he had to. He went and got down beside her, put his face in her lap, against her hands, resting his face in her lap.

Alys, he said, I love you. It isn't anything else. I've tried to reason with myself and make it something, something it isn't at all. You were a sort of intellectual quantity that I didn't get anywhere else. That was all I wanted. Like a lot of other illusions I've had for years. I've wanted something else. I haven't known what I wanted. I don't think many of

196

us do. Except very occasionally by a sort of intuitional flash. Sometimes it's a physical or material solution, sometimes it's spiritual, sometimes it's both. All of a sudden you know.

Yes, she said. Yes.

She moved and her hands touched his face, deliberately touching his face. She bent down. She wanted to touch him with her face, with her body.

Yes, I know, she said.

The rain was still coming down on the roof, a grey, infrequent sound of rain, that was no longer isolation, as in the hollow of the darkness their bodies touched. They existed in a kind of mutual agreement of touch, for which speech could find no expression, only the language of touch. After a groping with words you discarded these, and everything was suddenly explicit without.

She wanted to give him more than this. She wanted to give him everything, so that there were no barriers, and even more than that. She could not give him enough. She went into the other room, she took off her clothes, lying there in the intimate darkness, listening to him undress. She could hear him breathing. His belt as it hit the end of the bed. Her fingers moved on the sheet, almost a gesture of resistance before the intrusion of the unknown. In her room that had grown accustomed to the sounds of silk, a drawing on and off, or the brushing of hair, the feminine cadences of these, the masculine burr of leather had an altogether foreign tone.

Then he drew back the sheet and he was getting down beside her into the bed. She held her breath, conscious of a second shock, first the sound of leather, and now the notion

197

of a stranger getting into her bed. For it was not Oliver, the man she had talked to in the sitting-room, acquainted with his features, the accent of his voice, his form in a grey suit. This was a different person. Like the touch of cold water. She did not know. She did not want. She was afraid. And perhaps he would realize that she was holding her breath for all these reasons, because she was afraid, and that was why her heart worked like an engine inside her, banging away against her side.

He was touching her again, his arms, his whole body, now their mouths were exchanging breath, resistance gone. Now she was no longer afraid. It was Oliver again, this man with the unprotected body against her own, and she must bring herself closer to his, she could not bring herself close enough. She wanted him. They wanted each other. Her whole body seemed fragmentary with the tenderness that she could not give him in the measure she wanted to give. She felt she must cry out in little gasping breaths, forcing her love into his mouth. And nothing mattered now. No longer situated in the pattern of circumstance that was Happy Valley, they drifted almost unconsciously through a dark silence in which their united bodies were a luminous point.

Then the clock began to tick. He thought it was probably an alarm clock, that voluminous tick, and getting up to go to a lecture across the water, you lay in bed and frowned at the tyranny of time, at your own obedience not to time, but to a full-faced aluminium clock. At nineteen the clock was not even a symbol of time, was something personal, animate. But now you got up, symbols or not, you just got up. He drew back the hair from her face. She lay there, did not move, her arms curled loosely round his waist, the confidence of possession in her arms. He touched her face with his lips in the dark, that was no dark, that was Alys Browne, but no dark.

Well, he said, it's time.

Back to the inarticulation of words, he felt the inadequacy of his voice.

Mm, she said. I was almost asleep.

You'll be able to go to sleep.

Yes, she said. I suppose.

It's late.

He got out and started to put on his shirt.

Why didn't we before, Oliver? she said.

It wasn't the right moment.

It was a long time.

Of course it was a long time. But you don't regret it? he said.

No, she said. That is, regret what? What were you saying, Oliver?

Nothing, he said. Go to sleep.

Her voice, sleep-sheathed in the darkness, fell back on to the pillow.

I'm tired, she said. The sitting-room, did we put out the light?

Then she was asleep, or almost, her arms moved as he bent, were a pressure of recognition as he bent down to her face. He would leave her now, without any feeling of regret, for he would come again, always come, she would be here, she would expect him, they would expect each other, not

199

in words, but in waiting. There was no need to say you will come again, it was a necessity that you should.

Like waking to sleeping, he felt, when he stood outside on the porch. There were stars through the intermittent rain, and a cool breeze, and soon the rain would stop altogether. I have been asleep, he said. It is like waking. And I must remain awake, or at least conscious, conscious in one person of the whole. The others are asleep, perhaps will never wake. You go up on to a high hill and look down at them asleep. If you could go down among the sleepers and open their eyes, touching them with your hand, and hear their sigh as they turned, the sighing of people who slowly waken. Hilda stirring in sleep. I had forgotten Hilda. Of course. He began to fill his pipe. I ought to feel sorry, but there is no regret, which is perhaps a perversion of the moral sense, if finding yourself is a perversion, because this is what I have done. He lit his pipe, light fanned on his face, then the bud of light on his pipe's bowl. The world makes its demand, I shall run away from myself because of Hilda, I shall close my eyes. This is the world. This is Happy Valley. This is also not the world. I stand here, and it is cool, the stars are cool, and the rain which will soon stop. It is a long time since I have really been conscious of these things, felt their significance, conscious of the many rivers, the Delta of the Nile, water flowing into one water from the North Sea to the Pacific, no longer constrained by maps, and the people walking with upturned faces, looking for something that they do not find in themselves, always with faces upturned. I must remain conscious of these, he said. This is the world. There is a mystery of unity about the world, that ignores itself, finding its expression in cleavage and pain, the not-world that demands I shall run away from myself, that I too shall be a creature of cleavage and pain walking with my eyes closed.

He walked down the hill. I am being apocalyptic, or just plain romantic, he said. He went along and he did not think of much, he was tired, physically tired, but his mind was without qualm, rested on its certainty. The glow of his pipe went down the hill alone.

16

On the 29th of May Charles II rode into London with
a pealing of bells, read Willy Schmidt. Rodney Halliday
picked a stopping of blotting-paper out of a hole in the desk.
It made his tooth ache, that hole, where the chocolate got
in, and going to Moorang made it ache worse, the drill, as
breath swept down announcing onions for lunch. Dr Grey
had a wart on his face. Mother said, your teeth, Rodney
dear, are a kind of investment, your grandfather could crack
nuts with his when he was seventy-five, so you must tell
Mother if you think a hole, yes, Mother, he said, but the
drill touched, squirmed, was hot behind the knees. Willy
Schmidt's voice was limp and nasal, announcing a peal of
bells, though without conviction, it was after lunch, and
the air was brown with flies. Miss Purves rang the bell for
morning break. That was a peal of bells, for ten minutes'
freedom, or sometimes not even that, and Charles II had

how many years after he got the Roundheads out. Andy Everett was a Roundhead. Cromwell had a wart on his face. They made the fountains run with wine to show that freedom, like the peace procession, when Father had gone to the War, said Mother, and she wasn't married to Father yet, he was very young, and then there was the Armistice and Mother knew that Father would come back, and everyone in the streets, and confetti and lights, and Mother began to cry because she knew she would marry Father now, there were fireworks at night. The Restoration. They sent round the plate for two Sundays to restore the place behind the altar where Everetts' mare kicked a hole in the wall. Cromwell broke the glass. Andy Everett threw stones and they stung on your legs, sometimes ploughed up the skin. Mother sat on your bed after prayers, don't mind, Rodney, she said, because soon we shall go away from here, and Sydney will be a peal of bells, where you go as a boarder, Father drive us down in the car. Rodney Halliday drove into Sydney with a pealing of bells. St Mary's was a Catholic church, you did not go inside, they were always dressed in black. Mother wore a paste pin, that was something to look like diamonds, that Father brought back, at St James where George was christened, and they went to Leura for their honeymoon. George was born, they said come and see your brother, it smelt of powder and cotton-wool, and you didn't want to see, didn't, take me away, you said, to Mother lying in bed, she was under a mosquito net. Parliament had voted the King, read Willy Schmidt. That was Charles the Second, Charles 2. Father said to Professor Birkett, I've got two boys, Professor, the funny thing is it doesn't make you feel any different at all. In the encyclopaedia Charles II had Nell Gwynn, but not in the history book, that was Willy Schmidt's voice reading to the class. Willy Schmidt did not know that, or Margaret Quong, the day she came along the road and he was watching the bull over the fence, and Nell Gwynn had something to do with soldiers that were too old to do anything else. Father was thirty-seven. Mother said, go for Father, Rodney, he's wanted out at Ferndale at once, poor Mrs Anderson's broken her leg, he's just gone up the street, she said, and there was a hawker in the street, that Syrian whose dog had mange, and the penknives, your Dad's just gone up the street, Mrs Everett said, she had a clothes-peg in her mouth, he's gone up towards Miss Browne's, she said, and going to Miss Browne's did not want, knock at the door, I'll come at once, he said, and she had cool hands.

Three o'clock was a drone in the schoolroom from so many voices in an undertone in a wooden receptacle, with Willy Schmidt's voice pitched in a higher key, a solo instrument above the orchestration of sigh and whisper, the loud percussion of Molly Abbott's pencil-box falling bang on the floor. Ernest Moriarty closed his eyes against the glare of three o'clock, unavoidable though the drone, and it was better to make them read, avoid the necessity of explanation, drawing up words through the swollen channel of the voice. The little veins on Ernest Moriarty's eyelids were sharply red. He held his hand in a shade above his eyes, looking down at a page of the book.

That'll do, he said, when the paragraph sounded at an end. Next Gracie Philipps, please.

Rodney Halliday moistened a pellet of blotting-paper and stuffed it back inside the hole. Dr Grey had a nurse who mixed the stuff, she offered it on a piece of glass, he rammed it in, it was over, you felt pleased. The clock jerked, had cool hands. Nell Gwynn was a concubine, like in the Bible, only a good concubine with old soldiers, there were good and bad, it was difficult to know. I'll come at once, he said. But you needn't go, Rodney, she said. Yes, he said. He felt shy. There were big squares on her dress as she held out her hand, the stuff cool, and Father said, well good-bye, Alys, Mother called her Miss Browne, and you called her that when you were still too young to call her anything else. Father whistled going downhill. Father made you shy. If you had music lessons, only it was cissie to have music lessons, Father said it wasn't, but what would Andy Everett say, what would Miss Browne, Margaret Quong said Miss Browne was the loveliest person she knew. Her arms were cool as she opened the front door.

Rodney looked across at Margaret Quong. She was looking across. Their glances clung for a moment in the wilderness of bent heads. Then they looked away quickly, both, as if they had encountered a mutually intimate thought.

Margaret Quong scribbled on the edge of the page. There were scribblings all round the edge of the page, flowers that opened for no reason, a ship embarking into the print. To-day is a music lesson, she said. I have not practised, I don't care, and why should I practise, anyway, why play, go up there or stay away, play away the stay away. Her pencil furrowed the paper with a black line, inscribed

205

an A.B. on the face of a shield, shaded it, reduced it to black. She felt sick inside. It wasn't the heat. Mother said, you're looking yellow you want a pill. She wanted to cry. She went into the shed at the bottom of the yard and lay down on the hessian and cried. The hessian was rough on her face, it smelt of dogs, because this was where Bonnie had had her pups that Rodney Halliday came to see. But she did not care, she put her face down on the hessian and cried. It was wet when she stopped. It made her feel lighter to cry. She lay there with the hessian crumpled up in her hand, and there was nothing more to come, she was empty, she lay there like a shell. Rodney could not help it, did not know, had given her a shell. She wished she was at the bottom of the sea, if only you could wish, or a miracle like in the Bible, or that conjuror at the Show. It said something in the Bible about the sins of the fathers, were Rodney's sins, should hate Rodney, was wrong, because Rodney does not know. Mother said, I'll take you to the doctor if you don't sit down and eat your food, all this nonsense over good food, and who do you think you are, I could tell you that, my girl. He sat in the chair as she played a Beethoven sonata badly because he was there. He had his name outside on a brass plate, and some letters. Miss Browne had a plate without the letters. ALYS BROWNE, PIANOFORTE. She said, I almost went to California once, would you have come, Margaret, just the two of us together, we would have started a new life, two would have made things easier. Saying prayers for Miss Browne she took out a snapshot, kissed, that day on the hill as they picked harebells which she had in the box with the ivory rose, she kissed the snapshot and it was Miss Browne, holding harebells with a blurred hand. She had only kissed her once. He looked past her into the sitting-room, looking over her head, to see if Miss Browne was not there, and said, well, give her a message, will you, scarcely noticed her as he went away. Mother said, I'll take you to the doctor and he'll change your tune, my girl. She went out into the yard and was sick behind the block. Rodney said, my father's very clever, he knows Latin and Greek, he can play the piano too. The day she went up to the window they were playing a duet. He laughed, he said she was falling behind. Margaret dear, said Miss Browne, I'll make you a dress for your birthday, we'll go into Moorang and choose the stuff. She could feel her eyes beginning to swell, in her pocket Rodney's shell clenched. Rodney had had his hair cut and his ears stuck out, not like his father's grey hair playing a duet. She liked to play with Rodney. They made boats out of paper and sailed them in the creek.

Ernest Moriarty's lips were violet-blue. The sun lay hot on the chalk-dust, on the blotting-pad, on the earthenware bottle of ink with ink clotted at the top. He had not slept. He was tempted to sleep in the hot sun, letting his head fall down on to the warm blotting-pad, its white surface a field of sleep. The droning of children, of flies, was conducive to sleep. Sleep in the afternoon was a bitter taste in the mouth, and those warm dreams that swept up in a violent surge, the tower of white stone and the thick shadow that caught at your feet. He steadied himself on his elbow. He must not sleep. Children stare all those eyeballs all those stones in a catapult broke the wing and it lay there on the chalk gradually soaking in stamped on the ground a magpie

or she took it up in her hands as he put on a ring they
said the glove Daisy said the squeaking boots as they knelt
coming up the path Mr Hagan was a ranger in Nigeria or
Mozambique those oranges exchanged near Gosford but
the skin was scent a sample she said my eyes are running
not what you think shall we jump jump with me to show
it is bottomless my love it licks off if we fall the bells clap
lap. He must not sleep. He would go home later to Vic. She
would make him a cup of tea, That Hagan man said he
knew a man who was cured by a herbalist. Wouldn't that
be splendid, Ernest, said Vic. Splendid for Vic he hoped,
hoped more than himself, because what she went through,
and only sometimes irritable, and went out to the pictures
with—well, he was glad he could take her, the smoke always
made him wheeze, and she must have some entertainment,
she said. They went into Moorang Saturday night, there was
a dance at the School of Arts, you should have been there,
Ernest, she said, there were streamers and balloons, as if I
could go dancing about, of course, she said, and he dances
very well. He liked to see her enjoy herself, brighten up, if
only she didn't, but not Vic, was steady was Vic, was not
that Mrs Caulfield who ran off with the man who delivered
the milk, it was in the Sun, fancy, said Vic, lived a couple
of doors away from our Daisy and Fred, a quiet little thing,
had a kid too that she left, and off to Melbourne on a motor-
bike, I don't remember the man, was since my time, Daisy
said she couldn't understand, and the husband was a clerk,
and ever such a pretty kid. Vic said she would have liked a
child. Then she brought home that dog, Tiny she called it,
that died. She cried a lot. Poor Vic. He would have liked

208

a child, would have been different your own, not a room full of hostile eyes, that were not children, were only eyes. Hagan told a story and winked his eye. It made you cough if you laughed. Hagan said, trust her to me, I'll deliver her back without a crack. And what happened when they got to Melbourne on a motor-bike was difficult to say or perhaps didn't care, but he was a clerk, had known a man Berenger before he was married, insurance, but you got out of touch with people when you married, Vic said he made her sick, that was because he had a harelip. Vic said there was no dignity in a motor-bike, you wouldn't see her on a motor-bike. Hagan said perhaps a Daimler or a Rolls-Royce. She wanted a single-seater Ford, she wanted a pianola, and a backgammon set, and a perfume spray like Lucy Adelon advertised. Hagan said when his ship came home. He was a good chap. He was glad Hagan could take her about.

Now, he said, when Gracie Philipps had come to the end of the chapter, now you can go through that chapter again, taking notice of the dates. I'll be asking questions by and by. Arthur, put that orange away.

They hung their heads in lethargy. The roof cracked with the heat. Reading a chapter of history again was to take out from under the desk a bag of acid-drops or a hank of rubber tape. Ernest Moriarty shaded his eyes with his hand, intent on his desk, as the pencil scored imaginary exercises, stopped, quavered as the lead broke. It was too hot too too that story about a motor-bike he told she said he had a sense of humour on a motor-bike the fumes blind in a funnel in your throat they know that at seventy miles strewn with bottles of milk down a slippery slide never

never and the trees are dumb the signpost Happy Valley seventy miles like a voice through the megaphone that sings Daisy Daisy it was Fred on a bicycle built passing that pianola linoleum rolls from feet slip roll Vic Vic in a serge suit Hagan pianarolla on a pillion on a get you at the five mile if…

Look, said Andy Everett.

They looked. Ernest Moriarty's head was black with flies. Arthur Ball blew a raspberry. Somebody giggled.

Shut up, said Andy Everett. You'll have the old cow awake.

I'm goin' home, said Arthur Ball.

Go on! You're not, said Willy Schmidt.

Ain't I just. Just you see.

Arthur Ball got slowly up.

I'm goin' home, he said.

Betcha not game, Andy Everett said.

Yes, I am. I'm goin' home.

An orange rolled across the floor, rested by the table leg.

Hey, said Andy Everett. There goes my orange across the floor.

That's my orange, said Arthur Ball. You know it's my orange, he said.

Emily Schmidt giggled. She kicked the orange under a desk.

Oo-er! sniggered Gladys Rudd, as the orange settled under her feet. She kicked it at Rodney Halliday.

Rodney Halliday picked it up.

It's my orange, he said.

His lips were white with audacity. A time came when you did not care, that big coot Andy Everett, all hunched up with his red knees, and Margaret Quong turning to look. That's what David felt perhaps. And the stone hit him between the eyes, he was how many cubits, with David standing over him dead.

Andy Everett's round head bristled with slighted omnipotence.

I'll show you whose orange it is, he said.

Rodney Halliday threw. He did not care. He threw the orange at Andy's face. It hit the mouth with a stupid thud. It fell. It rolled roundly nonchalant and settled by Margaret Quong.

I'll give you what! Andy Everett gasped.

Emily Schmidt gave a little shriek.

Ernest Moriarty stirred. As they hit that stump shrieked out it was his name she had not forgotten looking back or whose name he thought Ernest could not tell or Clem as she clung against that stump his back sticking through his side and you couldn't ride fast with one hand she had and blood and that dust half blood clogging feet stuck shouting at you eyes as you stood in eyes of children turned up hate and began to scream those screaming eyes like a dream like a dream take off your coat and it is not a dream scream advance and touch her she is not dead yet on forward out of this scream.

It hit the mouth with a stupid thud. It fell. It rolled roundly nonchalant and settled by Margaret Quong.

I'll give you what! Andy Everett gasped.

Emily Schmidt gave a little shriek.

211

Vic, murmured Moriarty. Vic.

The eye glazed with sleep fastened on a reality, this orange rolling across the floor. Eyes stared at eye. They were staring, action arrested, as they sat twisted in seats, or hand raised, but everywhere a semblance of fear, of hate.

Vic, he whispered again.

Crashing against that stump. They might have been frozen as they looked at him.

What is it? he said. He got up on his feet, put his hand on the chair as he swayed. What is it? Stare at me, he said. Go on!

They recoiled from his voice. It was a strange voice. It made them afraid. Heads bent over books to disguise fear. They crouched.

Yes, he shouted. We know where we stand. There's no use beating about the bush.

He took up a ruler and beat on the desk. The way she looked back her face distorted, you knew it was a dream or not a dream, or all this, the stubborn faces fastened over a history book. He began to choke. Clinging to Hagan's back.

Yes, he shouted. It's all very well.

They seemed to crouch lower, were afraid now, of something that they did not understand. What has happened, the pulse asked, in the throat, what is the matter, the heart beat in soft, rubbery thuds.

He was going to have an attack. He felt old, sick. He was getting old sitting at a desk in Happy Valley. He wrote to the Board, which was officially unmoved. It was all very well, like walking up a shelving beach that rolled back, each

212

pebble a step, or a dream, or a dream. She would say, what is the matter, Ernest, and he would say, nothing, could not tell her it was a dream. Oh God, and what was going home and going home. To-morrow was going home. To-morrow was to-morrow was Shakespeare was. The trees were dead, those grey trees at the turn, and the wind clattering in a dead branch, sitting at a desk a dead branch tapping on the desk tap tap. That orange on the floor. Now they were afraid. The orange lay still. He would make them more afraid. Beating on the desk a ruler beat looked at the hand saw the centimetre beat.

Do you think it's any pleasure to me? he gasped, going down among the benches, his breath torn, a screech from his chest. Do you think it isn't misery for every one concerned? You or me, it's all the same thing. We all know where we stand.

Sitting on that bike with her skirt drawn up over her knees, his hand. His breath was a moan as he slashed, with the ruler slashed, slashed, did not care, make them afraid. Margaret Quong crouched over the desk, held her hands to her head. Emily Schmidt sidled away. The blows were falling on Margaret Quong. The edge of the ruler cut into her wrists. She sat crouched down protecting her head.

There was a silence of fear in the room. Waiting. Things began to integrate again, the other side of his spectacles that were no longer blurred, the room taking its habitual shape, brown and banal as it always was. It was no other afternoon, in fact. Just an afternoon. Only he felt sick, was spent now, standing there with a ruler in his hand. He went back to his table. He arranged the exercise books. He had

213

to hang on to the edge of the table because his breathing was bad.

Margaret Quong crouched still, feeling not so much physical pain as fear, and a welling of disconnected sorrow, the way an emotion fastens itself to a pretext that is not, properly speaking, its own. Emily Schmidt's face was white with momentary sympathy. She felt the pain of the blows that might have been hers. She turned towards Margaret a white face. But the others looked at their books. Margaret's look was a blank page, from wondering why this, she could not understand, or why it went on inside her the voice dulled by a bull's-eye in the cheek, beating, beating time, or why were you born, why this. She sat with her arms pressed into her neck. Alys Browne, she had written in the margin of the history book. It would have been easier if there had been the two of us, she said, as they walked up the hill, arm round waist, entwined, because when two were one it was easier. Margaret Quong's arm was numb with reflected pain.

Later on they went home, as they did any other afternoon, though quieter first at the door, then gathering in a tumult as they got outside, a little eddy of passion in the dust. Ernest Moriarty sat on at the table in the empty room in company with the clock. The room was empty. He could not think. His head was empty. He would go home up the hill, when his breathing grew easier, past the turn where those dead trees stood and clattered in the wind. The day they came Vic said, so this is Happy Valley, she said, I don't know why you've brought me here. He sat at the table and clenched his hands till they went knuckle-white.

Sidney Furlow walked beneath the plum-trees on her own. He had written to her, she had the letter in her hand, and she knew what it was about, that it would be like the others, so she had not opened it. The plum-trees were thin and black-boughed. They only bore fruit about once every three years. They were very old. But when there was blossom on the boughs you forgot their age, you put up your face against the cool, drooping boughs. She held the letter in her hand, unopened. It might have been a bill, a debt, as if she owed Roger Kemble something that she could not pay. Her face was sullen under the trees. She leant her head against a black trunk and felt the roughness of the bark. How long is this going on, she said, and what good is it going to do, whether I write to him or not, say I meant what I said, or say nothing at all. As if I had the power to make him happy, depending on me, something depending on me. The power. To hold his letter in her hand gave her a sense of power, and tearing them up, and the one she had poked into the incinerator, watching it curl brown, had quickened her pulse a little, though not very much. It was a pretty negative emotion that arose out of being able to control the life of Roger Kemble. She did not want this. People on the whole were pretty negative. The nice people you met at races and dances, whose niceness was about the only reason for their being, and consequently niceness had become an all-time job. But it left a pappy taste in your mouth, like coconut milk, and once you had tried it you didn't want to again. Only, only a sometimes hankering not to be Sidney Furlow at least, though standing outside would hate perhaps the you discarded, probably discover something as futile as niceness, something just as negative underneath.

She felt the bark against her forehead, scored and rough. She held the letter in her hand, tore it, following no design. The letter fluttered away in little jagged scraps. It lay white on the ground. It was the fourth letter she had destroyed. She did not even feel a sense of power now that she had destroyed the fourth. It had become a habit. Why it had ever been anything else. She laughed. In tearing a letter up. Or burning a letter and feeling that you were responsible, as if the fire. That time in the gully up near Ferndale was what you felt, what you could not express, when the fire ran down the gully from tree to tree and they felled a belt of timber to break the fire, and dug a ditch all night in a fever, all those men working like a lot of marionettes, up and down their arms, their faces black, and beating with branches to turn the course of the fire. There was something magnificent in the progress of fire. Then Roger Kemble wrote on white notepaper with a crest and asked you to marry him. She touched with her toe a fragment of white paper lying on the ground. He could not understand the leaping of fire against those trees, or why she had clenched her hands, or the way her heart, because it had a positive power that made men move their arms in abject unison like so many marionettes, it was pitiful to see, and exciting. She kicked her toe fiercely against the root of the tree.

Mother cried because she thought the fire would pass Ferndale and reach Glen Marsh, and you almost prayed for it with your throat dry to reach Glen Marsh. Mother making a family tree and hanging it on the wall. The crackle of green wood, the spitting of sap, they beat the fire with boughs. The Furlows of Glen Marsh perched on a tree, so many twigs to a branch. What a lovely fire, she said, what a lovely fire. Like saying, thank you for the *lovely* dance, only you did not mean it then, and this, this leaping of fire, your whole body worshipped the rhythm was the dance serpentine with flames. It did not reach Glen Marsh. It burnt itself out. It was not the men, nothing they had done, it just burnt itself out, a sort of hara-kiri of the fire. And Mother said, thank God, because she felt it would not be blasphemy to say it on such an occasion as this, so much saved, lives perhaps, and the way the men had worked, as if it had been the men, and not the fire that had died of its own will.

Sidney Furlow walked beneath the plum-trees. She walked over the scraps of paper that lay scattered on the ground. She went on towards the stables. She felt impotent.

A wilderness of hours lay between lunch and tea. The yard was a wilderness of silence. In the stable was the colt that Hagan had been breaking. He stood there dejected now with the saddle on his back, would stand there all day, smarting and galled, the flies jetting the corners of his eyes. He snorted when he looked across the gate of the stall. His flanks quivered. Eyeing her to see. That big brute riding the colt in the yard, she had seen, seen the horse ball in the air, shatter the ground, with Hagan unshaken on his back, then accepting dejection, and now standing all day learning the shape and purport of the saddle on his back. This was a triumph of man. The power of man, subjecting the brute to acquiescence, though not subjecting fire. A conflict for superiority between two brutes. He swayed a little as the colt struck the ground, then he was upright in the saddle again. The colt now eyed her to see.

Why not? she said. She opened the stall gate. The colt sidled, snorted, stared at her out of his white face, out of his bloodshot eyes. He was a big, muscular bay animal. He stood there, afraid, in the pools of stagnant urine and the piled dung on the stall floor. All that week Hagan had been riding him. He was still bewildered. He quivered when she touched the bridle rein. She did not give a damn what happened, what was said, what Mother said, as she led the colt, cautious in its step, across the yard. But she had to ride the colt. It was her funeral. She led the horse down the hill to a small hollow out of sight of the house.

There, she said, as she flung the reins back over his neck. She felt excited, the horse excited, blowing out his nostrils and spraying her with fear.

He was still when she mounted, quite still, only for a trembling between her legs, but he made no move, and she sat there tautly, waiting for something to happen, waiting for a thunderbolt. Touched him with her spurs then. She anticipated the shudder and the grunt, bent to the movement of the horse, as he hunched his back and curved in the air, her breath left her as he touched the ground. Oh but it was good, good, and she laughed, holding him with her spurs, turned him up the paddock, let the wind slip past and the blurred grass. She clung to the horse as he rooted back, she laughed, she spurred him on and they passed over the hill. Tried to shake her off and she clung to him, or hit him across the shoulder with her crop, striking the sweat bands and the white foam. There was foam on the leather crop. She could feel the straining of his mouth, straining at her hands. This was power. You could feel it in your hands. You could feel the hot air of the flames on your face. Something you could not explain. Something fierce and irrational, in the striving of the horse, in the progress of the flame. You became part of it, or overcame it and were swallowed up in a spasm of violence.

She drew him in on the flat. He reared up, beating the air. Then he stood still, hunched again, with his tail between his legs.

Taking him out for some air? asked Hagan.

Coming up behind her like that. Hagan approached her on his horse, riding in an easy jog with one hand planted confidently on his thigh.

He's broken by now all right, he said, looking ironically not so much at the horse.

You've done your job very well, she said. That goes without saying, of course.

I kind of irritate you, he said.

No!

She started the colt into a walk. He went pretty stupidly, in a daze. She was breathless, could not sort her emotions, coming up behind her like that, and blowing his trumpet, not that you expected anything else, not from Hagan, damn his eyes, skulking along, anyway she had ridden the horse.

You know how to sit him, he said.

I ought to. I'm not a child.

That doesn't follow.

She knew, and she bit her lip.

He looked at her, the way she hated him. She had guts though, riding that horse, he had said she had guts the day she ran down the hill, only he would not tell, he would not put ideas in her head, the sulky little bitch that wanted a good smack on her arse, running down the hill, there wasn't too much of it, but room enough for what it deserved. That was what most of them wanted, call me Vic and all that and then dropping you like a scone, to tune them up, this one too, only you wanted nothing like that, didn't want to get bitten, want...She could sit a horse though, you could see that, easy in the saddle. Didn't want that. Didn't want...

Going far? he said.

That depends.

I'm going up here to look at a fence.

She did not answer. But she rode along. She could turn off soon, but she would go a little. She was seated higher than Hagan on his rather stocky little mare. She felt a sense of easy achievement as she rode along. Her body swayed with the horse, soothed, or purged of the emotion that led her to take the horse from the stall.

He rode along beside her. He smiled to himself. Doing him an honour, Miss Sidney Furlow. She had a small waist inside that coat. She was neat enough in her own line, but a line that wasn't his.

I shall keep this horse, she said.

If you've made up your mind it's as good as yours.

His irony started to prick her again.

Don't you believe in getting what you want?

Yes, he said, I'm with you there.

Well then, she said.

Sometimes, he said, and he looked at her under the tilt of his hat, sometimes it's too damn easy, isn't worth having when you get it. That's what I mean.

Telling her something that she knew. Because she knew that. As if she wanted the horse, would say, Father, I'm going to ride that horse, she would have it, would not want it any more. It was always like that, was Roger Kemble, made you tear up the letter, made you feel a sort of contempt for anything you could reach straight out and take. Their stirrups clinked in the silence. Riding with Roger had been like this, a clinking of stirrups as toes touched. Only this was Hagan now. He sat confidently astride his horse, rather thick in the thigh. His hands moved with the reins, were square and coarse.

Hold on a minute, he said.

He suddenly put out his hand and held her arm. She

221

stopped. She did not understand. She felt the pressure of his hand, and the quickening of a pulse, and a confusion of bewildered thought, that wanted an explanation, to explain to her face that was red, she felt, why the pressure of this hand. But without explanation he had jumped down from his horse, was standing in the tussocks knee-deep, had taken a stick, was standing with his arm raised. Then she saw it was a snake among the tussocks, glistening and loosely curled. The colt snorted. She felt the quivering of his neck, of her own body as the snake loosened its loose coils, it was unwinding, straight and black in the yellow grass. He must get it, she felt, he must kill this snake. She leant forward in her saddle with the movement of the snake's body, that easy rhythm of glistening flight, she could feel a cry rising in her throat, not of fear, but rather of encouragement or more than this, she was directing his arm, it was her arm, she wanted to kill that snake. Then he brought down the stick. The snake writhed like a worm in knots. He struck it again on the spine, three times. The snake was a quivering of nerves.

Good, she cried. Oh, good!

She had to jump down from the horse and see, reins looped about the fetlock, steady him, and now see, it is dead, almost quite still. She ran forward and bent over the snake. It was not the first she had seen killed, there were many others, but now a pulse in her throat made it almost the first.

I wish I'd killed it, she said.

It's dead, whoever killed it, said Hagan, letting the stick fall,

Yes, she said, but I've never killed a snake. I've always

222

been afraid. But I think I could have killed this one. A snake nearly bit me when I was a child.

He looked at her, rather insolent.

That can't have been so very long ago, he said.

She looked back at him, insolent too. She laughed harshly.

A very long time ago, she said. But something apparently sticks in the mind.

This was Sidney Furlow showing off, the little bitch, if only he could take a lump of wood, treat her almost like a snake. But he looked at her and felt his throat go dry, he felt a bit small, though of course she was only showing off, and he was as good as a Furlow, would like to put her on the ground and show her a Furlow got off in the same place as anyone else.

She had turned away. She was bending over the snake, taut as her body crouched and touched the body of the snake.

It's quite dead, she said softly.

He couldn't stop looking at her. She made him feel very small. Often like this. Had to assert himself. There wasn't a woman made him feel like that, only this lean bitch.

She picked up the snake. She held it by a limp tail. Her face was half exultation, half disgust.

Put it down, he said roughly.

Why?

Because it mightn't be dead.

She shrugged her shoulders. With her other hand she slowly caressed the long body of the snake. She was fascinated by a dead snake.

Don't be a damn fool, he said.

223

He knocked it out of her hand. She looked at him, putting out her jaw a little, gathering force.

Why, Hagan? she said. I shall do exactly what I like.

Looking at him made him feel small, made him, made him...

But you, you, he said, he began to stutter.

What are you trying to say?

Smiling at him that way, and a word wouldn't come, the bitch, like swaying on that horse as much as to invite. He went at her suddenly. That thin month. He had her in his arms. He opened her mouth. She was nothing. She was no more than any of the others. Touching her he reasserted himself, was reinstated in his own esteem.

A second was a long time. She had no strength. She was opening up, her whole body, her whole life falling apart in two halves, and in the centre there was nothing, or air or languor, as she clung to his body not to fall, felt her arms put out tendrils, touched the roughness, wetness of his shirt. She closed her eyes. Helen said, no, not that, not, and she stuffed the sheet into her mouth. Her body was a shudder of disgust. She could only hear the quick clapping in her ears. She pulled herself away. Oh God, she said, and her whole mouth was twisted with disgust. She hated him, hated him. She hated him with her eyes, with her whole body that he had touched.

No, she said. No! You dirty brute!

As if the snake had not been killed by that raised stick. She could hardly find her breath. She took hold of her crop and hit him across the face, across his mouth, with a sharp hiss the crop falling, her breath, with all her strength, before

224

she ran towards the backing horse, took and mounted him, gashed him with her spurs. She did not care if he threw her, trampled her into the ground, this at least was clean.

Hagan stood watching her or not watching, he did not know, watching some act of woman on horse, a circus turn. His mouth was numb. He put up his hand to his mouth. He found he was standing with an open mouth. He felt he must shake his head that stupor clogged, holding air in his arms, this brief moment gone. Now she would go home and tell the old man perhaps. He did not care. He was touching her again, those small breasts tightly held inside the riding-coat.

The wind is wind is water wind or water white in pockets of the eyes was once a sheep before time froze the plover call alew aloo atingle is the wire that white voice across the plain on thistle thorn the wind pricks face the licked fire the wind flame tossing out distance on a reel.

She spurred the horse on across the flat, along the river-bank, where the tussocks cut past the horse's fetlocks and the air was clear with the cries of plover. She crouched against the colt's neck, feeling his coarse mane against her hand. There was no viciousness in him now, he carried her without protest, he almost seemed to associate himself with the inner purpose that drove her across the flat. She must get away, she said, she must get away, not so much from him as from herself. She began to cry stupidly. It came out of her mouth, broken, without a shape, and like most sounds that are uncontrolled, a little frightening to hear. The horse quickened. She heard herself blubber, broken by the wind, listened as if to somebody else, and it might have been, she had no control over herself. She put up a hand and held the fist in her mouth, biting into her fingers to stop herself. Because something had happened that was something dirty and she had wanted something dirty to happen all the time she had ridden past Hagan hoping not to happen because she was afraid hated herself and Roger Kemble she said take me away only not that I can't because as you see I am dirty I have always been am crying from my mouth his mouth pressed and feeling him that dead snake if only you could kill a longing for dead thoughts you have killed and buried that resurrect themselves and become tangible thought his back and I wanted to touch. The horse carried her through the wind, was wind, was power. She had got it now. She had forgotten the horse. She cried more quietly, the necessity for crying was almost extinct. And that big brute, hit him over the mouth, she had, and the way he looked she was stronger, even if he had killed the snake, killed him who had killed the snake. He had looked afraid, perhaps thinking, she will go home and tell the old man. She drew the horse down to a walk. I have him, she said, I can go into the office and say, Father, that brute, or I can say nothing, he will wait for me to say, I shall look at him waiting, both of us waiting. She felt stronger and controlled.

During the summer you looked at things with your eyes half closed, and the landscape was almost impressionist, colour and forms broken by the heat. But with the recession of the hot weather a line no longer wavered, was unequivocal. That sweep of the hill behind the town that had shimmered all summer was now static, classical, had the firmness of a Poussin in the afternoon. Late in the afternoon the sky, clarified by the early frosts, was a suave enamel blue. Autumn waited for winter with no storm of transition, only a peaceful air of anticipation was abroad to mark the change, this pause between two dominant seasons. You hardly took autumn into account. So little happened, apart from the steadying of outline and molten colour cooling off.

Sunday was still outwardly a long passage of tranquillity for Amy Quong. She lay on her bed after dinner, on the cotton counterpane, her eyes fixed half-way between consciousness and sleep. The Virgin Mary was a vague blur, soothing, the pink and the white. And now the week was over. Voices down in the street mingled with the clanking of a bucket in the backyard. She looked at the Virgin Mary. She was outwardly content. They had bought a plot of land below Harkers'. They were going to sow potatoes there. Potatoes, said Ethel Quong, that's all very well, that's you Quongs all over, thinking what you're going to get, but what about my child? Arthur said, Ethel, don't you fuss, which was singularly unusual for Arthur Quong, committing himself to so many words. In Amy's room, incense barely patterning the air, invaded the primness, the white and pink, and softened the crucifix of varnished oak. Her forehead was golden, polished wax. Mrs Ball said to Mrs Schmidt, I'd've give him in charge, if it'd been a child of mine. Exactly, said Mrs Quong, or tell the Inspector, or... Her arms were blue, Mrs Everett told Mrs Schmidt, you wouldn't think that little runt, must have been off his head. Arthur would plough the land himself. He would borrow a horse from Schmidts. He's a danger, said Mrs Schmidt, and what about us, what about Emily, don't like sending her down to school. A bell pealed on the hill from the Protestant church. Voices locked and unlocked in the street. Walter said, and he laughed, his belly inside his overalls, said a man had to keep his end up and not even Margaret was a saint. Ethel said Walter always said the opposite just because he wanted to annoy, and she didn't propose to stand around watching someone maltreat her child, because she *was* her child, both God and Walter knew, and she felt her responsibility, she couldn't understand these Quongs.

Later in the afternoon Amy Quong went and sat on the verandah in front of the store. Her face was a smile for people passing in the street, was Miss Quong, a symbol of respect, rocking in her chair with her feet not touching the floor. In the street a stagnation of Sunday with its silence of weatherboard, the long shadows on the road, gradually licking up the light, like the cat on the porch opposite licking at her paw with pink, voluptuous tongue. Occasionally people passed by, the unsubstantial Sunday forms, stirring the silence furtively. There were some of Rudds and some of Andersons and some of Maconagheys. Amy Quong smiled at them all. There was also Schmidts' youngest little girl. She was very fair and pink. Unlike Margaret, thought Amy, who felt herself sort of attracted to the pink and fair. But Margaret was a Quong. The day she went to see Ethel after Margaret was born she was glad the child was a Quong, though of course she could not have been anything else, what ever Ethel might have planned. Amy Quong rocked in her chair, nodding at the passers-by. Quongs had been at Happy Valley longer than most of these. The store that was built by old Quong squatted in its dirty crackle-pink, impervious to paint. Margaret was the granddaughter of old Quong. Coming one evening into the store, she cried on Amy's shoulder, she would not speak, she put her arms round her aunt's neck, and Amy experienced that almost demonstrative emotion that Margaret or Arthur sometimes stirred. Margaret's arms were a black-blue. He had hit her with the ruler, Margaret said. Good evening, Mr Turner, smiled Amy Quong, and the rockers of the chair made a crunching sound on the verandah floor. Ethel said she'd

229

prosecute the man, the brute, and that wife of his was little better than a Sydney tart. Amy trembling over Margaret's head. She and Arthur and Margaret who were Quongs, not so much Walter, and Ethel had only married in. A lustre bowl caught the light, twisted a face in tears. Amy smoothed Margaret's hair with her soft and almost boneless hand. What will it do, said Amy, sitting in the back room with Ethel, what will it do, she said, writing, or telling the Inspector, not very much, no, Ethel, we'll see, we'll wait a little, she said. Ethel grumbled. She went home. She never liked to be found at the store. The shadows got lower on the street. Amy sat with her hands in her lap, twisted them into a ball against the cold.

Dr Halliday drove down the hill out of the direction of Kambala, where he had spent the day. In the garden in front of Everetts' old Mrs Everett in her Sunday black nudged Mrs Ansell and winked. The lids of her eyes were a scaly red. I took Dorcas into Moorang, to Dr Burton, Mrs Ansell said, wouldn't trust that Halliday, not with any girl of mine, not if I was in the room meself. Halliday's car drove past contained in its own intimate hum. Oliver and Rodney sat in front complete in their own intimate thoughts. There were rifles in the car. Come on, Rodney, Oliver had said, we'll take out the rifles, we'll go on up to Kambala for the day, ask your mother for some sandwiches, and don't make it mutton again. Yes, Father, Rodney said. He lay on his stomach on the verandah, he was reading Antony and Cleopatra, the battles, and he could not unravel, but did not want to go to Kambala, was sure of that, to shoot rabbits with Father, he bit his lip. It isn't often we have a

230

day together, Father said. That made you feel shy. Driving up to Kambala was a long period of silence, of shyness, of searching for something to say and feeling a long way off, as Father sat at the wheel and you wished you were farther, on the verandah, or Egypt, and somewhere she put a pearl into a cup of vinegar and drank it right off.

They shot three rabbits. Then they ate their sandwiches in the shade. Rodney walled up a beetle in a tower of earth. Should they skin the rabbits, Oliver said. Rodney said he hated the feel of a rabbit that was skinned. Anyway, said Oliver, he was going to have a nap. He lay on his back in the shade with his hat tilted over his face, so that Rodney dared look at him, stretched on the ground, the way he sometimes looked at Father when he was asleep. The beetle dug its way out of a tower of crumbling earth. We shall be here all day, Rodney felt, I know that, but better at least if he sleeps, if I had brought a book, and perhaps I shall not be a doctor or even an explorer, I shall write books, only about what, that is where it gets hard, or about love, only you didn't know, and books were mostly about love, there was always an Antony and Cleopatra, even in the Bible that sort of thing, a concubine, or perhaps you could write a travel book, like Columbus, about a voyage, where there needn't be any love, if you had ever been for a voyage, but I shall go to Sydney soon. He looked at Oliver stretched out on the ground. A whip-bird called in the bush. We shall go to Sydney, Mother said. She sighed. But somehow there had to be love or it wasn't a book, that is, a proper book, not those ones about Red Indians that were being put away for George, those were for children, and I am growing up,

231

I suppose I shall have to marry, perhaps Margaret Quong, only she is Chinese, but that might be sort of Cleopatra, I am Antony, and Father Antony, she was a concubine. He dug a little hole in the ground. He put the beetle inside and watched it try to climb out.

It was very dull. They shot two more rabbits when Oliver woke. But still it was very dull. And Oliver knew it was. But I went there yesterday, he said, I shall not go to-day, the way Mrs Belper said, well, well, doctor, you here again? So he could not go to-day. The rabbits dangled, limp, their heads dark with the clotted blood. Rodney yawned and decapitated a flower. I am here and not here, Oliver said, that is why it is dull, and he knows, or does he, what does Rodney, never speaking, he is my son, Hilda's son, I have a duty towards him, have brought him up to shoot rabbits against his will. There is so much I want to say to Rodney, only I don't altogether know what it is. He is Hilda's son. Alys said, if I had a child I shouldn't mind, because it would be your child, like Rodney, who doesn't like me, I feel. Don't pull back that safety catch, said Oliver's voice, suddenly sharp. I'm not, murmured Rodney. He beheaded another flower. Alys's child. But Alys would not have a child, that he did not want, to pin the moment of perfection and then look down and see it dead, he wanted it alive and volatile, which alone was perfection, not with a pin through its back, she must escape this, even when they said things, because it had come to that he knew, they were saying things about Miss Browne and Dr Halliday. It made him feel savage, the glance of a face in the street. They were making it something different. Only Hilda said nothing, was silent. But you could feel a kind of silent opposition emanate from Hilda, which was only natural. She knew yesterday that the letter was from Garthwaite, that came with details of the Queensland practice, said he was willing to exchange, though not before August. That would be winter again. She came into the dispensary in winter with her hand. She was a patient. She had wrapped up her hand in a handkerchief, her mind in little artifices as a defence, and you peeled away, you probed, you knew her body and her mind, its perfections and imperfections. Before this you had not thought you could have loved someone for their imperfections, but somehow they made her more real. She was a core of reality in Happy Valley. And now they were beginning to hate, the people you passed, you could feel it. There is something relentless about the hatred induced by human contacts in a small town. At times it seems to have a kind of superhuman organization, like the passions in a Greek tragedy, but there is seldom any nobility about the passions of a small town, the undercurrent of hatred that had begun to flow about Alys Browne, or that poor wretch Moriarty. This had an unhealthy subterranean intensity. Which is what made these passions different also from the hatred between man and natural phenomena. You know how much to expect from fire or flood. You can't say the same of your fellow-men outwardly united in a small community. A city is different again, almost a natural phenomenon. The individual may get hurt by the general trend of mass passion but he won't be put on the table and deliberately slit open without any anaesthetic. Perhaps more acutely than anyone Hilda was conscious of this. Rodney must go to the city to school. Rodney must be saved, she felt. And now this letter from Garthwaite, inviting them to go away, to leave Alys Browne. The silence had grown oppressive, the sharp call of the whip-bird, and the pressure of the grey leaves. Rodney sat down underneath a bush and yawned. Want to go home? Oliver said. He could see that Rodney was relieved to return, to return to what, to answering Garthwaite's letter and Hilda's glance, wondering if that letter, he did not tell her, and the day had been a failure, he was a failure in relationship with Rodney, in relationship with Hilda. Alys touched with her hand your face and the material present dropped away, was immaterial. You began to breathe in a far more significant world. A far more significant world was yourself, but was also Rodney, was also Hilda, even George floating boats in a tub in the yard, each their own significant world. Responsible for these. The moon dropping molten from the earth, its origin, to cool and revolve, distinct. Rodney sitting in the car on the way home is very remote, like the moon revolving in another air, but it should not be altogether like this, for moon and earth have their seasons of approach, only I perhaps have failed to accept the possibility of this, I have made no effort, and going up to Kambala to shoot rabbits is not an effort but a feeble admission of failure. Going home a failure too. We are going home.

We are going home, said Rodney, that red tank up on the hill is almost home is a house and Father walking down the hill whistling those big squares on her dress and she said she was sick because Antony had gone because love in books seemed to make you sick and it was funny and why love and why Father.

They drove down out of the direction of Kambala, where they had been spending the day. In the garden in front of Everetts' old Mrs Everett in her Sunday black nudged Mrs Ansell and winked. The lids of her eyes were a scaly red.

Will you let me down here? said Rodney. I think I'll go up to Quongs'.

Oliver stopped the car.

Right, he said, and Rodney got out. Not such a bad day.

No, said Rodney. It's been a good day.

He stood there a moment uncertain, looking past Oliver's face. Then he turned and went up towards the garage, looking down and rather red. Oliver started the car. It slid forward comfortably, like a lie that masks an admission of failure, like Rodney going up to Quongs', relieved.

Rodney went up to Quongs' garage and hung about outside, because there was nobody in the garage and he never liked to go up to the house, the way Mrs Quong snapped. So he hung about and whistled a bit, and rattled a tin that was lying by the side of the road. He put some stones in the tin and rattled it aimlessly. But the street was still deserted, heavy with Sunday, for people had either gone down to stand at corners in the main street, or else were pressed into their kitchens, those Sunday groups, fitfully conversational and the faces vaguely melancholy that stare from the windows at the outside world. But at least it was better than shooting rabbits with Father and not knowing what to say. And Margaret might come out. He looked down the street stealthily. They laughed at him for playing with Margaret Quong, called him Dolly Halliday and asked him what they played. This no longer made his face go red, as if by saturation in shame he had become immune, and playing with Margaret was a release, like reading a book, was not going down to school, was the antithesis of Andy Everett and stones.

After a while Margaret Quong came out. She was sucking a sweet in the side of her mouth. She walked down the garden path, and her arms dangled long and bony, and her legs had a sort of bony grace.

Hello, said Margaret through her sweet.

Hello, he said back.

They stood together in the road, the silence lit with those random flashes of intimacy that will make a silence significant. And sometimes they talked and it had a sort of significance that was somehow not in the words, but behind, and whether talking or silent they were nearly always content.

We had duck for dinner, said Margaret.

I like duck.

I like turkey better, I think.

I like duck.

We had a turkey once for Christmas, and when Father cleaned it there were eggs inside.

He looked at her, pondering a mystery.

Were there many? he said.

Four or five. Some of them were soft.

Did you touch them?

She nodded. He paused a moment and wrinkled up his face.

236

Let's go into the garage, he said.

They went inside the garage. It was impressively mysterious below the girders, the shapes and smells and the patches of green oil. You could see your face in a pool of oil, like in a bubble, a bit out of shape. The pumps in the open doorway were gaunt and tragic in the frail light. Inside the garage it was getting dark. A voice made an echo, felt its brief and muffled way along the line of drums.

Let's make some aeroplanes, said Rodney.

They made them out of old circulars that advertised the Ford. He got up into the girders and he threw them down, so that in the half-light they fell fantastically at Margaret's feet, or they brushed her hair, or she caught them in her hands like birds returning.

Shall we pretend it's a war? he said.

No, she said, not a war.

All right, he said. Just as you like.

He climbed down out of the girders.

Fancy those eggs being soft, he said.

I don't know, said Margaret. It would have been very uncomfortable if they had all been hard.

He rolled up one of the circulars, trumpetwise, and began to blow.

I wish I could play, I wish I could play a trumpet, Rodney said. I'd play in the band at the Show. But I don't think I'm musical. Not like Father, anyway.

Margaret did not answer. He stopped blowing. It was pretty dark. Darker by silence too, by this sudden withdrawal of Margaret that he sensed, knowing why. There were so many problems enlarged by the silence in this creeping darkness. They were both conscious of these. But they did not speak. Just as they had not spoken of the incident in the school, their minds had taken it and walled it up, it was something enormous and inexplicable that you did not try to explain.

Margaret, said Rodney suddenly, I expect we shall marry each other later on.

Do you think so? she said.

Her voice smiled.

I expect so, he said.

I shan't ever marry, she said. I don't want ever to marry at all.

She said she said that it was so much easier the two and she might have been a nun playing that arpeggio before the hands struck on the keys could not move he looked said go on. She held her arms tightly against her breast. They had not hurt much, it was only inside, not Mr Moriarty at all, nothing to do with this.

Why? asked Rodney carefully.

What? she said.

Her voice came back out of the dark.

Why will you never marry?

You're too young, she said. You wouldn't understand.

As if he was a child. It was the first time she had suggested this. As if she knew a lot more. But he knew a thing or two himself that Margaret Quong knew nothing about. Resentment altered his voice.

Anyway, he said, we're all going away soon. Mother told me it won't be long.

Going away she felt, is not so much Rodney but

someone else, but what will happen, will not be the same. You did not expect that. You got older, and that was something you knew, it would not be the same. She held her arms tightly. There was going to be a frost.

Lights had come in the houses. Men were talking politics and sheep. Rodney Halliday going home trod through fragments of light that fell from the houses on the way, brushed without hearing the chance phrase, the clattering of dishes at a kitchen door. He was going home. They were going away. His mind was large with the possibilities of this, which were greater than a momentary resentment against Margaret Quong. And what would She, when Antony had gone, standing at her door with cool arms. This was a thread his mind slit, rejecting this as something superfluous to the ideal pattern of Rodney Halliday driving to Sydney in a peal of bells.

When he got in Mother said:

You shouldn't have stayed out so late, Rodney. I began to wonder where you were. Don't tear up that paper, George. Do you hear what I say? George! Now run along, Rodney, and wash your hands. Then I'll give you your tea.

I don't want any tea, he said.

But you only had those sandwiches for lunch.

I'm not a bit hungry, he said.

Oh dear, dear, she sighed. George, you'll knock that vase.

Rodney went out back to his room. The way people upset. He frowned.

Are you sure, Rodney? she called.

Hilda Halliday stood perplexed. She swept away a

mesh of hair with her hand. Her hand was large and bony, the wedding ring a little bit loose, because she was plumper when she received it from Oliver in the church. She was gaunt and narrow-chested. The wool sometimes caught in the skin of her fingers as she knitted socks for Oliver and the boys, or jumpers for herself. Her voice was the clicking of needles knit up with the vague protective softness of wool. Often now she stood perplexed, wondering how much she ought to know, or if there was really anything to know, and this only made her more perplexed, and at night she could not sleep, she coughed and turned about. Because morality was something you took for granted, you would not come into touch with the other, which was a quality in other people, the working classes or the very rich. She had been brought up like that, Hilda Halliday. You expected to come into contact with sickness, poverty perhaps, but never immorality.

George knocked his head against a chair and began to cry.

There, she said. My poor little boy. Come and let Mother make it better, she said.

She pressed George against her. His face was red and contorted with crying, his mouth gaping with sobs. She pressed his head tightly against her. George cried a little louder then, as if encouraged in his crying, as if he felt that she wanted him to cry against her chest.

There, there, she soothed. We'll look at this nice book. We'll look at it together, shall we? At the picture book. Look at the horse and cart, George. Look.

Oliver came into the room. He looked at her, was going

to speak, then went out to the dispensary. He looked angry, she thought, perhaps because of George. It made her cough.

Oliver, she called, she wanted to explain.

Her voice went out into the passage and came back unaccompanied. Holding George against her chest, his sobs, made her want to cough.

Look at the horse and cart, she said. That's a piebald horse. Do you see the spots?

George calmed down now, looked at the piebald horse, his interest in outside things revived.

Why is he pieball? asked George.

Because he was born like that, said Hilda weakly. George looked at the page. She stroked his hair. It was rather pale and thin. Oliver was very kind when George was born. He leant over the bed and held her hand. Oliver lying in bed at night, asleep while she could not sleep, she wanted to touch him, she wanted to make sure of what, assuring herself by her touch that could not assure. Oliver lay in bed, but so far distant, like Queensland distant, and perhaps there was really no means of bridging this, Happy Valley was permanent. The thought of winter made her afraid. And writing letters, she said, this is no positive assurance, we shall remain. We shall remain.

Hilda Halliday lowered her eyes. She did not let herself think about her, she would not let her exist, at least in the way that made you lower your eyes. Oliver scraping his boots too long on the iron mat. Oliver coming in. Sometimes it flickered up inside her, her anger, and Oliver coming in, as if she did not know, and the children crying in their sleep fed this anger, or softened it and she felt she wanted

241

to cry. Sometimes she cried to herself and her nose got red, only her nose. As if she did not know. And he tried to be considerate in other ways, and that made it worse, she wished she was dead.

Isn't that a fine big pig? she said, stroking George's hair.

If she were dead. It made her stroke his hair. Dr Bridgeman said, it's all right, Mrs Halliday, if you take care of yourself, you must rest, and I'll see to that, Oliver said. And now it had started again, when she moved the dresser to get at that spoon, the mahogany they bought at Beard Watson's was heavy on clawed feet, must drag, made her sit down, her handkerchief was red. That made her afraid, put up her hand to her chest, but if she were dead would not care, would Oliver, would Rodney, would George. It made her hold on tighter to George. It made him want to get away.

It's time you went to bed, she said.

George began to cry again.

Mother's very tired, she said.

I'm not tired, screamed George.

Oh dear, sighed Hilda Halliday. Her feet felt cold.

Oliver said they ought to light a fire. The forks clattered coldly on the plates as they ate their meal.

There's going to be a frost, he said. We're getting on for winter, you know.

Her feet felt cold.

Yes, she said. But the fire isn't laid. We'll have to leave it for to-night.

In his pocket the letter that Garthwaite had written lay warm, should tell her this that she was waiting to be told, that they would go away, but not yet, he could not tell her, go away yet. He hated himself. Hilda's face was hollow and tired as she turned up the wick of the lamp, the softness of the light hardening the contour of her face. It made him want to give way to pity, but pity was suicide. If I start pitying Hilda, that is to kill myself, he felt, the person that Alys has made, that is me, and now I must sacrifice it, I must pity Hilda, must go away. So he sat there hating himself.

Yes, she said. But it'll be warm up there.

What? he said.

In Queensland.

She was breathing rather fast, he saw. His hands tightened on the knife and fork.

We don't know yet, he said.

You haven't had a letter?

No.

As if she knew, she knew he had the letter he was hiding from her.

You didn't get a letter yesterday? she asked.

Why all this cross-questioning?

No, Oliver, she said, and her voice went softer, and he thought she was going to cry. No, I shouldn't, she said.

She looked away. He hated himself.

We'll go in time, he said.

The way you clung on, tightened up in opposition to Hilda, made yourself, as if there could be no reason for going, and Rodney and Hilda just incidental, or...He pushed back his plate.

What's the matter? he said.

I don't feel very well, said Hilda.

Her face was pale and bony in the circle of light, flushed on the bones, or perhaps it was the light. The lids of her eyes were heavy with shadow. She drooped.

Hilda, dear. Wait just a little longer, he said.

He stood behind her chair, felt her tremble as he touched her shoulders that were frail. If not as frail as the will, because you were weak, clinging on like this, there was no other word for it.

Why? she said, leadenly.

It fell into silence that there was no need for either of them to break. They knew the reason for silence. Then she began to cough, leaning with her elbows on the table and putting up her handkerchief.

Hiding from him something, this, that he knew, he knew it as she knew what she would not say, say to Alys, we are going away, Alys, because Hilda is very ill, she has been ill for a long time, or I am ill, the will, that is no will, sometimes it breaks or you give it to someone else, as I have given myself to you, and you have made me into something superior to myself, but which I must throw away, because of the world I must throw away because Hilda is the world, poor, sick, and there is no forsaking it.

I wish I were dead, Hilda said. Oh yes, I do. There's no use your opening your mouth to contradict me. I know it's best. We all know it's best. Then you could make something of your life. You and the boys. I'm only a drag.

There was a grey, hammering tone about her voice. He did not want to listen to it. But he was held there by necessity. He had to listen. And he would protest against her saying what she knew he knew to be true.

244

Then she began to cough again. She turned away. She put her handkerchief up against her mouth to stifle the coughing. He could not bear to see her cough.

Hilda, darling, he said, you mustn't talk like this.

He knew it sounded trite. He put his arm round her shoulder to try to atone for it. But she got up and went away, and he was touching air. There was a flush of red on her handkerchief. She went out of the room, still coughing, trying to hide the blood from him as she had done once before.

And it was no good. It would be better if she died. Just as she said. And Alys was up there, he loved her, he wanted her, there was something strong and productive about loving Alys. Loving Alys was not just existing, it made him believe in something more.

It began to grow hot in the cold room. His thoughts were hot, his head. Flapping its soft, plushy wings, that moth beat up against the lamp, pressing out of a dark sea towards a yellow island of light. Alys stood in a circle of light, the wave bent, the shore crumbled musically. What time was it by candlelight, she said, when the wax fell on her arm. He put his hand to his forehead, holding it there in a fist. He could not think clearly. He must not think like this, because he was undergoing some kind of moral disintegration. It was a matter of time and Happy Valley, their subtle corrosion of the will. It was wrong to love Alys. It was rotten and disintegrating, his love for her, and he was making her part of his own moral collapse. As Hilda saw, who was will to escape, unswerving in this. She also loved him.

That gramophone playing down the road dissolved. A still, soft playing, the stillness playing like insects, or a moth. He must go away. They must all go away. He went into the dispensary to write to Garthwaite, to say that in August he would be ready to leave.

A quarter, you said?

Yes, he said, a quarter, please.

He leaned up against the counter, steadying himself, she could hear him breathe, she could see his hand holding on to the counter's polished edge, she could see the bones and a meandering of veins. The peppermints rattled into the scales. The brass shone against the darkness of the shop, focussing the eyes, and she was glad, because she did not want to look up.

It'll soon be the races, he said. It ought to be good for trade.

We always do well in Race Week, she said.

His voice was tired. She did not, could not look up as she watched for the weight of the peppermints on the scales. She felt a sudden tingling of hate, a smarting. The peppermints fused in a white coagulated lump, then resolved slowly with the waning of emotion, and she put them into a paper bag, specially stamped at Moorang with an ARTHUR QUONG.

Thanks, Miss Quong, he said. We all have our little weaknesses.

She smiled, not so much at him as at the shining scales. Then he was going out. She looked up and saw the back of Ernest Moriarty stooped in the square of light. He was putting the bag of peppermints into the pocket of his coat. He was bent and a little tired. But his physical appearance made no impression on her, intent on this sudden emotional spasm that came up out of her body after weeks of almost indifference. She saw Ernest Moriarty going down the steps. She hated him. He went on down the street towards the school, walking slowly to save his breath. She could not pity. She stood still behind the counter and felt her hatred ebb slowly away, leaving no print on her small immaculate life.

Amy Quong's emotional life seldom came so close to the surface. Love or hate lurked, or stirred with a vague motion in the more secret depths. She was not intentionally secretive. She was not actually passionless. Emotion was just a mental state that she did not actively reveal, that anyone would sense instinctively, anyone at all close, like Arthur or Margaret, who were intimately linked up with the emotional life of Amy Quong. Arthur sensed it, in their humdrum, almost inarticulate intercourse, when she called him in from the stable through the smell of pollard and the quaking of heavy Muscovy ducks, when they sat on the verandah of a summer evening, or went leisurely over

248

the stock. Margaret too was conscious of a subtle emotional link, felt it as their heads bent by lamplight making up the books, felt it on the evening when she cried close against Amy's shoulder, at once both tender and hard, with its offer of intimacy and protection peculiarly expressed. Because there was a core of hardness in Army, as in most people who are self-sufficient. She could close up. She was a piece of stone. And there is no pity in stone.

She stood by the counter in the darkness of the shop. Moriarty went outside, passed into the light. She felt the weals on Margaret's wrists, the tears damp on the shoulder of her dress. She hated Moriarty. It was suddenly there. She could not help it. After these months, springing up at her out of this chance contact as she weighed out the peppermints. He came into the shop. She felt she had been waiting for this, some definite contact that was even more necessary than the sight of Margaret's weals. She heard him breathe. They said he had asthma. They said his wife was carrying on. She picked up the weights one by one and laid them down at the side of the scales with the clinking sound of brass.

Afternoon, said Hagan, coming into the shop.

She looked up at him, composed behind her spectacles.

Good afternoon, she said.

Her voice was quiet and soft.

What've you got in the way of chocolates? he asked.

Well, she said, it depends.

No, it doesn't. Not at all. The very best. That's what I want. A sort of occasion. See?

She looked at him unperturbed, as if he was trying to

rattle her and it simply wouldn't come off.

You'd better have a pound of these, she said. They're two-and-six the pound.

Make it two, he said. It's an occasion, after all.

He straddled across a chair, looking at her as she ladled the chocolates out of the jar, her brown hands busy in the coloured foil. A mousy, frightened little thing. He sucked his teeth with a mingled thoughtfulness and contempt. He had passed him going towards the school, exchanged nods without a tremor, because—well, you couldn't say it was the first time, and you got used, not like that cove in Moree, meeting him at the pub and looking down into the beer, Andy Walker the name, and what'll you have, he said, and call me Andy, he said, and she said, oh Clem, I'm potty, now don't be afraid, dear, I told you he's gone to Narrabri, looked down into the beer then as if that poor coot Walker might have known the way her suspenders snapped back against her leg. And Moriarty went down the street. Were two-and-six the pound. Who said a Chow didn't profiteer, the Chows and the dagoes, and nobody putting a spoke in the bastards' wheel, or what would she say this little brown mouse of a Chow if you did.

Seen you in town a lot this week, she said.

Yes, he said thoughtfully it came out in a lazy hiss, tilted down at the floor. Yes, he said. One thing and another, there's been a lot to do. Can't send in any of the men. They always hang round magging at the pub.

Her checks were dim and polished. He could not see her eyes. She was looking at him vaguely, not altogether conscious of his presence, except for what it signified. The chocolates rustled in the paper bag. Ernest Moriarty went down the street. She felt again that odd mounting of hatred inside her, that climbed up and took her by the throat, tightening it, though without any outer visible emotion. She felt out of breath. She felt her heart. They said his wife, that pink slut, that morning with the egg dried on her bodice, was carrying on with Hagan, so Mrs Everett, so Mrs Ansell said. Amy Quong's mind slid primly over the actual fact, the detail of adultery. As a fact it made her blush. It was too intimately connected with Walter Quong not to deal discomfiture. But she seized on the significance of adultery and Hagan and Moriarty's wife with a kind of inner exultation. She pushed the chocolates along the counter towards his hand.

That'll go down, Mr Hagan? she asked.

Eh? he said. Yes, you can put it down.

Put them down, but not the hard ones, Clem, she said, they stick on me plate, as she stuck her tongue up into a chocolate cream, licking out the cream like a rabbit, or snuggled up, or made yourself cosy, she said, and Clem dear, what I'd have done if you hadn't come, or wrote, Clem dear, Friday afternoon, I love you, dear, and didn't know what it meant to have something in my life and that night only I was afraid if someone came up the lane because I'm not really bad, Clem, and only because this is the real thing there was never any woman as happy as me so you'll come on Friday won't you Clem oh God it makes me crazy waiting for you and thinking that perhaps you won't, your loving Vic. The paper smelt like violet soap.

He looked up suddenly into the spectacles of Amy

251

Quong, behind which, in the darkness of the store, he could not see the eyes. He got up casually off the chair.

I've a couple of horses being shod. I'll have to be getting along, he said.

Hagan went out of the store, his body slabbed against the light, across the verandah and down the steps. Hagan went on up the road. Amy Quong stood in the doorway watching his casual walk and the way he tossed the paper bag in his hand. There was a sharpness about the afternoon that was not altogether autumn. Her fingers trembled. She clenched her hands in a ball. She seemed to he gathering herself into her small circumference out of which, on this autumn afternoon, a flow of unexpected passion had forced her to expand. Now, she said, now. She was a little frightened, a little unclean. She lifted up one hand and smoothed the white collar at her neck, brushing the shoulder to which clung the memory of Margaret's tears. Then her eyes became distant again, unconcerned with the figure of Hagan taking its time up the street and losing itself at the corner as he turned.

He tossed the chocolates up and down in his hand. On Friday, won't you, Clem. He felt he didn't want altogether, and the way they always went on like this and didn't know when to stop, until you said it's got to stop, any sane person'd see it couldn't go on for ever, though he wasn't the man to deny any woman her fun. Then they began to cry. Well, it hadn't come to that, not yet, though you could bet your life there'd be all that song and dance. Your loving Vic. Your hating Vic. A holy terror between the sheets Friday or Monday or whenever it was. Knew that night against the

252

fence that he knew her little game, had met it before. That was the trouble. It made you sick. He clicked the catch of the gate with the air of a man who knows that after all there isn't very much left to know.

Vic Moriarty inside heard the gate click, flattened up against the door, as she waited. It made you jump. However many times you heard it, though it wasn't really many times, it made you jump. Sometimes she said, I didn't really mean it to be like this. Lying in bed, and night, and it was only Ernest, his snore, she said it, but without conviction, she said who'd have ever thought it was going to be like this, that morning on the road, if Daisy knew, and all those people in Marrickville, that Mrs Who's-This with the stiff leg who carried on and said things when Mrs Caulfield ran off with the bloke on the motor-bike, as if it was any concern of hers. That was the trouble, and people didn't understand. Because I'm not real bad, Vic Moriarty told herself. She felt herself coming over in that queer way. Like opening the door to Him.

Hello, Lollipop, he said.

He smacked her on the behind that yielded with the soft report of complaisant flesh.

Oh, Clem, she said, not chocolates again!

No, he said. Oysters.

His hat landed neatly on an oak peg in the hall.

You're bold, she giggled. That's what's the matter with you. And I'm slimming, she said. Oh dear!

Go on, he said. You can tell me something else.

Really, she said. Look. I've taken off quite a lot from the hips.

She pressed her hands on her flanks. There were dimples on the backs of her hands.

I suppose there's no harm in a girl amusing herself, he said.

Then he put his arm round her waist, looked down in that way that always got them, was a sure fire, if you closed your eyes a bit you had them eating out of your hand.

Oh, Clem, Clem, she said, I'm glad you've come.

And why shouldn't I've come? he asked.

Pressed herself up, was easy as a house on fire, with violet soap, or whatever it was, or dusting herself with powder, that big puff with a pink ribbon she had in a jar on the chest of drawers, was like a big pink puff, or two.

Eh? he asked.

I dunno.

It was only Tuesday.

You don't realize, she said.

No. We never do.

She began to pout. The line of her lips looked wet. She had painted it in a bow.

You're cruel, she said.

He squeezed her face.

Want to go bye-bye?

No, she said.

It made you laugh, the way they carried on, when it didn't make you sick.

All right, he said. We'll go on standing in the hall.

She shrugged her shoulders, stood in the silence of linoleum squares, and the smell of pickles from lunch. Hagan began to laugh.

I think you're a swine, she said.

She went down the passage in a tap-tap of yellow linoleum squares.

Yes, she yawned, I think you're a swine.

When you turned over the bed wheezed sleepily. Lying
in bed at night, sometimes you were not quite sure which
was Ernest and which was bed. Poor Ernest, who was also
a twinge of conscience. A fly on the ceiling scraped its
wings.

What? he said.

Nothing. I meant to get this bloody mattress teased.

Had said to Ernest, and it was winter, not that night
going to the pictures, and perhaps she had a cheek to write,
but she couldn't hold out any longer so had to write and
say...

Did you get a surprise when I wrote? she asked.

When?

Silly! The first time, she said.

No, he said lazily.

I like that!

The bed wheezed as he turned over. Talking in the
afternoon was a bit too much of a good thing, and she
always had to talk, if he put up his shoulder as protection
would still talk over the ridge.

You're not very sociable, she said.

Her voice did not altogether mind. It stroked him, her
hand stroked his arm, tugged at the small reddish hairs.
There was an accent of voluptuous achievement in Vic
Moriarty's gesture, in the cadence of her voice.

You don't know what it means to me, Clem, she said. That first time. I thought I'd go crazy, Clem.

The yard droned with afternoon. He thought he would like to go to sleep. The room was a blur through half-closed eyes.

You're not going to sleep, Clem?

She put her arm under his neck, bolstered up his head in a way that could only be uncomfortable.

What do you think I am? he said. A machine?

Face looked over him sagged down, was a sag, was Vic Moriarty, a pink blur. He opened his eyes and frowned.

You needn't speak like that, she said.

Anyway, it's time I went. There's those horses waiting at the blacksmith's shop.

Have it your own way, she said.

Her breasts shook with resignation as she fell back on the bed.

And there's Ernest, he said.

Why d'you have to say that?

There's always Ernest, he said.

She looked at him as he got off the bed, stood with his back to her in the light quenched by the half-drawn blind. His back looked hard. She wanted to get off the bed herself, and touch him again, to make sure. Saying things like that. And he did not love her, she knew, was hard, like his body. He began to put on his pants.

You needn't bring in Ernest, she said.

No? he said, from the depths of his shirt. All right, then, we'll leave him out.

She turned away her head. She did not want him any

256

more. Talking about Ernest. Ernest's lips were blue that night. But she felt good. He made her feel good. She rubbed her cheek against the pillow and heard him putting on his boots.

Well, he said, Poppet, I'll be seeing you.

She looked at him.

When?

She did not care.

Some time, he said.

Lay there and weeks and weeks was an awful thought of Happy Valley like before and if this happened again and you heard that ticking mahogany clock and it got right inside you was sharp and said you did not care but you did you did and that was the awful part.

Clem, love, she said, you'll make it soon?

Clem Hagan looked down. Well, it was one way of passing the time, and you'd go off your rocker out at Glen Marsh if it wasn't for coming into town.

Yes, he said. Pretty soon.

In leaving you could promise anything. He tapped her on the shoulder and left.

Vic Moriarty lay on the bed, slackened, and tried to think and not to think, because if she thought, she thought of Ernest, or the things Clem said to hurt, or perhaps just said. She lay with her eyes closed. Her breasts moved stolidly with her breath. Now and again the distance clucked as reality became a hen, was no longer words spoken in half-sleep, I'm crazy about you, Clem, she said, that the room took up and gave back into her ears, making her smile, making her say it again. Vic Moriarty lay there smiling,

257

heaped in a dopey lump of female flesh that has abandoned its reserve and now enjoys the advantages of flesh that is really in no way partial to constraint. She smiled to herself with all the abandon of people indulging their intimate thoughts, the sort of moment that wears an expression of ultimate foolishness for all but the responsible, and these are mercifully unaware.

She lay there well on into the afternoon. She dozed. Then she began to feel cold. She woke, and there was goose-flesh on her arms. She shuddered back under the eiderdown. But she felt cold. I'm a fool, she said, lying here and someone might come in, or Ernest back from school, but if only you could lie here always, forget those plates in the scullery that Gertie didn't wash, and that it is going to be winter soon, he will come again, you don't mind how often come, even though sometimes he makes you want to cry, if only he come again, because if he doesn't he doesn't and he doesn't come he...Vic Moriarty clambered out of bed and put on a dressing-gown. It had big black poppies on a purple field. Ernest said, put on that dressing-gown, I like you in that dressing-gown, he said. Ernest would come home. Here am I lolling about, she said. Friday, Saturday, Sunday perhaps, or wouldn't come. She went into the sitting-room to get a cigarette. Her lips were tight on the cigarette. The smoke made her cough. I'm thinking like a tart, she said, but what's a tart anyway, and I do all he wants, darn those pants that I haven't finished yet, long pants on a man if you please, and there's always that stink of asthma powder in the place, what I don't endure.

But I'm fond of Ernest, she said, I'm fond of Ernest,

with the air of a woman defending herself against contradiction that did not exist. The cyclamen sprawled widely in the lustre bowl. She shrugged her shoulders and turned her back. Friday didn't exist, Sunday perhaps, turned his back and she could not see the way that hair ended suddenly on his chest, as if it was all over and he did not hear. Her breasts drooped against a purple field.

20

They had sent the car to meet him at the station. It was waiting outside surrounded by small boys, limpid with admiration before a large Packard car. Furlows' car. There was old Furlow now, he had been to Sydney, coming out of the station and going to get into the car. The spectators parted in two sections waiting to see Furlow pass.

Mr Furlow got into the car. He settled down. He was glad to be back. Moorang swirled past, the pubs and the dago's shop with the paper decorations behind the glass, the rolls of material at the draper's, the two kelpies, their ribs in relief, misbehaving themselves in the middle of the street. Mr Furlow took off his hat. There was a mark on his forehead where the leather had eaten in, and his hair was plastered down. He sighed. He began to feel his confidence return, a confidence founded on familiar things, the street at Moorang, the road out to Happy Valley, the gates the chauffeur would get down to open from there out to Glen Marsh. These were understandable and safe, the landmarks of discovered territory. So he was at his ease. Not as in the train when that commercial traveller, who shouted him a drink while they stopped in Goulburn, asked him his opinion of the European situation, as if Mr Furlow had opinions, as if there were a European situation. Though Mr Furlow had been to England. He had been taken over a brewery at Slough. It had impressed him very much, like the Lord Mayor's Show and the number of bowler hats.

I'm a simple man, Mr Furlow used to say. He used it as a defence, as much as to say, don't touch me now that you know the truth. Because he liked to be left alone. He liked to say, this is good enough for me. It absolved him from exertion, from opinions, from anything but a gentle meandering through a field of objective images. And that man bawling in the bar at Goulburn had upset his equilibrium. Now what about Mussolini? he said, and Mr Furlow did not know, he went cold down the spine, wondered what he ought to say, remembered that someone at the Club had said, ought to castrate the bastard before the trouble spreads. The Goulburn station bar was an isolated patch of discomfort in Mr Furlow's usually comfortable mind.

Had a nice drop of rain since you left, said the chauffeur.

Mr Furlow switched off, he was good at switching off, and returned to the immediate landscape between Happy Valley and Glen Marsh, to a mob of wethers in the hollow, to the fence that straggled out towards Ferndale, to all this, the comprehensible. His paunch stirred with the motion of the car, his mind with pleasurable anticipation of dogs running out from the house and Sidney perhaps standing on the steps. When she was younger she would run out too, with the dogs, and climb on the running-board of the car, and ask what he had brought. Her lips on his cheek were more inquisitive than affectionate, but the analysis of motive was not in Mr Furlow's line, and Sidney's mouth was still a kiss. He smiled. The bracelet in his pocket dragged down one side of his coat. The way she put her hand in his pocket was coming home, was Sidney's hand, was contact with the comprehensible detail of Glen Marsh, of Mr Furlow himself.

Not that he connected his daughter in any but an objective way, her face, her voice, with what he might, but didn't, term the comprehensible. The face, the voice, this brittle glass, he loved because they were familiar and time had made their contact mutual. But to penetrate the distant regions of his daughter's mind was something it did not occur to Mr Furlow to do. This remained a mystery from which occasionally there issued an indication of some conflict that, for her father, was more inexplicable than the activities of Mussolini or the European situation. He did not know. He did not want to know. He was a little afraid of something so remote and intangible. He would pick up his paper and go off into another room, forsaking an expression or a cadence that had caused him any discomfiture.

Driving up to the house, he put his hand in his pocket again, touched the bracelet that lay there in its leather jeweller's case. He liked to buy her diamonds. They showed very white and clear against her thin, brown arm. You spoil her, dear, Mrs Furlow said. That only added to his complaisance, in the way that certain rebukes do, and in fact are only meant to encourage the gestures they rebuke. Mrs Furlow's voice was moulded to this manner of rebuke, the mingled tones of martyrdom and delight, signifying, I don't count poor me, but won't Mrs Blandford be impressed when I write and tell her what you have done. Diamonds, for Mrs Furlow, glittered with the brightest social prestige.

Glen Marsh was so many years of prestige as the car advanced along the road. The house reclined, a little too perfect, among the trees, with its lap of green lawn outspread and an embroidering of round chrysanthemum beds. Soon the dogs would rush out, the servants peep from the side wing, the groom stop cleaning the harness at the back and come round to the drive. There was great satisfaction attached to such an approach to Glen Marsh. Mr Furlow sighed. He was heavy with the riches of the earth and a diamond bracelet that he would take right in and put on Sidney's arm.

Well, dear, said Mrs Furlow, kissing him formally on the cheek, I hope you haven't got a cold. You know the train gives you colds.

She spoke with the slight asperity of someone who has been left at home, for even a home such as Glen Marsh is less attractive as a constant reality than as an abstract idea. She did not like to be left at home.

Mr Furlow put down his hat.

Where's Sidney? he said.

She's in the drawing-room, I expect.

Anything wrong?

263

No. Nothing unusual, that is.

Mrs Furlow's face assumed the expression of martyred punishment that came to it always when her daughter was on the mat.

I can't understand her, she said, as if this at least were an unusual remark. She's been sulking for days.

He went into the drawing-room, prepared to encounter the incomprehensible, the slightly frightening aspect of his daughter, that made him go almost on tiptoe, accentuating his unwieldiness. The doors were open. It was cold. Of course, it was autumn, he said, of course it would be cold.

Sidney, he said. Hello, Sidney.

Back turned, she leant against the door, was looking down in the direction of the orchard, where the boughs of the plum-trees were a net of patternless black. Her dress was tight to her thigh. She looked very thin, remote, her face remote that turned from its preoccupation and touched him with a glance.

Hello, she said. You're back—in an accent that was without surprise, as if there were no more room for surprise, and why should anyone expect it.

Sidney is *passionately* fond of her father, Mrs Furlow always said, inaccurately gauging, like most parents, their children's emotional capacities. Now he stood there, a little uncertain. She looked at him as he hesitated, not only part of the moment, but of so many former occasions, some of them distinct, some fused in the general pattern, in which he stood or ran, picked her up that day she fell off Rose and the gravel was embedded in her cheek, talked embarrassed to Miss Cortine, or just his presence, or again his presence, linked to no particular incident. He is a succession of incidents, she felt, and going bald, and rather fat, the day the girls met him in the hall at Miss Cortine's, came in laughing because, said Helen, they had seen such a funny old fat man in the hall, so the cheeks burned, and going downstairs to find him looking tired, looked now.

Have you had any lunch? she said.

No. But I'll wait till tea.

All right. Just as you like.

Like lead the voice, but I am glad, I suppose, go put my hand on his arm or kiss, because I am fond, like the familiar bits of you, the nursery chairs or books, and tell him, tell him, that you did not tell, as you watched the moment pass, and it would be so easy to watch a trunk going down the drive, and he would know he had no more power than a whipped snake lying cool in the palm of the hand. She put up her cheek to her father. She felt languid. She felt the familiar texture of his cheek, the slight roughness. It was different pressed up against, and if only you had hit harder or with the handle, which was bone, perhaps to draw blood.

What's the matter, pet? said Father.

Nothing, she said.

She went and sat down on the sofa. She had begun to tremble. She would not think, isolate her body in a kind of envelope of passive indifference. Because why should I care, she said, that big brute, only it was dirty, rubbing your face in the stable in dung was cleaner than this, only why should I think about it at all.

Anything worrying you, darling? he said.

No. I said nothing—her voice rasping a little, as she

looked up and would have said, Father, send that swine away, that inevitably was not said.

Here, he said. I've brought you something.

She held the case in her lap, the lid opened on diamonds, on a sullen purity of diamonds that lay there waiting to be touched by her hands.

Thank you, she said. They're lovely. Thank you.

That's all right, pet, he said.

Then he went out, almost on tiptoe, half thankful for release from a situation that he did not understand. Her cheek burnt as he touched. Mr Furlow closed the door. It was disconcerting to brush against other people's emotions when they were not the same as his own. He drew in his breath. He did not want to penetrate any farther. So he went down the passage towards the office encased in the satisfaction of having done just what he wanted to do.

Sidney Furlow sat with the bracelet in her lap, touched with her hand the cool fire qui reflète encore calme dormant Hérodiade au clair regard de diamant, and would sit there without purpose, because there was no purpose in doing what in another room, seule, the evening coming home across the paddock a figure that made the blind fall on ma monotone patrie.

21

Hilda went about nowadays quietly, indomitably, nursing her certainty. She coughed, but she was not conscious of her cough. They would go away. He had written. They would go away. In Hilda's mind the remaining weeks were mentally ticked off. She lived exterior to these, or disregarded them as so many dead leaves, the bundle of an old calendar waiting to be torn off. The shortening of the autumn days, the first frosts, the ritual of the household, were part of an incidental mechanical process that scarcely touched Hilda Halliday.

Oliver watched Hilda. He could not feel any bitterness, she was more a stranger than anything else, who had no part in his life and who must be allowed to pursue the rhythm of her own. She had never been anything else.

Looking back, he said, Hilda has been nothing more than a sort of inevitable presence, appearing at the necessary moments in my life, and neither of us thought that this was wrong, neither of us imagined that we had anything else to expect, until something quite casual threw the emptiness into relief, and now we have not even the benefit of illusion, must recognize all the waste of emptiness. The children, Hilda says, there are the children, content to ignore the fact that they have sprung from an illusion. Hilda says this, it is part of her religion to say it, the religion of the world, of Happy Valley with its eyes closed to the possibilities of truth. Perhaps it is better like this. Perhaps Hilda is wiser. Only you regretted the sudden illumination in a face that was not altogether confined to a face, that overflowed and pointed out significant contours in the darkness. This was Alys. And on reflection you knew that this was right, morally, if not conventionally, was not a sort of moral disintegration as you tried to think in your thoughts, this was the world thinking, and you could not forget the world. Hilda would not let you forget, nor Happy Valley, that old woman virulent above a dead geranium in a window-box, no sap but the dead flapping of a conventional tongue that said, mind you, Mrs Ansell, was an eye glassy with hate, because afraid, because you are afraid to see other people give rein to those desires that you have never dared loosen yourself. So you let loose a wind of hate that flapped in the dead geranium leaves. Alys was untouched by this, did not seem to realize. That was the odd thing about Alys Browne, as if her consciousness of outer activity had become numbed by her intentness on an inner change. It was in her face. He loved her face. He had only to contemplate this, or no more than the recollection of it, to feel the conventional realities dissolve into a state in which the trivial and hard wore an aspect that was pitiable. I have learnt this, he felt, that it is pitiable, this Happy Valley, even in its violence that at first you thought deliberately destructive and cruel there is a human core that makes you overflow with pity for it. And this is not the pity of Hilda, which is founded on fear, a pity for man in his hopeless struggle against an ultimately triumphant force, not this that I have learned from Alys, is not Alys, compassion is not fear.

All this was taking place in Happy Valley the same autumn, which was superficially the same as any other autumn, as far as its natural details were concerned. But as I have said before, one of the most noticeable features of Happy Valley was its apparent remoteness from the human element, or perhaps an ironical half-recognition, laying a trap in the shape of its own activities and then letting things slide. Autumn was a season of preliminary cold and suppressed winds. Nothing much appeared to happen besides, though a lot was really happening all the time. Because it was at this moment that Amy Quong felt those dormant and really frightening passions begin to stir, that Clem Hagan was coming into town of an afternoon and going to Moriarty's house, that Moriarty felt things closing in, all those eyes and faces at the school, and that Sidney Furlow was trying to suppress the realization of her own desires. They each had their own problem, and nobody else had theirs, which is only natural perhaps, it is usually like that. And all the time Happy Valley was preparing for

269

winter, and those that were afraid of winter had begun to be afraid, which those who have not experienced Happy Valley in winter-time will certainly not understand. If you have you will know, you will realize the extreme brutality to which man can be subjected, whatever you may have experienced of this, of brutality I mean, in winter at Happy Valley it seems to be epitomized.

Oliver Halliday did not think of this. Before midwinter, said Hilda, we shall go away, we shall go to Queensland, we shall escape. So he could not but feel that time was arrested for the moment, that he would not participate in the coming phase. Nor did Alys think about winter much, because she had ceased to be afraid, come or not she did not very much care. That is the worst of arrested consciousness, because inevitably you must get jerked back. It was still autumn, not very long before the races, that Oliver went up to do it. He did not know exactly what he would do, or say, it was too painful to think about.

So he did not think. He went up the hill one evening to where Alys lived. I am going to break something now, he felt, all the best in me, not that that matters very much, only there is someone else involved. He walked up the hill. He felt rather old and out of breath, in a way that he had not noticed before. But, after all, it is only natural, he said.

Alys was on the verandah darning stockings when he came up to the gate. She glanced up, and down again, like someone catching sight of a person who comes a lot to the house, so often that you make no special stir or preparation, hardly move in fact, because this person has become a part of your life and this you accept as a matter of course.

270

Pull up that chair, she said. No. That one has a nail.

Has it? he said vaguely, watching the passage of her needle through the silk, with the smooth rhythm of silk. Her face, bent, did not notice him, only the inflections of her voice told him she was conscious of his presence. Sometimes he closed his eyes and listened to her voice.

Funny, she said. All these years, and I haven't banged in that nail.

All those years when I was waiting, felt Alys Browne, when it was so much waste time, and, looking back, really most of it has been waste, that convent in Sydney and living up here, which was also as good as a convent, not so much physically as mentally, accepting what I was taught to accept, but waiting as waiting is not so much waste time if it is part of a design. She drew the stockings through her hands. The air was getting sharp.

We'll have to go in, she said.

No, he said, don't go in.

He sat with his back against one of the verandah posts.

What have you got to tell me? she asked.

Nothing, he said.

Got to tell like a child that said nothing she made him feel when Aunt Jane and those apples feeling sick was reversed he said this Alys a child or a girl out of a convent got to tell was reversed and she put out a hand to help that she held up with blood and there was something to tell.

It'll come in time, I expect, she said.

He did not speak. She put her hand in a stocking and held it up to the light.

Alys, he said, Hilda and I have got to go away.

271

She held the stocking with an effort against the light, or it stayed there, she did not know, look, and it was getting dark, and the light, and Schmidts' cows lined across the hill dragging a rope of shadow, like words out of the mouth that would not come, or a numb thought. She felt isolated in a small patch of light. She had been jerked out of the succession of events, that had happened, that were passing on, but she had become stationary.

Yes, she said. Hilda.

Was an abstract idea, his wife, the woman that opened the door and said he was up at Kambala, without ever achieving much more personality than this, somehow she did not think of Hilda, and why, was more than a cipher.

I'm doing it for Hilda, he said. And there's the children. This is nothing to do with you. It isn't much to do with me. But we're going away. We're going to Queensland, he said, feeling the triteness of explanation in his voice, but perhaps it was less painful like this, details, like looking up trains. I'm exchanging practices with a man called Garthwaite, he said. Hilda can't stand the climate here. We'll leave Rodney in Sydney on the way. He's got to go to school.

The slowness of cows across the hill, cow-words as meaningful. But soon it would be dark. She waited for the darkness. Perhaps it would be easier then, or more difficult, because they said you said things anaesthetized.

We haven't spoken much about Hilda, she said.

We haven't had much time.

All time this woman was his wife until you woke up and saw, saw yourself and the callousness of women in love.

Why doesn't one think about these things? she said. Is

272

it that one's deliberately brutal, that one doesn't let oneself, or is one made to isolate oneself from what one doesn't want to think?

He put out his hand and touched her in the dark. She had hoped he would not touch her. It was easier to live in the intellect, in a sort of clarity of mental perception, almost not yourself. But he was touching her, bringing her back into the muffled region of emotional pain.

But I couldn't think, she said. I knew vaguely. But I just couldn't think. You see, when you know it's going to be something important, perhaps nothing so important will ever happen to you again, you can't throw it away. You can't, she said. You can't.

And now? he said.

Yes, she said. Now.

One word can make a silence silenter, he felt, her Now falling like a bead of lead through the darkness, right to the bottom of what, now what. He did not know. He pressed her hand and waited.

It'll still be that important thing, she said.

If you feel that.

Well, what?

That's what I've had to tell myself, Alys. If two people feel like that it can't be altogether negative.

They sat still, intimate, because it was all said. She hoped he would not speak again, would leave it like this, or perhaps to the fugitive comfort of touch that was so much more considerate than words. He would go away, with Hilda and the children, those three strange people, she could never think of them as being anything but strange, or

273

as having a greater reality than herself. They would go to Queensland. She followed her mind down the vague avenue of the future, only a little way, she preferred to stop, because it seemed meaningless and nothing would take shape, no definite image of Alys Browne either here or elsewhere, as if she had been discarded from the pattern of time. But I have meant something, she said, it is not altogether wasted if I have meant something, as he said, he said, this was my purpose, and it is something to have a purpose, to know it, above all that, to realize. She stroked his hand back and forth.

Alys? he said.

Yes, dear.

She put her hand on his mouth. She closed his mouth, her mind, in a little circle of the present that resisted the intrusion of time.

22

Happy Valley flickers up into excitement when the autumn race meeting comes round, kindled by a sort of self-importance and craving for display that you feel a week or two before the arrival of these two days, the Friday and the Saturday, not to mention Friday night when they hold the dance at the School of Arts, or as the bills have it, the Grand Race Week Ball. The posters are yellow, done by the local press, you see them cracked on a paling fence, or the smaller ones at Quongs' and in Hills' Tea Shop window, a rendezvous for flies, and washed paler by a yellow autumn sun. It makes you feel good to stand and look at the posters and think of the excitement of which they are the advance publicity. You can feel a hum blowing up in the wires between Moorang and Kambala, and Happy Valley and Glen Marsh, but centring in Happy Valley, you can also feel that. Stung to activity by the tingling of the wires, this is no longer so detached, as the press stutters at the office of the Happy Valley Star, as the girls sew the buttons on their gloves or a different flower on last year's dress, as the horses arrive in floats from Moorang in their yellow bandages and rugs, and the tempo is brisker in the main street.

By Friday they are all in town, and you can't get a room at the pub or scarcely lean an elbow on the bar for all the people that have come, the cockie farmers, the Kambala Chows, that little man with the broken nails and the cap, or broken-voiced bookies and their clerks, and the vaguer faces without purpose that peer from a corner over a dark glass of stout. In the smoke the remarks drift, on form, on the rainfall, on the wool clip, and somebody says that somebody said that Winapot was a cert. Dogs bristle in the street, a yellow bitch with her lip drawn under the dusty wing of a car. Somebody says it'll rain, or it won't, Saturday at least, because every third year it rains, and in 1928 Mitchell the bookmaker skidded on the Moorang road and they found his body under the car, you couldn't recognize his face. Looks in the glass and wonders if the green organdie, the pursed mouth censorious, if anyone can remember the year before, which a press would make as good as new, if only, if only. Dab a little here for certainty. Vic Moriarty examines her perm. Gertie Ansell squeezes a spot. And thought toys with a possibility of the fabulous, all the things you have put away for the best part of a year, twenty more pounds towards the mortgage, or that boy from the baker's in at Moorang, or the less specifically defined hopes that spring up out of the unconscious and flutter through the fever of two significant days.

It was like this then. Calmer on Friday, though working up towards Friday night when they opened the School of Arts, when the darkness got a bit reckless, that saxophone carving its way through the wall, and the ferns panting from their paper-swaddled pots, with a quivering of trifle, and whose giggle protesting against what. Music launched out, struck back deviously, got beneath the senses, and you danced, you danced, even if it got a bit too hot, and what was heat on Friday night, the light flare falling on a face in sweat, the floor glazed by the motion of feet, when you danced on that long and undulating skein that ravelled out of the accordion.

Chuffy Chambers plays so good, the girls said as they danced past, those crumpled flowers in taffeta who glanced up between his legs towards a smile that was Chuffy Chambers playing his accordion. Chuffy Chambers liked to play. He felt warm against the holy medals he wore next to his skin, felt important with smiles and the variations wrung from accordion stops. He could play all night on a glass of beer, or give way to the saxophone, the piano, and the drums, and just smile at the moving blur of sound. Only that boiled shirt said, walking up the hill to the pictures, chuffs along behind the girls, made the shame, the spittle come in his mouth, and a sudden creeping away down the lane, saw he was with her again wearing a blue dress, she had a sort of hoop in her hair covered with white flowers. The incubator rattled, asked his name, and Chuffy Chambers, he said, because he had never been called anything else, and what sort of a name, he said, till I get down. Hagan in a boiled shirt made Chuffy Chambers's pleasure recede. He looked down at his finger-joints jerking over the accordion stops.

The air was intricate with conversation. A door swung, that glass panel reflecting the back of Mrs Furlow, who wore only sufficient pearls to show what her position was.

This is like old times, Vic Moriarty said, her face warm against Hagan's shirt, a little too warm, it had moulded a saucer right in the centre of that complaining starch. Da da da-da-da-DAR, sang Vic softly against the shirt. We used to go out to the Palais, she said. Daisy and Fred and a boy I knew called Harry Jacobs. He was a buyer at Foy's. You should just see Harry dance a waltz, you've no i...What's the matter, love? You're as quiet as a church.

Mrs Everett said to Mrs Ansell said to Mrs Schmidt look now look putting her cheek and it isn't a shearers' ball but what could you expect from a woman that keeps open house.

A yellow moon rose above ferns, was Walter Quong as he watched her by the door standing there, her mouth tight, and fingering a diamond bracelet, but didn't talk to Lithgow, who was telling her how much polo he played, her face only melted into a yawn. She was thin and hungry-looking. She came up to the garage, didn't let fall a word, only how many gallons she wanted, and then the money into his hand, her red nails on the palm of his hand. Walter Quong sighed. He shuffled the money in his pocket and waned behind a bank of ferns.

Mrs Ansell said to Mrs Ball said to Mrs Schmidt she looked a sight about the eyes and what was she up to Miss Sidney Furlow with her dress cut down the richer you were the lower it got but you wouldn't want her on a plate that little piece hard as a nail.

Am I? he said.

Yes, she said. As quiet as a church.

Hagan began to hum. Got on his nerves all that clatter-clatch about a boy called Harry What's-his-Name, an Ikey Mo or something of the sort dancing a waltz, as if it was of any interest, and that was what you got from women, they never knew what would be of interest to a man, he sold or bought she said, women's underclothes she said, and got a bit flabby about the arms, said she was what age, just like a woman, cover up her age with lies, always had to cover something, or her face was thick, or say, oh no, you'll tickle me. Vic Moriarty pressed up against his shirt. The hall was a quivering of ferns, the paper looped back, the reds and blues that Mrs Belper had pinned up, she had such taste, and now vibrated with the music, the red and blue festoons. Hagan's shirt let out a sigh. Vic was all right, but, he said. Was a good sort. Was…

What are you thinking about? she asked.

It wouldn't be good for baby, he said.

She giggled up into his face. She wanted to say some-thing, wanted to say, how I love you, Clem, how you love me, don't you, only of course that Everett girl going by, and anyway you knew, or did you, how much did you really know?

Old Furlow talking to Mrs Belper, did not take his eyes off the floor, pressed his hands upon sciatica. Hagan avoided Furlow. He made him feel uncomfortable, even if she had not told, and she can't have told, because all those weeks, and Furlow said, put the lambs in the lucerne or drench those wethers for worm, did not say as you expected what the devil, Hagan, look at him out of those froggy eyes, what's all this about that Sidney told me, well it was like this. Sidney Furlow, he said. Giving her a man's name, and a diamond bracelet, and diamonds in her hair, showing off all she'd got, and a bit more, looked at you as you went past, but wouldn't shrivel you up, and that was what made her feel sore, if you asked her to dance, if you asked...Hagan felt Vic Moriarty growing soggy in his arms, a lump. She stood by the door in that green dress, or silver, a sort of silver-green. She did not dance. Somebody talked about polo. Hagan felt a bit small. She made you feel small. But he wanted, he wanted, he wanted to go down to the basement and get a drink. The way that red mouth looked into his eyes.

Between dances the random remarks the breath recovered sifted gently where music had been and the band wiping its mouth that laugh coiling out whipped up and fell back exhausted as if it had taken fright at the paper shades gasped shall we go out or stand on steps that circle of children no more than faces inquiring or a whisper or a silence as feet crunch down the road into distance they are tuning up that long roll of a drum which says keeping a beat with a glove beat smells of camphor and hair escaping casually from control.

Alys Browne said that she would not come, had come, wished that she had not come, though come or stay was immaterial, was the same preoccupation. I shall not look, she said, in a certain direction in case, till all directions

280

became heavy with danger, a face detaching itself from its surroundings, just this and nothing more. How easy it was to say in the numbness of a moment, yes, you must go away, you must not come here any more, it will be simpler like this, until you go. All this time, she felt, I have been waiting for this one occasion to watch a face, and this only a few weeks, which are a fraction of what is going to be, and am I strong enough. Sitting at home, it is easy enough to say I am self-sufficient, to contradict the glass.

Her hand encountered the thorn on a rose. Looked down, she saw the drops, not under glass, and red, these had not dried up, dried by the kisses beyond glass, these were flowing fresh, and would heal without relic. There is no relic of pain unless you want it, place it in the personal reliquary, awaiting the admiration of the constant adorer, self. The drum beat, drop by drop. It flowed on. It flowed on. Till time will begin to flow on, will not congeal in permanence. Tell yourself this, she said, tell yourself the music is not so banal that it will not flow, washing of the blood, in blood. It lay upon her finger eyeing her.

Why, Alys, said Mrs Belper, you're spoiling that rose.

Yes? she said. It got crushed.

Watched the petals fall beneath somebody's feet.

Such a pretty rose, Mrs Furlow said. Doesn't the doctor look tired, poor man.

She spoke with the cruelty of innocence, Mrs Furlow on top of her wave. She bowed with the air of one, not stinting her benevolence, but conscious of its worth, while her hand wandered down her pearls, chaplet-wise, in gratitude for yet another social success.

281

Such fun, these country dances, she murmured to Mrs Belper. They always go with a swing.

Though Mrs Belper would understand, her cousin was secretary at Government House, would of course understand that a country dance was no more than a relaxation from the more ardent ritual of Mrs Furlow's life. Mrs Belper, in the glow of being patronized, would have understood anything.

The head began to ache that heard twelve o'clock issue dimly out of the darkness and the Protestant church. It was cooler by the door. Oliver Halliday wiped his forehead and watched nothing in particular. Marking time at the training camp, the drum, before the streamers fell down into the sea and Hilda's voice waved, said I don't think I'll go to the dance, Rodney has a cold, will keep warm in a thermos, in the dispensary, don't forget when you get back, when the War stopped in Paris, and going into that church was to feel suddenly complete, like touching a face in the dark, like...He shifted his feet. They grated on the floor. These are the feet, he heard, he said, the opportunities you have not taken, that turn under the pillow with the closed hand, as turning over you reject again, and think, is to reject, is to think, and then the heart starts out on a one-two at the dancing class with powder in his gloves, pink, pink, pinking over, or red. Red. She must not crumble that rose. He wanted to shout, Don't. He felt he would shout out something, and it would be that sensation of standing on your head in church, everyone thinking you mad, and you had to hold on to the pew to stop before you found it was a dream. He put up his hand to his head. He had to stop.

He had to put up his hand against the well of music that would tumble if...He felt weak about the knees.

Go outside, she said. Into the air.

I'm all right. .

Go outside.

She pushed her hand under his arm, and the stem of what had been a rose. She was leading him outside.

I thought we said...

Yes, she said. I know what we said.

He let her lead him, felt the relief of waking from a dream and reality cool upon his face.

I said it might be better if we didn't see. Until we go.

Yes. But come outside.

Mrs Ball said to Mrs Everett said to Mrs Schmidt the doctor doesn't look well and what's she doing well well leading him out she knows the way you can see it isn't the first time that somebody's opened the door.

The music swirled in gusts, or in the intervals between the dances, the conversation, right through the body of the building that bent before the passage of sound, jostled out of its tranquillity. Because the School of Arts was seldom used, had grown dusty and complaisant with neglect, dozed the year through in cold or heat, and felt the darkness rub up softly against its scabby face. It was old. Built after the store, it had a medallion with a date over its portico that stamped it with a greater sense of permanence than the weatherboard dwelling-houses had. But there was something ironical about that date, as if somebody had thought the building would last, and now it must make an effort without very much wanting to. Still, it enjoyed a sort of sleepy importance, even if seeming to doubt the virtue of permanence. It eyed the darkness yellowly and rumbled in the basement where the supper-tables were.

Amy Quong, polishing glasses with a cloth, watched Hagan getting his breath after a glass of beer. It was cool in the basement, the coolness of beer and ham and a concrete floor. Amy Quong's hands were cool in the belly of a moist glass that caught her small rounded face and pinched it capriciously out of shape. Her cheeks were flushed, across the brown, perhaps from the music, or perhaps from something else, though she liked to listen to the music and the feet sliding overhead. Her glance drifted over Hagan and back to her own reflection in the glass. When anyone spoke to her she started up. Her eyes rounded with surprise behind her spectacles, as if she were coming back out of her private thoughts.

Thought, flowing smoothly through Amy Quong, twisted Clem Hagan's lip. He felt better after the beer, though not altogether satisfied, still with that bitter disappointment beer leaves in the throat. He hitched up his trousers, because he wore a belt, couldn't stand anything but a belt, and his hand touched the surface of his wet shirt that had almost lost its shape. He frowned at the convention of a boiled shirt, at dressing up for what. And somebody wore diamonds. No wonder there was revolution, if only to rip the diamonds off a woman's throat. His hands felt rough. Vic said, who was a good sort, put your hands here, Clem, but did not want to think about Vic, getting a kick out of hands. He felt ashamed of his hands. Diamonds made you ashamed, and if you went up and said, you had a damn

284

good mind, you were just as good as diamonds, wouldn't she have a dance, just for old times' sake, yes, that was it, and she'd know, the way that whip stung, what you were smiling at. He trod a cigarette into the concrete floor. Miss Furlow, you'd say. What the hell was the use of waiting, and feel the sweat come on your hands, when you hadn't been killed this far there was no harm in trying again. The floor was undulating overhead.

They've put too much stuff on that floor, Mr Belper complained.

Standing on the edge, disconsolate, rather bilious about the eyes, it was the remark a man makes to comfort himself, not really meant for anyone else, not that anyone else would have bothered to reply. Mr Belper soothed the collar eating into his neck. He had an expression of bottled-up concern increased by his environment. All he could think was, what will Cissie say, that purple lace, without daring to linger on the subject of his wife's displeasure. Mr Belper hunched his shoulders, a man protecting himself from a cataclysm that nobody else could suffer. He had lost all desire to slap anyone's back. He went outside to make water in the dark.

It Couldn't be November, It Wouldn't be December, but Some-dhay panted with persistence from the saxophone, with the crushing optimism of a saxophone, moved the foot to measure not time but boredom traced in powder on the floor. Her foot, describing an F, had smudged the S. And Mother will talk to Mrs Saunders, and Mrs Lithgow, and Mrs Bligh. She took a mirror out of her bag, noticed with some bitterness the smudge that was her mouth, and slashed it into shape again. Three hours of watching a lot of louts enjoy themselves inclines the face to wilt. I look bloody, she remarked mentally. As if it were the result of being looked at by a lot of louts, who if they weren't louts would be worse, that mauling prerogative of men of your own class. Or someone else. The way he danced with that little tart in the blue tulle. Oh, God.

Sidney Furlow looked up quickly with a suspicion she had said something aloud. There was no indication, no quiver of Mrs Furlow's back. Her foot slid again, sighed along the floor, on the margin of the dance. The bracelet melted into her wrist. Who was Mallarmé, some old stick, to know better how you felt than you did yourself, or what did you feel exactly, only wanted to hit out, that day at a snake, or sink down against blue tulle, those hands, they were rough, catching in the tulle perhaps, to tear. Helen said it did hurt a bit. She pressed her foot against the floor. Encountered feet.

Will you, he said, how about?

His voice began to disintegrate, as it had that day, as if it were afraid, Hagan afraid.

She looked up into Hagan's face. She felt herself shrinking in. She felt herself shrinking right in, gathering herself to strike. And he stood there, foolishly, trying in spite of his voice to ask her to dance. She got up without speaking, looked over his shoulder, she could feel his breath on her neck as she accepted his arms.

Mrs Furlow smiled at Hagan. After all, she was conferring an honour, not Sidney but she. Then her smile slid away as her mind encountered Roger Kemble and that terrible afternoon.

They make a fine couple, Mrs Belper said.

Er, what was that? Mrs Furlow murmured faintly, though of course Mrs Belper did not mean, only a stray and rather vulgar remark, because poor Mrs Belper was slightly vulgar in spite of her cousin at Government House.

A waltz clung turgidly to the air, making Mrs Belper nod her head, heavy with the vague nostalgia of a waltz and the fumes of a late glass of beer. It was the sort of waltz that made you love a waltz, if you were that way inclined. It strayed outside where the darkness obstinately refused to produce a moon.

She was leading him anywhere, through the dust, he could feel his feet in the dust, and the peeled stem of a rose, and the fluctuating phrases of a waltz. He did not mind where she led him, was too tired, was dust, was waiting for this, to be led by Alys out of a dilemma, and all the unreal frustration that lies hidden in the banal phrasing of a waltz. Hilda loved a waltz. It made her talk about old times.

Where are we going, Alys?

I don't know, she said.

She did not know. It was dark, and sufficient in that. We are losing ourselves, she felt, if only we could succeed and lose ourselves sufficiently, but there are the windows still, and that facade and a street, but touching his arm I am proof against all these, against all those doubts that I haven't been able to avoid since we are going away, Alys, he said.

I'm all right now.

Rest, she said.

His hand was touching stone, or brick; he could feel the cement between the cracks, supported by Alys and a brick wall.

Do you think anyone noticed? he said.

Noticed what? There was nothing to see.

No, he said. I suppose, I suppose not.

Her voice convinced, soothed. He steadied himself against the wall. The darkness straightened, placid on his face, was without words. That waltz came out lurkingly, more potent because so banal, and made her feel, I must be careful of myself, this is not the same person listening to a waltz who decided how many weeks ago which was the way out. She heard words launched that approached inevitably, now approaching, now removed by the music. She felt a rushing of the darkness, stationary, then coming to grief on her face. To close the eyes was only to close the eyes on something without form, already she knew, even in choosing a last gesture of mechanical resistance she realized the futility of this.

What I told you, he said. We were going away. As if I could go away. I believed myself at the time, because I wanted to believe. It had to be true, because Hilda. But, Alys, it isn't, it isn't true, anything of what I said.

The words strung along Oliver's voice running together in her head.

Yes, she said, Oliver, it was true.

You don't think I could go away?

Yes, she said, I do.

His hands, touching brick, felt her voice that was bending, bending. As in that hall the lights bent, your head, you were trying to resist before something licked out and you were going the other way.

Listen, Alys, he said. We're not as strong as all that, we never shall be, it isn't worth the attempt. All my life I've tried to resist something just a little bit stronger, without getting anywhere at all. There's a kind of moral satisfaction attached to the effort to resist, at least we think, we make it so, it's got to be. Because we must have our illusions, drug ourselves, they're the one consolatory compensation for what we know to be the ideal state. So we fasten on to the moral satisfaction. Man the Moral Animal. And that's why I said Hilda and I are going away. Going away to what? What's a moral satisfaction?

This isn't what we agreed, she said.

Her fingers snapped the stem of a rose.

We'll leave out all that, he said. This is what I am. That's what I ought to be.

Because nobility, he felt, is one of those games played by Corneille on a stage set that has not the dimensions of Happy Valley.

Or perhaps, he said, it hurts to see what I am?

Because after all it was much easier to love someone for their imperfections than to discover these afterwards. Now she would not speak, was a point of silence in a distant waltz.

No, she said, and her voice came closer. You know it isn't that.

I think I know what it is.

And if we went away?

She wanted to speak of Hilda Halliday, whose voice

289

reproached opening a door, or in the street always a reproach, that child looking away when she touched his hands. The eyes would not close on Hilda Halliday. Her hair strayed untidily like the strands of a colourless waltz.

Voices were going up and down the street and uniting with bodies in the splash of light that the door had let fall upon the steps. Mr Furlow stood upon the steps smiling at no particular face, his smile half sleep and a glance backward into the hall where she danced, that dress, and a bracelet on Hagan's shoulder. She did not see him, but he was perfectly content. It was enough for Mr Furlow to have launched a casual bubble and to pat it airwards with an occasional glance. Mrs Furlow had very quickly imbued her husband with a reverence for other people's pleasures. And this was Sidney enjoying herself. The label was stuck on, and nobody, least of all Mr Furlow, dare attempt to scrape it off.

Sidney Furlow danced against Hagan, giving herself without grace, he could feel this indifference in his arms, or as his leg encountered the taut V of her thighs, and it made him uneasy, dancing with Sidney Furlow, because he was holding something that he did not quite understand. The collar began to grow soggy round his neck. He wondered if he ought to make a joke.

This is something like a dance, he said, feeling his resources fail in an opening remark.

I never cared much for dancing, she said.

And that was as far as you got, because one way or another she hit you over the face, and it stung, and you could feel her like a piece of wire, and that scent mounting

290

up and up, the number of unfair advantages women took. That night he walked past her room, and she stood against the blind, he had wanted to go in. Vic Moriarty over there looking as if she could kill. Damn Vic Moriarty, he said. His hand shifted on Sidney's back, cautiously exploring the skin. But you never got closer than a shadow on the blind that moved away, or tried to shift from under your hands as if it was taking a liberty to touch what anyone would think was an invitation, the way it was cut down. His hand was unperturbed in the hollow of her back.

Not dancing, Mrs Moriarty? Mrs Belper beamed. And what have you done with your husband to-night?

Vic Moriarty, torn between graciousness and distraction, twisted up her handkerchief.

Poor Ernest, Mrs Belper, he isn't feeling too bright, you know. So I left him at home with a book. Ernest's always happy with a book.

Looked over to where that girl, dressed like anyone could dress if they needn't remember the baker's bill or Chows coming in to dun, didn't have to put up with that, was dancing with Clem. Vic Moriarty in her blue tulle, the powder caking about her face, wilted on a brown varnished chair. She would, if she could, have given him a look, though she didn't want to monopolize, and what was a dance, but Clem, and he said, of course I love you, Vic, like that, it made you wonder if leaving the room he wasn't coming back again. Vic Moriarty's looks foundered on Hagan's face. It made you understand the papers, the woman they found with her mouth on the gas with perhaps a note from your broken-hearted Vic, only the smell of gas, and what was the use if you weren't there to see the effect of the note, if there was, if there wasn't, if he tore it up and said, Miss Furlow, how about the next dance. She looked at Amy Quong and frowned. You couldn't escape from Chows. It made you want to have a good cry, Chows and Happy Valley and Clem, and oh damn Ernest, enjoy yourself, he said, as if that was an easy thing. She got up and went to the ladies' room to see what was happening to her face.

Mrs Moriarty's gone, said Sidney.

She did not move her head from his shoulder. Her voice was level with his ear.

And why shouldn't Mrs Moriarty go?

She hummed a bar or two of the waltz. She felt a kind of exultation watching the retreat of blue tulle.

And why shouldn't Mrs Moriarty go?

I'd like to dance on and on. I'd like to die dancing, she said.

Her breath was sharp in his ear. They swung up on the peak of a waltz as he felt her grow softer, a little, the motion of her breasts. It made you wonder what was her game. You walked past a window and a shadow was peeling off its dress. He pressed his arm into her waist, that quivered, she was trembling, holding off. He bit the inside of his cheek.

She knew she was trembling, wanted to snatch away or press up, press all resistance out of the body that the motion of a waltz, and his breath, and the palm of his hand had decomposed. No, she wanted to say, stop, and the music, to put her finger on that nerve that jiggered in her cheek, that she could almost have laid against, and closed the eyes,

292

known the warm throb of a waltz touch with its hand the valley of her breasts that melted the spring at Kosciusko with the snow which showed the grass and she lay down before midday on the grass. Music faltered in a last sigh. She was almost stationary in the angle of a tightening arm, straightened against him, Hagan, who was only Hagan, she must remember it was Hagan.

He looked at her, smiling, at her eyes grown cold with composure that showed no vestige of smouldering. She stood there erect in the stream of disbanding dancers and said, almost between her teeth:

I think Mother looks as if she wants to go home.

These last moments the collected wraps the regrets stealing out furtively with a yawn as the piano lid falls touch a sort of depth that makes you walk past it is over and not glance back at figures dancing in retrospect in sleep that lamp hanging heavy and only asking for extinction says it is over it is over sighs the light at cock-crow.

If you're not afraid, Oliver said, we'll go a long way off. We'll leave all this. We'll go to America, he said. I'll settle what I've got on Hilda and the boys. Some people are only happy when they're safe. Hilda's like that. It's something I've never been able to give her, just that feeling that she wants. Now she'll be able to find it perhaps, for herself and the boys. It'll be better like that. Certainty.

So it was America then, as she sat with pamphlets on her knee, wondering if California.

No, Oliver, she said. I'm not afraid.

We shan't need much, you and I. And I couldn't touch anything that was Hilda's. I want to get right away.

293

To speak like this without reason, he felt, was to give way to some long-shelved desire that was too foolish to contemplate before, its distant probability, or because the consequences made you afraid. He did not think of consequences now. The future was America, not what you would do, not the carefully docketed plans of people living in houses. He did not want to think like this. He only wanted to get away.

We shall go when? she said.

It reassured him to feel himself taken for granted. But Alys was like this, coming to her house she had taken him for granted, waited for him to come again.

To-morrow, he said. To-morrow night.

She did not speak. She felt no quickening of emotion. It would be like this, she felt, all this time I have been waiting for the inevitable. It is part of what I have expected of Oliver and me. All the time we have been going to America.

It was no longer morning climbing the hill, no specific hour that the cock crew, or voices inquired going home, that trailed feet and the vestige of a streamer. Houses yawned out of the silence, the blank faces, the heavy eyes. The signpost pointed nowhere, not to Moorang, nor to Kambala, because in the half-light these had grown purposeless. A white balloon, fallen in the grass, rested on the dew.

23

It blew up cold for the second day of the races, the wind teetered through the grand-stand, and especially underneath, where beer lay in cold pools on the zinc top of the bar. It was the third year, somebody said, it always rained on the third year, and in 1928 Mitchell the bookmaker skidded on the—— We all know that, another said, and went out to look at the sky. It was terrible bad, a head shook, raining on the Saturday, raining special for the Cup. That big bastard Interview that they sent from Sydney, a ball-faced gelding, won a race at the Farm, they said belonged to a cove near Bombala, was stopping off at Moorang and Happy Valley to clean up a pool or two on the way home. So says you, says that stream of spittle plopping dustwards. Might've saved theirselves the trouble taking that bloody camel out of the train. Somebody said it would rain. And what did Arthur Quong think he was doing with that little colt, and young Stevie Everett up, already peeing his pants he was that afraid. Beer belched placidly or rumbled into surmise or grew glassy in a fixed stare. The fragment of a cigarette hung in tatters from a lip. They said the Handicap was pulled, Smith and Morefield between them, frigging about at the corner, you could see it plain with only your eyes, and that caution Morefield smiling all over his face at the scales, his mother was an old black gin up Walgett way, but that was by the by, and nobody said he couldn't ride, that of course when he wasn't fixed. Somebody looked out and said it had started to rain.

The crowd moved without design in the space behind the stand, shuffled on the torn cards and the spare grass, yellow still with summer, turned a yellow face to voices shouting the odds. The pulse of the crowd quickened. The throat dried. There is something desperately emotional in the voices of bookies shouting the odds, in a vein swollen above the collar stained by the week before. Chuffy Chambers stood with his mouth hanging loose. He felt his head swaying to the measure of a voice. He felt the first drop of rain run like a shiver down his skin. It was a shame, they said, a shame, raining for the Cup, and all the more shameful perhaps because no one could be held responsible. A clerk hunched his shoulders to the wind, wiped his nose with his left hand, and transferred the snot to his ledger with no degree of concern. It was 2 to 1 Wallaroo, even money Birthday. A voice tore and became a cough. Oswald Spink swore it wasn't worth the fare, for all the money you took in a joint like this, to catch your death in a mackintosh and shout out your guts for a couple of fivers and the fun.

The horses were going out for the second race when Vic Moriarty, not wearing the hat she had got for the Cup, the big straw that the rain might spoil, walked inside the turnstile with her eyes half-closed looking a little vague, because she had discovered just that morning it suited her to look a little vague. But it was too bad, the rain, and that big straw that drooped down, giving her face a frame, like the coloured supplement of the Empress Eugénie or someone she had seen. The rain and all, she felt bad, not sleeping a wink after that dance and the way Clem went on. Vic Moriarty played with the idea of what she would say to Clem. Oh, she would say, you, and go and have half a sovereign on Spider Boy or just inquire the odds, she wasn't sure, because she wanted to have a flutter on the Cup, but anyway she'd make someone look sick, only it was a pity she hadn't the straw, she looked quite elegant in a big straw, and Mrs Furlow looking over, there was a pity indeed.

The horses were going out for the second race, nervous and elastic against the rain. The little nervous snorts they gave as the jockeys caught them with their heels made you lean over the fence and hold on tight to your card. Vic Moriarty felt rather gay, high up on her heels and willowy at the waist, quite elegant in fact, in spite of her mackintosh and a felt. If only they had a band, like at Randwick where you walked up and down behind the stand and people said things about your dress, and sometimes if you were lucky someone was good enough for a dozen oysters and a glass of stout. But this was Happy Valley of course, and Ernest cranky at breakfast about that egg, as if you could know the history of an egg right the way from the hen, you said, or get inside and look, I like that, but nobody's going to spoil my day not about a bloody egg. A jockey glanced down. She smiled just enough, at her card. If only there was a band, there was nothing like a band for making, even Ernest, went to the park and he held your hand and said there was almost enough for the ring as they played Carmen, it was Sunday, and Ernest had had his hair cut the day before. That was the sort of thing that made you feel sorry for Ernest, but you couldn't spend your whole life feeling sorry and nothing else, because look what it landed you in, if only Daisy hadn't pushed, and those stamps, it made you laugh, going into Moorang to read a paper on stamps. You go along, Vic said, stop talking about that egg, everyone'll feel better when you get on to the stamps.

That was eleven o'clock. They had breakfast late. Because it's a Saturday, Vic said, yawning out of the bed. He was going into Moorang in the afternoon to read a paper in the evening to the Moorang and District Philatelists' Club. Ernest Moriarty on Perforations, it had come round on the circular. Though what anyone sees in a stamp, said Vic, spitting a mouthful of toothpaste froth into the toilet bowl. The bowl was festooned with roses, they were pink, the toilet set a present from Fred. Ernest broke his braces. Here give them to me, she said, what you'd do without me is something I'd like to know. Ernest stood in his underpants and watched her sew.

Ernest stood, no more than stand, his hands hung down, watched her hands irritated by a needle and thread. Vic, he wanted to say, Vic. He heard the postman knock again and letters on the hall linoleum, stooped again in the hall to pick them up, re-enacted what was painful many times. Then his braces snapped. Give them to me, she said. There were some bills and a circular. He put the other in an album in the sitting-room. He put it out of sight. Walking through the hall, the lozenges of light were yellow-green, pale and empty the linoleum squares where letters might not have fallen, only the rattle of the postman's footsteps, and he had put it in the album in the sitting-room. The thread wove in and out the ink, words that said without date or signature or compromise, I don't want to intrude, said ink, only there are some things somebody ought to know that everyone knows and Mr Moriarty it's like this your wife far be it that I want to intrude have you ever opened your eyes to see even if it is painful but then it always is for the good of the town and your position if nothing else that Hagan and your wife that Hagan and your wife will forgive me for wishing you well.

You do look a sight in those pants, said Vic. Here are your braces. Now you can put on your trousers and cover them up.

Thank you, he said. Thank you, Vic.

Now what's the matter with you? You're not going to have one of those attacks?

No, he said.

Because I don't want to have your pleasure spoiled. And you say you get some pleasure from stamps. I should think you'd better stay in there the night. There's no use busting yourself, she said, getting back God knows when. We've got to think of your health.

Yes, he said.

Brushing out her hair, Vic had dimples in her back, where the shoulder-blades met above the camisole. I want you to meet my wife, he said to Berenger, whom Vic did not like because he had a harelip, and Moriarty's wife they said, or Mrs Moriarty that clerk when they signed the register, she said, Ernest, can't I sign mine, I love writing my name. He felt bones, flesh, and a little breath, thought he would fall perhaps, though as if it had nothing to do with him, he had nothing to do with himself any more. He went back to the postman, to the floor, and going into the sitting-room. It was in that album, only he didn't want to look. Hagan said, leave her to me, as taking up her coat he held it out for Vic, holding the coat and Vic, poor Ernest, she said, I don't like to leave, only you know what it's like if you come in all this cold. Hagan said, Hagan said, Hagan said the pictures. Hagan said, your wife will forgive me for wishing you well. Ernest, putting on his trousers, bent down and looked at the floor, wished he could fall. But the effort was not his, he was doing this without effort, putting on the trousers was not his arm.

Gertie! called Vic, clucking her tongue. We haven't forgotten those eggs, even if you have. What I have to put up with, she said. It's a wonder I keep my patience at all.

He went into the sitting-room.

Ernest! she called. I'll put your pyjamas in the bag. You can take a room at the Crown. I didn't sleep a wink, she said, and I'm not going to lose to-night.

Gertie Ansell brought him an egg, sulking, she had not washed her eyes, and stove-black on her hands.

No, he said. No. I don't want the egg.

300

She looked at him in surprise. Then she went out of the room leaving the egg behind.

Ernest Moriarty sat staring at an egg. The letter said, forgive me Hagan for wishing you well said take your pyjamas said just another case of anonymous adultery tapping her knee and laughing at a joke. This was Vic then, or not Vic, could not be Vic. He wanted to say this is not you, Vic, that the letter said. He wanted to say this. He sat in the chair groping at no word that came heard her voice singing in the next room, and the rattle of a tray as she shifted it off the bed. When he said, Vic, I want to tell you, in Daisy's front room, all right, Ernest, she said, I know just how you feel, so just you take your time and he did not know what to say, when Vic held his hand, he could not see from his glasses, only Hagan and that gold tooth, and a smile, or Vic's smile that was Hagan's smile over on the music stool. Not this, he said, not this, taking up the spoon. He felt something come in his throat. He took up the spoon and beat the egg. It went chip chip chip chip, like that. Hagan laughed. Because it stank, the room was stinking like an egg.

Vic! he screamed. Vic!

She came tumbling into the room in her dressing-gown, it was half off, those big flowers, and her face looked a little afraid.

What on earth's bitten you now?

She began to frown, was no longer afraid, as she looked at him trembling in the chair. He knew he was trembling. He had no strength to say.

Well, she said, what a way to carry on! Anyone'd think

301

you didn't know there was such a thing as a phoney egg.

It stinks, he said.

He could feel the glasses tremble on his nose.

Would you like me to go and talk to the hen? It wasn't me that laid the egg.

She took it away then. Her dressing-gown opened up as she bent down and took up the egg. He wanted to put his head on the table and close his eyes, he wanted to stop his heart.

Ernest Moriarty sat in the sitting-room all the morning. It was Saturday.

I put your notes in the case, she said, poking in her head. Now you're not still sulking about that egg?

People started going down the street to the races, wearing their best clothes.

She put in her head and said:

Do you want any lunch before I go? There's a nice piece of cold pork. But you'll have to hurry up, she said. You don't want to miss that truck.

No, he said.

He sat there. He heard her heels going down the path. I am going to Moorang, he said, she said the key under the mat, and not to miss the truck. He got up, felt along the wall, because it was time, it was time to take the case, his notes and his pyjamas, she said.

Vic Moriarty hung over the fence and watched the horses sidle out. Voices picked the winner, invited to a drink, and little Bernard Schmidt dropped his toffee-apple in the mud. The poor kid and how he cried. His nose ran down his cheek. Sound swallowed up, ran along the fence to the grand-stand, or splintered into rain, the hissing of rain on canvas. The flag laboured on its pole. Vic Moriarty looked back over her shoulder, a ten-shilling note crumpled in her hand, and wondered if Spider Boy, if Hagan, stuck up there in the stand perhaps or holding an umbrella for someone to make a bet, the way some people can skite. But wait, she said, wait. She did not know for what exactly, and that was what made her sore, and the water coming through her shoes. The world was very unjust.

Over at the stalls Arthur Quong rubbed the hocks of the bay colt, his hands running brown and nervous along the skin that sensed his touch, he could feel the skin moving with his hands. What price Arthur's colt, they said. But Arthur smiled. The horse seemed fretful in what was not the brownish gloom of the stable at the back of Quongs' yard. He kicked at the earth floor with his hoof. He picked at Arthur's sleeve and worried it gently with his teeth. All right, all right, Arthur said, not exactly to the horse, as the sigh of the crowd following the second race, from the stand or the fence, penetrated through rain and stopped short at Arthur Quong. Like the children playing down the street, looking at Arthur and stopping short. Perhaps it was his eyes, those white circles, that enclosed not only the iris, but the whole secret being of Arthur Quong. The colt whinnied into the rain, where a kind of depreciating mumble announced the finish of the second race.

Mr Belper watched his economic assurance flutter with the fragments of two torn cards, Comeagain and Rosabelle, down from the stand. Though after all the second race was only the second race, was not the Cup, was Interview was still a cert. Mr Belper's first chin rested on the red flap of the one immediately below. His eye, no less bilious than the night before, fixed itself on the reminder of Come-again and Rosabelle, now lying in the mud. Mind you, Mr Belper often liked to say, punting at a country meeting, then allowing a pause for a change of key and the attention of his audience, punting at a country meeting, he would say, is nothing but a fool's game. This did not, however, prevent Mr Belper from playing the fool. He sat on the stand now and a sickly little tune came trickling out from between his teeth. Because what was a fiver here and there. Cissie said, you've got a liver, Joe, gave him something out of a glass. He wanted to think this. He went into Moorang and they talked about the Crisis as if it were some new kind of disease. Only the trouble was you couldn't take anything out of a glass. You said that Things Would Pick Up, or the Tide was on the Turn, or even Every Cloud, not that this was much of a comfort. The fact was that Mr Belper, in spite of his taste for generalization, those evenings at Moriartys' when he talked with gusto on natural resources and the canalization of energy, found that Brighter Slogans were no longer in his line. He sat and stuck out his lower lip. Joe, said his wife, you give me the creeps, we're All in the Same Boat, she said. But how well, or in which boat, was something Mrs Belper did not know. He had not mentioned Deucar Steel or Newcastle Incorporated Coal and Iron. It was this that made her husband poke out his lip and stare at the fragments of a bookie's card.

Hagan brushed past Mr Belper, that heap of troubled mackintosh, on his way downstairs. He did not stop to

304

speak to Belper, had seen that hat on its way down, and a face. Hagan hurried after a face. He would perhaps have called out, only in this case you couldn't, a bit of class. So instead he jostled, and what did he think he was at, they said, unimpressed by the contortions of a man trying to be recognized. A face turned in the rain. It looked past Hagan's head, resting casually not on Hagan, those eyes, looking for what in the rain. It made you want to swear. He bumped out of the crowd and went into the bar.

Walter Quong was giggling. He was already rather drunk.

Hello, Hagan, said Walter, quaking like a gin-something that he held in a yellow hand.

A double Scotch, Hagan said.

Then I said, said Walter Quong, it isn't far to the cemetery. Oh, she said, you're telling me. Nettles sting. It was the Sunday after they buried old Mrs Falconer. She was covered with dead flowers.

Walter sighed. There was a bubble on his mouth.

Hagan drank his whisky. It had the limp, watered flavour of the whisky you get in country bars, not worth spitting out even. He felt, like the whisky, kind of flat, clenched the glass that did not, would not break, splinter into the hand. He wanted to break her. She danced round, and you put your arm round her waist, she was that small, and bent back, the sort of face that came just a certain distance and said that Mother was going home. She looked past, you might have been air, or something she didn't want to touch, even if last night you could have sworn, against your face, and Mrs Moriarty's gone, she said. He had forgotten Vic, was whisky standing too long in the glass, was time to throw out and go sober, you wouldn't get drunk on vinegar.

Furlow's mare's in form, said the barman.

Furlow? he said. Not a chance.

He slammed down his glass.

Too full of tricks, he said.

She looked past his face in the rain. He wanted to lam that girl.

Arthur's won the Cup, said Walter Quong.

The Cup? said the barman. Listen to Walter. The Cup hasn't been run.

Walter's mouth plunged on a glass.

Oh well, he said, Arthur's going to win the Cup. She was covered with dead flowers.

Hagan was feeling wild. To listen to a randy, drunken Chow made you feel—white. He went outside.

Oh, said Vic Moriarty, it's you!

She sauntered over to Oswald Spink and began to inquire the odds. Because that will fix you, she said. And Sir Galahad, Mr Spink, she said, no, I'm not taken by the name. Looked back to see if Clem, if Clem had stood. She could feel the water soaking through her shoes. Didn't it make you cry, the races, when back turned said nothing, and you wanted to say you didn't mean it, really, Clem, whether the horses went out or stuck in the mud or what, because who cared if a horse. Vic Moriarty crumpled ten shillings in her hand. I've got to get hold of him, she said, listen, I'll say, honest, Clem, you don't know what it means, and he's going to Moorang, just to-night, because then I won't care any more. Vic Moriarty's face was crumbling under its beauty hints.

Even money Interview, they called.

The horses were going out. That glint is steel is eye turned is his first race Stevie Everett and shirt sticks to the skin the orange conjunction with green where the barrier stirs a nerve and Furlow's mare with all that weight treads mud said Interview the paper said balancing a cloud on flagpole feels his stirrups stretch to what depth to what underneath whether muscle or air or Quong's colt keeps the store the awful twisters these Chows in a country of possibilities and ideals at 2 or 5 to 1 the collar sticks on a lozenge from shouting from stretching the neck to see the starter's two-day importance lead into place a bridle when the balloon goes up.

They shuddered in a bunch against the barrier, then streamed out, that long trajectory of colour against an indifferent landscape, the muscle whipped by rain, by the sudden emotional compact of breath and wind. They urged into the wind and the flat, grey with trees. The colour broke fiercely on the grey. It whipped round the bend. The horses coiled back in a long elastic thread. You could hear their hoofs dulled by the mud. You could hear the approach of frantic breath. You could almost hear a flash of colour breaking through a clump of trees. And the crowd leant over the fence, drawing the horses on with their hands, so many puppets on so many strings, of which the jockeys, balled up on their saddles, had no ultimate control.

Arthur Quong held on to the fence. Upright, he did not breathe with the crowd, was something apart, or part

307

of the colt, could feel his muscles, touched in the stable, stretch out, watched that coloured bead move on the string and fuse with the one ahead. He felt the wind. Hoofs dealt mud on his face. Hoofs ebbed in a wave of sound. Interview was done, they said, with the mud, with the weight. They swirled out on the second round. Arthur Quong fixed his eyes ahead, felt a singing singing, as he waited, felt himself smiling, tapping his foot, as he waited, as he clung to the fence. He had stopped breathing. Because this was no longer Arthur Quong, was out there threading through the trees one green and orange bead. That colt of Arthur Quong's, they said, was leading, they said. Did not hear this, but the whinging of breath. They eased up slower along the landscape. He felt a kind of long lassitude, almost closed his eyes, if it were not for the motion of air that pressed open lids. The ears heard the approach. Stevie Everett's face was pale against the neck of a bay colt. Arthur Quong dropped his shoulders. The wind died.

A Chow! somebody shrugged. It's the day. No horse could carry weight in all that mud.

Mr Belper tore up two more tickets. Who would have thought that the Cup, that Arthur Quong...

Almost touched Vic Moriarty, Arthur leading in the winner, she looked up, saw the nostrils blown out pink, and a horse was going past, and vaguely she knew the Cup was over. She looked down, she had a ticket in her hands, Sir Galahad, she had asked for only so that she could turn, turned and was no one but backs closing. She let the ticket fall from her hands. I got to see him, she said. She pushed past Mrs Everett, who had a newspaper over her head because of the rain. She went round the corner of the stand by the urinal. She went along the line of stalls. I got to see him, she said. She heard her feet plopping in the mud. It went on jabbing in her head, one idea, I got to see, I don't care, but I got to see. He was standing at the back of the bookies' pitch lighting a cigarette.

Clem, she said. Clem. I've been looking for you everywhere.

I haven't been so many places, he said.

Don't get wild, Clem, she said. I didn't mean it.

Mean what?

Giving you the go-by like I did.

He caught in his breath. She was mauling his arm. Vic Moriarty making a scene, when as if he would have given a damn whether she thought what she thought he thought. He looked hard at his cigarette. A drop of rain became smoke on its point.

Did you? he said.

Yes, I thought.

Well, I didn't. Now let go my arm.

She wanted to cry.

Clem, she said, don't be hard.

Sidney Furlow walked past. Her hair was plastered at the sides against her face, that did not see, was cold eyes with the lids half dropped. He could have run after her, twisted her round, and said. He did not know what he would have said. He looked down.

Damn you, he said. Let go my arm.

She began to whimper, the rain on her lips. Sidney Furlow got into a car. He wanted to run, stop, stop, firing its exhaust. And Vic was holding on to his arm. God, what a sight. The car moved slowly out.

Now, he said, are you satisfied? Now that you've had your scene?

I didn't want to make a scene.

No, he said. You couldn't help yourself.

But last night, and to-day, I wanted to say, Clem, I had to, you'll tell me when it's finished, Clem, you won't walk out, you can't.

Words in a whimper made her lips swell plumped out face and wet in the cracks. A mouth said Mrs Moriarty's gone. He wanted to press on a mouth his mouth not this plumped out for a song.

Ernest's gone to Moorang, she said.

She watched him, anxious to suggest, or seize the expression in his eyes. Her voice halted for this.

We can't stand here like a couple of fools. You'd better do something about your face.

His voice at least was flat.

But Ernest, she said. You will, Clem?

She stood and waited.

Yes, he said. We'll see.

Would go perhaps because nowhere else, and you could not wring a neck that wasn't there to wring, and Vic what a sight was still nothing wrong, if only he got that out of his head and could not feel her dance.

The crowd, its stare glazed, its emotions spent, trampled cards underfoot, the Cup was run, the day without expectation after this. They wandered without much purpose waiting for another race. It was over, or as good

310

as over. Thought hung limp like a flag on its pole. It was over for another year, they said, all that had happened and that had not happened, the money lost and the hat worn. But they waited without animation, for some last-minute frenzy perhaps, for some sign that it wasn't time to go home. Because going home is acceptance of the ultimate defeat.

I took my girl to the races, sang Walter Quong.

He was lurching about behind the stand, trying to catch the rain.

24

Being alone made her feel a bit afraid. That zooming of a moth over-life-size on the wall, or two moths, shadow and substance, had also the implication of dead things, a moth or a bird, that she could not bear to touch. When Tiny died she could not touch him, lying in a shawl, though I love all dogs, she said, and when you think of the affection of a dog, but before it goes stiff of course. Ernest took Tiny by the hind-leg, she cried to see her poor pet, he was almost a whippet, hang stiff like a flying fox, in the Museum with Ernest, who said that the flying fox was a curse, with the rabbit, the prickly pear, and the briar, and none of them aboriginal except the flying fox perhaps. Though Ernest liked Tiny. Oh dear, my poor Tiny, she said, I wish we could have had a child, because Tiny dead makes you feel there is nothing else left. Ernest said yes. He shuffled in his slippers and coughed. She had embroidered slippers from a pattern, two pairs, but the first hadn't come off, so it shows my industry, she said, that I didn't give in on one. Ernest called it application.

He had forgotten to take his slippers to Moorang, they lay under a chair, she saw, because Gertie had forgotten to move, Gertie always forgot. It made her sort of guilty looking at the slippers. She looked away. She thought of a flying fox. They hung upside down from the fruit-trees, or brushed through trees, and squealed. The zooming of a moth made her twist her hands. If he comes as he said, she said, I shall hear him coming up the path, if he comes. The slippers made her feel guilty. She took them from under the chair and threw them into a cupboard, where they made a softish thud. Perhaps I'm fonder of Ernest, she felt, hearing the slippers thud, fonder than I, at least after standing in the rain, and you couldn't move his arm, only touch his arm, and that was what Ernest would not understand, what made you want to hold on to Clem, when he touched you in the bed. That's lust, Ernest would have said, all right, she said, it's lust that makes you wait for feet coming up the path. Like the Bible, and Daisy giggled at the curate reading the lesson, that big brass eagle standing on balls, and she said at the bazaar the ice-cream slipped down her throat when he touched. She wished she had lit the fire.

Vic sat twisting her hands. There would be a frost, an injustice when you woke up, alone, or perhaps Clem would stay. A moth hitting the wall made her shudder into herself. She had to think of that flying fox. Or a bat, they said, landing on your hair, made you bald. She picked a leaf off the cyclamen. It was withered, brown, it rustled in her

313

hand. She used to play a piece called Autumn Leaves when she was at Marrickville, a descriptive piece she bought in a music pavilion at the Show, that she played with feeling, and Daisy said it made you feel the autumn leaves, it made you sad. But the cyclamen sat up straight with sap, its pink ears shivering, the way that plant behaved. She saw her face in the bowl. She patted her hair, her perm not quite, and Clem you could see by the way he looked, but what could you expect in the rain. And that girl.

Vic Moriarty clenched her hands. She went and leant against the mantelpiece, pressing herself against the mantelpiece, where glass was cold on her forehead. It was Ernest's clock. Go on, she said, go on, tick tick, I can't help it, she said, you egg, tick tick. The way there are certain things that open wounds, any wounds, such a thing was Ernest's clock. She saw that girl get into the car, as if she could help notice when the number-plate drove off and he said, all right, we'll see, relaxed. You might be a bundle waiting, without feeling, for the train. On her hands her face was hot.

When he came he threw down his hat. It stirred her up to hear the hat.

Coming to your funeral, I suppose, she said.

That's right, he said. Without the flowers.

He began to kick the fender with his toe. Some soot fell down the chimney, on to the paper fan in the grate where Gertie should have lit the fire.

You're doing me an honour, she said, having it in my house.

Oh dry up, Vic.

Or perhaps you're having two.

He looked at her. His eyes made her cold.

Hagan kicked the fender with his foot, wanted to kick through or take with his hands, the way you pressed a sheep and the bleat came out, those white lashes on their eyes. Killing a sheep, or time with Vic, was the same, a bleat. And you killed a sheep, it meant nothing, or chops for breakfast, or...Why the hell couldn't she stand still? She was talking about the Last Time, even if it was this she said. It was something he had heard before.

Even if you hate me, she said, you'll always know I love you, Clem.

She fiddled about with the tablecloth. Her voice came out in lumps.

Well, we'll let that be understood, he said. You needn't rub it in.

Even when She, she said.

Who?

He shouted her pale, and looking like that.

No one.

Her voice fell in a whimper on the tablecloth, was plush.

Then he went and took her, she felt limp, it made him feel wild, wanted to shake, or kiss, was kissing a limp mass.

All right, he said. If it's what you want.

His voice came against her teeth.

In the other room the candle flame was long on the wall the wax fell in slender silence, lay whitening in pools. He lay on the bed, his head against his arm, after a fashion satisfied. She smoothed his forehead, moist, with her hand.

315

But he did not want to open his eyes and see Vic Moriarty, white and passive like a pool of wax. As if the flame had burnt down. She was a flame that danced with her face against his cheek. You could not touch, put out a hand but could not touch. Or stop as the car moved out, was steel and touching steel was cold, resistant. It made you hot and cold to think, so you closed your eyes, felt the hand of Vic Moriarty, of no one else.

It bewildered Hagan to think. It was a fresh experience. Sidney was a hard name. He resented his bewilderment.

Out of this silence that was like lying with a dead body by candlelight, Vic heard her breath rise, no more. She was not afraid now, even if not being alone was almost like being alone, the way he lay. But her arms were warm, her eyes rested that glanced along the line of his shoulder and closed upon his neck. What was this before her sleep fell and a key rattled she did not know her flying fox that she wrapped up in a shawl that night Ernest took the stick and said I'll go out to turn off the tap in the frost he took the shawl but not that no is covered up not to see it isn't what you think the light on leaves is not the pedal Daisy that he pressed was dead it feels funny like a leaf is being dead is the frost on the tap oh cold all right you think no pity in a voice said she had on had on diamond when the dog barked only turning off a tap but not in a shawl is dead Ernest only not to look at its face you see Ernest turn back the shawl it's cold looking at your face Vic he said is dead.

Her voice stumbled out of sleep.

Clem, she said. Clem.

He stirred.

316

It was a dream, Clem. It was queer.

She sat up and saw herself touching her face in the glass.

You're a caution, he said.

The bed grumbled when he moved. He felt hungry. He yawned. Going up north, the night train, there were frankfurters at Werris Creek with the girl sleepy against the bar, and she rubbed her eyes, and the steam told you how hungry you were, not girls, not Vic or any other bit. But his jaw tightened all the same. He got up sharply off the bed and began to put on his shirt.

She looked at him standing in his shirt. She began to feel bitter again.

You're going? she said.

It looks like that.

She wanted to talk, she wanted to talk about anything, because that furniture was one long creak, the leg of his trousers made the shadow bend.

I knew a girl called Edna Riley, she said.

She wasn't quite sure of her voice. She had to speak.

Why Edna Riley? he said.

Oh, I dunno. She just came into me head. And you would have liked her, Clem. Edna was a good sort. She was clever too. She'd passed a lot of exams and things. She wanted to be a stenographer. When her father died she was going out with a man I knew called Lassiter, insurance I think he was. But Edna, that was what reminded me, Edna had a book on dreams. Got it at the circus, I think she said. There was a woman with a handkerchief over her eyes that read your thoughts and things. And dreams were a sort of side-line, see? And Edna bought the book. And you worked it like, suppose you dreamt of a black horse, well you looked it up and it told you what it meant, a journey or whatever it was.

She had to talk. She couldn't stop. Her voice fluttered in the candle flame.

And what about Edna? Hagan said.

He was tying his tie. He had a scarf-pin once, that he lost, with an artificial pearl.

Edna? she said.

Her mind bumped round. She had to speak. A dream made you feel queer, like looking at your face in a mirror when you turned back that shawl.

Don't go, Clem, she said Not yet.

Her voice rose, flickered, on a candle flame. Edna and all, it made him laugh.

And what happened to Lassiter? he said.

God, how it made him laugh.

Then it began to go round. They heard it going round and round. They heard it one two, or drag and stop, or hit against the skirting-board, as it went round, in the sitting-room. It was a noise, a foot noise. The feet went round and round the sitting-room.

25

Rodney Halliday trailed about in the yard. There were a few stars, and the suggestion of a clothes-line, the smoke went up from the roof. He felt a bit alone, for it does increase your sense of isolation watching smoke go up at night. Smoke by day has substance in comparison. Rodney stood watching the smoke. He knew that some day he would die. He had not realized this before. Poor Mrs Worthington's dead, said Mother, we must write to the girls, we must wire for flowers, a sheaf I think because wreaths are like a funeral. The Worthington girls in black, and Mother put her hand to her chest, and they were eating eggs and bacon, it was breakfast time, you went on eating in spite of death. Death was in the cemetery with a smell of laurels and those crossed hands on Mr Peabody's grave. It happened somewhere else perhaps, but death reverted to the cemetery, enclosed by ivy, the gate grated on a rusty hinge. Going down the hill ivy droned. You went on down the hill to school and hoped you would not meet Andy Everett. Effie Worthington had chapped hands. She gave you a gingerbread cake at the farm, and you bit in, it was sticky inside, and a glass of milk afterwards. But death was not here, in the hen-cluck, in the blue shadow of milk on the glass. You would die, but not yet, not yet. The gingerbread.

You knew you would die, and you did not know, it was like that. The smoke wreathed up against a star. You stopped breathing because it suddenly caught you, death. You knew what it meant in the yard, in the dark. You wanted to run away.

Rodney Halliday stood still. This moment when death assumes a personal bearing, no longer the Worthington girls in black, is a moment of significance. It was perhaps the first significant moment in Rodney Halliday's life. Over against his fear, a sense of importance. Fixed upon this sheet of black, like a star, in his own distinct circumference, his life, till the intervention of death. He was himself. Oliver, Hilda, and George, the idea of corporate safety, were no longer this, were distinct too. The safety line is broken by the consciousness of death.

Growing up then was like this. You were ten. The moments crept, with a scent of apples at eleven o'clock, was always another eleven o'clock, or the afternoon asleep in the sun, incident loomed large in the sun detached from its shadow, there was no skirting round this forest of incident and its solid, waiting forms. This before you knew. Then time began to race down an avenue cold with stars. You wanted to put up your hands. He wanted to go and tell

Margaret Quong, tell her what. Because this was something you could not tell. It happened. You knew it. That was all. Like a scent or sound, you could not tell. Or Mother crying in her room, you went in, you went away, knowing. And She said stay, waiting on the steps of the verandah with cool hands. Father stood in a corner of the dining-room, where is Mother, Rodney, he said. You looked away. Went to the window and knocked out his pipe upon the sill. You looked away. Mother closed her door when you went past, closing her door on what you knew was not changing her dress. He took it up to the post to send to Mrs Worthington, the parcel post, because Mrs Worthington is poor, she said, and an old dress, is dead. She was wearing mauve. A car came up the road out of the direction of Moorang, he could see its lights, with the unimportance of lights on a passing car. I shall grow up, I shall go to Sydney, he felt, I shall do things, I don't know what, until. The night was very large and black. Father stooped in the dispensary, his shadow stooped, would have said, what are you doing, Rodney, if he knew, but you did not know what to say to Father, or words just came out. Father sometimes made you afraid. Father would die, the shadow on the window wiped out.

Rodney went inside. He did not know what he would do. He wanted to go to the dispensary and say, Father, I want to sit in here for a while. He felt his way along the passage to the door. He stood at the door and waited. He did not know what he would do.

Oliver opened the door and stood there looking out.

Is that you, Rodney? he said. I thought you were in bed.

No, he said. Not yet.

They stood there looking at each other, or not looking. Rodney wondered how he could say what after all you couldn't say.

It's late, said Father. You ought to be.

Yes, he said.

Standing there in the passage, could not stay, or stand, because Father would not understand.

Yes, he said. I thought I'd say good-night.

Father's kiss was rough, like tweed, the suit you touched and wanted to stay, say you knew out there in the yard. But tweed was no longer protection after this. You went down the passage biting your lip, it was a long way from the lamplight and Father closing the door.

Oliver went into the middle of the room. He stood with his head bent, wondered, what was I doing before, he asked. The drawers were open on his activity, the papers scattered, and the diary with the pages torn, he held the pages of a diary in his hand. Then Rodney came to the door. Good night, Father, he said. Tearing pages from a diary, the lamp caught the leaves, grew brown, months, weeks, coiling into smoke, this was the past, as if contained in the pages of a diary and easily destroyed. Then Rodney came to the door. Rodney was also the past. This is all going, Oliver said. He tore up a bundle of papers. He slammed a drawer. It went to savagely, with half its contents hanging out. The way you clung on to papers for no reason, or old emotions, cluttered yourself up with these and had not the courage to clear them out. Well, he said, this is the clearance now, now I can start to breathe, now I am standing before the future, there is no reason for the past. Rodney is also the past. There is no reason, he said. There is no reason. His face halted in the glass. If you could see your conscience, he wondered, what form would it take? That smooth, stethoscopic Jesuit. He began to laugh. He found himself thinking of broad beans.

Round the walls the photographs, their expressions growing mat and yellow underneath the glass, stared with their customary stare, the always-with-you look of old family photographs. This was one evening in many, except for the litter on the floor and a certain emotional disorder perhaps. It might have happened any time, on any evening just as this, packing the bag before a case and going out. He would only take a bag. He didn't want anything else, nothing connected with leaves lying brown against the fender, these belonged to somebody else. He was washing his hands at the basin. He saw hands fold round each other, unfold. It was like this. The hands. He saw the water, the soap, and the towel hanging on the rail. Then his hands fumbled in the towel, he must go, he felt, at once, quickly. The photographs stared down with a sort of faded surprise. He was moving in jerks, must go, must get outside before the mechanism broke. The spring strained that controlled the mechanical washing of hands.

In the hall he tore the tab of his overcoat. The house was quiet. Looked down stupidly at the coat, the torn tab, at Hilda saying, Oliver, you can't go about with your clothes like that, would say that people would wonder how, would Hilda look a needle say. Because Hilda was conscience, that dark phrase in undertone when Rodney came to the door, recurred, till you wanted to put your head on your hand, lean forward with the weight and pray for the strings to lift up the head, it was by Sibelius, Birkett said, you waited for the strings, for some clarity of tone, not this phrase that ebbed, your whole being flowed backwards into the past, into the throats and the far baying of the horns. Then you saw the programme creak against the floorboards, escape in one flutter, when you had not the power, or the careless sweep of paper, even when the chairs moved, were still there, locked in a past moment that withstood hands and the flowers. But this was music, was ten years that the mind dragged back. This, he said, is dead. Heavy with his coat he opened the door, saw the stars, there was frost upon the step. It was more than opening the door. He did not think back. The frost was brittle underfoot.

Rodney, lying in bed, heard Oliver go. It was like any other night, a case, and Father going out, you heard the car start from the garage after the scrape of the garage door. Mother moved in her room and coughed. But he had to sit up in bed, he had to sit up in the dark, as if it would do any good, because sitting up was dark. Somewhere water dripped on zinc. It was no dream this, that Mother's hand smoothed sitting on the bed when you woke up, whether Father took the car or not, was still a long way off. He had never felt like this. Slipping away, slipping away, the foot met more than darkness drawn from the sheets as it moved, the blur burr of a car, then breath.

Waiting, waiting for what, Happy Valley waiting in the dark, is the question without answer. There is no collaboration between human curiosity and the attitude of inanimate things, least of all in the dark, when the answer to the question in the dark might prove a momentary, if not the

324

ultimate solution. So there is no choice but to fall asleep, as Rodney Halliday falls asleep, crumpled up against the wall. There is always this advantage in sleep, you cannot feel you are cheated, until of course the moment of waking, and that is a long way off. So Rodney Halliday sleeps, and his face is once more ten years old. So Walter Quong stirs in the grass at the side of the road and his world is non-dimensional, escaping the nettle's touch. His dream is unimportant, except as a dream.

Alys Browne sat with her bag in the sitting-room. She waited. She heard the car coming up the hill. All this that I am leaving, she felt, has fulfilled its importance, there is no sorrow attached to discarding objects that are no longer necessary, it is right that I should touch nothing, that I should simply walk out. She thought a bit about Mrs Stopford-Champernowne, the wind blew through the grass in the Park, and on Sunday afternoon the Salvation Army played, she thought a bit about the convent and the face of Sister Mary and over the wall the violet sparks from trams, all this was a dream, she felt, and Hilda Halliday. Then her mind stopped short. She got up. She wanted to walk about. It is wrong to dream, she said, Oliver is reality. She found herself clenching her hands. I want to live, she said, I have a right to this as much as Hilda Halliday, I shall not be possessed by this half-life, this dream, or is it a dream, or is it a dream, or is Oliver a dream. Oliver is coming up the hill. We are going away somewhere, only somewhere, there are no labels, and here we shall live. This is right.

Alys, Oliver said, it was his voice outside.

It was right, his voice said, as she turned down the

lamp, turned it right down, and it was dark, she could see no longer the Alys Browne, part of books and pictures accumulated in a room, an apology for life, or the lack of it. Happy Valley is asleep, she felt, I am no longer part of Happy Valley, this poor dream, this substitute for reality.

Alys? Oliver called.

Yes, she said. I'm coming.

She stood alone in the darkened room, the shreds of past emotions slipping away. There is nothing I regret, she said, there is nothing I, not even Hilda Halliday. These are part of sleep.

26

They heard it going round and round. Two figures detached by fear were large in candlelight. There was no connection now between Hagan and Vic, for the moment not even the connection of a voice. Fear was a personal preoccupation. While feet trailed round the sitting-room.

Hagan felt his heart bump, then go on its normal way. It made him snort. It wasn't as if you were afraid, it wasn't that that gave you a bit of a start to hear. It made him angry to think anyone thought him afraid.

How do you like that? he said, and his voice came with a snort. That's old Who's-this back. Makes a cove look funny, he said.

Vic sat on the bed. She did not speak. The sheet streamed floorwards from her breasts. She held it to her breasts, that escaped, hung yellow and static in the candlelight. He was speaking what she did not hear, she felt, she heard the feet.

Well, I guess I'll push off, Hagan said.

Felt a fool skulking out, though your pants were on, it might have been worse meeting someone in your shirt. He stood in the passage, waiting. His hat. The sitting-room door was an enamel knob. He waited for the knob. He heard the feet. There was no sign. He wasn't one to look for trouble out in the middle of the road. So he took up his hat. He went down the passage away from the door, almost on his toes. It was easier to breathe in the yard, easier in the lane, where your eyes still waited for the turning of a knob. He began to whistle softly. It was company. A waltz something, that you didn't mind if Sidney Furlow, you were satisfied, it almost mightn't have been Vic, she said, Mrs Moriarty gone, and good night, Sidney, you said. She lay on the bed in a funk. Though it gave you the creeps, Moriarty in that room, like a circus horse on the track, or a broken-down cab-horse with gammy knees plodding along William Street, and if that knob had turned you would have said what. Christ, he said, Christ. His breath whistled through his teeth. Not that you were afraid, or anything like that. A white blur was no knob, was moving up the dark, was what.

Who's that? he said, his voice hollow in the lane.

His eyes fixed upon a white blur that would not take more definite shape. He stopped against the fence.

Eh? said the blur. It's me.

Then that loony Chambers lumbering up the lane. Hagan saw his face drift past, or the white suggestion of a face. Said his name was Chuffy Chambers, the bulging eye, and they let it go round loose. It made him swear as he went on down the lane.

Chuffy Chambers, lumbering in the dark, felt his skin tingle at a voice. Sometimes he could not sleep at night, he wandered up and down, his feet were soft in the nettles that grew at the side of the road. Hagan, he said it over, rough against his tongue. He could feel himself beginning to shake, with Hagan, with a name mouthed, and holding on to the fence the light at Moriartys' danced. He felt he must spit out a name that, winding round his tongue, stuck. He must get it out. It trickled down his chin. Then he began to feel better, purified in a way. The stars flowed back. He used to lie on the verandah, when it was summer of course, and count the stars, but he never counted very far.

Chuffy Chambers meandered along the lane, like a name meandering in his head, though only the shape of a name, no emotion now attached. He heard the call of a cat, raucous with love, saw the black pool that was cat elongate and press itself through a hole in Moriartys' fence. The call echoed frostily. It pierced through the skin with a little shiver, reaching out to touch Ernest Moriarty's back stooped in the sitting-room. He heard the cry of the cat. He straightened up. He stared at the pattern of familiar objects that were only just there, for the first time taking shape, knew all these again, though different. They pressed down like the pressure of a clock, he had heard, heard, in the pace of feet walking, were his feet, stopped. He knew he had been walking round the room, but why, but why, and why the clock. Then he remembered the hat. His mind pitched back. He was calm enough. Even if the hat.

She said, you'll take your pyjamas, and the Crown, you'll wear your pyjamas, the egg, she said, and of course it must rain because of my straw hat. But going into Moorang you forgot that this was Vic, or a straw hat, or the rain, was a pain in your chest that truck that jolted over the ruts, and your head swam past telephone poles, or wires in loops of telephones that said the voice anonymous. It was in the album, now perhaps, pressed against Senegal, only you did not look, see the lamp you lit when the match broke. He could not remember lighting the lamp. You will read a paper on stamps, they said, in the circular, and that was why in Moorang, in the main street, would read a paper on stamps, afterwards coffee, with a discussion, that this must be remembered or written down in a book with an imposition from Arthur Ball when the ink fell on the floor. But not Vic. Ink fell on a name, obliterated a face. Then he was going round and round, he felt he had been going round and round, his head or his feet, of which there was no trace on the carpet when looking, only where the coffee fell, but someone had been walking where there was no track. Or sign. No hat in the hall. All those faces at the school waited for a talk on stamps, and that was why you were there, the moustache and the twitching eye, or Miss Porter who would pour out coffee that did not fall, like ink, like not in school, because this was not the school, because Miss Porter said the advance of history commemorated by the philatelist by a cup of coffee or a stamp, take care Mr Moriarty, she said, a cup of coffee will pick you up if you fall, it's tiring to read a paper, she said.

Ernest Moriarty felt the room sway. It did not hit him on the head. He parried the ceiling with his hand. It settled down like the pressure of misery, like a cat calling in the

330

dark, the deep swell of pent-up misery. I am here, he said, not Moorang, I have come why, because there is no longer a paper to be read, all this is over, like so much. You could feel it crumble as if a drink, and sitting in at Moorang having a drink, you would not stay, Miss Porter, you said, because Vic says I must go to the Crown, and that is the state of affairs, to have a drink, to feel a chair crumble and the shape of table in a glass of port, though not port said Vic, she said, you know, Ernest, how your chest, even at Christmas-time when Uncle Herbert sent what he would not have sent if they hadn't given him commission on a bottle or two of port, but drink, Ernest, it's only for your good that I say, the barman said it was fine old tawny, his wife was expecting, and sitting in at Moorang the face dissolved that expected nothing much.

The lamp had a milky china shade. It was an Aladdin lamp in the catalogue. He felt bad. He felt bad in at Moorang drinking fine old tawny port. His chest was a ravine of pain, the breath rare and hot that struggled up, he could not get up far enough, he could not drag a weight. And the voices, they went on, the voices in a bar, the random voices that said, that commercial in a check suit, the mechanic who had lost his mother the week before, said he was strung up and it bloody well served him right, because her head was beaten in, and it must have been a hammer, they thought, anyway she didn't last long, not after the doctor came, and they caught him in the train near Scone, it was his second wife, she had a little money put by, she once had a pub in Singleton, anyway the bloke was strung up, took what was coming as cool as if, and it wasn't as if there was reason for what he done, but then if you read the papers you often wondered what entered people's heads, there wasn't reason for much. Cripes, said the barman, you're looking off, he said. Then they turned, the random faces in bars. The looped wires of telephones said, the voice said, anonymously, I don't want to intrude because Hagan is expecting your wife, so let's go, Ernest, let go, let go of my hand, it's only the port and you see it's like this, my chest and to-morrow geography, must go. They put him on the floor and shot water on his face. I'll be better, he said, I'll be getting home, I'll be getting back to Happy Valley, somehow this, even at night, before the water soak, I had no business drinking port, even at Christmas it doesn't do. Collins was starting for Happy Valley, they said, out in the garage now, would a lift, would do, the barman said. He still felt queer, his chest. But he had to go home, had promised this. He left his pyjamas at the Crown.

All his life Ernest Moriarty had been going round and round, the small circles of habit, that yet was not as satisfactory as going round and round in a room, not so comfortingly blank. All your life you had been going round in circles for a purpose, at least you thought, you did not know it was non-existent. Now you had come to a stop, the purpose gone. He felt that coming home in Collins's truck. The wind was black. He felt it was all over, only a few straws of habit clung, you could not shake them off, like coming home, like opening the gate, like wiping your boots on the mat. He put his key in the lock, heard it rattle, wondered what he was waiting for. The frost. He went round to turn off the water-tap. The time the wash-house tap burst there was no end of a mess, and it's washing day, said Vic, it's a pity you're not a plumber, Ernest, she said. It was a pity he wasn't what he wasn't. But there was no reason for him to be—well, anything, or what was the reason for anything when he hit her on the head. Or a hat in the hall, or a light. He went into the sitting-room. It all shelved away, and there was no reason for a lamp to walk round, round, breaking a match to find how frail, and so many more in the box, thirty or forty perhaps, as frail as a match.

He looked down at the fragments of a broken match. He looked at the lamp. He stood in the fragments of thought that the evening had strewn round, and momentary anaesthesia wrapped soothingly in black. Before it had returned, the room, that was also Vic, and not Vic, had slipped into the next room and there was...The breath rose in his chest. He could not breathe, move, heard the door, the footsteps, the rattle of his own breath. He could only stand in the sitting-room, where her hand trimmed a leaf, she said, there's something saucy about this plant, they say you've got to keep it moist, though God, I'm tired of this suite, I'm tired, I'm tired, when I used to care for pink, but look at the spots, and the hole that Belper burnt, and why've we got to stay here all our lives, it makes me feel like suicide, only nobody would care. Vic's life in a room was this, was pink, her hand touched, tied a bow. We're making this, you said, it's us, and I'm glad, Vic, you said, because... The cyclamen looked a waxen pink. The petals fluttered in his breath, that came fast, were without defence. His legs began to move.

He began to go into the other room. It was no longer

the bedroom, this, it was the other room. Two separate worlds. I've got to go in, he said. He could feel the sweat on his chest. It ran down cold. It was a long way, and the silence, and the sounds that break through silence made it longer still. But he opened the door, he stood, she watched him stand, there was only the silence between them, and the candlelight.

She could not speak. There was nothing to say now. She sat on the bed still, as if Hagan had only gone and fear had arrested a sheet in its passage to the floor. She thought, if Fred, if Daisy, if Clem going down the street perhaps for the last time, and the time that Tiny died she cried the dream she had with Ernest's face the shawl. This made her hand stir, touch her skin, she was naked, sitting there, with Ernest in the doorway, and his face, and his face.

Ernest, she said, and it came out as if her tongue was sticking to the word, afraid to release it on a doubtful errand, let it go out towards a face that was not Ernest's face.

Waiting for the moment that would break the tension, it must come soon, or something break, Vic Moriarty pressed back against the wall and Ernest Moriarty standing at the door watched each other crumble away, the face known, the personality, all eliminated except the basic flesh and bone and the passions that actuated these. And that is what made her afraid. Because this was not Ernest here, the face altered in line by the passing of a few hours. She began to make little convulsive gestures with her arms against the wall. The shadow followed laboriously.

What are you standing, why don't you move? she said.

His face looked blue. Her voice stopped, thickening with fear.

All right, she rasped. All right then, we know, she rasped.

The shadows bent down. Perhaps it was the shadow on his face that she could not properly see, was not the expression that she thought.

Ernest, she said, Ernest, wailed against the wall, beat back her voice into her mouth, her fear. If only you'll listen, she said, I'll tell you. Ernest, it was like this.

He stood there. Her mouth froze.

Then she watched him coming forward. His arms were stiff. He was coming forward. She could look into his eyes. Oh God, then it was this that you did not like to think, or dream, as you lay on a bed and felt his breath coming hot, his hands.

No, not this, Ernest, she screamed. I didn't. No. I'll tell. But not this.

He got her up against the wall, felt her quiver, her body afraid that lay on the bed, they said the letter said, if only he had the breath to press, as looking into an eye it came up close, it swam, it flowed, and light delved down, he must press down with all his might, and they caught him in the train, and they strung him up, with the loops of telephone wire cutting right into the throat, snapped.

There was no sound in her throat, as if words had solidified, had stuck. Her hair hung floorwards. She drooped. This thing on the bed. He looked at it through the blur of his almost exhausted breath. Then it slipped down, the hair drifting and the sheet, it fell lumped upon the floor. He

335

looked at it. He wanted to crush out, the hands on neck, all semblance of a lie, even if his lungs tore and this was his last act. Because if she was not dead, he said, if she was not dead...His hands fumbled, stopped.

Ernest Moriarty looked down. He was kneeling on the floor beside. The sheet was red. He looked down at a face and the tongue swollen, clapper-wise, that he held in his hand protruding from the mouth of what had been a woman, like the face, was no longer this, this thing, no longer Vic. I have killed Vic, he said, she is gone. He pulled savagely, impotently, at the tongue of the thing that was no longer Vic.

Now that it was all over his strength flapped, his nerves, yet he felt a strange freedom, a reserve of strength. He went into the sitting-room. The silence grated, was out of key with this strange exultation almost musical in his head. He listened to glass fall, felt the splintering of glass on his hand still red. He looked at his hand. It did not seem important, whether it was red or not, only to destroy this and this, was all that was left, was right. It was all over. It had served its purpose, this room. He found himself crying into his hands. Give me your braces, she said. Blood on his mouth. He cried. But the only alternative was to go round and round, and going round and round for how many years, was a lie. He looked at the cyclamen that lay crushed upon the floor, he had lifted it out by the stem, out of the lustre bowl, and it lay bruised, surprised, its pink ears full of query still. He crushed it with his heel.

He would go out now. There is a dead woman in the other room, he said aloud. It was one of those things you could not believe. It made him laugh. He looked back over the debris of the sitting-room, the mahogany clock that the Smiths gave, the cyclamen crushed upon a field of glass, all these symbols that had fulfilled their purpose in the life of Vic and Ernest Moriarty. Ernest Moriarty was the man, he said, and what sort of a man, and why to kill his wife.

He began to walk out along the road in no particular direction, just to walk. The air tightened his chest. Vic said, burn a powder, dear, you'll feel better, she said. Was the wife of a man called Ernest Moriarty. He taught in the school. It wasn't as if there was a reason for what he done, the paper said, the checks, you wonder what enters people's heads. Ernest Moriarty walked on. The chief reason was there was no reason. He began to cough. It tightened up, his chest, his life that straggled out over years, as if someone had pulled the reel, and with a jerk, was at least a purpose, to feel this. He was walking. He was walking. Feet sounded on the metal, told him he was there, and the thin crackle of ice. Then he stopped and he was not there. There was no evidence that Ernest Moriarty was even a name until he walked. Out of his eyes water ran, not tears. For tears are personal. Walking or not, he was the dark. That slow darkness. His hand felt towards ice, did not try to reject what it became.

The light wedged into darkness, split it up into two sectors, with the car spinning down the path of light. Houses, no longer the real structure of houses, were pale beside the road, the paper facades, or masks representative of sleep in a kind of silent allegory. A rabbit crossed the road, lacking in substance, to join the dark. Only the car in fact, you felt, had some reality or purpose. They had given it this with their bodies that sat up straight. They had not relaxed yet, like people going on and on in a car, on journeys that might be without end to judge by the expression of a face, They still sat up straight with a rigidity of purpose. We shall get somewhere, they said. This is why we are doing it. Even if the luggage be without labels there is nevertheless a goal.

Though what this is, said Alys Browne, sitting here with Oliver, if not Oliver what else, America or Africa, but it is still Oliver, still, is always this. She began to relax a little, into a smile that was half sleep and thought that winds round the irrelevant, a cup of coffee, or the stockings left behind. But she felt warm. She could feel his coat jutting into the half-reality of a dream world and making it almost tangible. This is real now, she said. It is only just beginning, asleep, awake, is still Oliver.

I'm hungry, Oliver, she said.

We'll stop in Moorang, at the station, and get some coffee, he said.

Yes, she said, that half-sleep. Coffee at the station always smells.

She did not mind. Talking of this with Oliver, the ordinary things, and their whole life, begun already, would be a succession of ordinary things that touched on the personal shore and became significant. She smelt the coffee in a station cup, warm in her throat, she felt warm.

He felt her relax as talk of coffee sent the mind back, right back, that bistro in the Rue de, he forgot, there was nothing between the moment and this, to sitting in a rainy night where khaki smelt, and the khaki coffee, or she asked for a café crème, were inseparable because wet, they clung, the fold on leg, and going out into the rain you knew that you were going home, the War was over, the long years, and time stretched out blank waiting for an impression that you would make now. It had waited for this. The other shapes were not, that you thought, that you imagined before Alys Browne.

Oliver Halliday, driving his car from Happy Valley to Moorang, swung out to avoid something that he was not sure, on the road, if this. The trees were grey and sharp in

339

the stationary light, the wheel solid, he felt steel, anchored to this the returned thought.

I'll have to go back and look, he said,

Hearing words, she knew they had returned out of another world. He would go and look. She closed her eyes. She did not want to look, not so much at something on the road, as at the sharp outline of trees. Opening the eyes the light stopped short. She could not see along the road, because it ended that leaden ridge, so very heavy in the headlight, the car clamped down. There was no connection with motion in the passive body of the car. Or herself. Or herself. She could not move, she would never move out of the shackles of the present moment, she could not even unclasp her hands,

Oliver went back. It was Ernest Moriarty lying on the road. He was dead.

A bird flapped, slow, out of a grey tree.

He stood looking at the body of Ernest Moriarty, dead some little time, it was almost cold, like any other body, stiff and a little ludicrous in its unconsciousness. The insignificance of Moriarty was somehow underlined by his being stretched in the middle of the road. There was blood on his face, the fall. Death made you feel in a way detached, looking down at Moriarty like this. Moriarty walking out along the road from Happy Valley and falling dead, this automaton, was no more automaton than, only you did not fall dead, you stopped short, returned to the inevitable starting-point. You did not escape from Happy Valley like this. That bird flapping brushed the mind free of stray impossible thoughts.

340

He went through the gesture of stooping, of touching the body again. He would take it back, the doctor, they would want to ask. Hilda's face drawing the curtains would twist in pity because, and Moriarty pity, Hilda and Moriarty who were joined in Happy Valley by a link of frustration and pain. Only Moriarty was dead, not Hilda. He put his arms round the body to lift it up. Hilda tried to hide her handkerchief that he knew was stained with blood. He wanted to cry out into the face of the dead man who weighed him down with his weight, that he must drag back, back, that he must take back to Happy Valley. Then he stooped under the weight.

It's Moriarty, he said. Something's happened. He's dead.

She heard the door close. She did not speak. We shall go back now, she felt. She did not question death, or wonder at something felt already in her leaded hands. She did not turn to verify the fact. It lay in Oliver's voice, in the live moment, in what they were doing, as well as in the body of the dead man. And this, this Moriarty who is dead, walked down the street yesterday. We shall go to America, we said. She felt the cold weight of the impossible. It lay behind her in the car. She heard it bump as they drove along the road.

Alys, he said, we'll have to stay. They'll want to know. Just for a little. I want you to understand that.

She heard no conviction in his voice. She did not expect it.

I'm glad he didn't have to lie there long, she said. I'm glad we came.

341

She did not want to talk about what was now, she did not want to recall this. They drove along the road to find Moriarty, the reason was this.

Then they were driving up the street, without stir, that had not noticed their departure. No dog barked at a return that was almost without a setting out, no expression of surprise on the face of house. How dead the houses, and unreal, she felt, though it is we that are unreal, slipping back like shadows, carrying in the back of the car the body of a dead man. And all these plans we have made. The words we have spoken are dead, yet without the reality of this dead man. He has achieved something where we have failed.

Oliver opened the door of the car.

I'll have to take him in, he said. If you wait a little I'll drive you back.

This was Dr Halliday. She sat and listened to him speak. Mrs Halliday told her to wait. His eyes were grey, no, blue, his professional manner cold. She watched the doctor carry up the path something that made him stoop, as if he were an old man. She did not feel at all bitter. It did not make you feel bitter to trace the natural course of things. But she felt she was going to cry, this sudden release of emotion, somewhere out of her the tears, out of another person left back on the road.

Oliver, manoeuvring the body of Moriarty in through the hall door, knew he must face something, what he did not know, but the silence, but the lamplight trailing across the linoleum squares, and this open door, dark in the face of the house, were more than superficial detail, made his heart beat. That cyclamen bruised black across the pink and the tangled mechanism of a clock in the hearth. Moriarty lay on the sofa in what had been the sitting-room, perfectly serene, and unconnected with all this, once so intimately his. He had cast it off. And Mrs Moriarty? He stood in the doorway of the back room, watched this thing that had been a woman, now unmoving, the pulpy face, and the sheet slipped, and the candle dim in its pool of wax. He did not experience horror, it was too far removed from any human element, this heap of cold flesh, the breath gone from its mouth. Then it began to come back, the situation in which he stood, he and Alys and Hilda and the Moriartys linked in this frail wooden house. Our bodies similar to these, though moving still, the same passions, the fears, of face that said, Ernest must write to the Board, she said, Ernest must escape, because I love my wife, poor Vic, what she puts up with, doctor, before the needle plunged and the face relaxed in temporary peace. Peace out of chaos, out of Happy Valley, we must look for this, we must go to Queensland, Hilda said, because Happy Valley is pain and the kind of irrational impulse on which the Moriartys have come to grief. The flame of the candle sank in its pool. He watched the body lose its shape. He stood in the dark.

It flowed round him, his impotence, in no way alleviated by this removal of forms. She was still there, and Moriarty in the next room, and the debris of furniture. They have tried to cast off the insuperable, they have broken themselves, he felt, and Alys and I slipping down the road, headed for what vague dream, are just as irrational perhaps. He could not suppress his anger that rose against no definite cause, was a groping in the dark. It was this that made you want to beat your head against the wall, substituting wall for the intangible. Or Happy Valley. A clock in the distance drew him to the present. He was cold with sweat.

Go down the street, tell, he said, tell Hilda and the others you have won, only not you, something thrown in the road as a sort of ironical gage to pick up and carry back, they let you get as far as that knowing you would return, impotent. Because you cannot cast off the shell the ways and customs, except in death, as Moriarty has. You substitute fortitude, like Hilda, who is fortitude, sleeping in her wooden room, and call it a moral victory. He felt all the bitterness of a moral victory that was not rightly his.

Moriarty lay in the frail remains of what had been his outer life. Oliver bent in the sitting-room, fumbled through glass, to pick up the fragments of a clock. The sitting-room was hideous with the lack of consciousness of a room desecrated and left, in a way undisturbed, in a way that you felt Moriarty's was only a part success. The spring of the clock straggled loosely in his hand. Sitting in the Botanical Gardens, it was summer, he pushed back a strand of Hilda's hair beneath her hat, her face broke up when he read a poem, banal as a poem at sixteen, she said, Oliver, I know now what it means. He was breaking Hilda, for what, for slipping down the road with Alys, whom he loved, towards some greater, though still undefined certainty. Hilda must stare at the remains, like a broken clock, listen for the tick, with the expression of Hilda looking at something she does not understand. I love Alys, he said. It was not a protest. It did not sound like this. Unlike Hilda and the fragments of

Moriarty's house, Alys would remain intact.

He went outside to where the car stood in the dark.

Alys? he said.

He found, half expecting, she had gone. Emotion could not unravel itself out of a sudden weariness. You accepted this. You could not think.

Then he went up the street to the police-station and rang the bell.

Sidney Furlow got out of bed. That finger of grey was too
much, pointing out of the dark. She pulled at the curtains
and they closed, she stood holding the dark, her feet were
hot on the floor. It was now what time, as if time had any
bearing on night, what time it was when it was still night.
Waking up with the sheets twisted, you were seven, you
could not move, you wondered if night would ever, if you
could move a finger ever again. But that at least was waking
up, not wondering if you held your head in the basin under
a tap, or sheep, or an aspirin. Mother said aspirin had a
capital A. Mother and Father were two names, capitals or
without, and you wondered, you wondered what else, and
what went on beyond a person's face that was better not
to see.

She went and lay on the bed again. The sheets were
still hot. Going past the cottage was no light, said I'll go

for a walk before bed, but of course in a coat, it's cold, and my head, and it's not far just round and about, the way they watch you to see what, and nothing to see, no light, you knew that, but had to see, and walk round and round, remember at the races, and this, it was this now, why shouldn't Mrs Moriarty go. She turned over and forced her face into the pillow that was soft and hot. It gave. It was so easy. You pressed your face and it gave in. Was feathers, or tulle, and crying in the rain. But now there was no rain. She lay on her back and listened, heard nothing, no horse. She felt exhausted, though without the capacity for sleep.

Or anything at all, wondered what this is for, as touching with the fingers the breast and thighs, these instruments of languor and passion, wondered for what if not, if not, what you did not like to think, and thought, watching for people to recognize, like Mrs Moriarty, you knew at once, he knew because riding into town, did not say Mother is going home, but take me, I want this, I want to feel. She twisted her fingers in the sheet. Sidney Furlow, she said with contempt. She wanted to throw a bomb into all this, to destroy, or tear a sheet. Lacking the means, you lay back, were a Furlow, which was nothing, or as good as nothing, or a name and a house and occasional paragraphs in the papers. This was not power, like fire that swept down the gully, or you pressed your feet into its sides, felt the wind move. This is what I want, she said, and the other, say take me, when his voice fell, saw he was afraid. He is afraid, of me afraid. There is something contemptible about a man afraid, and at the same time desirable, you want to possess this fear in a human body, his arms when

347

he danced, but above all the body which you know is so much masquerading strength. Breaking a horse, he laughed to see it stand cowed, feeling it tremble between his legs. Hagan, she said. It had a rough, clumsy sound in her mouth. She found herself thinking of Roger Kemble. That was the difference perhaps.

Somebody speaking in sleep was a long way off.

Sidney Furlow got out of bed and put on her fur coat, felt the soft voluptuousness of fur against her neck. Mrs Furlow had paid a lot, not so much for the sake of the fur as for the privilege of paying a lot. But there was also something of the swings and the roundabouts in Mrs Furlow's attitude, take my daughter, take my mink, it was something like that. We shall settle this, Sidney said. It gave her some satisfaction to say it between her teeth, in the dark that was sleep, her mother asleep, and her father, skipped over that, walked down the passage towards air, she must have air. The coat was heavy. She had burnt it once with a cigarette. She moved inside it, her body, as if she were something apart or withdrawing from the contact of fur when she slipped out on to the verandah. You could smell the frost. She began to shiver. She felt at once hot and cold, certain and afraid, it was always like that. Inferiority Furlow, Helen said, inferiority damn, that made you break the mirror at Helen's feet, shiver it cold on the floor, and Helen laughed, because she was a whore, or a whore slipping out in fur between the trees. She could feel in her hair the twigs, the plum-trees. If you were a whore to want the not-want, feel the boughs of trees, press yourself against a tree, was hard and sterile a tree. The plum-trees bore fruit about once in

348

three years. Not even this in bed you lay, waited, speaking words the dark heard, Hagan said, a whore in tulle or a fur coat. Mother said, always remember who you are, as if you could remember and forget at once. What if I am a whore, she said, what if I want something in the place of nothing.

She walked and felt the grass sharp against her legs, twigs pause in her hair, slip, she was walking beyond trees, would walk up and down till light, she knew where it came beyond that hill, where you looked for light when you could not sleep. In the stable something stirred chaff, a cat perhaps, or mice. The sleepy sound of chaff that fell beneath rafters. She was very remote from this, and horses feet mounting out of a well, up and up, they came up the hill with no body, she looked out to attach some form to a sound.

Getting off a horse was the chime of steel, a voice. He was getting off a horse. Hagan stood on the gravel. She knew. She held herself against a door, very flat, heard the horse shake itself free of the bit.

What, he said, brushing with the saddle, she felt the flap brushing her side, what the devil? You! he said.

Yes, she said. I couldn't sleep.

He went on into the saddle-room. She stood holding her coat.

You ought to go back to bed, he said.

His voice not intent on the present, she felt, was not on her, his head bent, was thinking. She dug her nails into a crack in the door.

Yes, she said. I ought.

Hagan, she wanted to say, now, as she heard him go

349

down the hill, as if she did not exist. Something heavy in his step, was not there, was gone.

She ought to go back to bed, trail across the yard a coat, not more, that was softly remonstrative against the skin. It was still not morning, not anything, to lie, Sidney Furlow in bed. She pressed her mouth into the pillow, soundless, conscious of sheets that had grown cold.

Thinking you have not slept is almost as good an excuse as not having slept for complaining about the toast. She felt awful, her head. Her eyes were heavy, dark about the lids.

This toast is awful, she said. It's soft.

Ask for some more, said Mr Furlow.

Mr Furlow sat in the rustle of yesterday's paper and the scent of marmalade. He felt at his best at breakfast, which they ate at half-past eight, because it salved Mr Furlow's conscience to eat his breakfast early if not to do anything else. It was a matter of principle, like eggs and bacon as a standing dish and kidneys or something else besides. And the men would go out to work. They were Mr Furlow's men. He sat with his back to the log fire. He was very satisfied.

Sidney crumbled a piece of toast, conscious of the warmth of the room, suspended in this, a sort of cloud. She wanted to close her eyes, to protest against the solidity of the furniture and her father's composure as he passed up kidneys into his mouth. Coming into the dining-room, she had kissed him on the cheek. You did this, it was eight-thirty, and a kiss, and Father asking you how you slept. To cut it out of the succession of days there was nothing you would have missed. Father's face smelt of soap. It made her

350

feel dirty. She wanted to cry. The fire sizzled, a damp log.

Your mother's got on to the telephone, he said.

It was not a reproof. Mr Furlow was really too far immersed in the complaisance arising from kidneys to feel anything like a reproach. Besides, he liked to sit with Sidney, sometimes alone, to know that she was there, physically at least. They understood each other, he felt, not that he would have admitted this to his wife, not that he would have been able to explain the nature of this understanding, or even on what it was based. Mr Furlow avoided explanations as savouring of intellectual enterprise. But it was there, this understanding, all the same.

He looked at her over his glasses and said:

How about some kidneys, pet?

It was his contribution to the relationship.

No. I feel like lots of coffee, she said.

It made her look down into the cup, this glance. She was ashamed. Father sitting in his chair, was a chair, it was like loving a chair, a habit acquired over a space of years. At the seaside once, they sometimes went to Terrigal, she trod on an anemone and crushed it into the rock. Then she crushed two or three more. It gave her a sensation of mingled pity and horror watching the shreds of jelly on the rock. She stirred her coffee. She was afraid of thinking like this.

Mrs Furlow came into the room. Something about her slapped right into the atmosphere, upsetting any equilibrium at once. For Mrs Furlow was perturbed. She was twisting her wedding-ring.

The most terrible thing, she said.

Mr Furlow shielded his plate with his hand. He objected strongly to being upset. There was a helpless protest in the shape of his hand.

Really a shocking thing, she said. It appears, so Mrs Belper says, that Mrs Moriarty is dead.

Here Mrs Furlow paused, not altogether unaware, whatever her agitation, of dramatic possibilities.

Sidney felt her heart twist. A sort of exultation. She got up, she could not sit.

And Moriarty, announced Mrs Furlow, with the clarity of a Greek messenger. They found him lying in the road. Quite dead. A cardiac seizure, Mrs Belper says.

It began to penetrate beyond Mr Furlow's face.

Yes? said Sidney. Yes, what else?

Because there must be something, she did not know, because walking down the hill, the head bent, and you ought to be in bed, he said, a voice that in the dark, was no connection, but…She heard the fire singing in the grate.

Yes, said Mrs Furlow. If it were only that. Of course I never liked the man. His look. You could see there was something. I remember the day he came, sitting in the office in that big coat. And Mrs Belper says the poor woman's face was simply pulp. They don't know, to be sure. But supposing, why, Stan, suppose if they send the police? They're sure to send someone out.

For what? said Sidney.

Her voice came out hard and strong. It made Mrs Furlow stare.

For Hagan, of course. Fancy, Stan, the police!

352

Mr Furlow's mind closed in despair with a wandering thread of argument.

But what about Moriarty? he said.

Moriarty? The poor man's dead. And then that brute. There was something going on, Mrs Belper says. She says they're sure to send the police.

Of course there was something going on. Mrs Moriarty was Hagan's mistress.

Sidney *dear*! The woman's dead. Mrs Belper says she was covered in blood. There'll be an inquest. They're guarding the house. And a trial if Hagan...

If Hagan was there.

She felt very taut and erect. No nerve now to bleat the voice to think what because to think and say above all say.

But Hagan was. So Mrs Belper says. The Chambers boy saw him in the lane. Just at the time it all took place.

And Moriarty? Mr Furlow said.

Moriarty is dead.

Mrs Furlow dabbed her face more with her fingers than with her handkerchief.

Sidney took the back of a chair. She felt the smooth mahogany scroll. It had belonged to Mrs Furlow's grandmother, or a great aunt.

The Chambers boy, she said. And what evidence is that?

Well, we know he's a little soft in the head. But in the lane, Mrs Belper says.

Sidney Furlow gathered her breath. She went to the window, tracing with her finger no particular pattern in the mist, in which the trees swam, then took more definite shape.

There will be a trial, she said, and Chambers will give his evidence. A half-wit.

She watched the cold stems of trees, frost silver in the grass.

But Hagan was not there, she said.

But Sidney, *dear*!

Hagan was in my room. I slept with Hagan, she said.

The brutality of words shattered the silence and a coffee cup. She did not turn. She stood watching the trees. Then voices penetrating, no longer congealed, flowed, the coffee, its drip drip, or the protest of a voice, she did not know.

Mrs Moriarty was Hagan's mistress, she said. I love Hagan. I slept with him. I love him. I shall marry Hagan, she said.

Mrs Furlow's world spun. Words were no words, were a mouth open stupidly.

I don't care, Sidney said, it beat out on the window pane. Whatever Mrs Moriarty was, I shall marry Hagan, she said.

She turned and faced the debris of human emotion in the dining-room. She held herself very straight, her cheeks drawn in. She did not belong to this, could watch like the shreds of jelly on a rock, the contour of a face or the angle of a shoulder, from which she was separated by kind and substance. Mrs Furlow began to cry.

Sooner or later, Sidney said, it would have happened like this.

Wondered why she said what, without explanation, must remain a riddle for faces, or always a riddle for faces that could not understand the gradual accumulation of years and waiting for the ultimate explosion. Mother's face crumpled without the protection of hands, sat there, Father, this is also Father. She could not look at her father's face. She smoothed the back of a chair, following with her fingers the curve of a mahogany scroll.

Mr Furlow tried to get up from his seat. The heat of the fire and the sight of messed-up kidneys on his plate. He could not get up, stared at the plate, tried to marshal his thoughts that flapped wildly in a morass of half-delineated images of which Sidney was the focus point. To a rudimentary mind all shock is at first almost physical. This is why the collar clung, the tongue swelled, in the ears a roaring of blood. Then in the confusion, Sidney, or Hagan and Sidney, Sidney and Hagan, or Sidney, Sidney. Saw sprawled in the mud that was not kidney, the face torn by gravel, walked past the door at night on tiptoe, where a night-light in its saucer wavered, went past, past this to the drawing-room, the air was cool before fires, like diamonds on a hot wrist, or the ice-cream spooned up on a high stool. He began to mumble something that was not anything at all. For Mr Furlow the impossible had happened. His eyes were groping round the room, from object to object, these material stays on which his life had rested until this, finding no explanation, there was nothing on which the glance might rest secure.

She could feel this. She could feel it pressing down on her, and at the same time she was breaking away, out of her immediate environment. She could feel a certain ebb and flow of pity, though faint, as if this were the death, not without regret, of a deep emotional undertone. But she must free herself, she must get away, discard pity to live.

She went out of the room. It meant very little now, or the house, or the servants she heard in the kitchen quarters conducting the ritual of the day. Because she had to go down the hill, there somewhere would make the next logical move. The air on her face was keen with purpose, like her step. She walked past the stable and the insignificant figure of a groom. Down the hill the shed, where he had watched, where, closing the door, she had stood in a kind of stupor against the ploughs, escaped from something in the house and still wondering what, and what was her life but a succession of days, or her body, of which she was afraid, that she pressed against the arm of a plough. She went past the shed. There was no question of defeat, the issue already palpable in her mind.

Hagan stood over by the wagon shed giving orders to the men. She saw his back and the mesh of a knitted jacket that he wore. No fear now, but power to turn a back, and watch, and see.

Hagan, I want a word with you, she said.

His hat cocked over an eye that sized her up, wondering what now, wore an assurance that could not deceive her confidence. It made her laugh, the way a man always put out a hand to take as his due what was sometimes air. This will be my party, she said. It allowed her to look him in the eyes.

Well? he said.

Smiled that tooth, as much as to indicate, and the legs

apart, planted on the ground that nothing would shake. She looked through his body, holding back a moment the words that would blast. The fold of his arms brought him physically close. There was no tremor in sensing this.

Mrs Moriarty is dead, said Sidney Furlow.

Watched the skin for the pallor that crept up. This is Hagan afraid, she said, I have made him afraid, now dependent on my words.

And Moriarty dead on the road. He must have walked out and died. They say it was heart. A perfectly natural death. But his wife, his wife was murdered, she said.

Hagan looked as stupid as—well, a big man suddenly afraid.

Moriarty murdered his wife? he said.

Hagan's voice halting, uncertain, had given her courage once, though not now, there was no necessity for this as, watching his face, she said:

Perhaps.

At a little distance one of the men was standing cracking his whip.

She's dead, he said stupidly.

Sidney Furlow saw his throat move, the motion not of compassion, but of fear, she felt. There is great absurdity attached to the Adam's apple in a man's throat.

Death pinned itself to Vic lying naked on a messed-up bed. And don't go yet, Clem, she said, with the knob waiting to turn, and that little runt waiting inside, mad, because he must have been mad, going round the room like that, you heard, and a mad china eye of knob, not a bull on the mantelpiece that you killed before it was meat,

357

you killed the bull, its blood, was murdered she said, was standing over the bed in the lane, was going down the lane away, perhaps she said was Moriarty or not perhaps, or who was in the room. She stood close to him, watching. He could feel her eyes.

You don't think, he said. I didn't do it. I didn't. Listen, Sidney, I'll tell you how it was. But if you think…

I don't.

She stood very firm on the balls of her feet, playing his emotion, sensing the tug.

But Chuffy Chambers was in the lane. Chuffy Chambers saw.

Walling up a beetle or a cockroach as the earth fell in its scramble, that you finally took in your hand and set free.

You've got to listen to me, Sidney, he said.

He had to find a way to say, he wanted to go away, he wanted to hang on to something that was not brick, a word, you done it, they said.

Why? said Sidney Furlow. Why should you be afraid?

He looked at her, asking for release.

Because you were not there, she said. Who is Chuffy Chambers? Think. Was there anyone else?

No, he said. No.

Then you weren't there. You were in my room, she said.

Sidney Furlow you wanted before going cold the room she took off her dress was shadow when you went past and could not touch she was Sidney Furlow mad Moriarty dead and Vic and this was what that she said. His hands were helpless at his sides.

You must have gone crazy, he said.

358

I'm making you an offer.

Looking at the ground, his head bent, for a sign that was not there of what she meant.

And what after that? he said.

His voice was distant and still. She heard him laugh at a broken colt.

I'll make you a second offer, she said. I shall marry you. We'll go away.

Your father?

I do what I want, she said.

At a little distance one of the men was slowly cracking a whip. It cut in with a steady stroke like Sidney Furlow's voice. It sang in his ears.

Do you understand?

Yes, he said. It was not Hagan's voice.

She heard it going back up the hill, he stood kicking the ground with his toe, and yes, he said, or she, speaking for Hagan, was Mrs Hagan, living up north probably, would buy a place, you must ask my husband she said, my husband sees to my affairs, will buy or sell, though on my initiative, it is understood. She felt very self-contained. I have done this, she said, I, I is me is he but me. They would have some children perhaps. You may come in, Clem, she would say, open the door, don't be afraid, would touch with her mouth a mouth that waited, always waited. Going up the hill she stroked her arms with her hands. She felt the texture of her dress. She touched no tremor, only the firm substance of her arms.

The eruption of passion in Moriarty's house stirred up the stagnant emotions surrounding it. The leaves of the geranium, that heavy green, could not disguise the face that peered, the breath on glass, the indication of a quickened pulse, as come here, Maud, the voice said, there's the sergeant going in. Or they stood in the street, outwardly static, by the fence, the faces bared by expectation, the mouth drooped. There was no awe. The hush in the street in front of a murderer's house is never so much the sign of awe as of exultation, as if we have been waiting for this, to be lifted out of the trough on somebody else's wave. Who'd have thought that Moriarty, or Hagan if it was, they said. The mind of the crowd dramatized the situation, peopled the scene with vague shadows of its own, substituted with a shiver, because after all it might have been. It made the spittle come in your mouth, the possibility of this. The geranium quivered behind the glass.

The emotion of Happy Valley had flowed to a certain point. Drained of this, the rest of the town stood high and dry, the landscape dead, removed. Oliver Halliday saw from his window the desolate line of the hills, jagged in the higher reaches, then falling to a slow curve, describing the course of a fever, it could have been this, on a large scale, or not so large, on which you might read the action of the pulse, sense the tick tick of the brain, visualize the shadow bending down that the hand resisted, passed through, became a scream or the fixed cavern of a mouth. All this was last night, or farther, but really last night, he said, was opening the door on what the papers will call a murder, that you might in ordinary circumstances read without a qualm, because that is different, somebody else's murder is not the same. He began to smile. It made his face twitch. Because the awfulness of murder is relative to the moment and the circumstances, becomes a joke in the train or looms in the dark room, dependent perhaps on the digestive juices. But the act is insignificant, and those concerned. Like the significance of two people running away from themselves, the dwarf figures that magnify their own importance, tossing out a reply to the world, this is what we think, they say, as if they existed except on sufferance as part of a design. Alys Browne, said Oliver, tracing with his pen, and all that we have thought and felt, all this, like a murder, is a relative experience, perhaps a joke in the train. Or not. Or not. He felt his anger swelling inside him. No, he said, no. He dug the pen into the desk. But it increased his sense of impotence.

Oliver Halliday sat in the dispensary waiting for words to formulate a decision, it would be no more than this, a formality, he would write, he would say, Dear Alys. Then he stopped short. The life of the house flowed almost in its habitual stream, except that Hilda was making a list. We shan't take everything, she said, all that distance, the expense, but we'll take the dining-room table and chairs, they were a present from Aunt Jane, and the tea service, it's good, and the mirror in the sitting-room. Oliver Halliday's mind was blank, like a sheet of paper, because it was less painful, a business letter or a blank. Hilda wrote spasmodically. She would not think, not since the Moriartys, and the car she heard was not a dream that set out and returned, and finding Moriarty on the Moorang road. Her hand jerked with the pricking of a thought. But she would write, she would make a list, this would be some assurance. Oliver said that Garthwaite had a little girl. She had gone in to look at George before the car returned. It was only last night. The couch in the dispensary had broken springs, it was not practical to take, because Queensland such a way. Oliver said that Moriarty was dead, and the glance faltered above bacon, it was breakfast time, and the mind sickened not for Moriarty, who was dead, chronic asthma affects the heart, he said, cut up the bacon in pieces on his plate, she could not cut, piecing in her mind the fragments, going in to look at George, and the car, she must mend the tab of his coat, she would take the Chinese vase and the carpet in the sitting-room, were moths in Queensland like anywhere else, heard the car rumble and stop, Moriarty's heart or her own, and the possibility of

362

Queensland. Hilda Halliday made a blot.

Soon it would be lunch, Rodney coming home from school, and boiled mutton and caper sauce.

Oliver looked for assistance at a photograph. It was Hilda's face. She sat on the edge of a chair waiting to spring up. Hilda's face receiving the news of Moriarty's death, he had told her at breakfast, turned to Alys, because Hilda knew, fumbling with her plate, said it was fortunate you went along the road, he might have lain there all night, which was uttering words, like writing a letter to Alys dead, and the emotions he must kill, because only in this way it was possible to write. Dear Alys and the date. Time frozen on the 23rd would not flow, the words, or the hand move across the page.

He got up and walked about. He heard Hilda in the dining-room. They were laying the table for lunch. Alys would receive a letter to say Hilda and I are going away together with the furniture and the accumulation of habit contained inside this shell of a house, this is our life, it will continue like this, in Queensland or anywhere else. A bald statement on a blank page. Emotion destroyed both confidence and conscience, even life, and for this must be suppressed, the way she lay on that bed without Hilda's face, was nothing divorced from the debris of a clock and a broken cyclamen, the fragments that Hilda clung to, they were hers, we shall take the tea service, Oliver, she said. We. It was Hilda's life. It was planned.

He sat down and took up the pen, conscious of words, it must not be more than this, like Dear Alys, a name. Then he began to write.

Perhaps I would have said last night what I am going to write now. It might not have been so difficult. I don't know. But I came outside and found you had gone. Perhaps you thought it was best, I mean, to go without saying any more. Because all through this you've been so much more aware than I of what we were doing and what we ought to have done. It was my fault, my weakness, that I wouldn't let you follow your own judgment. I did not want to face the truth.

He looked up through the window where the clothes-line cut across the sky, the drops of moisture on the cable, and beyond it the valley swept back, very tangible, no longer receding into a cloud that the mind substituted. He was free of this. The valley was earth and rock, he saw. His elbows pressed into the desk.

I hope you realized, going away, what I think you did. I went into the house. She was, of course you'll have heard, dead. There was all the futility and pain of wilful destruction about that house and two people trying to escape from the inevitable. Talking of the inevitable may sound defeatist perhaps. We might have escaped down that road to some form of personal happiness. But, Alys, I can't, I won't willingly destroy, after facing the meaning of destruction in that house. Man hasn't much of a say in the matter, I know. He's a feeble creature dictated to by whatever you like, we'll call it an irrational force. But he must offer some opposition to this if he's to keep his own respect. I don't know why I'm talking like this. You knew it all before. You realized and I didn't. Now I do. That is the difference. So I want you to try and accept what you were willing to accept before.

Words these with Alys rounding behind words put out her hand sitting on the verandah before dark and touched. Emotion drifting back pressed the eye, must not, must write, reject the images you wanted to construct.

In a couple of weeks Hilda and I shall have gone away. I don't think of the future. I know it is there, without any great significance. I can't take any other view after what we have experienced, you and I. I tell myself it will still be there, that this is something which no passage of time or external pressure can destroy. Perfection is never destroyed. I would like to thank you in more than words for all these weeks of happiness, for all you have helped me to see and feel. My darling, I could never thank you for this.

In the dining-room they were laying the table. He forgot the scratching of a pen.

It is too much, impossible, like trying to assess the future, which I accuse of emptiness without a second thought, forgetting what I have already and shall always have. Because I love you, Alys, still. This is my existence, loving you. This is its whole point. Going away is only going away, a mere exchange of environment. Because I love you, my darling, and I want you also to remember that. Once I have said this there is nothing left. I have said as much as I can.

Alys dear, Alys, in the halting of a pen. Knocking, the door was opened, a voice said:

Lunch is ready, Oliver. Don't let it get cold.

He sat staring at a written page. She watched him from the door, his back, beyond it sensing that this, she did not know, but felt, it made her hold her breath.

Yes, he said. I'll come. But I want to run down to the post first.

Hilda watched from the door. She wanted to come forward and say, yes, Oliver, I know, to say the things that you never said, and not even now. Pity on Hilda Halliday's face strayed with her hair, wavering, was ineffectual, like her life, sometimes she realized how ineffectual she was. You put up the strands of your hair that almost at once fell back again. So she halted by the door, wondering, she could only see his back, wondering what she could say, felt her achievement lie heavy, this exultation that said then this is Queensland and now we are really going away. Happy Valley stretched out beyond the window, grey and emphatic, but she felt safe, she had her hand on certainty.

I wonder if the Garthwaites would take some of the furniture, she said.

It tumbled into the room. It was not what she would have said. Her hand tightened on the knob.

I dare say they might, said Oliver.

The voices of George and Rodney mingled in the dining-room.

Well, hurry up, dear, she said. There are the boys.

Oliver Halliday went down to take a letter to the post. He avoided the house where the Moriartys had lived, and the figures bunched in the street beyond the fence. The town was very quiet beyond its focal point, all emotion concentrated upon this centre of extinct desires. It was quite dead this house, whatever any spectator might do towards fanning it with his stare into a semblance of life. It sickened Oliver Halliday. He felt he was part of the house.

All that day, in the apparently unconscious body of the town, a fever burned, excited by the mingling of surmise and fact, and articulated in the afternoon by the wind that blew up, cutting a phrase here and there, so that a word stood out hot. Mrs Belper, speaking through the stammer of the telephone, as if the wires were infected too and eager in their delirium, told Alys Browne how Dr Halliday, called to a case along the Moorang road, had found the body of Moriarty and had brought it back. Dr Halliday and It. She had ceased to play a part, was disconnected from the flow of events, surmise as well as fact when, in the late afternoon, it was dark and she had drawn the curtains, Mrs Belper reminded her that this and this had occurred and perhaps she would like to know. Alys Browne was glad that it was dark, and that the dark voice of Mrs Belper was only the telephone.

Like Oliver and Hilda Halliday, Alys had been left high and dry by the ebb of emotion into the town, until now this voice penetrated, wandered when she hung up the receiver like a theme through her returning consciousness. That a murder had been done, the voice said. That Dr Halliday returned along the road. Alys Browne, the negative coefficient, cancelled out to provide what, for Happy Valley, is the solved equation. I have always been this, she felt, the negative coefficient in Oliver's equation, Oliver, Hilda, and Alys Browne. So why now, why this bitterness starting out of the telephone? I am still the same person, she said, that played Schumann haltingly, that groped through the tangle of experience, feeling her way, without asking is this really the direction. There were very few questions. And does time become, with experience, the perpetual question? In the convent questions were under lock and key, that smooth air, she looked back, like laurel leaves, rubbed against itself and did not encounter more than the grating of a tram and this in distance. There is an agelessness about the faces of nuns that I regret, she said, and the lock-and-key existence of nuns. Or I regret those afternoons before, playing Schumann at five o'clock, with the always clear perspective of five o'clock before the intrusion of experience, which is also the recurring question, the why, the why. I sit up here and think, time is no longer the bemused acceptance of events, this is what Oliver has done. This is why I am bitter, she said. I cannot accept this, that Oliver should have given me a mind, that is part of Oliver's mind, the constant reminder. She wanted to say, let me go. She wanted to escape, as she had in Mrs Belper's voice, from the flow of events. But Oliver was there, if not in substance, it was still Oliver. She pressed her hands into her face, she heard again the dark stammer of the telephone, or was it the ringing of a bell, the bell.

A letter to hold, or to open, it was immaterial which, would have no bearing now on the life of Alys Browne. She sat holding a letter in her hand. She lived by herself on the edge of the town, giving piano lessons or running up a dress. This, she said, is Alys Browne, this must be her purpose that shall not alter, but fixed like a water-tank on the rim of the hill, almost, though without the utility of this.

The issue already settled in the mind, there was no need to open a letter that crackled in the hand, that the hands

368

opened, that the eyes read. Reading words, she said, this is apparently also me, for someone else, is it really me, sitting in a car last night what I am going to write now, because all through this you've been so much more aware, walking in a dream and still aware, perhaps, because I love you, Alys, still, this is my existence, loving you, this is its whole point. This is Oliver. I am this to Oliver, despite the pressure of time, and going away is only going away, a mere exchange of environment, or light for shadow, or light for light.

Alys Browne sat by lamplight holding in her hands a letter that was more than this. It was moving, moving, she could not touch with her hands the circle of light that receded, without circumference, there was no limit to the endless efflorescence of light. Happy Valley was dead. I shall go away, she said, to California, perhaps, but always into the light. There is no fear attached to going away by oneself, there is nothing that can destroy, no pain that is final. Then she realized she was crying with the shreds of paper in her hand.

A man or woman murdered ceases to be an entity, the same with the murderer, they are names or a column in the news. It is difficult to fasten motives and passions to these that legal inquiry has stripped and print depersonalized. You are finished with the human element. Ernest Moriarty, school-teacher, forty-four, murdered his wife, Victoria Mabel Moriarty, thirty-five, at Happy Valley, and subsequently died of heart-failure on the Moorang road. That is all. Eustace Wing, commercial traveller, propped his paper up against a bottle of tomato sauce in the Narrabri station refreshment room, hoped that his indigestion, hoped he would catch his train. In Sturt Street, Broken Hill, Mrs Euphemia Richardson cut up her Sydney Evening Moon, with a view to the earth closet, into conventional squares. There was a picture of Victoria Moriarty in her wedding dress. At Newcastle in the tram Herbert Kennedy, coal-miner, going home with a pound of brisket, read from the parcel that William Chambers, twenty-three, mailman and lorry driver, had given complicating evidence.

On the night of the 23rd, said William Chambers, I was in the lane back of Moriartys' when Hagan came out of the house. He seemed kind of upset. You could see. Just one minute, said Mr E. G. Filey. You could see. But surely it was dark? Well, yes, it was dark. But you could kind of see, you could see Hagan was looking queer. I ask you, said Mr Filey, is this the kind of evidence the jury can respect?

The jury, composed of Antonio Lopez, fruiterer, Arnold Winterbottom, publican, James Thripp, grazier, Stanley Merritt, horse-dealer, and various others, was inclined to laugh. They knew, Winterbottom at least, that William Chambers, they called him Chuffy out at Happy Valley, was not right in the head, though driving the lorry, a sober boy, and his mother told Mrs Winterbottom herself, poor Chuffy, she said, he's simple, but he's good, and that you could see in the box, his head was a size too big. I saw Hagan come out of the house, Chuffy Chambers said. His lip was a size too big, trembling, and confused. You saw him come out how many times? asked Mr E. G. Filey in the act of blowing his nose. Everybody laughed.

And the man Hagan, this name? Gertrude Ansell, seventeen, employed by Mrs Moriarty as general servant, twisted her hands, they were very red, and played with a wart on her left wrist. Mr Hagan came to see Mrs Moriarty on and off, Gertrude Ansell said. What did she mean by on and off? Twice a week. She thought they were friends. What did she mean by friends? Well, she did not know. Gertrude

Ansell went red. Anyway, Mrs Moriarty sometimes had sandwiches cut, and glasses put in the sitting-room, and Mr Hagan brought chocolates, and sometimes they went to a dance. There was nothing else that the witness had seen? Not exactly, said Gertrude Ansell, feeling herself perspire.

Mr Filey complained that his client was being need-lessly involved. He would like to draw the attention of the jury to statements already made by Miss Emily Porter, matron of the Moorang Hospital and president of the Philatelists' Club, and by Clarence Westrupp, bartender at the Crown. On the night of the 23rd, Miss Porter said, Moriarty read a paper on perforations, seemed nervy and preoccupied, and after the discussion went away refusing a second cup of coffee. His hand was shaking, she said. Clarence Westrupp stated that Moriarty looked like death when, in the bar-room of the Crown, he went right out to it, and fell flat on the floor. They threw water on his face. When he came to he spoke kind of queer, said he would go home, they got him a lift in Collins's truck.

The novelty wearing thin, Antonio Lopez, fruiterer, felt his collar pinch, James Thripp, grazier, was conscious of Winterbottom's breath. Was twelve o'clock, was that grey monotone the official voice stating that Moriarty was a mild man, sober in his habits and respected by authority. Was only seven minutes past. Yet Moriarty had been subject to fits of unaccountable anger, as parents of children attending the Happy Valley school were able to testify. There was, however, the evidence of William Chambers, not without a snort from Mr Filey, and of Gertrude Ansell to be taken into account.

Winterbottom knew that cove Hagan, that big skite lounging over the bar between stories and sometimes breaking a glass, knew how much to expect, whether Mrs Moriarty or not, had pinched the missus, she said, her behind, and now stood in a funk, you could see, as if he'd got something in his throat.

Clement Hagan, thirty-one, overseer at Glen Marsh, denied that he had been in Moriarty's house on the night of the 23rd. Chuffy Chambers trembled, inarticulate on his bench. Well, Mr Hagan perhaps could give some idea of his whereabouts? The silence is a clock, is a cough, that foot rasping on the floor. Miss Emily Porter sneezed. Clement Hagan looked at air and said he was at Glen Marsh. And in support of that statement could Mr Hagan provide? Mr E. G. Filey swept with a rustle of papers through the silence and said that Mr Hagan could.

To read the case in the papers, which was without particular point for Eustace Wing at Narrabri, for Herbert Kennedy of Newcastle, or for Mrs Euphemia Richardson in Broken Hill, made Mr Furlow uncomfortably conscious of an element that all his life he had tried to avoid. For reality is not a parcel of the mind of such as Mr Furlow, who reads his paper ordinarily in the office after lunch, half-way between the furniture and sleep, finds that something has occurred in another hemisphere, finds that a fly, his face, his nothing, because by this time Mr Furlow is asleep. But now the news has a fresh and alarming significance, rounding a known face, and encroaching on Mr Furlow's own exclusive territory. Because you had to see if, to read, then Miss Sidney Furlow was called, even if the stomach queasily protested against this reconstruction and the eye wanted to reject what it had seen.

Because Mr Furlow had gone into Moorang for the case. I can't face it, Stan, Mrs Furlow said, with unusual access of affection that made her husband uncomfortable. Then Miss Sidney Furlow was called. You sat and looked at the floor, or a face, or the floor. Miss Furlow, said Mr Filey, with the unction of a conjurer about to introduce to his public the most infallible trick in his hitherto shaky repertoire. Mr Furlow, touching the seat, it was pine, you could feel the grain, heard the voice, the account for the whereabouts, the splinter prick, on the night of the 23rd, before the silence lifted up his face to look.

Yes, said Miss Furlow, I can. Stung the air, the faces raised, James Thripp and Stanley Merritt, because this was expectation, and Miss Furlow of Glen Marsh, and you waited for the breaking, the wood crack. Mr Furlow watched a wrist, without diamonds, tauten against a bag. Miss Sidney Furlow said that on the night of the 23rd, no equivocation in this, Hagan was in her room. The pencil frayed, Leonard Woodbridge of the Moorang Advocate already worked up mentally a good connection with Truth. And could Miss Furlow's family vouch for the statement she had just made? Miss Emily Porter felt a tingle in her spine. And what did old Furlow over there, looking at the floor, say when the light went out? The jury sat up straight. In the circumstances, said Miss Furlow, no. Arnold Winterbottom bit his nails, because—well, well...Could Miss Furlow explain just a little more clearly perhaps? The splinter pricked in the hand, the voice, darling, I haven't a

374

bean, the face on shoulder was Sidney's face. Hagan is my lover, Miss Furlow said, I can't explain more clearly than that. Leonard Woodbridge, toying with possible headlines for Truth, decided on Wealthy Grazier's Daughter Risks Fortune and Honour for Love. Slim, pale Sidney Furlow, popular member of Moorang and Sydney's younger sets, spoke up courageously to defend her man. Mr Furlow's hand relaxed on the bench. This is Sidney, he said.

In the street even if dinner was late was worth it and didn't she have a nerve a girl a man could admire and what was that Chambers boy almost throwing a fit and anyway it was always established that Moriarty done it himself wrecking the room and all the police had it fixed only what the Chambers said was what you called a legal formality having Hagan in court a half-witted boy like that but what price Furlows now the Glen Marsh bloody Stud come on Gertie I was that scared you was brave she done up her face look if she hasn't a cheek and what'll happen now.

They drove back to Glen Marsh, Sidney and Mr Furlow. They did not speak.

Hearing her go about the house, Mr Furlow assured himself if was over, though reading papers you wondered if it was. Don't be sick, darling, she said, it had to happen like this, and when we're married we'll go away. If not already gone, this strange person that he could not altogether connect with a figment perched on soda-fountain stools, that made up her face when she said I am now eighteen, or stood against the buff panelling, it was pine, in the Moorang court house when Miss Sidney Furlow was called, was reported in the papers, connection with the

Happy Valley murder, it made Furlow pick up the paper again because things had always happened outside a certain radius, a strike in Sydney or a financial crisis or even beyond the seas, in Europe a war, which was safe, but never in Mr Furlow's immediate environment that he defended with tradition, a bank balance, and so many acres of land, only these were no longer a defence, the papers indicated, and a firm step walking about the house, these were negative assets after this. Mr Furlow was without protection. Sitting in the office reading the papers, facts were no longer news, but swelled out into full dimensional forms, you could feel the immanence of these. Mr Furlow said, I am sixty-five.

Marched about the house that step linking room to room in a state of preparation. I shall be Sidney Hagan now, she said, in the glass her face that was slightly supercilious, because Hagan was my lover or husband or whatever you like. Whatever it was already consummated if not in fact, she felt this, the words spoken, felt it die down the room with all those faces above a bench, dropping into a silence the old emotions, almost as if his body had touched her in the court room in at Moorang, could she explain, she could, for the benefit of the law if not for herself.

Sidney Furlow did not try to explain to herself. She looked through drawers wondering what she would take. They would go to Java for their honeymoon. But her mind was apathetic where an explanation was concerned, much as if a fever had released the mind from a turning and twisting in hot sheets, the past year like a twist of clinging sheets that she had cast off, her body now accepted the future with tranquillity. And Hagan, loving Hagan? Her face was supercilious in the glass. This man was afraid in the box, on the night of the 23rd I was at Glen Marsh, he said, waiting, and she stepped up, Hagan in my room, she said. She saw his eyes.

Sidney Furlow went outside. A red cock, sad-combed, pecked at the hard ground in the yard, because it was a stiff winter and the earth did not thaw even in the middle of the day. She went across to the stables, where Hagan was saddling a horse. There was a scent of dung and the ammoniac stable smells. She watched him fasten a buckle against the belly of the horse.

Clem, she said.

Watched him turn.

Hello, he said, with the bewilderment of one not yet used to a situation that had formed without any effort of his.

Hagan was not sure of himself. This girl you had wanted, falling into your hand like a pear not yet ripe, those breasts you had scarcely touched, and it made you wonder what, made you a bit afraid. On the night of the 23rd I was at Glen Marsh, you said, and it wasn't exactly funk, but something, twitching under your waistcoat pocket, because why should she speak up, what you could not understand, Vic and the others, but not this. So Hagan was puzzled. His hands fumbled with the buckle of a girth, or with his hat in the office, she said, Father wants to talk to you, Clem, now don't be a fool, he won't eat, you've left all the rest to me, so why won't you leave this, we'll go to Java, we'll have a place up north. But sitting in the office had fumbled with his hat, watched it roll on the floor, and old

377

Furlow speaking, you could hear his breath wheeze, it was an effort to say, well, Hagan, well, whatever happens we must think of Sidney's happiness. Then he stopped short with the hat. They both sat and looked at the hat that was also something else. Because I want Sidney to be happy, he said, whatever she takes it into her head to do, even if I can't quite understand, not that he said, but you saw, and you did not understand yourself, anyway it had happened, and you weren't such a bloody fool to turn down a good thing. I know of a place up near Scone, he said, Sidney fancies the north, and yes, sir, you said, there was nothing else that you could, and the old coot, it made you feel sorry, did not want to mention anything that might, it made you feel uncomfortable sitting on your chair and listening to old Furlow speak. It's nice country round Scone, you said. Yes, he said, good country for cattle, and I want to make Sidney happy, like a wheezy old parrot that you taught a couple of words that it couldn't forget. It made you glad to get outside, when the door banged, and she said, she was waiting, well, it didn't kill you, she said, and in the passage you wondered what she wanted, or wanted now.

I thought I'd come over and see what you were up to, she said.

I'm going to ride the Ferndale fence.

She stood looking at him. He could not see her face. The horse shifted its weight.

Well? he said. Anything else?

Because he felt awkward, to know what she wanted, to touch her or what.

Come here, she said.

378

It was queer, Sidney Furlow, and you touched her mouth, and you touched her mouth, and you wondered if this was Sidney Furlow that you really touched. But you weren't such a bloody fool to turn down a good thing when it was put right into your hand. You had always wanted this, to kiss Sidney Furlow, to...

She felt his body. She was holding him. She felt a certain bewilderment in his mouth.

I can't understand, he said.

What?

What you've done. In there at Moorang. You were crazy, he said.

She laughed. It sounded clear and remote in the stable, beating off the stones.

I always get what I want, she said.

Then he kissed her again, she made him mad, couldn't get hold of her, only her mouth, and you wondered what she thought.

Not any more now, she said.

She watched him gather his breath.

I like the sound of the place, she said.

What?

The place that Father's going to buy. I shall breed shorthorns, she said.

And sheep?

His voice vague.

Oh yes, and sheep. But I'm more interested in cattle, she said. It's going to be fun having a place.

He wanted to kiss her. She saw his face preoccupied, groping, moving towards. She opened the stable door.

Mother and I are sorting things, she said.

The daughter of Mr and Mrs Stanley Furlow of Glen Marsh will leave with her husband for their honeymoon in Java before taking up residence near Scone. He watched her go across the yard, feeling she had not told him what he must do next.

Mrs Furlow had ceased to write to Mrs Blandford. Since the night of the 23rd she had forgotten to put any cream on her face before getting into bed.

Rodney went down to the store. They were going away soon. He beat the wire fence with a stick, heard a humming in the wires, stopped to listen to it running down the hill. Though perhaps the telephone wires overhead, perhaps these, he thought. But it did not matter very much, because Mother said, dear me, Rodney, how you've grown, we can give these shirts to Mrs Schmidt, held up a shirt to see. It was the telephone wire after all, and not the fence. He looked up at the telephone lines, followed them past a knot of birds that sat frail and bunched in the wind, followed them down the plain, his eyes picking out their progress through the tussocks, always the black line. The telephone wires were fastened to the outside world. Time and Happy Valley had given this a legendary tinge, and the telephone murmuring of far events was nothing short of oracular. Until said Mother, what do you think, we're going, Rodney, in a voice that suggested more than Moorang and the dentist or a picnic in Kambala on Sunday afternoon. The line of the horizon moved in Hilda Halliday's voice, moving to embrace. He felt her hair. And Mother sometimes cried. It's nothing, Rodney, she said, because now we are going away, we shall leave you in Sydney to go to school, we shall buy you some new clothes, these will do for the Schmidts. He felt the nearness of a voice. They were very close, he and Mother, in the silence of unfolding shirts. They looked out of the window, before it became dark, and watched the line of hills slowly dissolve. Rodney Halliday drove into Sydney in a peal of bells. She put her hand on his shoulder and told him he might light the lamp.

It made him want to sing now, often he felt he must sing, or make a noise without words because these did not matter, or the words in telephone wires. Going down to Quongs' he struck at the fence with his stick, listened to it burr, opened his mouth and sang into the wind. He wished he could play a trumpet, or like Chuffy Chambers, the accordion. The Moriartys were dead. There had been a trial. You walked past the house where they had lived, and your heart beat pretty fast, at night you wanted to run. There had been a murder. If you said it at night the shadows were big on the wall, making you sit up in bed and listen for a voice. A voice in the next room was life, was not walking in the yard telling yourself that death, some day you would die, but not now said the voice, as you slipped back against the pillow and fastened your eyes on the candle flame.

Rodney Halliday's preoccupation with the idea of death was no more than spasmodic because—well, they

382

were going away. This was a release from the immanent shadow on the wall, the group behind the urinal, all those fears that Happy Valley implied. These would not exist in that vague but soothing state the future, somewhere behind the hills, and to which the telephone wires were mentally attached. He went on down the hill. His mind was absorbed, not in the moment, the corner of the street, the flapping of a piece of iron on Everetts' roof, but in a series of barely defined events that time and Rodney Halliday would form out of a fresh material.

Good evening, Rodney, said Miss Quong.

She sat in the store behind the counter, crocheting a collar for a dress. She smiled. He felt the warmth in the smile of Amy Quong.

I've come to see Margaret, Miss Quong, he said.

Margaret! she called. She's out at the back, Rodney, she said. You can go through the back room.

He liked Miss Quong's voice, like her smile that was round and soft, when you came in from school to buy some bull's-eyes, some marbles, or else a liquorice strap. He halted behind the counter and said:

We're going away, Miss Quong.

Yes, she said. I heard.

Her hand was busy with the crochet hook. It did not stop. It played out silk into a stitch, the weaving motion, in and out, that took no account of the departure of the Hallidays. The boards of the floor were old and rough. They had lain there many years, under the feet of old Quong who had sold laces in the mining camp, of Arthur and Amy, and Margaret, the boards were a fixture, they had the stolidity of old unpolished wood. Rodney did not know what he waited for. Only he was fascinated by the motion of Amy's crochet hook. He felt a little bit sick in his stomach. They were going away, he had said. Farther and farther as the silk streamed, as the car. You came in from school, out of the frost, sat on a stool by the bacon machine. It was warm and safe.

But I expect you'll come back, said Amy Quong.

Yes, he said. Perhaps.

Though not with conviction. He did not feel this. I shall come back, said Rodney, I shall marry Margaret Quong, anyway, perhaps. The intention lay cold.

He met Margaret on the back steps, in the yard the quarking of heavy Muscovy ducks and the sound of Arthur Quong who was grooming the colt.

Hello, Margaret, he said. I thought I'd come, I thought I'd...

They stood about in the yard. There did not seem to be very much to say.

Margaret Quong hummed to herself, thinking this is Rodney, I like Rodney, but really what can you say, Rodney is very young. She had all the composure of one who had just put up her hair, only she had no hair to put up. But the feeling was there all the same, something secret and complete. It was different now. Because Margaret had taken things into her hands. Mother, she said, they were drying the dishes after dinner, and Ethel Quong's bitterness fell with a dull sting into the water in the sink, Mother, I'm going to live at the store, just like that, before she hung the dishcloth over the stove. Anyone'd think, said Ethel Quong, forgetting her past regrets in a moment like this, that I wasn't your mother, that I don't count, but I'm not one to be bandied about, you can put that idea right away, Walter, what do you think of this, did you ever hear the like! Ethel's grievance beat on her husband, but did not penetrate. He went out of the kitchen and crawled under the car, squinted up at the axle where the grease, where Gertie Ansell said, I'm not the kind of girl to go joy-riding round in cars, but perhaps for half an hour if you promise to make it that. The kettle hissed in the kitchen like the voice of Ethel Quong. Margaret put on her hat.

She went to live at the store. She would leave school and help Aunt Amy with the books. On washing days, when the sheets were heavy with grievance in the yard, she helped her mother iron, and the words of Ethel Quong evaporated in a thin and bitter steam, they did not touch Margaret, they never had. After all I've done, said Ethel, after all I've been through, and your father, and the shame, they picked him up in the street again on Saturday night, who'd've ever thought at Government House, I've got those Stills to blame for a lot, and now Mrs Ansell says she'll have the police. Was smoothed out by the steady pressure of the iron. Here are the handkerchiefs, Margaret said.

The circumference of Margaret's life was closed, except where it touched on Arthur's and Amy's, fusing unconsciously with these. But the box was untouched now in the drawer, with the harebells, the photograph of Alys Browne, and Madame Jacquet's shell. This was over now, like crying in the shed upon the heap of hessian, feeling the texture of hessian, biting your hand against the tears. I shall

385

die, you said, I shall die. You lay against the ground and waited for this, before it was two o'clock, the light choking the crack beneath the door, sound stifled by the sun. It was hot in the shed. The skin of your cheeks was tightened with dried tears. You were still alive. At the store they opened a tin of herrings for tea. The glass was a little ashamed. Those Moriartys, Aunt Amy said, as the tea plopped, brown, or red as it caught the lamp, you could have them in court, said Aunt Amy, before they'd pay.

But now the Moriartys were dead, the house closed before the next tenant, the photographers had gone. Margaret did not think much about the death of Moriarty and his wife, after the first stupor, that is, when the known face is removed, leaving a gap in the habitual pattern of one's life, because this is inevitable, but the Moriartys were of no greater purport in the life of Margaret Quong. Even Moriarty, that face connected with a ruler and sudden fear that descended as you held your arms above your head, waiting for the pain of which Moriarty for the moment was an active instrument. Felt on your arms the blows that were not from Moriarty, no physical pain, but the accumulation of misery that spilt itself in tears as you lay on the hessian in the shed. This was the significance of Moriarty in Margaret Quong's life.

But you cried no more. Moriarty was dead. On Sunday you heard the bells first from the Roman Catholic, then from the Protestant church. Aunt Amy went to Mass. On the verandah waiting, it was Sunday, that was almost perpetual now, though you sat on a bench at school with Emily Schmidt and Gladys Rudd and another hand wrote

386

with chalk, he's ever so good-looking, said Emily Schmidt, he's boarding with Mrs Ball, and, Margaret, don't you think, that was a question or a breath of Parma violet as Emily Schmidt bent. Margaret Quong watched the meandering of chalk. Soon it will be over, she said, soon I shall leave school. Heard the deferential voice of Emily Schmidt you can come up on Sunday, Emily said, no longer a favour when now you had stopped caring whether Sunday or the Schmidts, when you would go back to the store and it was always Sunday afternoon.

Something had happened to Margaret Quong. They could sense it, Emily Schmidt and Gladys Rudd, a sort of superiority that would not be imposed upon. Something had gradually taken place, evolving out of experience, that you did not notice at the time, not until you felt that Margaret Quong was invulnerable. Voices no longer sang going up the road, My mother said I never should, because really Margaret Quong, she wasn't such a bad sort, only she was queer, a Chow, and you couldn't get very far. But Margaret Quong kept her distance, as if her defence were hardly won.

Moriarty was dead. Hallidays were going away. She felt nothing so positive as exultation, not even the negative emotion of ordinary satisfaction. Because these two events no longer had any bearing on her life. She went past the fence where the brass plate said ALYS BROWNE, PIANO-FORTE, or she went up and said, Miss Browne, I shan't be taking lessons any more, because I really haven't time, I am going to help at the store. A face was like a photograph, put away in a drawer, having some meaning in the context of

387

the past, but very little when removed from this. The room was bare of emotions where you sat and talked, where the music on the piano, open at another page, did not point back towards two heads bending by lamplight above the keys, before a knock swept the sonata into a volume of confused sound. I played very badly, thought Margaret Quong, I shall not play any more, even if the Hallidays go away, there is no point in any of this, or touching a hand that is now only a hand.

They were standing in the yard, Rodney and Margaret Quong. The tin clattered with the bran mash that Arthur was feeding to his colt. Rodney played with his knife. He could feel the reserve of Margaret, a deepening of the light, of the noises in the silence of the yard.

Let's play at something, he said.

What do you want to play? she asked, out of the distance her voice.

She was taller than he, bony and composed. She made him feel very young.

Poor Rodney, she said, going away or coming to play, as the paper fluttered down, white, the aeroplanes from the girders in the garage roof that you caught in your arms, held, settling in the dark. There was a shell, her name was Madame Jacquet he said, it came from the bottom of the sea, which is a very long way off. It lay on the floor of the ocean in a fluttering of weeds, or in a box upstairs untouched.

Yes, she said quickly. What shall we play?

Oh, he said, nothing. I just thought.

That it would be easier to play either aeroplanes or houses than to stand, because Margaret just stood, was sort of different, and anyway you would go away whether Margaret Quong, when you said you would marry, stayed, and Sydney was a long way from the bacon machine rasping and the frost, when you came inside it was warm, she said, would you like a glass of milk, only that was the summer, the milk cold, before Mrs Worthington died, and the Moriartys, and Margaret did not know that to die. He looked up. She was tall. She had folded her bony arms, and leant against the door like the women you saw along the street leaning against their doors and talking in the green gloom that the dahlias made. Only walking in the yard, it was night, and the smoke unravelled, and the stars, this was more than Margaret had realized. Margaret does not know this, Rodney felt, looked up with the compassion of one harbouring a secret experience.

I've still got the shell, Margaret said.

Oh, he said. I'd forgotten the shell.

Forgotten that Margaret or the shell, as the car streamed out, would stay, all this, and Andy Everett, the knife with the bone handle that Andy Everett broke, with which he played, cut his hand, and it bled and healed, so that after the itching you forgot, even that white scar, it was like a grub, don't touch it, George, it's a grub, just to see the face wrinkle up, it was only a joke, or Miss Browne said, doctor, look there isn't even a scar. Broke off there as if. But even this was finished.

Margaret and Rodney stood in the gathering dark, conscious for the moment perhaps of a mutual thought. Looking at a face you knew. They had never spoken of this that was silent like a white scar.

In Queensland there are pineapples, Rodney said. And sugar-cane. I shall go up there for the holidays. Father says it's a long way. But I'll be eleven soon.

He walked in the gloom of sugar-cane, the heat, and the murmuring of flies. At eleven o'clock the sun was a shining disc in the sky. Columbus, a word, tumbled on the tongue, lumbered in the Gulf of Mexico, where the sun. He would be an explorer perhaps, touching like Columbus on a new world. He would do things while Margaret Quong stood in a doorway with folded arms. He could no longer see her face.

32

Mr Belper drew a fanfare from his nose.

The crux of the matter is we're stony broke.

Which was at least a relief, to realize in words what had stuck for the past few weeks, with the collar tight like a halter round your neck. Now Mr Belper felt deflated, waiting on his wife's silence, what Cissie would say, because Mr Belper, although refusing to admit any positive quality in woman, other than a prowess in the house, or more specifically in bed, secretly respected the oracular talents of his wife. Those talks they had at night, muffled by the pillow and proximity, were tinged for Mr Belper with an admittedly Delphic significance, even if he might cut them short with a shut up, Cissie, how you jaw, under the dictatorship of love or sleep.

But now all Mrs Belper could say was:

Oh dear, Joe. Oh dear, oh dear; and make a sucking noise with her plate.

Under the frill of a chair a fox-terrier snuffled heavily. The room with its garnishing of pokerwork, those silhouette shades that Mrs Belper had worked herself, the pouf in morocco leather, and the blue suite, all those attributes of a hitherto well-upholstered life could not disguise the frailty of walls or of the aspirations these contained.

Oh dear, Joe, Mrs Belper said. You shouldn't've been so rash.

The miraculous behaviour of stocks and shares, if still no less miraculous, disturbed Mrs Belper's confidence. She remembered how once, she was sixteen, it was at her aunt's, she dropped a wedgwood sugar-bowl and watched the fragments scatter on the floor.

It's the Crisis, her husband said.

Because often in the past platitude had helped him out of a conversational hole, was something to cling to at home or at the club, where the Crisis was answerable for much, it gave you a feeling of being not altogether to blame. He even ventured to glance at his wife. As Mrs Belper's confidence ebbed Mr Belper felt his own return. You shouldn't've been so rash, she said. Mr Belper, wiping his forehead, found some comfort in picturing himself as a rather impetuous male.

We'll pull through somehow, Cissie, he said.

And who'd have thought that coal. Why, everyone burns coal.

But in a time of crisis, said Mr Belper, the courage that comes from words thrust his hands into his pockets and sent him stamping about the room, in a time of crisis, he said, even a commodity like coal.

How a commodity like coal behaved Mrs Belper did

392

not hear, did not stop to ask herself what a commodity could be, like those terms he sometimes used and of which you made a mental note to look up after in the dictionary. Joe was clever, Mrs Belper said, intent on labelling all her possessions with some sort of satisfactory excuse. He talked about things being at par, he read a leader in the Herald, and told you what was happening to the franc. Even Mrs Furlow was impressed. But this is just why Mrs Belper quailed.

It's only a matter of time, Mr Belper said, and as he assumed the upper hand the candlesticks joggled on the mantelpiece. Australia's the country of the future. Australia's bound to come out on top. Look at the interior, he said. I ask you. What a chance for development.

For even if his confidence returned Mr Belper felt it wiser to avoid his personal predicament. So he plunged inland. He clung for assurance to the tail of words. Mrs Belper's corsets groaned.

And what about the Salvage Bay? she said.

Which was irritating to return. It made Mr Belper cough.

The Salvage Bay has gone into liquidation, he said.

He tried to jingle the money in his pocket, discovered only a two-shilling piece. Like a key dropped down your spine, for hiccoughs, she said. He felt the rim of this solitary coin, encountered its mute reminder, that nuzzled there in his pocket making him stick out his lip.

Always a chancy business, pearls.

Mrs Belper recollected a different story, told in bed if she remembered, or was it sleep, when pearls cannoned heavily in the corners of the room. She looked at her husband, at his red face, at poor Joe. With Mrs Belper superiority turned to compassion. A man was a fool perhaps, but—well, you couldn't let him flounder, even a fool.

That was only a flutter, I expect.

Yes, agreed Mr Belper, grasping at the opportunity and closing his mind to the rest. We must have our little fling, Cissie. I ask you. After all.

Mrs Belper began to laugh. Because Joe looked such a fool, and as if she didn't know, and he knew that she knew, and it was all so damn silly, even if Mary had to go, she could make a very good scone herself, they could live on potatoes if it came to that, and the way he talked about a corner in jute, all that mumbo jumbo that you swallowed as if...That was why Mrs Belper laughed.

Her husband looked offended and said:

I don't think this is a time to laugh.

No, screamed Mrs Belper. No. Only it is so funny, Joe. You and me, and—come here, Trixie, on to Mother's lap. What shall we do about Father? Eh?

Mr Belper traced the rim of his solitary two-shilling piece, a little shocked by the facile explosion of so many weeks of suspense.

Well, he said, if you can laugh...

Of course I can, heaved Mrs Belper. No one's going to do me out of that. And what about a cup of tea? she said. I'm just as dry as dry.

It was on this particular morning that Alys Browne came down to see Mr Belper at the bank.

Well, Alys, you're a stranger, Mrs Belper said. We were

just going to have some tea. Weren't we, Joe? Now what's the matter? I thought we'd got it all off our chests. You aren't proposing to mope?

No, said her husband quickly. No.

Then pull up a chair for Alys. The girl isn't a ghost.

Alys Browne had put on her hat and gloves, because this was something in the nature of a formal visit, because at last she had come to the decision, she would go to California. Oliver loves me, she said, heard it in the house, her voice, walking up and down these past days, because she had to walk up and down. This is not chaos yet, she said. But outside the hills were grey, and the plain, they pressed in, just pressing quietly with a gentle, slow pressure, until her hands clenched, and she longed almost for some form of eruption rather than this grey, still pressure of the hills. Oliver loves me, she said, to reassure herself. Then there was a storm of rain, at night, beating on the iron roof, with the wind, a black chaos. I am alone in this house, she said. It was a statement almost without emotion, either self-pity or fear, that she heard come back in the beat of the rain. She watched the furniture, the passive droop of the tablecloth, she could feel herself watching for some move, that was not made, there was a final cessation of motion in the house, cowed by the beating of the rain.

She knew she must resist the inertia of this house. She wanted to protest. It surged up inside her with a slow beat, from room to room as she walked about. She looked down at her waist and saw her hands clenched. So I shall go to California, she said, the wave beat, was a wave, the turning of wheels, slipped oily in the night through the shrill steam and the halt with cold voices calling the time, but the wheels must move, the wave, the little islands, those pointers towards release as the water flowed. And now she could listen to the rain, its small significance. She would go to California. It burst out in a strong, glistening theme that she could grasp, like a leit-motif returned from out of the beating of the drums, that she had heard first in the drawing-room at Mrs Stopford-Champernowne's, wondered, then as it became submerged forgot, until walking in this still house she caught on to it again.

Her face returned an expression in the glass that was triumph and something else, it made her turn away. In the drawing-room at Mrs Stopford-Champernowne's a young man sat with chocolates, from a bank, would she come to Vaucluse Sunday or the pictures Saturday night? There was wistaria at Vaucluse. She yawned, because this was unimportant, though her face grave, as a girl it was almost always grave, and expectant, though without much faith in expectancy, as if nothing would happen, eating a chocolate or reading pamphlets from a shipping office, even if she went across the sea, because what was this. A Java sparrow in its cage was cracking seed, discarding, and the intention slipped, there was no need, not now, for California, this little frail theme like the cracking of seed. This was not her face in the drawing-room, now in the glass, or was, and the returned theme, was larger, this glistening cable that she touched, gathering importance and momentum as it rushed out, she must seize it, this was its purpose, she felt, looking in the glass.

So in the morning she put on her hat and her gloves.

She would go to the Belpers'. She heard the cool morning sounds, smoothed her gloves, experienced the round tranquillity that sometimes follows a decision made. Because now it was settled. The house lay behind her on the hill, like a shell discarded overnight, walking up and down in the dark she had cast it off.

Mr Belper, I've come to talk business, she said. I want to ask you about my shares.

Mr Belper, looking down, wondered how deep a teacup, how red the rose. Mrs Belper's stomach rumbled danger. Well, she thought, and Alys too, this is not so good, because Mrs Belper, inside her casing of corset and superfluous flesh, was fundamentally a Good Sort. Even Mrs Furlow had granted her that.

That's funny, said Mrs Belper. We were just talking about shares.

Yes, said Mr Belper. Yes.

Clinked his spoon and looked to his wife for some telepathic miracle. The way you reach out, straining to catch it in its flight, catch at nothing and coil back. Mr Belper returned to a state of deflation after his moment or two of grace as that rather impetuous male.

Because I want to sell, said Alys. I want to go to America.

America! Mr Belper said. A fine country, Alys, to be sure. A country of opportunity.

Not without a glance of, you see, Cissie, where I am, and this is all you can expect, this is what I am, but what now?

Mrs Belper poured tea in a fine, compassionate stream.

It was gratifying to sense your power, though not to know you were powerless at the same time. Mr Belper stirred his cup. The veins were swollen on the back of his hand.

Alys, she said, do you mind very much?

What, Mrs Belper? Mind what?

As if now, sitting with your hands in your lap, you would mind what Mrs Belper was trying to suggest. As if all emotion had drained away leaving a dry receptacle. There were cherries in the cake.

Because Joe has some bad news. Tell her, Joe.

Mr Belper's eyes clung to his wife's wavering glance.

Yes, Alys, he said, it's bad. The Salvage Bay is bust.

Alys Browne sat in the Belpers' sitting-room, the Belper faces faintly red, heard this without moving her hands. She did not feel the need to move, or say, or say...Because this exchange of environment, he said, is only an exchange, or California, it is like this.

Oh, she said. I only thought, thought I might go. It wasn't very important, she said.

She had wanted to feel the ship move, to move with it, into distance, away. This was wrong perhaps, only an exchange of environment, this would make no difference, was what Oliver's letter had said.

We're all in the same boat, murmured Mrs Belper, you heard the murmur of her voice borrowing her husband's phrase. We were going to Manly for the summer, she said. Joe's sister has a cottage there. That's Fran. And the children, it's nice for the children to be by the sea. Because Sydney's very trying in the heat. Fran's just had her appendix out.

Mrs Belper's voice pursued its stream of narrative.

When anyone died Mrs Belper always believed in not keeping to the point. She was not really insensitive. She just believed in sweeping you on, no matter where, but on, pointing to the incidents that swirled past, till you were out of the danger zone. She pinned her faith to narrative. In fact, Mrs Belper's own life was an endless stream of narrative, of more or less connected fact. Alys Browne, listening to her talk, thought that she understood Mrs Belper better than before, saw her pitching on this stream that she had wanted for herself, going to California, making her life narrative. But to furnish your life with incident was no ultimate escape, except for a Mrs Belper perhaps. She had never moved in the current of Mrs Belper's stream, a pool rather, and you looked down, aware of the reflected images, frightening sometimes, but never distorted by the slurring of a stream. It was better like this, the truth of the undistorted images. There is nothing to fear, she said, even in contemplation of the depths.

Mr Belper was talking about time, and the way things picked up, all of which was irrelevant.

Well, said Alys Browne, and she laughed drily, I'm sorry for us all.

Because it was the sort of thing you said.

Poor Alys, said Mrs Belper.

Going home, Alys Browne felt calm and detached. She trod on a frozen puddle and heard it crack. I wanted to escape, she said, this, after all, is California, its true significance. Understanding, you felt no pain in your body, that ice did not touch, in your mind that was a fortress against pain, and Happy Valley, and because of this you lived. She began to think about Oliver, who was a moment in the past, but also present and future. I shall not live altogether in the past, she said. This is still alive. This is interminable. This is what I wanted to deny in taking the boat. She saw nettles powdered with frost. They stood up sharp and fragile beside the road. People were going about their work, the faces that she passed, the faces hurrying, as she walked slowly home. I shall not hurry, she said, I shall shape time with what I have already got.

33

Packing up and going away, that box in the passage, the overcoat that won't go in, the rime of newspaper on the edge of the hall, the echo of voices calling from room to room, whether in tears, or just the even stream of an officiating voice, is not without its nostalgia and regrets. Oliver Halliday straightened up. You felt them, these last moments that were without a clock, only the dusty shadow of a clock projected on to the wallpaper. In spite of yourself you felt this, and it made you smile, not without bitterness, at this instance of the fox his hole. The sun was watery on the floor. It sifted over the boards and the bough of a tree that waved in substance in the yard. In the empty house sound was swollen out of all proportion to its significance: the maundering of George perched on his island of luggage in the hall, the rasp of Rodney's knife as he carved his initials on the kitchen door. R.H. wavering to commemorate, though without the date, because this was too difficult, and you had to take care, falter on the H as you looked round to see, Mother said it was vulgar to carve initials on trees.

To commemorate what we have experienced here there is now nothing, Oliver felt, as he leant against the windows in the dispensary, unless you can impregnate a place with all you have suffered and enjoyed, leaving these as a heritage for the tenants who come next. Altogether he did not envy Garthwaite his lease, if this were in fact possible. And feeling your chin that you had shaved so badly this morning, Oliver, said Hilda from the bedroom, we must try to get away in good time because the children must not stay up late, you wondered what was left of the confusion of emotions beneath the tissues and the bone, you thought perhaps that these after all had been imparted to the house or, if not to this, floated volatile in the Happy Valley air. Because in a way you were swept clean, the bare boards with the bough of a substanceless tree stencilled on the winter light.

Oliver, Hilda said, as she came into the room, have you brought round the car?

Yes, he said. When you're ready we'll go. I don't think there's anything we've got to do.

No, she said. The sooner we—I mean, the boys will be getting out of hand.

Hilda's voice penetrated with more purpose than you expected, it did not waver now, it was a core of reality in the shadows of this room. Like Hilda, a voice that said, it was night, Oliver, with an effort in a voice, I want to talk, it's the last night, and we've never talked about this, there's very little we've talked about. Whether on an iron seat in the Botanical Gardens in a heavy summer light or lying beside Hilda in bed, in the dark, all those years you had not talked about much, penetrated the surface word, though after all very few people achieve this, but Hilda was making an effort in the dark, you felt it in her hand, the fingers with the ring that time had loosened, touching you with more than Hilda's hand. He looked at Hilda now. He looked at the face that had been this voice, when he had been glad of darkness and the touch of Hilda's hand. Because I know, Oliver, how you feel, it came to him from a great distance, then closer, it was very close, you mustn't think I don't understand or that I'm saying this because it's all over. She was speaking of Alys, not by tentative allusion, but making a direct approach. It was an undiscovered quality in Hilda, that she had just discovered for herself, you could still sense it in her voice, the note of discovery groping towards confidence. And because it was strange, he wanted at first to resist, because it was touching on something they had never mentioned, more than touching, it suffused a whole experience. Hilda could now identify herself with this, joined to Alys by a link of pain. Lying on your back, you did not resist after the first moment, this intimacy with Hilda that you had often tried to achieve and in which you had failed, it was Hilda who had accomplished it, speaking in the dark and opening with courage an old wound. But Hilda was always fortitude, an abstract virtue, you wondered what else until, feeling her voice, her hand in the dark, you knew. It will be hard, she said, as if she spoke to Rodney, there'll be lots of nicer little boys, so Rodney, dear, but not Rodney, it will be hard, though when we go away we'll try, we'll both try, Oliver. Feeling in the

403

darkness when your head touched, you were not Rodney, it was Hilda, it was not Alys, or all these welded together by Hilda's hand. I love Alys, Hilda, you said, or Hilda, or Alys, it was immaterial, to darkness or a hand. You would sleep. You felt Hilda's lips falter in a kiss that was sleep, that you wanted to say, Hilda, this is all over for better or worse, some purpose perhaps that we can't discern, because it is dark, it is anywhere, not Happy Valley, it is anywhere.

Now they were standing in the dispensary.

We'll start, shall we? Hilda said.

Mother! screamed George. Rodney won't give me his knife. I want to have Rodney's knife. Rodney's cut his name on the door.

No, George, Hilda called, you mustn't have Rodney's knife. Father's ready. We're going now.

Rodney sat in the car. They were going away.

Where's the thermos? Hilda said. George, you sit with Rodney in the back. And don't lean out of the car. You must promise Mother not to do that.

Dr Oliver Halliday got into the car. They had taken the plate off the fence, stripped off this label that would be stuck on somewhere else. Dr Henry Garthwaite would arrive the following day. The house waited to receive a life, or stood giving up a ghost, whichever way you liked. The car drew away down the hill.

We're going! We're going to Queensland! shouted George.

Rodney felt his skin prick. He looked down the street, that was now almost another street, its sole importance withdrawn. The plum-tree by Mrs Heffernan's fence stood in another morning. The letter-box at Perrys' was blue, blue, not green that you thought. It was another street with Perrys' blue letter-box marking the transition from the known. He always thought it was green. Come here, Green-face, they said, that you skipped, you smiled to see the fence roll past, hitched to something beyond the town. It made you wonder if your breath, tumbled in your chest, was coming or not, and that sick sick, ticking away in your stomach, made you press with your hands against your belt. In Sydney there were trams, at the Circular Quay the peanut man. You swam down through the water, opened your eyes, it was morning there, yellow against the sand. Rodney Halliday's eyes, fixed beyond the present, were the eyes of the swimmer under water opening on another world.

Oliver made the turn.

Slipping away the ghost gives the live part of the body purged if it were possible to accept this the wind alive on the face on Oliver Halliday on Hilda Halliday his wife on George and Rodney Halliday that are baptized afresh by wind that points down the valley beyond the post the so many miles that are just so many miles into the future that is Rodney and George may I be an explorer Rodney said if there is anything left to explore that woman's face with the dead child you looked down and saw a chart which did not indicate much more than pain and its possibilities but not the life until Moriarty relaxed and you saw the hinterland indicated in the flesh was more than plunging a needle was Alys shading her eyes Oliver look I can't offer you much only my life that is also the life of all these people the Moriartys the Everetts the Schmidts moving beneath the lens the house front the geranium.

There are Quongs, Rodney said.

They stood on the store verandah, Amy, Arthur, and Margaret Quong, a little consolidated group. Margaret waved. Sometimes you thought that the Quongs were exotic, foreign to Happy Valley, but not as they stood outside the store, this first and last evidence of life. You never got beneath the Quongs, the brown, aloof faces, the silent glance. The road down the valley was a brown curve, distinct and aloof like Amy Quong. In spring the hillside flickered up, in winter died to a dull grey, there was not much more evidence of any emotional quantity. Amy Quong lay on her bed, Sunday afternoons, watched the smoke from incense dwindle in a lustre bowl. She had bought it for five shillings at the sale, it was now hers, the only tangible sign of any inner confusion that may have been. The bowl reflected nothing of the past, that other face, and the rain that morning on the window-pane. Possessions are tragically adaptable. Amy Quong saw her room suspended in the lustre bowl, her life rounded and intensified. To touch the bowl was to touch not conscience, but achievement, but the moment, because the dead woman was hardly this, or the letter, the pen hesitant before a word, that was only anonymous after all, that was only means to an end. Amy linked her arm through Margaret's. Looking back through the window of the car, you saw the Quongs recede.

Hilda held her hand to her chest, less as a safeguard than from habit.

I hope the plates will be safe, she said. I packed them in plenty of straw.

406

Oliver saw the road move, heard Hilda say the things that she always said, because this was Hilda, also a voice speaking in the dark, Oliver, I understand. Hilda has found something that I have yet to find, though perhaps I am closer, moving along this line of wires, you can hear their hum, the almost disclosed secret of telephone wires, the rock with its meaning hidden, the harsh contour of the hills. Rodney, George, and I, together, are for Hilda a defence against uncertainty, at the same time wrapped against breakage in the straw of her solicitude. Oliver looked at Hilda. He saw her smile, heard her voice say, we shall try, no longer expressed in words, but a glance. He looked back through the windscreen at the road. Trees moved in the gathering rain. A flux of moving things, like experience, fused, and Alys Browne, he felt, is part of me for all time, this is not altogether lost, it is still an intimate relationship that no violence can mortify. This is the part of man, to withstand through his relationships the ebb and flow of the seasons, the sullen hostility of rock, the anaesthesia of snow, all those passions that sweep down through negligence or design to consume and desolate, for through Hilda and Alys he can withstand, he is immune from all but the ultimate destruction of the inessential outer shell.

We shall be at Moorang in no time, said Hilda.

Yes, said Oliver. Quite soon.

Hilda, brushing against his shoulder, took her hand away from her chest.

The car furrowed the road, lapsed into distance and the moving rain.

THE HISTORY OF VINTAGE

The famous American publisher Alfred A. Knopf (1892–1984) founded Vintage Books in the United States in 1954 as a paperback home for the authors published by his company. Vintage was launched in the United Kingdom in 1990 and works independently from the American imprint although both are part of the international publishing group, Random House.

Vintage in the United Kingdom was initially created to publish paperback editions of books bought by the prestigious literary hardback imprints in the Random House Group such as Jonathan Cape, Chatto & Windus, Hutchinson and later William Heinemann, Secker & Warburg and The Harvill Press. There are many Booker and Nobel Prize-winning authors on the Vintage list and the imprint publishes a huge variety of fiction and non-fiction. Over the years Vintage has expanded and the list now includes great authors of the past – who are published under the Vintage Classics imprint – as well as many of the most influential authors of the present. In 2012 Vintage Children's Classics was launched to include the much-loved authors of our youth.

For a full list of the books Vintage publishes,
please visit our website
www.vintage-books.co.uk

For book details and other information about the classic authors we publish, please visit the Vintage Classics website
www.vintage-classics.info

www.vintage-classics.info

Visit www.worldofstories.co.uk for all your favourite children's classics